Ancora

The Fog Banshee's Curse

By Miriam Pittman

ILLUSTRATED BY KELLEY McMORRIS

MEMPHIS, TN

Published by IngramSpark 2020

Printed in the United States of America

LCCN 2020919781

BISAC: JUVENILE FICTION/ Fantasy & Magic | JUVENILE FICTION/
Action & Adventure |JUVENILE FICTION/ Family/ Siblings | JUVENILE
FICTION/ Girls & Women | JUVENILE FICTION/ Monsters

ISBN 978-1-7357965-0-5 (paperback)

ISBN 978-1-7357965-1-2 (ebook)

For my own three adventurers:
Mary Chase, Kathryn & Jane
And for Chase,
who always believed

Thanks so much for reading! I hope you enjoy the adventure ☺

Miriam Pittman

Contents

PROLOGUE

The night was cold and perfect for magic.

The Spellbinder rubbed his icy hands and drew close to the fire, his ears alert for any unwelcome sounds—the hoot of a screech owl, the careful shuffle of a raccoon, even the low growl of a mountain Blood Wrecker crouching just beyond the blackness. The crack of a branch punctured the silence and he whipped around, his dagger slicing the air. At the forest's edge, a deer paused in its grazing to study him warily. The Spellbinder half rose, as if to chase it, but changed his mind and turned back to the fire. Deer were harmless—stupid really—and wouldn't reveal secrets. The same could not be said of other creatures in Ancora.

He sat quietly for a minute more. Not a sound. He was alone, the only human for miles, which was perfect. The Spellbinder removed a bottle from a satchel at his feet and swirled the contents around, admiring the scarlet liquid sloshing inside. He glanced at the sky. Two shadow moons. Yes, everything was perfect. The old woman had done her best to stop him from making this potion, but she had been foolish to think she stood a chance against him. A pity. He didn't enjoy killing people and he tried to do it as little as possible.

His fingers twitched as he poured the liquid into the flames, his arm moving in a graceful circle. There was a smoldering sound as the flames weakened and disappeared into the embers. For one horrifying second, the Spellbinder wondered if the old woman hadn't beaten him after all and he was out here in the middle of nowhere, pouring a perfectly useless potion into a perfectly good fire, wasting both and looking like an idiot. Then, as though marked with an invisible brush, the fire began to change colors.

It raced from red to purple, then green, blue, back to red with dizzying speed. Flames licked upwards, forming curls and ribbons that streaked into the night, twisting and bending as though alive. Blue flames merged with yellow ones before exploding in showers of emerald that colored the air. Other flames wove in and out of one another, creating strands so vibrant that the Spellbinder's eyes ached. It was beautiful and terrifying at the same time but he couldn't look away. As the fire climbed higher, the Spellbinder heard a low chanting coming from deep within the flames. The chanting grew louder until it filled, not just his own ears, but every nook and cranny in the forest. For hours–or perhaps only seconds–this bizarre scene played itself out until, with a burst of sparks, the chanting stopped and the fire vanished, leaving only charred logs. The Spellbinder watched as a ribbon of blue smoke wafted up into the night, growing steadily larger until it blocked out the trees. In the center of the smoke, two red orbs flickered, then pulsed. The Spellbinder smiled.

The fog banshee was here. The search had begun.

Chapter One
The Three Adventurers

In the beginning, the Harper sisters did not set out to have a full-blown adventure.

They did not plan to insult magical creatures (Kat), ride on the back of something with enormous teeth (Rosie), or find themselves in a net twenty feet off the ground (Lulabelle).

And they most certainly did not intend to battle evil fog banshees that wished to suffocate them slowly and painfully.

That's not to say they never had adventures at all, but there's a big difference between bumping into a small, tidy adventure by accident and running after one as fast as you can until you feel like your lungs might explode. Sort of like the difference between tripping over a hole in the ground and jumping off a cliff. The Harpers had never had a jumping-off-a-cliff kind of adventure, with the exception of Kat Harper, who literally jumped off the roof of their house on the morning of her tenth birthday. She had just read the story of Icarus and decided that now was as good a time as any to fly. Like Icarus, Kat had made her own set of wings. Unlike Icarus, she was determined not to die.

She built her wings out of whatever was lying around: old clothes hangers stretched out to provide a frame, her mother's new bed sheets to maximize gliding, and a lot of brightly colored feathers to make the wings seem more authentic. She imagined her family sitting at the breakfast table while their mother made Kat's favorite pancakes (caramel and banana), when Rosie, who was eight, would leap out of her chair and cry in a voice full of wonder, "Look at Kat! Isn't she magnificent!" That Rosie had never in her life used the word "magnificent" was a minor detail. Kat then pictured herself making a grand birthday entrance to loud applause and extra pancakes.

Unfortunately for Kat Harper, this particular adventure did not end well. Once on the roof, she realized it would be impossible to get a running start. There was also a slight chance that she was deathly afraid of heights. By then, however, there was no turning back, especially with Rosie firing questions at her from the front lawn.

"Are you scared, Kat? You're very high up."

"I know I'm high up, I'm on the roof . . . and I'm not scared," Kat added, rather unconvincingly, even to herself.

"What if you fall? Are you planning to land on your head?"

"Nobody plans to land on their head, Rose."

"You might if you smash into a tree. Have you thought about smashing into a tree?"

"Of course I haven't!" snapped Kat, now picturing herself smashing into a tree.

"You're just standing there—aren't you going to move?"

"I'm waiting for the wind conditions to be right." Kat closed her eyes and imagined herself soaring into the sky. "No more talking, Rose, ok? I have to concentrate!"

Her concentration was promptly broken by Lulabelle, who came running out to see what all the noise was about and discovered Kat, wings extended, ready for flight.

"Kat!" she shrieked in horror. "Are you insane? Get down from there!"

Kat sighed and gritted her teeth. In her dreams of flying, she had envisioned a lot more wild applause and a lot less arguing with the spectators. She wondered if she would be featured on the news, maybe given a nickname, like Falcon Girl or Kat the Condor.

"Kat, are you listening to me?" Lulabelle paced back and forth, talking rapidly and making wild gestures, the way she always did when explaining a concept foreign to her younger sister, like the law of gravity or following rules. "I once read that fifty people die each year from tripping over their own two feet."

She didn't say how she knew this but Kat believed her. Lulabelle was basically a talking encyclopedia with blond hair and a peanut butter addiction. "If all those people can die on the ground, think about what'll happen when you fall. Because you *will* fall, Kat. Fall, not fly. It's against the laws of science and just plain idiotic."

Kat wrinkled her nose and considered Lulabelle's advice for a good five seconds. Nice try, Lu. She wasn't going to be talked out of this history making moment that easily.

"Anyone who's dumb enough to die from tripping over their feet wouldn't have a chance anywhere," she called back. "And it's not that far down, I probably won't have time to die." She adjusted her wings, preparing for takeoff.

Lulabelle's mouth fell open. "Don't do it!" she screeched. "You will plummet to your death! Do you hear me? TO YOUR DEATH!"

She turned and raced away. Great. It was only a matter of time before their parents got involved. It was now or never.

Kat looked down at Rosie, who gave her a thumbs up and an encouraging, "You can do it! And don't listen to Lu, I bet you won't break *all* your bones!"

Kat took a deep breath. Showtime.

As if on cue, Mrs. Harper came running out the back door followed by Lulabelle. "Katarina Juliet Harper!" she said in a shaking voice and Kat knew she was in serious trouble. "Stay right there and don't move! Lu, tell your dad to get the ladder!" Lulabelle dashed off, relieved to be away from the crime scene and off the hook for whatever happened next.

"Rosie!" Mrs. Harper turned to the small figure standing meekly in front of her. "How on earth did your sister get up there? Why didn't you—KAT!"

Kat had taken advantage of her mother's turned head and shuffling as fast as she could along the ridgepole, she leaped bravely off the edge of the roof, flapping her wings with all her might, and landed with a loud thump in the azalea bushes. Amazingly, Kat escaped with minor scratches and a sprained ankle, although the wings didn't survive nearly as well. She spent a good part of her birthday at the doctor's office while Rosie, the accomplice, spent the rest of the morning in her room. Worst of all, the caramel and banana pancakes burned.

Three months had passed since the birthday fiasco. As Kat stared out the window of her family's car, watching the landscape fly by, she felt an itchy restlessness that she couldn't explain, like a mosquito bite on your back that you couldn't quite reach. Next to her, Lulabelle sat motionless, her face behind a book. Kat was convinced that their car could launch itself into a river, sprout flippers and swim downstream, and Lu still wouldn't notice the fish swimming by her window. In the back seat, Rosie was sketching something in a notepad, her small, heart-shaped face frowning with concentration. In the front of the car, Mr. and Mrs. Harper argued good-naturedly about whether they had missed the turn, with Mrs. Harper insistent that they had and Mr. Harper insistent that they had not and if the map said they had, then the map had made a mistake.

Mr. Harper was an English professor, which meant that he liked to quote long passages from very old books and was constantly misplacing his glasses. Mrs. Harper was an artist, which meant that her clothes and hair were always streaked with paint and she spent most of her day behind an easel. Of all the Harpers, only Rosie had inherited her mother's talent, although she looked like Mr. Harper with her delicate features and big brown eyes. Lulabelle was eleven and loved books and school like her dad, but she and Mrs. Harper shared the same curly hair and lanky arms and legs. Kat, it must be said, took after no one in looks or interests. Her freckles and unruly honey-colored hair resembled neither of her parents, and Lulabelle had once remarked, after a disastrous show-and-tell that earned Kat yet another trip to the principal's office, that she had done the math and there was a ten percent chance that Kat had been raised by a pack of rabid squirrels and dropped on the doorstep ("It was only a baby opossum!"

Kat retorted. "It's not my fault the whole class panicked!").

For the past month, Mr. and Mrs. Harper had talked of nothing but going to the country and the cabin they would be renting for the summer while Mr. Harper taught at the local college and Mrs. Harper worked on her painting. Lulabelle, Kat, and Rosie, it had been decided, were to spend the summer doing what children were supposed to be doing, which Kat suspected meant entertaining themselves and staying outside. Her parents were so enthusiastic, though, that it was hard not to share their excitement. Lulabelle had decided to keep a science journal listing all the plants in the forest by their Latin names, while Rosie wanted to spend her time drawing scenes from nature. Not surprisingly, Kat had dismissed both ideas as uninteresting, and in Lulabelle's case, hopelessly boring. For her part, she was hoping to catch and tame a bear.

Mr. Harper found the turn at last and steered the car onto a gravel driveway and down a hill where their cabin sat nestled in a cozy tangle of trees. While Mr. and Mrs. Harper unloaded suitcases from the car, Kat and her sisters took in their new surroundings. Through the trees a lake glistened, the water sparkling like a field of perfect diamonds. Far away came the unmistakable drone of a motorboat and Kat wondered briefly where they could find a boat and whether ten-year-olds were allowed to drive them.

She turned her attention instead to an enormous tree just beyond their cabin. This tree wasn't tall and straight like the others, but was wild and knotty, its limbs splayed out in all directions as though struggling to keep its balance. Kat exchanged glances with Lulabelle and Rosie and all three of them grinned. Racing to the tree, they began pulling themselves up through the branches.

The limbs were thick but Kat easily found footholds as she pulled herself from branch to branch, loving the raw smell of the leaves and the scratchy bark against her palms. She wished she could climb forever. She positioned herself with her back against the trunk, arms grasping the branch above, and gazed out at the forest, lush and seemingly infinite.

"Kat, please be careful," came Lulabelle's muffled voice. "You're making me nervous."

"Where's your sense of adventure?" Kat called down into the leaves. "What if a pack of hungry wolves was chasing you and the only way to escape was up a tree? You have to think of these things, you know."

"But I read once that tree impalement is the nineteenth leading cause of death in Estonia—"

"You're making that up."

"I'll climb with you, Kat," chimed in Rosie. "I want to be chased by wolves!"

Kat opened her mouth to reply but it was then that she saw it. At the top of a nearby hill, something glittered. She squinted, trying to get a better look. What *was* that? Could it be treasure? Jewels, maybe? Kat's heart began to pound as she scrambled to climb down the tree (admittedly a much harder, less fun process than climbing up it). Buried treasure on their first day in the country! Or, maybe——her thoughts spun wildly as she hit the ground and dashed up the hill toward the sparkles, Lulabelle and Rosie's voices echoing behind her—maybe it was some sort of signal—maybe jewel thieves had hidden diamonds and were on their way to reclaim them. *The jig is up you scoundrels*, she shouted triumphantly to herself. A policeman had said that in a book—or was it a pirate? At any rate, it seemed fitting. She ran faster.

"Don't go far, girls!" she heard her mother call. "Remember to stay together!"

Kat reached the top of the hill in record time. The sparkly thing was nestled in the crevice of an enormous black rock. Kat reached into the crevice and grabbed for it just as Lulabelle arrived, panting heavily, followed an instant later by Rosie.

"What got into you?" Lulabelle gasped. "Why did you take off like a crazy person?"

Kat started to speak but, glancing at Rosie, she saw with alarm that her younger sister was bent at the waist, her face pale, her breathing ragged.

"Rosie, are you ok?" Lulabelle's concerned expression mirrored Kat's own. "Did you bring your inhaler?"

"Yes, I have it, but I'm fine." Rosie took a deep gulp of air, her small chest straining. "I'm fine," she insisted. She took another breath, nodding at Kat's closed fist. "What did you find?"

Kat opened her hand to reveal a slender silver chain with a circle the size of a quarter. It wasn't beautiful but Kat found herself fascinated all the same. Holding it up, she saw that the circle was decorated with a series of intertwining loops and squiggles.

"It's pretty," said Lulabelle, studying the necklace. "A little odd, but pretty." She turned her attention to the rock formation. "What is this, do you think?"

Kat stuffed the necklace in her pocket. It wasn't treasure but it was close. Besides, whoever had left it there didn't seem to want it, judging by the dirt on the chain. "What do you mean? It's a rock. Anyone can see that."

"I know it's a rock, but what kind of rock? Have you ever seen anything like this?"

The rock was black with specks of white. Oddly shaped bulges protruded from it, as though something had tried to force its way out. The rock stretched for fifty feet along the hill and looked impossible to climb (Kat's first thought) since the sides towered at least ten feet over their heads before forming a smooth slope that leveled out on top.

"No, but all rocks are the same, aren't they? You're the only person in the world who would care about that sort of thing."

"Lu, Kat, over here! You have to see this!"

Lulabelle and Kat followed the sound of Rosie's voice around a large, jagged piece of rock that jutted out like a wall. At the base was a small opening, wide enough for a person.

"Rosie, are you in there?" Kat called into the opening, feeling a bit silly.

"Yes, I'm here!" came Rosie's muffled answer. "It's unbelievable!"

Kat got down on her stomach and peered into the opening. Lulabelle crouched beside her.

"Are you going first or am I?"

"Well, you're older and bigger so if you make it through then we'll know it's safe for me."

"Thanks a lot."

"Where are you?" Rosie called. "What's taking so long?"

"Hold on, I'm coming." Kat took a deep breath and tried not to think about small, enclosed spaces. Digging her elbows into the dirt and pushing off with her tennis shoes, she wiggled through the tunnel.

She got to her feet, brushing spiderwebs from her hair, and felt her mouth drop open in a very undignified way. The tunnel opened into a vast cave that was five times the size of her bedroom back home. The sides of the rock extended so high that Kat had to strain her neck to see the ceiling. Sunlight streamed in through numerous cracks, giving the cave a warm, airy feel and Kat could see a chunk of blue sky just beyond a hole at the top.

"Isn't this amazing?" Rosie's voice bounced off the walls. "It's like a rock castle!"

"It might be limestone," said Lulabelle, getting to her feet and shaking the dust off her jeans. "Maybe marble. Probably not volcanic, although that would be cool. I wish I'd thought to bring my science textbook with me, I'm sure there was something . . . "

Lulabelle launched into a rambling speech about the wonderful world of rocks, but Kat, having learned long ago to tune out anything that sounded remotely like school, heard none of it. She had noticed a tunnel off to the side that led deeper into the cave. Curious, she wandered over to peer into it. Lulabelle stopped talking about the important role of igneous rock throughout history and watched her suspiciously.

"Please tell me you're not thinking of going in there."

Kat was silent, a strong indication that she was, in fact, thinking of going in there.

"Kat, are you insane? You can't go marching into some dark tunnel that goes who knows where. You might get lost—"

"We won't get lost," scoffed Kat, although she couldn't help but relish the idea. "These aren't caves that go on for miles in all directions. Rose, don't you want to see where this goes?"

"Yes!"

"There could be bats," insisted Lulabelle, "or snakes . . . or spiders . . . or flesh-eating mushrooms!" Kat gave her a disbelieving look but Lulabelle was undaunted. "I saw it on a documentary."

"Fine," retorted Kat. "Rosie, don't eat anything in this tunnel, ok? Especially if it looks like a flesh-eating mushroom. Lu, you stay here and wait for us. If we're not back in five minutes, we were probably attacked by bats. Ready Rose?"

Rosie shivered with excitement. "Hold my hand?"

She clutched Kat's arm as they inched their way into the tunnel, Kat keeping one hand on the rock for support, while listening for any sounds that might belong to unfriendly animals. She guessed flesh-eating mushrooms were pretty quiet. They had only gone a few feet when Lulabelle's footsteps echoed behind them.

"Oh for goodness' sake!" she huffed, unfastening a small flashlight attached to her belt loop. A faint glow illuminated the passage, casting eerie shadows along the walls. "If you insist on walking through a dark, creepy tunnel filled with snakes, bats, or something else with teeth, we might as well see where we're going." She took Rosie's other hand and shot Kat a fierce look. Kat tried her best to disguise a grin. As much as Lu pretended otherwise, Kat knew her sister hated being left out of any adventure.

They continued in this way for some time, making their way deeper into the tunnel. The gentle thud of their tennis shoes on the rock was the only sound Kat could hear, an unnerving reminder that they were alone. Or were they? What if a prehistoric cave monster was lurking in the shadows, waiting to bite off their fingers? What if she had to fight it?

Lulabelle stopped suddenly and Kat blinked as the image of the cave monster vanished with a poof.

"I don't understand," Lulabelle remarked, holding her watch up to her eyes. "We've been walking for almost five minutes, we should've come to the end by now. It wasn't that big."

Kat frowned. They *had* been walking for a long time. "Maybe we're zig-zagging back and forth so it's taking us longer."

"I don't think so, look." They turned to follow the flashlight's beam behind them. "We've been walking in a straight line the whole time, we haven't turned a corner once."

Rosie's eyes widened. "Are we lost in the rock?"

A small shard of uneasiness caught in Kat's chest but she pushed it away. No sense in worrying Rosie, not when they could easily go back the way they had come. No, this was a much bigger rock than it appeared, that was all. Lulabelle seemed to read her thoughts because she chuckled nervously.

"Of course we're not lost, Rose, I'm sure we're nearly at the end." She handed the flashlight to Kat and Kat took her turn leading the way through the tunnel. When more time had passed with no sign of the tunnel's end, Lulabelle glanced at her watch and whispered in Kat's ear, "It's possible we're going down instead of across. That would explain why we haven't come to the end of the rock."

"Down? You mean like down into the earth?" Kat pictured a staircase descending for miles into the center of the world. Lulabelle nodded.

They walked in silence for another minute. "I once read about some hikers who got lost in a cave for weeks and they ended up having to eat each other's—"

"Stop!" Kat was in no mood for one of Lulabelle's horrifying stories. She glanced at Rosie. "Let's give it another minute and then we'll turn around."

Almost as soon as the words were out of her mouth, Kat noticed that the darkness was fading. At first she thought her eyes had adjusted to the tunnel, but gradually it grew lighter and lighter until the flashlight became unnecessary and Kat switched it off.

"I think we're coming to the end," she announced. Sure enough, up ahead was daylight. Kat had never been so glad to see the outside world as she was at that moment. Hopping down from the rim of the cave, blinking furiously, Kat felt a sudden coolness envelop her body. Although the cave had not been unpleasant, the sun on her face and the grass under her feet were a good reminder that she much preferred fresh air to a musty cave that smelled like old socks. Kat sniffed, detecting the faintest whiff of cinnamon on the breeze. Still blinking, she squinted into the light.

And promptly felt her heart crash down into her stomach.

For one long second she felt like she was falling. It wasn't possible. It couldn't be possible. They must have taken a wrong turn back in the tunnel, despite what Lulabelle had said, and ended up . . . where? Not on the hill with the black rock, that was certain. Kat looked frantically at Lulabelle, and her panic only grew when she saw that her sister had turned white.

"Where did all the trees go?" Rosie said slowly. Kat opened her mouth but found that her words had disappeared into her stomach along with her heart. She whirled around, hoping to see their cabin and the lake, but there were only hills stretching as far as the eye could see. Mountain peaks towered in the distance, snow-capped and majestic, the kind Kat had only seen in pictures. Where had *they* come from?

Looking down at her feet, Kat noticed that the grass was darker, nearly blue, and thicker than she remembered. What had happened? She sat down hard, her mind spinning. Their cabin, the forest, the lake, all of it had vanished. But the strangest thing, Kat thought as she looked out on the hills before her with growing dread, were the two moons that hung suspended in the sky like a set of pale, glowing eyes, watching them.

"Lu?" Kat tried but failed to keep the tremor from her voice. "Where are we?"

CHAPTER TWO

The Harpers Have to Run for It

T here's a rational explanation, there has to be."

Lulabelle paced back and forth while Kat and Rosie huddled together on the ground, trying to come to terms with their situation. Kat knew Lulabelle was fighting to stay calm but the frenetic pacing didn't inspire confidence.

"The tunnel must have gone down into the hill instead of through the rock," Lu continued, her words tumbling over each other. "We've come out a mile or two from home, that's all. If we retrace our steps, we'll be fine."

"What about those mountains?" Kat avoided looking at them. She hoped that, given enough time, they would tiptoe quietly away.

"Obviously they're an illusion!" Lulabelle sputtered, her voice cracking. "There wasn't enough oxygen in the cave and it's affecting our brains. The mountains are a mirage, playing tricks with our minds. That makes sense, right?"

More pacing.

Kat didn't think anything about their situation made sense, but Lulabelle was clinging to the possibility like a life raft. She pointed at the two moons. "And those?"

"Double vision," replied Lulabelle confidently. "Lack of oxygen to the brain can cause a person to see double. Everyone knows that."

Kat closed her eyes. She wanted to believe her sister's explanation, but it wasn't only the mountains or the fact that the forest, the lake and their cabin had inexplicably vanished, or even the two moons. Everything felt unsteady and off, like a picture that was out of focus. She couldn't tell Lulabelle, though, not when Lu was so sure she could explain it all away, and Rosie would only worry. At any rate, they couldn't stay here. If Lulabelle was right, retracing their steps through the tunnel would take them back to the forest and home. She tried to say as much but Lulabelle shook her head so hard that Kat worried she'd get whiplash.

"No, if the oxygen in the tunnel is low enough to make us hallucinate, going back in could damage our brains permanently. We have to hike back."

"Fine, which way do we go?"

Lulabelle motioned toward a ridge of trees on the other side of a meadow. "That must be the forest. If we go that way, I'm sure we'll find our cabin."

With shaky legs and even shakier hearts, the Harpers headed down the hill and across the meadow, their eyes casting around for anything familiar. Maybe it was the cool, perfumed breeze or the warm glow of the sun, but Kat felt her spirits lifting, in spite of the strange circumstances. She stopped abruptly as a shadow passed over them, followed by more shadows one after the other. Kat looked up in time to see four black objects streak across the sky. From the opposite direction came a larger group of black objects, which joined up with the four in what was clearly some kind of formation. Were they birds? Kat felt her blood run cold. They couldn't be birds. They were too big and too fast.

And they were heading straight for the Harpers.

There was no time to run. Grabbing Rosie's arm with one hand and Lulabelle's shoulder with the other, Kat dragged her sisters to the ground just as the flying creatures careened over their heads (or where their heads had been only moments before). Kat fought the urge to bury her face in her knees and instead chose the much braver approach of covering her eyes and peering through the cracks in her fingers. The creatures took no notice of the Harpers, but continued on their journey, their enormous wings sending wind ripples across the meadow. Kat squealed as one landed mere feet from the Harpers; with a flutter of wings, it rose back into the air like a furry helicopter and took off after its herd. When the creatures had finally gone and the Harpers could trust their legs not to give way, they got to their feet, trembling.

"*Horses?*" Lulabelle was staring open-mouthed, astonishment written across her face. "Please tell me those weren't horses."

"No, they were definitely not horses." Kat gulped. "They were flying horses—you know, horses with wings."

This wasn't happening, she told herself. Those sorts of creatures weren't real. They belonged in the pages of books, preferably with knights, swords and safe, happy endings.

Lulabelle gaped at her as though Kat was speaking Sanskrit. "Horses don't fly," she whispered. "It's not possible. Nothing about this is possible." Her eyes glazed over and she went silent. Kat couldn't help but think she would have made an excellent mannequin.

Rosie gazed after the creatures, now dark specks in the sky. Unlike her sisters, she didn't seem bothered by the fact that she had nearly been trampled to death by something that couldn't exist. "They're beautiful," she said softly, eyes glowing.

That was one way to look at it, thought Kat. But beautiful or not, the Harpers couldn't stand here forever.

"Come on Lu, we should keep going. We're almost to the trees."

Lulabelle stared at her, wild-eyed. "Have you lost your mind? We have no idea what this place is! What if there's . . . I don't know—dragons!" Kat was impressed at how quickly her sister could pivot from shock to panic. "No, absolutely not! We should go back the way we came."

"You said there wasn't enough oxygen in the tunnel. Which is it, Lu? Permanently damaged brains or the chance we might meet a monster?" Kat crossed her arms and watched Lulabelle hesitate with the decision. She supposed Lulabelle's teachers would be proud that Lu considered dragons preferable to bad grades. Kat decided to press her advantage.

"Let's go a little farther, up to those trees. We'll still be able to see the cave from there. Maybe we'll find someone who can help us."

"Please, Lu," begged Rosie. "I want to see if there's anything else magical."

Lulabelle cast a pained look at the cave. "Okay, but only to those trees, and only because I know you'll go anyway and I want to keep an eye on Rosie."

They reached the top of the hill and Rosie paused to catch her breath while Lulabelle and Kat pondered their next move. From this high up, Kat felt like an explorer at the top of the world. Before them lay the meadow, stretching into the horizon, the blueish grass swaying slightly with every delicate breeze. Behind them, the forest smelled of pine and earth, the trees tall and spindly with delicate branches. The forest floor lay covered in shaggy moss that spilled over onto rocks, logs, and anything else that had managed to fall in its path. Lulabelle put a finger to her lips, as though she were listening. Kat listened too, not sure what she was listening for, but after a few moments, she detected the sound of water moving over rocks. There must be a stream nearby.

"I'm not sure this is a good idea," said Lulabelle when they had journeyed a little way into the forest and found the stream, brimming with clear water. She gestured towards the trees. "We don't know what kind of dangerous things live in there."

Kat knelt by the stream and splashed her fingers. "But we haven't had anything to drink and it's a long way back home. I'm thirsty and so is Rosie, aren't you Rose?"

"Yep."

"I'm thirsty, too, but we don't know what's in that water. It might be enchanted . . . or filled with toxins. I for one would rather be dehydrated than break out in boils or something."

Kat gave her a withering look. "Don't be stupid, it's not a cauldron. Fresh water is fresh water no matter where you are. Nothing's green or oozing."

She cupped the water in her hands, pausing long enough to imagine herself as a gigantic, toxin-filled boil with a ponytail. Kat took a sip and smiled up at Lulabelle and Rosie. "See, perfectly safe."

Rosie knelt down beside her and scooped up the water, letting it dribble down her chin. Reluctantly, Lulabelle joined them, encouraged by the fact that neither sister had transformed into a hideous mutant. Even the water was different, Kat realized, as the cold liquid coursed down her throat. Softer, if such a thing was possible.

"Eek!" Rosie scrambled to her feet, her eyes as big as saucers.

"Rose, what is it? What's—AAHH!" Kat and Lulabelle jumped up at the same time, their shoulders knocking into each other.

Something small, furry and very much alive was bouncing up and down on the sandy bank in front of them. It was blue and pear-shaped, with no arms or legs, but two enormous eyes that looked out of place on its tiny body. Although it didn't appear to have a mouth, a high-pitched squeak was coming from somewhere inside it. Lulabelle took a step back, pulling her sisters with her. The odd little creature followed, growing more excited with each bounce.

"How adorable."

Shaking off Lulabelle's arm, Rosie knelt down. With a happy squeal, the bouncing thing plopped onto her outstretched hand.

"Rosie," Lulabelle said with forced calmness, "put that down. We have no idea what that is."

Rosie smiled at the tiny blue creature bobbing on her palm. "It's not dangerous, Lu, it just wants to play." She stroked its furry back.

It gave a contented purr, then resumed bouncing. Kat and Lulabelle edged closer.

Kat stared, amazement elbowing out any fear. "What *is* it? A fur ball with eyes?"

The creature squealed once more, then disappeared in a puff of smoke. In its place lay a smooth blue stone. The Harpers gasped. The stone vanished in another puff of smoke and there lay a twig with blue-tinged leaves. After several seconds in which Lulabelle, Kat, and Rosie remained still, their eyes fixed on Rosie's palm, the twig exploded yet again and the little creature reappeared, bouncing harder than ever.

"I think it must be a shape-shifter. I've read about them, of course, but only in stories."

Lulabelle reached out a trembling hand to pet the creature. Its eyes fluttered and it made a purring sound. Before long, all three Harpers were giggling and tickling the odd little shape-shifter, who alternated between happy purring and excited bouncing. It leaped out of Rosie's hand and onto the ground, where it shape-shifted into a blue stump, than an enormous turtle, followed by a rabbit as tall as Rosie.

All of a sudden, the little shape-shifter froze. With a shudder, it turned and bounced off into the bushes. The Harpers waited.

"Do you think it's coming back?" Kat strained to catch a glimpse of blue fur but the bushes were too thick.

Rosie frowned. "It looked upset. Do you think we scared it?"

At once there came a low rumbling sound and the trees began to shake. Something was crashing through the bushes. Kat could see branches snapping like twigs. She lunged for Lulabelle and Rosie's arms, pulling them away just as the unseen creature burst out of the trees.

"I think THAT scared it!"

The creature let out a deafening roar, revealing a mouth full of razor-sharp teeth. It was the size of an ox and covered in dark, shaggy fur. Two horns resembling upside-down question marks protruded from each side of its head. It stomped the ground with its massive paw, sending a tremor through the forest, then snapped its jaws and lumbered toward the Harpers. Kat took that as a clear sign.

"We have to go!"

The Harpers sprinted into the forest, Kat in the lead. She had no idea where she was going or what they might be running into, only that they had to get away from all those teeth. She looked frantically around for some place to hide, but everything was a blur, the trees blending together as they plunged deeper into the forest. What should they do?

Behind them came another roar. The ground trembled and the trees seemed to bend, as though they too wanted to hide. Kat stumbled over a branch, regaining her footing just in time. Lulabelle had grabbed Rosie's hand and was practically dragging her along. The monster was getting closer.

Ahead, the ground dropped off and Kat could hear the sound of gushing water. Without stopping to think, she reached the edge and leaped over the side, landing with a thud on the sand below, followed by Lulabelle and Rosie. Lulabelle motioned for them to follow her across the sand to the bank, where vines and ivy had created a natural covering. Lulabelle parted the vines, revealing a shallow nook, and the Harpers scrambled in, pulling the vines over themselves. Rosie fumbled for her inhaler and immediately began to draw short, quick breaths.

The Harpers sat motionless for what felt like an eternity. At last, Lulabelle got to her knees.

"Do you think we're safe?"

Kat poked her head out far enough to see on either side. "I don't see anything. I don't hear anything either, but let me take a look."

Using the vines as ropes, she pulled herself up the bank and peered over the top, praying that nothing was waiting to drag her away. She breathed a loud sigh of relief when she saw that the forest was still, with no ox monsters in sight.

"I think we should find another way out of the forest," Lulabelle said after Kat had reported her findings. "We don't want to run into whatever that was again."

Rosie nodded. "I think I'm ready to go home now." Her

breathing was almost back to normal. "Do you know where we are, Kat?"

The truth was that Kat had no idea where they were. In the chaos of the moment, she hadn't paid much attention to either direction or distance. Now all the trees looked the same and it was impossible to tell where they were in relation to the black rock. How big was this forest? What if it went on for miles?

As though sensing Kat's uncertainty, Lulabelle cleared her throat. "It looks like the river has gotten bigger as we've moved deeper into the forest, so I think the best thing is to follow it until it becomes a stream again. From there we should be able to find the meadow and the black rock."

Kat glanced at the bank above them. "I think we should stay down here, though, just in case."

"So where are we?" asked Rosie as they made their way through the sand and rocks in the direction they hoped led back home. "Is it some kind of magical place? And if it is, how did we get here? Did something happen to us when we were in that cave?"

"I don't know, Rose," Lulabelle replied, her eyes darting from side to side for any sign of the ox monster. "Somehow, that tunnel in the black rock took us from our world to here . . . like a portal."

"A what? In English, Lu."

"A portal, Kat. A passageway from one world to another one." Lulabelle scrunched her eyebrows together. "This is crazy—there's no possible way this is happening!" She glared at Kat and Rosie, daring them to disagree. "It makes no logical sense," she announced again.

"I know," Kat agreed cheerfully. "How soon should we come back, do you think?"

Lulabelle swung around, colliding with Rosie. "Come back? To this place? Are you crazy? Did you enjoy running for your life just now? Was it fun when we almost got trampled by a bunch of flying horses? We're not coming back, it's far too dangerous! Mortal danger could be waiting at every turn!" She glanced around the forest, as though expecting to see mortal danger peering at them through high-powered binoculars.

"What's crazy is leaving and never coming back," insisted Kat stubbornly. "This is a once in a lifetime chance. How many kids can say they've been to a magical world? Ok, there's some scary things here, but there might be amazing things, too . . . like unicorns . . . or . . . or dragons!"

"Wonderful—let's head straight for a fire-breathing dragon! If we're lucky, maybe we'll get cornered by a bunch of hungry minotaurs."

"You have no sense of adventure, Lu."

"And you have no sense at all, Kat."

"Do you think other people live here?" Rosie interrupted, hoping to prevent an argument. The sandy bank had narrowed and they had to walk single file to avoid sloshing through the water.

Kat shrugged. "I doubt anyone wants to stick around if they know they might get eaten."

"Well, they're smarter than we are." Lulabelle paused again to listen for suspicious sounds. "We've been here less than an hour and we've already done a lot of running. I hope we can find our way back before dragons invade or the trees come alive and eat us or something else horrible happens."

Kat made a face at Lulabelle's back. Lu could be so grumpy. She took her role as oldest sister far too seriously. If she would only relax, she might see how amazing this place was. A sudden thought hit her.

"Did you hear that?"

Lulabelle froze. "What? What did it sound like?"

"Shh!" Kat put her finger to her lips and knelt down on the sand. "There it is again—can't you hear it?"

"No!" Lulabelle looked like she was about to have a heart attack.

Rosie squatted next to Kat. "I don't hear anything, either." Kat gave her a quick wink and realization dawned on Rosie. Stifling a giggle, she reached for her inhaler and blew into it with gusto.

"It's getting louder every second." Kat jumped to her feet. "It sounds like a bazillion angry bees, don't you hear the buzzing? LU, IT'S ALL AROUND US!"

Lulabelle spun around so fast Kat thought she resembled a large blond pinwheel in the middle of a hurricane.

"I don't see anything!" Lulabelle's voice bordered on hysteria. She picked up a rock and hoisted it over her head. "Tell me when you see it, this may be our best defense!"

"I think it's coming from the trees!" Kat could hardly get the words out over the laughter welling up in her throat. "I think they're alive and they're about to attack! QUICK, LU, BEFORE THEY SUCK OUT OUR INSIDES AND HANG OUR BODIES IN LEAF COCOONS!"

"AIEEEE!"

Lulabelle shrieked and hurled her rock at the nearest tree, managing to scrape off some bark. Running over to the unfortunate tree, she karate-chopped it for good measure, which impressed Kat because she knew her sister hated violence and she assumed that included attacking plants. Lulabelle reached for another rock but froze at the sound of poorly concealed laughter coming from Kat and Rosie. She straightened up, the rock in her hand, her eyes murderous.

"Are you serious? You think that's funny? Kat Harper, WHAT IS WRONG WITH YOU!" Lulabelle threw the rock, thankfully at the ground, and stormed off.

"I hope you're happy! I should make you find your own way home."

Kat and Rosie hurried to keep up with Lulabelle's furious pace, still giggling.

"Oh, come on, Lu, don't be mad. I'm sorry you were scared, but you have to admit that *was* kind of funny, especially when you threw the rock at the tree."

Rosie snorted. Kat found that it was very difficult to apologize when she was trying not to choke with laughter.

"Please don't be mad at us, Lu!" Rosie managed to gasp. "We're sorry we scared you, honestly."

"Don't be mad at Rosie, be mad at me! I thought a joke would make us feel better, that's all."

No response. Kat tried again.

"Please, Lu. I'll let you have my dessert tonight." She thought that was more than fair, since she was sure dessert would be sweet potato pie, Lulabelle's favorite.

"Would you stop talking? I can't think about which way to go with you blabbing on. And I'm not mad at you, Rosie, you can't help that Kat's a bad influence."

Lulabelle increased her stride and the conversation appeared to be over. Kat shot a sideways grin at Rosie, who grinned back. They both knew that Lulabelle's wrath, while intense in the moment, tended to be short-lived. Throw in sweet potato pie and it would no doubt vanish as quickly as it began. Kat stopped walking, her attention suddenly distracted. There was something odd about the path up ahead. Something she couldn't put her finger on. What was it? Kat started to call out to Lulabelle again, but at that moment she felt a prickle on the back of her neck. The prickle made its way down Kat's arms like a lit fuse moving toward a firecracker.

Someone was watching them, she was sure of it.

The prickle grew stronger and Kat found it hard to breathe. She scanned the forest for a glimpse of the unseen watcher. Nothing. But she knew he was there.

Out of the corner of her eye, Kat glimpsed Lulabelle as her sister stalked silently in front of them. With a flash of realization, she realized what had struck her as odd about the path. While most of the leaves lay scattered haphazardly, wherever they had fallen, the ones covering the path formed a single even layer in the shape of a diamond. It was a shape that couldn't possibly be natural. Something was very, very wrong.

And Lulabelle was heading straight for it.

"Lu!" she cried, breaking into a run. "Lulabelle, wait! Stop! Those leaves don't look right!"

"Nice try, Kat." Lulabelle quickened her pace. "I suppose they're alive, is that it? They're planning to jump out like bandits and kidnap us?"

Lulabelle reached the part of the path containing the diamond leaf pattern and bounded into the middle of it. For one moment, nothing happened. Then, out of nowhere, came a soft whirring noise and the leaves exploded into the air like confetti, exposing an enormous net. Lulabelle screamed as the net shot up into the trees, taking her with it. Kat and Rosie stood helpless, unable to do anything but watch in horror.

"Lulabelle!" Kat yelled over the roaring in her own ears. "Lulabelle!"

CHAPTER THREE

Aidan

While it was possible that the situation could be worse, Kat found it difficult to imagine exactly how. Now that the trap was sprung, the leaves fluttered back to the ground where they resumed a more natural position. Lulabelle, after her initial shriek, pressed her face against the net, attempting to speak over Kat's yelling.

"Kat! Kat, shut up a minute and listen! I'm fine, but we have to get me down before whoever put this here comes back. I need you to stop screaming and start thinking." For a person who found herself in a trap, presumably to be someone else's dinner, Lulabelle was remarkably calm.

She struggled to a crouching position and gave a little bounce.

The tree branch wobbled but remained firm. "I have an idea that might work," Lulabelle called down. "If you can find something sharp and get it up to me, I might be able to cut away the net. I don't think it's quite as strong as it looks. Kat, are you listening?"

Kat, who had most definitely not been listening, took several deep breaths and tried to focus on Lulabelle's words. Right. Find something sharp to cut the net.

"Rosie, be careful. There might be more nets. We don't want to get trapped, too."

Rosie flattened herself against a tree trunk, her worried eyes on Lulabelle. "Won't she get hurt if she jumps out?"

Kat let the question hang uncomfortably in the air with Lulabelle as she raced over to the river bank, her eyes scouring the ground for anything sharp. She picked up several rocks but rejected them all as not lethal enough. A glint of color caught her eye and Kat saw a small reddish shard sticking out of the water. It looked like it might have been part of a bottle or jar.

Kat gamely threw the glass shard in the direction of Lulabelle's outstretched hands, but after several unsuccessful tries, she doubted whether this would work. It didn't help that Lu had never been good at hand-eye coordination, particularly when it came to catching baseballs, tennis balls, or in this case, jagged pieces of broken glass.

"Do it again," ordered Lulabelle, her eyes narrowed in concentration. "I almost had it that last time."

Kat aimed carefully and tossed the shard at Lulabelle, who lunged for it, caught the sharp edge and fell back into the net, clutching her hand. The shard disappeared into a pile of leaves and Kat and Rosie scrambled to retrieve it. Kat was so intent on her search that she didn't notice him at first until Rosie's warning.

"Kat!"

A boy with red hair and bright gray eyes was leaning against a tree, watching them in astonishment. He wore faded brown trousers with patches carelessly placed on the knees, as though whoever had sewn them either didn't know much about sewing or didn't care to do a neater job. The boy's white shirt hung on his skinny frame. A tan satchel was slung across his chest, from which protruded a suspicious pair of furry ears. The boy stood up straight.

"I'd say you little birds got yourself into a bit of a pickle."

Kat and Rosie looked at each other. No one said a word. The boy cleared his throat.

"Do you not understand me? Have some trouble with your ears?" He took a step toward them, lowering his voice sympathetically. "You weren't kicked in the head by a mule, were you?"

"No, no we understand you," Lulabelle replied quickly from up in the net. "We were on our way home and I walked into this trap. If you have a knife we could use to cut me down, we would really appreciate it."

"Well, I suppose that's one way to go, but it's an awfully good net and I'd hate to ruin it like that when it took me so long to make it." The boy stared hard at Lulabelle. Kat noticed the corners of his mouth turn up, as though he was trying not to smile. "I don't suppose you'd be open to staying up there, would you? Just until I can muster up enough rope to fix Maud, of course. It would only be a few weeks, and as you can see, the view is massive."

"A few weeks?" The shock of meeting this strange boy had worn off and Kat was indignant. "You can't leave her up there for a few weeks! THAT'S MY SISTER!"

As the rest of his words sank in, she felt her face grow hot. She jumped to her feet, eyes flashing.

"Are you saying that *you* set this trap? This is your fault? She could've been killed . . . or . . . strangled! Who leaves a dangerous trap lying around anyway? It's . . . " She racked her brain for the appropriate word and settled on one that Lulabelle was constantly throwing at her, " . . . Irresponsible! It's totally irresponsible! And probably against the law, at least where we come from." Now she really sounded like Lulabelle. "YOU GET MY SISTER DOWN FROM THERE OR YOU'LL BE SORRY!"

"Whoa now little bird, no need to get your feathers ruffled." The boy held up his hands, not even trying to disguise his grin. "It so happens that I'm the chief net cutter-downer around these parts. If you want your sister on the ground that badly, I suppose I can sacrifice Maud for the greater good, much as it pains my heart. But to be fair, I think we should give your sister —what's her name, by the way?"

"Lulabelle," Kat hissed. "Her name is Lulabelle."

"How is it, Lulabelle?" He called up to the net. "It looks cozy up there, I must say. If you're worried about missing your afternoon tea, you have my word that I'll personally serve you a fresh cup every day." He scratched his head and looked around. "Biscuits and jam'll be a sight harder to scrounge up, but we can always hope, can't we? Power of positive thinking and all that." His gray eyes twinkled and Lulabelle managed a tiny smile in spite of herself.

"No, thank you. I think I would rather have all that on the ground."

The boy shrugged. "Suit yourself, but you're missing a plum chance to start a new life in the trees. I'm sure if Maud could speak, she'd agree, and not just because she's hoping to avoid a cut or two."

He began rummaging through his satchel.

"Who's Maud?" asked Rosie curiously. "Is that your net?"

"Sure enough, I name all my nets, and a dependable girl Maud is, too. I can always count on her to bring home a tasty meal. Not like Fiona—now she was temperamental." The boy chuckled, shaking his head. "I had a time with her, that's the truth. I declare she thought it a nuisance to actually catch a critter, although she did manage to snare the sweetest little rabbit, I'll give her that."

Rosie's eyes lit up. "Did you keep it as a pet?"

"Nope, ate it for dinner that night."

The boy pulled a knife out of his satchel with a flourish, looked it over appraisingly, then secured it in the back of his pants and grabbed hold of the lowest tree branch. With the practiced agility of someone who had done this before, he swung himself up, grasping each branch with strong, steady arms. He reached the limb holding the net and scurried across it as easily as though he was on solid ground and not twenty feet up in the air. Straddling the branch, he whittled away at the thick cords.

"You know Lulabelle, I'm a bit surprised you want to join your sisters after that nasty prank they pulled on you," he said in a cheerful tone, as though everything about the scene was perfectly normal. "You seemed a mite eager to get away from them—not that I blame you—and now you're asking me to sacrifice my best net . . . You'll forgive me if I'm a little puzzled."

"You were spying on us?" Kat felt her indignation growing by the second. "You were watching us the whole time and you didn't say anything? You could've warned Lu before she stepped into the trap! What kind of person hides in the woods, waiting to catch other kids?"

"Now hold on there." The boy looked at Kat with a hurt expression, although she suspected he was enjoying this immensely. "I was minding my own business, looking out for my traps, when I hear you three crashing though the woods like a grand May Day parade.

Scared any critters I might have caught, so you'll forgive me if I was a bit surprised."

He nodded at Lulabelle. "Of course, I never meant for you to wind up here, but you moved so fast and I'd be lying if I wasn't a mite curious whether Maud would work on a person. The biggest thing I've caught in her was a muskrat, and a small one at that." He beamed. "Guess we know what a right good net she is."

"We feel so lucky!" Kat retorted. "Are you done cutting the ropes?"

"Nearly there, these things take time, you know. Anyway, how do you think I feel? I was looking forward to a bit of venison roasted over a fire, and now I'll have to hope for some Hill province trout, and they're on the wee side this early in the summer. All right there, Lulabelle, you're about to go for a ride."

The rope fell to the ground, releasing part of the net. Without warning, the boy leaped from the branch down onto the net, clinging to it with arms that were clearly stronger than they appeared.

"Awkward meeting this way, but it can't be helped, can it?" He winked at Lulabelle. "Hold tight, little bird. I'll have you out of your cage in no time." With one smooth cut, he tore an opening in the net, then replaced the knife in his pants and leaped into the open air. The Harpers gasped as he dropped to the ground, landing gracefully on a pile of leaves.

"Right then, Lulabelle. Sit on your bum and dangle your legs, then hold onto the rope and ease yourself out—nothing to it."

Lulabelle gave him a tortured look that plainly said she thought there was a lot more to it than his simple instructions. She inched forward, opened the tear, and peered down at her sisters.

Kat crossed her arms nervously. She doubted Lu would have the courage to jump out of that net; she could barely walk off the end of a diving board. At this rate, the only way to get her out was to annoy her into action.

"Hey Lu, if you stay up there, I'll have to take Rosie home and that means I'll get your share of sweet potato pie. Do you really want that?"

Lulabelle's face clouded. Kat smiled up at her.

"Then I'll have to borrow your books for my summer reading, and you know I tend to lose things, or bend the covers, or draw little faces on the pages so I can make those cartoons when you flip through the book fast." She paused. "I may even highlight everything!"

"Stop, just stop!"

Lulabelle gritted her teeth, turned over on her stomach, and slid out of the net. She tried to think about landing on the world's softest pillow, and let go.

She landed with a thud, not as gracefully as the boy, but

without breaking anything important. Blushing, Lulabelle brushed the leaves from her jeans and gave Kat a pointed look. "You owe me your piece of pie."

"Deal." The knot of worry that had been growing in Kat's stomach began to unravel. The boy was smirking at them, which she found very annoying.

"Now then, Lulabelle, have I made amends for being a plonker? Safe and sound, no harm to speak of, and a grand story to tell them when you get home."

He tilted his head. "Speaking of, where exactly is home? You don't sound like anyone from the Hill province, that's a fact." He rubbed his chin. "You could be from the Mountain province, I suppose, but you're a sight far from home. Definitely don't have the look of the Central City or the Sea . . . Hmm, quite a mystery. A little far to be from the Southern province, although you—" he pointed to Kat, "—have the temper of a Southie."

Kat glared at him. She had no idea what he was talking about, but it sounded like he had just insulted her.

"Aha!" he exclaimed. "The Lake province! Process of elimination and all that." He looked pleased with himself. "How did three little birds like yourselves end up in the Whispering Woods of the Hill province?"

"Stop calling us little birds—we have names. You know Lulabelle, that's Rosie and I'm Kat." Kat scowled at the boy, although he appeared unfazed by her hostility. In fact, he seemed to find her very amusing.

"Kat, that explains it, sure enough."

"What's that supposed to mean?"

"Nothing." The boy winked at her, which only irritated Kat more. "Just that your da was a prophet, wasn't he now? I mean, he didn't name you Ducky or Puppy, that's a fact."

"You haven't told us your name," interjected Lulabelle before Kat could respond. She stepped forward and held out her hand, as much a gesture of peace as an introduction. "We appreciate you helping us and we're sorry that you had to cut your net—I mean, Maud. It was very nice of you."

For the first time, the boy looked embarrassed. He wiped his hand on his trousers and shook Lulabelle's with some hesitation, as though unsure what to do. He dropped it quickly and ran his fingers through his hair.

"Aidan's the name, pleased to meet you." He didn't volunteer a last name and Lulabelle didn't think it polite to ask.

"Well, Aidan, we're a little confused. We're not from any of those places you mentioned, at least, I don't think we are. We came out of a cave over by a meadow. There was a tunnel, from our house to—to here." Lulabelle stopped, flustered at how ridiculous her words sounded.

Aidan nodded slowly. "Aye, I know the bit of rock you're

speaking of, out there in the meadowlands. Never knew it to be a cave, though." He scratched his chin and frowned. "So you're saying you're not from *anywhere* in Ancora? That you got here through a bleedin' cave?"

"What's Ancora?" Rosie asked. Aidan's mouth dropped open. He took a step back, flabbergasted.

"What's Ancora? This! This is Ancora!" He gestured in all directions. "Everything you see for hundreds of miles! It's a country, sure enough, and you three are telling me you stumbled in from another place entirely?" He looked suspicious. "You're not pulling my leg? Taking a shot because of the whole trap thing?"

"No, we're not kidding, honestly!"

Lulabelle launched into the story of how the Harpers had come to be there, beginning with the discovery of the black rock and ending with their escape from the ox monster. When she finished, Aidan gave a low whistle.

"That's a load to drop on a fellow. There are legends of course, about other worlds, but no one actually believes them. And now you little birds—" He grinned at Kat, "—beg your pardon, *young ladies*, are proving they were true the whole time." He took a step forward, studying them. "I thought you looked different, your clothes and all, but another world?" Aidan shook his head. "Amazing! You look so human."

"We *are* human," said Kat, gritting her teeth. "We're exactly like you, only we're from our world, not Ancora."

"And we were going home," interrupted Lulabelle, shooting Kat a warning look. "So if you would point us in the right direction, we'll be on our way and you can go back to hunting."

Aidan looked disappointed. "Are you sure you don't want to stay? People might pay a fair price to see strangers from other worlds." His eyes gleamed. "Do you have any costumes from your land? Maybe with some sparkles? Or a headdress?"

"We're not in the circus," said Kat huffily. "Just tell us which way to go."

"Suit yourself, it's that way a fair piece." He pointed towards the woods behind them, although to Kat it looked like nothing but trees. "I'll walk you back myself, but I have some traps to check first, if you don't mind waiting. Who knows, maybe I've caught more children from other worlds."

The Harpers exchanged looks of alarm. They knew nothing about this Aidan, but the thought of traipsing through the woods alone was not a fun prospect.

"Okay," Kat said, in a voice that sounded braver than she felt, "we'll go with you."

"How old are you?" said Lulabelle as the Harpers hurried to keep up with Aidan's long strides.

"Thirteen," replied Aidan, studying the ground for animal tracks.

"Where do you live?"

"Here and there, depends where I can find shelter."

"Don't your parents mind you being out here alone?" asked Rosie.

"I suppose, if they were alive." An awkward silence ensued. The Harpers found themselves engrossed in watching for Aidan's traps, although Aidan himself didn't seem bothered at all. He made his way through the trees, whistling a tune under his breath.

"Tell us more about Ancora," said Lulabelle at last. "You mentioned provinces, I think?"

"Yep, eight of them." Aidan shook his head. "That's right, you don't know a jot about Ancora, do you? Well, it's a big country, hundreds of miles, maybe more. I never went to school myself, but I've seen maps here and there and Ancora's something fierce." He sounded proud, as if the size of the country was a positive reflection on its inhabitants.

"Some provinces are bigger than others—land wise—and some, like the Central City, are small but with lots of folks packed in. I haven't been to all of them, but I get around."

Aidan puffed out his chest, enjoying his new roles as ambassador and tour guide. "This here is the beginnings of the Hill province. Horse country, most call it. Fairest province of them all in the spring, when the wildflowers bloom the colors of the rainbow. People aren't a bad sort either. A few nosy old biddies, but most are decent about giving a lad odd jobs here and there. One of them took me in when I was a wee lad and a kinder soul you never saw." He looked sad all of a sudden, but didn't say more.

"What are the other provinces?" said Rosie. "Didn't you say there was one with lakes?"

"Aye, the Lake province, east of here. It's green too, but flat, and surrounded by a fair number of lakes. Some are so deep they don't have a bottom, with water as smooth as glass. But don't let that fool you. There's all kinds of critters below the surface—Asrai and Pixie Lights and Will-o-wisp. If you're not careful, they'll grab your ankles and pull you down, never to be heard from again." Aidan winked at Rosie and she couldn't help but smile back, even though that sounded like a terrible way to die.

"The Mountain province is that way." He made a vague gesture to the west. "Never met anyone from there myself. I know a chap who claims to have seen their leader, Ragnar, and said he was like a king of old, sure enough. I've heard their great hall—Vallengard it's called—is a grand sight, made of stone and ice and carved into the mountain.

"I'd like to visit the Mountain province," Aidan continued jovially, "if only to catch sight of a Blood Wrecker."

"What's a Blood Wrecker?" asked Lulabelle with revulsion. Anything with a name that unpleasant couldn't possibly be a good thing.

"Terrible big creatures, bit like wolves, but as smart as they are nasty. They say a Blood Wrecker can creep up on you in the dark and tear your throat out before you even know what's what, on account of the fact that it used to be a man, a long while ago, and still has its human brain. But I'm told they stay pretty well hidden, so you've not much chance of crossing one."

Aidan sighed, apparently disappointed by the utter lack of bloody danger. Kat couldn't resist a smile. She was doing her best to stay mad at him, but the more he talked, the more she felt her anger dissolving. It was hard not to respect a boy who survived on his own in a dangerous forest. Plus, he had such a cheerful way of talking that you couldn't help but like him. She ventured a question, instead.

"What about the other provinces?"

"The Cave province is behind us, but that one's a real puzzler. They keep to themselves and don't have much to do with the rest of Ancora. Sea province is south, don't know much about that one either, except they live underwater—"

"They live underwater? Do they have gills?" blurted Lulabelle and instantly turned red. Aidan didn't laugh, but seemed to consider the idea.

"Haven't the foggiest," he admitted. "I've only seen one of them from a distance but I wouldn't be surprised. They're thick as thieves with the Forest province and that place is full of magic, good and bad. I went through there awhile back and it was brutal on my heart, sure enough. The trees are so big and black, you feel like they'll swallow you alive. I never saw a soul, but I could tell they were watching me, daring me to come too close. I've never moved so fast in my life and my heart didn't beat right until that place was behind me."

Aidan lowered his voice. "They say a good many Spellbinders came out of the Forest province, and that's why it has so much dark magic."

"What are Spellbinders?" Rosie whispered. Aidan knelt down to study a paw print, nodded with satisfaction, and continued walking, the Harpers right behind him to catch every word.

"It's all hearsay, mind you, patches of stories I heard growing up. But a long time ago, long before I was born—long before everyone was born—Ancora had a dark age, with all kinds of treachery and black magic and provinces fighting each other. No one trusted anyone and there was a whole lot of betrayal and murder before it was all over. The Spellbinders were the worst of the worst—sorcerers trained in the most powerful dark magic—and they did their level best to turn everyone against each other and take over Ancora. They were finally driven out, at least the ones that weren't killed. Like I said, they're just stories, not even half true, and if there were

Spellbinders, they're long since dead and gone. But they do make right good tales around a campfire." Aidan stopped to give the Harpers a serious look. "And you'll not find me going through the Forest province again.

"Further south are the last two—the Southern province and the Central City. Central City's not bad, impressive buildings and good food, but not my cup of tea. Didn't care much for the people, either."

"What's wrong with them? Are they mean?" said Kat.

"Oh, they're respectable enough," said Aidan, in a voice that implied he didn't think much of respectability. "Not as bad as the Southern province. I spent a week there once and that was long enough for me. A bunch of lazy, stuck-up, good-for-nothings they are, with tempers to match their high opinions of themselves. And quick to turn up their noses at anyone who's not from those parts, the insufferable gits."

Aidan spoke with such contempt that the Harpers decided right then that they couldn't stand the Southern province and its horrible people. Lulabelle made a mental note to look up the word "git" and see whether it was appropriate to add to her vocabulary. Kat tried not to feel offended that Aidan had compared her to the Southern province earlier, while Rosie wished with all her heart that she was from the Hill province and could despise the South the way Aidan did. They were so lost in their thoughts that they didn't realize

Aidan had stopped walking. He held up a hand for quiet. Ever so softly, there came a faint whistling from the trees above them. As the whistling grew louder, Aidan motioned for the Harpers to step back.

"Right," he said, opening up his satchel and rifling through it, "this may be a problem. Stay where you are and don't look scared— it can sense fear. Don't look it in the eyes, either. And don't make any sudden movements, no matter what it tries to do."

"Why? What's happening?" Lulabelle exclaimed just as Kat said, "What can smell fear?" But before Aidan could answer, the whistling grew to a painful crescendo that made Rosie cover her ears, and the "it" swooped down from the trees and landed right in front of them.

Whatever Kat was expecting, it wasn't this.

The creature was huge and wore a ragged cloak that hid everything but its face and hands, great gnarled claws that looked like tree roots. Its face was pale and wrinkled. Instead of eyes, black sockets peered out from the cloak. Both the eye sockets and the teeth dripped blood, which streamed down its cheeks and chin. The Harpers stood frozen as the creature loomed over Aidan.

"I can't watch!" Rosie whimpered, her face hidden against Lulabelle's chest. Lulabelle, remembering Aidan's words, tried her best not to make eye contact with the creature, although since it lacked eyes, she wasn't sure if the black holes counted. Kat found herself mesmerized by the bloody teeth. Her legs appeared to have turned to jello.

"All right, madam, you've caught us, fair enough," said Aidan, his voice clear and calm, without a trace of terror. "No doubt we'd be a tasty snack for you, but there's far better things in this bag of mine." The creature made a low whistling sound. The dripping blood had formed a pool at Aidan's feet.

From his bag, Aidan pulled out two small white cubes, which he placed in the pool of blood. The creature sniffed at the cubes, then popped them into its mouth. Kat fought the urge to gag. Aidan nodded knowingly.

"I'm not surprised you fancy that, who doesn't like a bit of sugar? Now, if you don't mind, we'll be on our way and we shall leave you to a pleasant afternoon."

The creature smacked its lipless mouth but didn't move. It let out the same high-pitched whistle and lunged toward Aidan, swiping at his face with its claws.

Lulabelle squealed. Before she could stop herself, Kat yelled, "Hey, leave him alone!"

Aidan ducked in time to avoid the claws, but the combination of Lulabelle's squeal and Kat's shout made the creature notice the Harpers for the first time. It bared its teeth, raised its claws, and flew at them, screeching wildly.

With a burst of speed, Aidan leaped between the Harpers and the creature, throwing up his satchel as a shield. There was a tearing sound as the claws cut through the leather, then an outraged hiss. Aidan peered out from behind his shredded satchel.

"You win, madam. I admit I've been holding out, but there's no need to drag these nice little birds into this mess."

He lowered the bag, pulled out a dead rabbit, and placed it at the creature's feet.

"There you are, a Hill province hare, biggest of the season. It's all yours, if you'll let us be on our way." Kat held her breath, praying the creature preferred the taste of rabbit to children. It hissed again, grasped the rabbit in its mouth, and shot up into the trees.

"What *was* that?" shuddered Kat as Aidan hurried them away. Lulabelle had her arm around Rosie, who kept looking over her shoulder anxiously. Aidan fingered his shredded satchel.

"A Bloody Bones, one of the nastier creatures around here and that's saying a bit. It likes to jump down on unsuspecting travelers who've wandered off the road."

"You were so brave," said Rosie, running up beside Aidan and pulling on his sleeve. "Weren't you scared?"

Aidan looked surprised, then flattered by the compliment. He patted Rosie awkwardly on the head. "No worries, little bird. I knew I'd have something it fancied. Here we are, all in one piece—except for my bag, of course." He began to whistle breezily, but Kat noticed that he was sweating quite a bit for someone who claimed not to be afraid.

"I wish you'd been with us before," continued Rosie, "when we got chased by that awful ox monster. I've never been so scared in my whole life . . . until right now."

"Ox monster?" Aidan raised his eyebrows. "You mentioned that earlier. What ox monster?"

As Rosie described the shaggy creature with the question mark horns, Aidan's puzzled expression changed to a broad grin and then a snort of laughter. "I'm sorry, I don't mean to laugh," he said, although he didn't look sorry at all, "but it wouldn't have harmed a hair on your heads. More likely to give you a slobbery kiss, that's all."

"Harmless?" Kat retorted. "Why did it chase us through the forest then?"

"Hoping you'd play with it, I imagine."

Aidan laughed at the Harper's unbelieving faces. "It was a Parandrus you ran into, sort of a nature spirit in these parts. I can see how it might look fierce at first, but it's a right gentle soul. It's small, you see, nothing more than a puff of fur with eyes. It works its way up to the ugly brute you saw before starting all over again. Rather boring after awhile."

"There *was* a little blue animal right before the ox monster appeared," said Lulabelle slowly, "but we thought it was scared and ran away."

"Nope," replied Aidan, "just getting ready for its grand finale. It's not the smartest thing in these woods, and I don't believe it knows how ugly it is. Bit of a disappointment, I'm sure, when you jumped over the river bank."

Rosie looked crestfallen. "Poor little thing! I hope we didn't hurt its feelings."

Kat flung another look over her shoulder. "Aidan, back there, you called that creature 'madam.' How did you know it was a girl?" It hadn't exactly been wearing a necklace and hair bows.

Aidan shot Kat a sly look. "Well, I can't say whether it was a lady Bones or not, but it did look an awful lot like the ladies I met in the Southern province—almost as mean as some of them, too." He smiled at her, and for the first time since she'd met Aidan, Kat smiled back. Maybe she was going to like this boy after all.

The Harpers spent the rest of the morning following Aidan around the forest. Along the way, he pointed out various spots where he claimed to have faced all manner of fearsome creatures. Lulabelle and Kat doubted whether any of his stories were true, but Rosie hung on every word, gasping and cheering in all the right places. This only seemed to encourage him.

"It tried to pull your ears off!" shrieked Rosie when they paused under a misshapen old willow tree. "How did you get away?"

Aidan stuck out his chest and assumed a knowing look. "Oh, it almost had me, no doubt about that. I thought my number was up that time. But I knew that the Puca hates fire and it so happened that I had stol—-that is, I had found some matches lying around and I lit one and dropped it to the ground—right where you're stand-ing—and it formed a fiery circle around me. Then, I took my rope and threw it up into the highest branches there." Aidan pointed to the topmost branch of the willow tree. "The rope caught the branch and took me right off the ground! And I sat at the top of the willow, watching that ugly old Puca stamp around until it ran out of time and had to go back to its hole for another thousand years."

When they finally arrived at a dirt road that cut through the woods, Aidan glanced at them regretfully. "That's the way back to the meadow and the black rock," he said, pointing to where the road disappeared over a hill. "I'll walk you back a piece, make sure you don't run into anything unpleasant. At any rate, I'm out of luck with my traps."

"What will you eat if you can't catch anything?" said Kat.

Aidan shrugged. "I'm sure I can rustle up a plump chicken or two, there's usually one lying around someplace." Before any of the Harpers could ask him where he intended to find a chicken, Aidan put a finger to his lips.

" Someone's coming. A Hill wagon from the sound of it."

As if on cue, the scratchy sound of wheels on dirt rose from behind the hill. Aidan looked back and forth between the empty road and the forest, then sighed, looking apologetic.

"I'm afraid this is where I leave you. I'd prefer not to run into someone from the Hill province at the moment. And if you could avoid mentioning my name, I'd be most obliged."

"But, I thought you were going with us," exclaimed Lulabelle in dismay. "What if we run into another creature?"

"You'll be fine if you stick to the main road, hardly anything ventures out into the open." Aidan was backing up into the trees. "I'm awfully glad I got to meet you. Sorry again about all that trouble with the net."

"Why don't you want to run into someone from the Hill province?" Kat yelled after him, but he had already disappeared from sight.

CHAPTER FOUR
Kat Learns an Unpleasant Truth

I think they've seen us," said Lulabelle, drawing her sisters to the side of the road. "Let's be polite and friendly and maybe they'll leave us alone. Kat, that means I do the talking and you stay quiet, ok?"

"I can be polite and friendly," muttered Kat as the wagon lurched to a stop in front of the Harpers and a man stared down at them in surprise. He was a medium-sized man, with a high forehead, leathery skin and kind eyes. Seated next to him was a girl with flaming red hair that hung down her back in two braids. She gazed at the Harpers with interest.

"May I ask what you young ladies are doing in the Whispering Woods?" asked the man. "Have you lost your way?"

• 58 •

Kat and Rosie looked at Lulabelle.

"No sir, we've been out for a walk and we're headed back to the meadow. We live just beyond there." Kat noticed that Lu made no mention of Aidan, or the fact that, "just beyond there," meant a completely different world.

"These woods can be treacherous, child," said the man with concern, "especially for young ones. Where are your mam and da?"

"They're at home," replied Lulabelle truthfully, "but we've been gone a long time and I'm sure they're waiting for us. We'll head that way now." She motioned for Kat and Rosie to start walking.

"Wait." The man held up a rough hand. "It's a dangerous hike to the meadowlands. A moment ago I saw a hobgoblin through the trees." The Harpers looked at each other in alarm even though none of them had heard of a hobgoblin until that moment. "Why don't you come with us, have a bit of lunch, and then we'll take you back to your home."

"Oh, you don't have to do that," said Lulabelle hastily. "It's fine—we're fine—to walk back." Her voice trailed off as she looked at the empty road. Kat knew she was imagining all the unseen monsters, hobgoblins and otherwise, hiding in the shadows.

The man shook his head. "It's past noon already, and it'll be one before you reach where you're going. Are you sure you're not a wee bit hungry?"

"No sir, we had a big breakfast."

Rosie's stomach let out a low growl of disagreement, which she tried to hide by wrapping her arms around herself. The man's lips curled into a smile. "Right, perfectly full you say."

He turned to the girl. "Maeve, be a good lass and pop up the wagon for them." She nodded and hopped down from her seat, unlocking the back of the wagon so that the wooden side dropped with a bang.

"Our cottage is not far and my wife is planning a grand feast in honor of our homecoming. I assure you there will be plenty to share. We couldn't call ourselves good Hill folk if we didn't offer a bit of hospitality to strangers now and again." Sensing their hesitation, his voice softened. "I promise you, children, we mean no harm. It will do my Maeve good to have company her own age to chatter with. My ears need a long rest after the jabbering she's given them."

"Da!" The girl blushed and smiled shyly at the Harpers. Lulabelle smiled cautiously back, then turned to Kat and whispered, "I'm not sure what to do. We can't walk back to the black rock by ourselves. You heard the man . . . it's dangerous. There could be a hobgoblin—whatever that is—or one of those bloody things waiting for us. Anyway, I don't think we have a choice. You-know-who left us and we have no way to get back safely. Plus, you-know-who said the Hill folk are good people."

"Yes, but you-know-who forgot to mention that they don't like him!" retorted Kat, but Lulabelle had turned back to the man. "If you're sure it's not too much trouble, sir, we'll go with you after all."

"Excellent! We are delighted to have you as our guests." The man gestured for the Harpers to climb into the back of the wagon. The red-haired girl climbed in beside them and they were off with a jolt.

"I'm Liam Stewart," said the man over his shoulder, "and this is my daughter, Maeve." Maeve held up her hand in an embarrassed wave. The Harpers introduced themselves and the four children settled into an uneasy silence.

"I'd never been to the Central City before yesterday," Maeve told them after several minutes had passed and it became clear she was dying to talk. "It's a grand place, it is. All those buildings full of people, wearing the fanciest clothes I've ever seen. And the rose garden filled with real swans? Amazing!" She rested her chin on her hands. "I would love to go back at Winterfest and see the fountains change color. Have you ever seen it?"

"No, we haven't. We live . . . er . . . near the big meadow . . . um . . . where the black rock is, and we . . . we've never gotten around to visiting . . . er . . . although we hear it's lovely in the spring . . . " Lulabelle faltered and Kat made a face. Lu was without a doubt, an exceptionally bad liar. Mr. Stewart turned in his seat, eyebrows raised.

"Near the meadowlands, you say? I wasn't aware that anyone lived in those parts. What is your family name, child?"

"Froggybottom. Our parents are Maximillian and Roberta Froggybottom," replied Kat, without blinking an eye. Lulabelle looked stricken. "You wouldn't know them, though. We just moved and . . . and we haven't met any neighbors yet."

"I see." Mr. Stewart's eyebrows rose higher. "And which province did you come from, if I may ask?"

Kat's mind cast around for one of the provinces that Aidan had mentioned. "The Lake province!" she shouted, hoping she didn't sound too desperate.

"Really? The Lake province?" Mr. Stewart smiled. "What a coincidence. I go there often to trade so I know many of the families. Tell me, who's leading the Lake province right now?"

Lulabelle made a noise somewhere between wheezing and gagging. Rosie slid lower in her seat. Kat crossed her arms and gave Mr. Stewart a defiant look.

"They were in the middle of an election when we left, so we can't tell you that," she said firmly, determined to stick with her story. Mr. Stewart nodded, still smiling.

"I see. Well, we're glad to welcome you and your family. I hope you're settled soon." He turned back in his seat and Kat let herself relax. That was easier than she thought.

"Just out of curiosity," came Mr. Stewart's calm voice over the lurching of the wagon, "was your home in the Lake province spared during the dragon rampage two months ago? We heard all about it. Such a terrible waste."

"Oh yes," replied Kat without hesitation. "It was terrible, really terrible. Houses burned to the ground, bodies everywhere, lots of screaming, begging for mercy. That's a dragon for you, though—" she broke off at the sight of Lulabelle, who was signaling to her, a panicked expression in her eyes. Maeve looked confused.

"But there haven't been dragons in the Lake province for ages," she said. "Isn't that right, Da?"

Mr. Stewart pulled on the reins and the horses came to a stop. He turned again in his seat and regarded the Harpers. "No, Maevie, there haven't," he said in a serious voice. "Would you little birds care to tell us where you're really from and why you felt the need to deceive us?"

Rosie looked nervously from Lulabelle to Kat, whose mind was working feverishly to come up with a more plausible untrue story. Lulabelle's face reddened .

"Yes sir, I'm sorry. We didn't mean to lie, and we *did* come from the meadow, but . . . . it's a little complicated. I'm not sure you would believe us if we told you because we're having a hard time believing it ourselves—"

"Why don't you tell us and then we'll decide," said Mr. Stewart patiently. With a nervous glance at her sisters, Lulabelle began to explain, for the second time that morning, how they had found their way into Ancora, although she left out the part about getting trapped in a net and meeting Aidan. When she was finished, Maeve shook her head, her eyes shining.

"It's too incredible to believe! My gran used to tell me stories about other worlds, but I never really—that is, it's all so . . . " She let her words drift away, as though unable to hold onto the right ones.

Mr. Stewart was quiet, his face pensive. "The black rock you say? You found a tunnel from your world to Ancora through the black rock? You're not from Ancora, you're strangers . . . travelers here." It seemed to Kat that he was talking more to himself than to them. "I appreciate your honesty," he said finally, "and we would still be honored if you joined us for lunch. I assure you, a dragon rampage is unlikely." He turned back to his horses, but as he did, Kat saw a worried expression flit across his face.

If her father was somber, however, Maeve was downright giddy. "I can't believe it!" she repeated, beaming at Lulabelle, Kat, and Rosie as if they were shiny new toys. "How lucky that we ran into you! I want to know all about your world. What's it like? What do you eat? Do you have a wagon, too?" Her excitement was so infectious that before long, all four girls were laughing and talking as if they had known each other forever. It seemed like only minutes had passed before Mr. Stewart called back, "We're coming into the Hill province, children. We're nearly home."

Stretched out before them was an ocean of emerald green hills, some so large that their grassy tops disappeared into low-hanging clouds. Sounds echoed from the valley below and Kat spied a herd of cows on a nearby slope, their bells clanking as they meandered through the lush grass. Dotting the landscape were cozy looking stone cottages with brightly colored doors and shutters. Kat could see neat rows of flowers and vegetables growing behind most of the cottages. As the wagon made its creaking way into the valley, the grass gave way to more cottages and more people, until it became clear they were leaving the countryside entirely and entering a town. A young woman sweeping her front porch with a toddler at her feet waved as they passed. Three middle-aged ladies with baskets huddled together chattering, their voices blending like a gaggle of excited geese.

In the front yard of one cottage, a group of children were playing a game that involved a red ball and lots of yelling. They turned to watch the wagon and one of the boys called out, "Who you got there, Maeve?" Maeve waved back but didn't answer. The Stewarts seemed to know everyone and as the wagon rumbled by, they were bombarded with greetings and good-natured teasing.

Although many people were smiling, Kat couldn't help but notice that quite a few others glared at them suspiciously, and one old woman slammed her door as they turned onto a narrow dirt path, marked with deep, bumpy ruts.

The Stewart's house was at the end of the path, a white stone cottage with a blue door and shutters and window boxes full of pink and purple flowers. Moss covered one corner of the house while rose bushes formed a protective hedge around the small front yard. Kat thought it looked just like a fairy tale.

A tall woman, who resembled an older version of Maeve, appeared in the doorway. With a gleeful shout, Maeve hopped from the wagon and ran to her. The woman kissed the top of Maeve's head, regarding Lulabelle, Kat, and Rosie with a pleasant but bemused expression. As Maeve introduced the Harpers, Mrs. Stewart glanced questioningly at her husband.

"Maeve and I happened upon these little ladies back in the woods. We couldn't abide them eating crabapples and tree bark, so we brought them along with us for a true Hill province feast." Mr. Stewart winked at the Harpers, but Kat saw him lock eyes with Mrs. Stewart and unspoken words seemed to pass between them. Maeve's mother must have understood, because turning to the Harpers, she smiled with genuine warmth.

"We are delighted to have you. Maeve, why don't you fetch a blanket and you and your new friends can eat in the pasture."

The Stewart's cottage was small but inviting. The wood floors, although old, were clean and polished. The main room was divided into two parts: a sitting area with a love seat and two rocking chairs, and a simple kitchen. Against the back of the kitchen was a stove on which several pots were bubbling, and in front of the stove, her back to the Harpers, was the oddest little woman Kat had ever seen. At least, she was dressed like a woman, but when she turned to face them, Kat suddenly wasn't so sure.

The woman was no more than a foot tall and floated above the ground, her legs trailing under her as though treading water. Her skin was very wrinkly and she had large eyes and a sharp beaked nose. When she saw Maeve, her wrinkly face broke into a smile and she made a noise that sounded like the tinkling of bells.

"What is THAT?"

Kat spoke the words without thinking, and the little woman's face went dark. Glowering at them, she began to chatter furiously in her unknown language, her meaning clear even if her words were not.

"Kat, that's rude!" hissed Lulabelle, elbowing her sister in the ribs. "You don't ask someone 'what' they are—apologize!"

Kat opened her mouth but the little woman was carrying on so loudly and persistently that she couldn't get a word in. Maeve held up her hands to calm the woman, who took a deep gulp of air, her big eyes bulging.

"Now, now, Alberta, she didn't mean anything by it, truly she didn't. These are new friends of mine and they're not even from

Ancora, can you imagine? They come from a place very different from here, and they've probably never seen a brownie, so please try to be understanding."

The little woman snorted and said something else in her tinkly language, to which Maeve replied, "Yes, but it was only a slip of the tongue, and of course, we all know how valuable brownies are, not to mention graceful and lovely to look at."

Kat thought that was pushing it a bit, but since she had started this whole mess, she wasn't in a position to disagree. In her best imitation of Lulabelle, she nodded, trying to look apologetic.

"I'm really, *really* sorry. I didn't mean to hurt your feelings. Maeve's right, I've never met a brownie before today. I've never even seen one. I mean, I've eaten them, of course, we all have—"

Alberta looked terrified. Maeve made a choking sound.

"Wait, that's not what I meant!" Kat gasped, struggling to undo the horror of her words. "Brownies are different in our world— they're not like you, they're sweet—not that you're not sweet! But I would never eat you! You're chocolate—I mean, they're chocolate!"

Alberta glowered at her. This was going from bad to much, much worse.

"Quick, Kat," Maeve was murmuring out of the corner of her mouth. "Pay her a compliment—anything!"

"Um . . . " Kat's mind went blank. "I love your—" What compliment could she find for this grumpy, ugly little woman whom she had accidentally threatened to devour? "—your beautiful, silky hair," she finished lamely. This was clearly a lie, as Alberta's hair bore an uncanny resemblance to a clump of weeds. The little woman crossed her eyes and stuck her tongue out at Kat. She turned back around to the stove, but Kat noticed she patted her hair several times and made a satisfied noise. Maeve breathed a sigh of relief.

"Right then, nice work, Kat. That bit of flattery should last a good long time. We'll leave her to the kitchen and get that blanket, shall we?"

"So, that . . . lady in your kitchen," Kat could tell Lulabelle was trying not to sound rude. "Who is she?"

Maeve laughed as she spread the blanket down on the grass next to the Stewart's cottage. "That's Alberta, one of our brownies and—like all brownies—she's mighty proud of that fact. Much better than us lesser mortals." Maeve removed her socks and heavy shoes and stretched out on her stomach.

"What's a brownie?" asked Kat, kicking off her own shoes and socks. The grass felt cool and tickled her toes.

"I don't know exactly and I'm sure no one else does either, except maybe the Enchantress. They're related to fairies in some way, or is it trolls? I can never remember which it is. Da bought this cottage and land from Alberta and her husband when I was a baby. A few years later, Alberta showed up at the front door with all her bags. She told us that her husband had died and she was moving back in . . . we could stay if we liked." Maeve laughed, remembering. "She threatens to turn us out at least once a month, but I don't know what we'd do without her. Brownies are a cheerful lot, for the most part, unless you hurt their feelings, which is quite easy to do. But they're also incredibly vain, so one good compliment works wonders. Ah, here's Mam with lunch, looks splendid!"

Maeve jumped up to help her mother carry a large basket laden with all kinds of delectable foods. From the basket, Mrs. Stewart brought out a plate of roasted pork with a red, fruity plum sauce, buttery potatoes, fried eggs, bread drizzled with honey, freshly picked strawberries, and cabbage stew, which the Harpers accepted politely, but turned out to be so delicious Kat had to stop herself from lapping it up like a dog. Mrs. Stewart was as kind as her husband, but Kat couldn't help but notice the same worried look in her eyes. Once or twice she gazed out at the hills, as though her thoughts were somewhere else entirely. She returned to the cottage and the children ate in contented silence, the only sound coming from a distant cowbell. When Kat had eaten all the honey bread she could stomach, she lay down on her back and closed her eyes.

"Maeve, you said something about an Enchantress. Is she like a witch?"

"No, at least, I've never thought of her that way," Maeve replied. "She's part of a circle of Enchanters who watch over Ancora. They're as old as the hills and they've got powerful magic. I suppose they're like our guardians. The Enchantress watches over the Hill province. We don't see her very often, but with all the bad stuff that's happened—" Maeve stopped talking abruptly. She looked as though she had swallowed some sort of nasty bug.

"What sort of bad stuff?" Kat sat up. "Is that why people in your town seemed mad that we were here? I saw one lady shut her door when we passed."

"Are they scared of us?" asked Lulabelle in surprise. Rosie stopped trying to catch a blue and yellow striped butterfly to listen.

"No! That is, not really." Maeve picked at a loose thread on her dress. "We've had a bit of hard luck, that's all. But it's nothing to do with you!"

She bit her lip and immediately changed the subject to other provinces and what they were like. Maeve had yet to travel anywhere beyond the Central City, but she was eager to share everything she had heard with the Harpers, who in turn, were eager to hear more about Ancora, beyond the little information supplied by Aidan.

"Da only took me to the Central City because he promised that when I turned eleven, he would take me, and I know he thought I'd forget, but I didn't so then he was stuck and had to do it! I'm good and determined to go to all the provinces before I'm eighteen, sure enough."

"You're eleven? I'm eleven," said Lulabelle, and both girls beamed at this newfound camaraderie. "What's your school like?" Lulabelle asked and Kat immediately lost interest.

Feeling restless, she got to her feet and picked up the picnic basket filled with empty plates. "I'll take this back," she said, wondering if Alberta was still in the kitchen and whether the comment about her hair had lifted the brownie's dour mood.

As she approached the door, the sound of urgent voices stopped her. Mr. and Mrs. Stewart were in the kitchen and through the open window, she could hear them clearly. Although Kat knew it was rude to eavesdrop on other people's conversations, she couldn't help but listen, especially when it became clear at once that she, Lulabelle, and Rosie were the topic of conversation.

"It could all be a coincidence, couldn't it?" Mrs. Stewart was saying. "The children coming after everything else?"

"I'm not sure I believe in coincidences anymore," replied Mr. Stewart. "Not after Birdie's murder and especially not after this spring. By themselves, maybe, but together? It's too much."

"But they're only children—nothing but wee birds. How could they possibly have anything to do with our trouble?"

"I don't pretend to know the answer to that, but then that's the problem, isn't it? We've never really known . . . we just assumed . . . "

There was a silence.

"There's black magic at work here, Colleen, no doubt in my mind. Ever since the winter, the ground's been saturated with evil. Even before it came. I fear if anything else happens . . . " Mr. Stewart didn't finish his thought but let the words dangle ominously.

"Should we tell the children? Warn them in some way?"

"No, not until we know more. Perhaps I'm wrong and it's a coincidence, as you say. I do know this, though—we found those little birds wandering alone in the woods and they claim to have come through a tunnel from their world. I suppose they could be telling tales, but it's more than that. There's something different about them. If I were a betting man, I'd wager they're no more Ancoran than a kelpie is tame."

There was another silence during which neither Mr. or Mrs. Stewart spoke. Then Mrs. Stewart said quietly, "Does this mean the other legends are also true?"

"I don't pretend to know the answer to that. But she will, if anyone does. And she said we should send word if anything else happened."

"Do you think the children to be in danger?" Mrs. Stewart sounded distressed.

"Until we have some answers, we must assume the entire Hill province is in danger. Only the darkest sorcerer is capable of the black magic we've seen. No one else could have summoned it."

"Maybe it won't come back, maybe it's gone for good. What else could it take from us that it hasn't already?"

"We'll know more when we talk to her," said Mr. Stewart in a placating tone. "For now, I think it's best to say nothing." Kat heard the sound of a chair scraping across the floor as he rose to his feet. "But this much we do know—someone truly evil is out there. If this person believes the legends and finds out that three children have mysteriously arrived in Ancora, I don't know what they'll try to do, to us or to them."

Her heart racing, Kat clutched the picnic basket and darted around the side of the house, trying to make sense of what she'd heard. Bad things were happening in the Hill province, black magic was involved, and someone named Birdie had been murdered. There were also legends that might or might not be true and a mysterious "she" that the Stewarts trusted. But the most urgent thought that kept banging around in Kat's head like a very loud drum was that a dangerous, evil person was out there, and as long as that person was free, she and her sisters were in terrible danger.

CHAPTER FIVE

The Harpers Manage to Agree

After lunch, Maeve disappeared into the cottage and immediately returned with the news that Mr. Stewart had agreed to take them through the village on their way back to the meadow. "We'll have such a grand time!" she declared, clapping her hands. "I can't wait to show you off!"

After the conversation she had overheard, Kat wasn't sure she wanted to be "shown off." If there was a dangerous person lurking in the Hill province, that person could be anywhere. What if he saw the Harpers? Kat watched Mr. and Mrs. Stewart talking quietly as Mr. Stewart got his horse and wagon ready. She tried to move closer in the hopes of hearing their conversation.

"—More suspicious if we take the children and leave," Mr.

Stewart was saying as he fitted the bridle on his horse. "Half the village saw us come home, including Neala Moloney and Saffronella Quigley, so that means all the village by now."

Mrs. Stewart said something that Kat couldn't hear, to which Mr. Stewart replied, "I agree, but best to treat it casually. I'll take the long way through town, but we won't dawdle. My hope is that—" The horse gave a loud neigh and the rest of his words were lost. Mrs. Stewart looked up and Kat quickly turned her head.

When everything was ready, Mrs. Stewart removed a small cloth bag from her apron and carefully counted out a few silver coins, which she gave to Maeve with instructions to stop for a sweet at Piddlewick's. They climbed into the wagon and Mr. Stewart turned to look at Maeve, his face grave.

"If anyone asks, tell them that our new friends are from north of the Central City and leave it at that. Let's not be mentioning caves or another world or anything of that nature, understand?"

Maeve frowned. "You want to lie about where they're from? Why?"

"Not lie exactly," Mrs. Stewart interjected, "just a bit vague on the details. We think it best to let people believe Lulabelle, Kat, and Rosie are from Ancora, especially with the . . . eventful spring we've had. The less said, the better."

"Yes, Mam," said Maeve quietly and Kat knew Maeve understood more than she was letting on.

The town itself was unlike anything Kat had ever seen. The street was made of cobblestones and the buildings were tall, narrow and all different colors. Kat felt like she was flanked on both sides by very large, long rainbows. Flower boxes adorned the windows of most shops and the sidewalks were filled with people, although Kat spied glimpses of wrinkly faces, similar to Alberta's, fluttering through the crowd.

Three men in beards and red hats stood outside a shop called Flanagan's Elixirs & Restoratives, each playing different oddly shaped instruments (Kat had to do a double take at the sight of bubbles floating out of one tuba-like horn) and stamping their feet in time to the music. A tired looking woman was pulling a wailing child out of a shop called Fiona's Finest Flowers, her shopping basket filled with vivid blue and gold petals that appeared to be singing. Next to the flower shop was a green building with a purple door and sign that read Gilded Thistle: Quenching Your Thirst For Over 50 Years! On the sign was a picture of two smiling mugs that were dancing a jig. A brownie who looked to be the proprietor floated just outside, tinkling a greeting to everyone who entered. Raucous laughter echoed from within the open windows. A few shops down, a portly young man was standing on a ladder, polishing a gold lantern while a small dog pranced around him, nipping at his pants. As

Kat watched, the little dog leaped into the air and sank its teeth into the portly man's backside. With a childish squeak, the man toppled dramatically into a wheelbarrow. Shaking his fist at the dog, he chased it down the sidewalk, unaware that his pants were torn and his pink undershorts were on display for all to see.

Mr. Stewart stopped in front of the shop where the portly young man had been and handed Maeve a piece of paper.

"Quickly now," he told her. "I'll stay with the wagon if you want to take our guests inside." Under his breath, Kat thought she heard him say, "The bakery should be safe if nothing else."

A chime sounded as the Harpers and Maeve entered the bakery, a cheerful, light-filled shop with pale yellow walls. Several people stood in front of a narrow counter on which were stacked rows of mouth-watering breads and pastries. A large, pleasant-faced woman in a pink apron moved back and forth, taking orders and laughing heartily with her customers.

"That's Mrs. MacDougal," Maeve told them. "She's one of the kindest souls you'll ever meet. Also, a terrible gossip. Mam sells Mrs. MacDougal fruit from our garden and she's quite fond of me, so if we're patient she might slip us something tasty."

"Maeve dear!"

Mrs. MacDougal beamed as they reached the front of the counter. She smoothed her graying hair back into its bun, leaving a streak of flour.

"How are you this fine day? Do you know, I made the most delectable tarts with the blackberries your mam sold me. Folks couldn't get enough. Why, Olive McCutcher was simply irate when I told her they were gone, although Olive always looks like she swallowed a hedgehog, poor dear. I simply won't allow you to sell anywhere else, especially not to Killian's, because I know for a fact they don't use actual butter in their pastries and I shudder to tell you what's really in them—"

Kat felt like she was standing in front of a large, happy fan that was blowing directly into her face. Mrs. MacDougal went from one topic to the next without appearing to draw breath or expect any answer in return.

"And I heard about the terrible business with your chickens." Mrs. MacDougal made a clucking noise, like she was a chicken herself. "What is this world coming to? And right on the heels of our recent misfortunes, I declare! One of these days we'll be killed in our beds, you mark my words!"

She stopped to take a breath and Maeve quickly introduced the Harpers, explaining with a slight hesitation, that they were recent acquaintances from near the Central City. If Mrs. MacDougal was suspicious, she didn't let on, although she did fire off a volley of questions that made Kat feel sure the baker would have been an excellent interrogator for the army, if only she wasn't so cheerful.

At last Maeve managed to break through Mrs. MacDougal's

torrent of words with a hasty, "I'm afraid we must be on our way, Mrs. MacDougal. Da's waiting for us in the wagon."

"Bless me, I almost forgot! Puddy MacDougal, where are you?"

The shop door opened and the portly man burst through, his face flushed. "Yes, Mam, do you need something?"

"Of course I need something, Puddy my boy, why else would I be calling you?" scolded Mrs. MacDougal good-naturedly. "Make yourself useful and bring me the chocolate cake from the store-room. Don't even think of swiping a taste of frosting!"

Puddy grimaced. Kat realized he must have discovered his pink underwear was showing. Flattening himself against the wall, he shuffled comically around the perimeter of the room, hands glued to his rear, until he reached the safety of the bakery counter and fled into the back room. Maeve and the Harpers tried not to laugh. He returned, clutching a package, which Mrs. MacDougal presented to Maeve, a nervous smile on her lips.

"He was so kind, your dear father was," she stammered. "When I think about what would've happened—-my poor Puddy might've—and risking his own life—" Mrs. MacDougal pulled out a handkerchief and blew her nose with the force of a charging rhinoceros. Maeve stared at the floor, embarrassed.

"Well, enough of that." Mrs. MacDougal smiled again and handed Maeve a small brown bag along with her other purchases. "Here's a tasty to keep your strength up. And stay away from the cheese shop—rumor has it that the latest batch soured and now half the village has diarrhea!"

As the Harpers followed Maeve out the door, Kat heard Mrs. MacDougal's voice boom, "Puddy MacDougal, what do you mean by parading around in your under drawers?"

"What was Mrs. MacDougal talking about in the bakery?" Kat said when they were back in the wagon. "What happened to your chickens? What was the terrible business? I didn't know you had chickens. And how did your dad risk his life?"

"Kat, stop being so nosy!" whispered Lulabelle but Kat ignored her. How would you ever find things out if you didn't ask questions?

Maeve sighed as she opened the bag from Mrs. MacDougal and passed out fruit tarts. "We don't have chickens. We used to, but someone pinched two of them a few weeks ago and another one three nights ago. We depend on those chickens for eggs, and since they're my responsibility, I'm allowed half the money." She took a ferocious bite of fruit tart, her face grim. "Now we're down to three young hens, so it's bound to be months before I can afford anything nice. All because some plonker was too lazy to buy his own chickens!"

"That's terrible," murmured Rosie. "You have no idea who stole them?"

"Oh, I have ideas!" retorted Maeve. "I'd bet you a bag of geldings it's that no good redheaded boy that does odd jobs around town.

You can tell by looking at him that he's a shifty one. I wouldn't be at all surprised if he's behind the other thefts, too."

The Harpers felt suddenly uncomfortable. Surely Maeve wasn't talking about Aidan? Maybe there was an army of red-haired boys who did odd jobs of one kind or another. "What other thefts?" asked Lulabelle, forgetting her own advice about nosiness, but Maeve had already hopped out of the wagon.

She led them into a store with a purple awning and a wooden sign that said, "Piddlewick's," in fancy red letters. Inside were the tallest shelves Kat had ever seen and rows of twinkling silver lights hovered above the room like hundreds of fireflies. As far as she could tell, the twinkling lights weren't attached to anything. The counter-top was made of marble and behind it hung a board on which a gold pen with an enormous feather added numbers, as though held by a giant invisible hand. Mountains of candy were stacked haphazardly around the room, some reaching all the way to the ceiling. Lulabelle bent down to inspect a mound of chocolate butterflies and jumped back in surprise as the butterfly candies rose into the air and floated around the shop in a single graceful line.

"Hallo?" came a faint voice from behind the marble counter. "Is someone there? Show yourself you rascally scoundrel or I'll turn the candy on you!"

The Harpers looked at Maeve in alarm but she laughed and

called back, "Mr. Piddlewick, it's Maeve Stewart and I come in peace! No need to turn us into chocolate frogs!"

"Can he do that?"

Kat was torn between fear and an overwhelming desire to see Lulabelle transformed into a large chocolate frog. From behind the counter came a scraping sound, as though someone was moving boxes and then a crash, followed by a muffled cry.

"Finnegan's fanny! That hurt!"

The sounds grew louder as papers flew into the air over the counter. Each bump resulted in more muttering by the unseen Mr. Piddlewick and one barely audible oath that made Maeve gasp, "Mr. Piddlewick, language, please!"

Kat was about to decide they were better off not meeting the mysterious (and seemingly accident-prone) shop keeper, when a shower of golden sparks exploded into the air and Mr. Piddlewick landed on the countertop.

"Maevie, my girl! What a delight to see you! I was taking inventory of my sleeping sugar snaps and . . . well . . . I'm afraid I couldn't keep my eyes open. Hazard of the job, don't you know?" Mr. Piddlewick turned pink. "That wasn't so bad, but I was also sampling a new fruit drink that I'm planning for the Midsummer festival—Cokeley's Creative Juice, guaranteed to bring out your hidden talents—and apparently I built a replica of the clock tower and trapped myself inside." He bowed. "But of course, I take the risks so my customers don't have to. And it really was a remarkable clock tower. Very architecturally sound, even if I slept through the actual building of it."

Standing in front of them was the funniest man Kat had ever seen. He was two feet high and dressed from head to toe in a gold suit. He was very stout, with red cheeks, a brown beard, and a pair of eyeglasses that kept slipping off his nose. Kat took a step closer toward Mr. Piddlewick and before she could stop herself, asked the first question that popped into her mind.

"Are you a leprechaun?"

Behind her, Lulabelle sputtered, "Kat!"

Mr. Piddlewick glared at Kat over the rims of his eyeglasses. "My dear young lady," he said icily, "I am most certainly not a leprechaun. Please don't insult me by asking such a ridiculous question." Bowing again, Mr. Piddlewick returned to his jovial self. "I am a clurichaun, you see. We're an entirely different clan!"

"Okay." Kat was relieved that she hadn't hurt Mr. Piddlewick's feelings too much. "Is that like—I mean—what's the difference?" She heard Lulabelle sigh in exasperation.

"Oh dear, here we go," muttered Maeve. Mr. Piddlewick's eyes twinkled.

"For starters, we are at least three inches taller! We practically tower over them, poor, tiny, stunted little souls." He hooked his thumbs in the lapels of his coat and puffed out his enormous stomach. "Then there is the matter of color. Leprechauns have an absurd fondness for green, which I fear makes them look like large stink bugs. Not at all a happy comparison. Clurichauns, on the other hand, are much more open-minded toward the color spectrum." He smoothed his suit. "I myself am partial to gold. Not only is it slimming for, uh, certain body types, but I'm told it brings out my eyes." He batted his eyelashes at Kat and she couldn't help but laugh.

"Now, Maevie, my girl," he said, when Maeve had finished introducing the Harpers, "as delighted as I am to see you, I suspect you're not here to chat with a forgetful, sour-faced old bag. Besides, Mrs. Piddlewick is out for the day!" Mr. Piddlewick laughed so hard he hiccuped. "Bertram's bloomers, I'll pay for that when the missus gets home!" he gasped between cackles.

He wiped his eyes with the cuff of his coat, still chuckling. "So, what will it be my friends? Sunflower Suckeroos? Firework Fizzies? One of my Yummy Gummy dragons? Careful how you eat that last one. I put enchantments on a few and they actually breathe fire. A pity I can't remember which ones."

Maeve laid the silver coins on the counter. "Please Mr. Piddlewick, may we have four Honeyfizzes?"

"Excellent choice! You can never go wrong with a classic." Mr. Piddlewick swung his arms back and forth, as though conducting an orchestra, while behind him bottles of different sizes and shapes mixed together with a great deal of clanks and spills. Four bottles of amber colored liquid floated out on a tray and Kat hesitantly took a sip of hers. It tasted sweet and thick and delicious, but it was more than that. It reminded her of sunny days, grilled hamburgers, the beach, and riding her bike all mixed together. Next to her, Lulabelle's eyes were closed, a contented smile on her lips while Rosie swayed back and forth, keeping in time to music only she could hear.

"I see you too are fans of Piddlewick's famous Honeyfizz," beamed Mr. Piddlewick. "I made that particular batch after Mrs. P and I enjoyed a delightful picnic in the hills. Most restorative! I daresay it's infused with enough happiness to lighten the most downtrodden soul."

"Do you mean Honeyfizz is magic?" Lulabelle asked, her eyes popping open. "It makes us feel happy because you were happy when you made it?"

"Something like that," nodded Mr. Piddlewick, bouncing on the balls of his feet. "I use a very special honey, you see, from bees kept by the clurichaun for centuries. I suppose you could say that it soaks up my feelings at the time of harvest and brings out similar feelings in the one who drinks it. A most wonderful magic, indeed." Mr. Piddlewick's expression darkened. "Of course, there was the unfortunate batch I made while struggling with a mortifying stomach ailment. I won't tell you what sorts of feelings it brought out in my customers, but I did have to give a substantial refund with that one."

The Harpers said their goodbyes to Mr. Piddlewick, who waved his hands in the air, sending a burst of sparks over their heads that turned to snowflakes. As she reached the shop entrance, Kat noticed a peculiar pile stacked against a wall. This pile wasn't made of candy, but was a mishmash of jewelry, clothes, china cups, a pair of bookends, and a large model ship. A few pieces of elaborately wrapped chocolate sat on top.

"Mr. Piddlewick, what's this pile? Do you sell other things besides candy?"

The shopkeeper turned sharply as the feather pen toppled to the ground. Maeve drew in her breath. Several seconds of awkward silence passed before Mr. Piddlewick blinked and replied in a loud voice, "Just a bit of summer cleaning the Missus and I are doing. Time to sweep out the old, bring in the new, that sort of thing. Nothing at *all* out of the ordinary, I assure you."

"What was that about?" whispered Kat as she, Lulabelle, and Rosie followed Maeve out of the store. "Didn't you think it was weird the way he got nervous when I asked about that pile by the door?"

"Yes, it was weird," said Lulabelle thoughtfully. "You know what's weirder? When someone tells you everything's fine and there's nothing to worry about. Grown-ups only do that when something is very wrong. Remember Poopsy?"

Poopsy had been the Harpers first pet, an overweight guinea pig whose talents were sleeping, eating, and not much else. Kat remembered the day four years ago when Poopsy had stopped eating. Their parents had gone out of their way to reassure them that Poopsy was probably fine and just needed a checkup from the vet. They buried Poopsy the next day.

"It's not only Mr. Piddlewick," continued Lulabelle, as two women coming toward them abruptly crossed the street, their faces wearing identical suspicious expressions. "Other people are acting strange, too. I think . . . ." She hesitated. "I think they're afraid of something."

Kat bit her lip, remembering the Stewart's conversation. She would tell Lulabelle everything when they were alone, but not here. She cast her eyes around nervously, wondering where this sorcerer was, and if he was watching them at that very moment.

Mr. Stewart was deep in conversation with another man when the Harpers and Maeve climbed back into the wagon. The man was short and balding, with a round, babyish face, and wore the same brown trousers and white shirt as Mr. Stewart, although his stretched considerably over his pudgy middle. A red hat perched jauntily on his head and he wore matching red boots. Kat had a fleeting thought that he looked like an overgrown elf.

"—Simply madness to cancel it!" The man was saying in a bleating voice that reminded Kat of a sheep. "The Midsummer festival is the biggest event of the year! But no one wants to risk the chance of dying horribly. They won't sign a release for that!"

Mr. Stewart cleared his throat and the man stopped talking. The worried look on his face was replaced by a broad smile as he noticed the Harpers.

"Ah, the young ladies themselves! Liam was telling me all about you, my dears. Aifric Digby, mayor of the Hill province—at least until the next election, eh Liam?" He nudged Mr. Stewart.

"I hope you've enjoyed our simple village," continued Mayor Digby cheerfully. "We may not have as much excitement as other provinces, but no one can best Hill folk in our hospitality towards visitors!" He clapped his hands and leaned forward. "From what I understand, some visitors come from much farther away, do you not? Perhaps, *worlds away*?"

"Don't worry, children," said Mr. Stewart soothingly, as Kat, Lulabelle, and Rosie exchanged panicked glances. "I trust Mayor Digby completely. We've been friends for over thirty years."

"Quite right," nodded Mayor Digby sagely. "There's no need to worry. We don't want all of Ancora coming to gawk at you, after all." Lulabelle gulped and Kat knew she was imagining millions of eyes watching her. It would be Lu's worst nightmare.

"I must say, it's incredible!" Mayor Digby said, removing his hat and twirling it around. "I owe my dear sweet mother an apology for laughing at the stories she told me when I was a lad. Stories of other worlds, and all true, she said! And with the recent dark events, the fact that you children have come seems like fate, like the prophecy—"

"Aifric!" said Mr. Stewart, a warning tone in his voice.

"Naturally, by dark events, I'm referring to the extraordinary amount of rain we've been having!" the mayor stammered. "Wonderful for the plants, but it creates a melancholy mood among the Hill folk. That's all I meant."

"I think we've stayed long enough," said Mr. Stewart, giving Mayor Digby a meaningful look as he climbed back into the wagon. "You and I can meet later to discuss the festival, Aifric."

"Of course, everything in good time!" agreed Mayor Digby, nodding and bowing as though controlled by invisible strings. "No worries, Liam, we'll sort it out when you get back. Safe travels, young ladies. I do hope to see you again!"

The forest was quiet as the Harpers wriggled out of the black rock and sprinted down the hill toward their cabin. Kat beat her sisters to the back door and flung it open. "We're back! We had the most incredible morning, you're not going to believe it!"

Mrs. Harper looked up from a chair by the window, a partially drawn image of the lake on an easel in front of her.

"Hello, yourself! I'm glad you've had a good time. I haven't heard so much as a peep from any of you. Your dad left for a meeting at the college a little while ago. Have you been exploring the rocks at the top of the hill?" She glanced down at her watch. "Good heavens, where has the day gone? I guess you were having fun if you missed lunch!"

"It's fine, mom," said Rosie. "We're not hungry at all."

"She's right," agreed Kat. "In fact, we found the most unbeliev-able—ouch!"

She had been on the verge of spilling the whole story of the black rock, Ancora, Aidan, Maeve and all the rest, but Lulabelle had abruptly (and quite painfully) stepped on her foot.

"A cave," interrupted Lulabelle. "An amazing cave, Mom. It's perfect for a fort. We'll probably spend all our time there. And Rosie's right—we're not hungry, honest."

"If you're sure." Mrs. Harper smiled at her daughters. "This forest is such a magical place."

"You have no idea," muttered Kat to Lulabelle, who elbowed her in the ribs.

"It does explain things," said Lulabelle that night after Kat had told her about the conversation she'd overheard between the Stewarts. They sat cross-legged on their beds, the moonlight throwing silvery shadows against the wall. "Something bad is happening in the Hill province and whatever it is, it's really bad . . . so bad that only a very evil sorcerer could be behind it." Lulabelle hugged her knees. "And somehow, our coming has made it worse, whatever it is. That's why Mr. Stewart was so serious when we left."

Kat nodded. Mr. Stewart had made each of them promise several times that if they returned to Ancora, they would come straight to the Stewart's cottage and nowhere else. Then he had made them repeat the directions to the Hill province until he was satisfied they were sufficiently terrified at what might happen if they disobeyed. Even then, he had still seemed uneasy about letting them return; in the end, Maeve had volunteered to meet the Harpers the next morning and show them the way herself. Mr. Stewart was still looking somber when they left.

Kat and Lulabelle were silent for a few moments until Kat blurted out a thought that had been hiding at the back of her mind.

"Lu, you said this morning that Ancora was dangerous and we shouldn't go back. Do you still think that?"

Lulabelle hesitated. "I know I said that, but that's when we were alone. We hadn't met Aidan or the Stewarts and everything seemed scary. Now that we know them, I don't feel quite so scared."

"I agree," said Kat. "I don't think Mr. Stewart would let anything happen to us." She took a deep breath. "Lu?"

"What?"

"We discovered a secret, magical world today!"

Kat and Lulabelle looked at each other, then put their pillows to their mouths and screamed, careful to muffle the sound. Lulabelle held out her hand so Kat could see it trembling.

"It's insane!" Lulabelle whisper-shrieked. "It's completely against logic or science or anything. Another world, Kat! With people and magic and who knows what else!"

"And it's our secret!" Kat whisper-shrieked back. "No one knows anything about it!"

"You're right, it is our secret," Lulabelle said, frowning suddenly. "Yours, mine, and Rosie's. If we go back to Ancora, we have to tell her everything."

"No way, it'll scare her to death. She's too little."

"It will not scare me to death!" came a voice from behind the bedroom door. The door opened to reveal a small, pajama-clad figure with crossed arms and an indignant expression.

"Rosie, were you eavesdropping?" said Kat, equally indignant. Rosie bounced onto Lulabelle's bed and snuggled up to her sister.

"Of course I was. How would I know what you were talking about if I couldn't hear you? And I'm not scared," she added. "Well, maybe a little scared, but I still want to go back. They're in trouble and maybe we're not the ones who can help them, but we should at least try." She crossed her arms again. "And I'm NOT little!"

Kat and Lulabelle tried to hide their smiles. Kat patted the bed and Rosie bounced over to her. "Okay, Rosie, whatever you say, you're the boss."

"I've also been thinking," said Lulabelle, "I don't think we should tell anyone what we found today. I think we should keep Ancora a secret between the three of us."

"Not even Mom and Dad?" said Rosie. "Why?"

"For one thing, I don't think they would believe us. A magical world? That sort of thing doesn't happen here. And if they did believe us, I'm sure we wouldn't be allowed to go back, especially if they knew it could be dangerous."

"So it's our secret," whispered Kat with an air of finality. "We tell no one, right?"

The Harpers gazed at each other, each aware that this moment was extremely important. In years to come, they would feel the weight of this decision in their bones, like an anchor tethering a ship to a harbor. From now on, their lives would be very different. Finally, Lulabelle and Rosie nodded.

Kat took a deep breath and looked at her sisters. "Our secret then—only ours. Tomorrow, we go back to Ancora."

CHAPTER SIX

Aidan Does Something Dangerous

The next morning, Kat leaped out of bed and threw on her clothes in record time. She paused to clasp the circle necklace with the intertwining loops around her neck and tuck it safely into her shirt. Since it was the reason they had discovered the secret tunnel to Ancora, she regarded it as her special lucky charm; with the dirt and grime gone, it actually looked pretty. Kat pounded downstairs and into the kitchen where Lulabelle was scrambling eggs in a pan while Rosie buttered slices of toast.

"Here, take this," said Lulabelle, shoving a plate of eggs and toast toward Kat. "Dad's already left and Mom's setting up her easel on the dock." She handed Kat a sheet of paper on which was printed, *"Supplies for the fort."*

"Now," said Lulabelle, pulling out her own sheet of paper, "if we're going back to Ancora, we need to be prepared. Rosie—"

"Supplies for the fort?" asked Kat, munching on her toast. "What's that?"

"I couldn't take the chance that Mom or Dad might find these lists, especially yours Kat, because—let's face it—you tend to lose things. I thought it might sound better this way. Plus, the black rock *is* a cave so it's basically a fort, however you look at it."

"Very sneaky, Lu," nodded Kat. "I like it."

"Rosie, you're in charge of medical supplies, like bandaids, things like that. I think everything's in the hall bathroom."

"Can I bring vitamins?"

"Vitamins? Sure, you can bring vitamins. Kat, you'll—"

"Why do you need vitamins, Rose?"

"I don't know, they seem like a good thing to have."

"Maybe you should bring a saw in case Lu gets run over by one of those flying horses and we have to take her leg off!"

Rosie giggled. Lulabelle sighed. "That's ridiculous and gross. No one's getting their leg sawed off. Kat, you're in charge of snacks, but only if you promise not to eat them all before we get to Ancora. Also, don't bring only chocolate bars. I'll be in charge of flashlights, extra batteries, whatever else might come in handy. It's not like we'll need everything, but we should be prepared."

At that moment, Rosie spotted Mrs. Harper coming up the

hill and they hastily put away their lists and concentrated on eating breakfast as fast as they could.

Ten minutes later, the supplies had been located and Kat's backpack was nearly full, but she sifted through the snacks one last time. She tossed in some bottles of water and considered whether to bring peanut butter crackers, which she knew Lulabelle and Rosie preferred, or another chocolate bar (just to irritate Lu).

"Kat, hurry up!" called Lulabelle from outside. "Make sure you bring apples, they're first on the list!"

"I've got them!"

"I listed everything alphabetically if that helps!"

"Thanks, Lu, I said I got it!"

"Rosie left her inhaler on the table so bring that, too!"

"Fine!" Kat answered distractedly, trying to resolve her snack dilemma. She decided to err on the side of more snacks and stuffed them both into her backpack.

"Hey kiddo," said Mrs. Harper, coming into the room with a small canvas in her arms. "I'll be painting on the dock if you need me. Lu says you girls are going to play on the hill by the big rock?" Her mother was smiling and Kat had to remind her heart (which seemed to be doing backflips in her chest), that Mrs. Harper's question was perfectly innocent.

Kat nodded. "It's a great fort. We'll be up there most of the day."

"Okay, be careful. No jumping off that rock or anything dangerous. And please watch out for Rosie and make sure she doesn't overdo it."

"Kat, where are you?"

"Mom, I have to go." Kat threw the door open. "I promise we'll be careful. Have fun painting!" She took off before her mom could think of any more instructions.

The sky was the same radiant blue when the Harpers emerged from the tunnel into Ancora. Once again, the two moons stared back at them, but this time Kat felt entirely different emotions. Now she was struck by utter amazement that it was still true, that Ancora really was here and it was their secret.

Lulabelle set her backpack down and scanned the hillside. "I don't see Maeve yet," she said, checking her watch.

Kat reached into her own backpack for a snack. "Why do you think Maeve and Mr. Stewart couldn't see the tunnel yesterday?"

"I don't know." Lulabelle looked thoughtful. Despite the Harper's insistence that there was, in fact, a gaping hole in the middle of the rock, neither Maeve nor Mr. Stewart had been able to see anything other than a solid black wall. It was one more question in an ever growing list of questions.

"For crying out loud, Kat!" Lulabelle snatched the bag of chips out of her sister's hand. "We just ate breakfast—these are for later!"

"I'm hungry now!" Kat protested, but was interrupted by Rosie.

"Maeve's coming!"

A lone figure was moving at a brisk pace toward the rock. At the sound of Rosie's yelling, she broke into a run, arriving breathless and beaming a minute later. They set off together in the direction of the Hill province, Maeve chattering all the while.

"I know we're going to have a grand time this summer! There's so much about the Hill province that I want to show you. I'm awfully glad you're here. If you hadn't come, Mam would've made me play with Birnie Sullivan, down the way, and all she wants to do is sit at home like a grown-up lady and stitch needlepoint on pillows or monogram her socks."

"That sounds horrible!" said Kat with feeling. "Who would want to do that?"

"Exactly what I say," agreed Maeve. "Who wants to waste their time being elegant and stuffy when there's life out there waiting to be lived?" She flung out her arms in the general direction of the sky.

"Aren't we going to your house?" said Lulabelle as Maeve veered off the path and guided them towards a large hill covered with yellow flowers. "I thought we were supposed to go straight there if we came back."

"We'll get there before long," replied Maeve breezily. "The Cahir are practicing today, and you simply have to see them. I wouldn't be a proper hostess, otherwise."

"What are the Cahir?" said Kat, her curiosity aroused. "Is that another creature?"

"Not in the way you're thinking," laughed Maeve. "The Cahir are warriors—guardians of the Hill province. I don't know how you become one because they're quite secretive, but it's a great honor to be chosen and it doesn't happen often. Their horses are the fastest and most beautiful in the hills. They say that a Cahir and his horse are so connected they can sense what the other is thinking. I don't know if that's true, but the horses are special, no doubt about it. Some of our old ones even claim there's magic in them. It's great fun to watch the Cahir practice and they don't usually allow an audience so we're in luck."

"Is this ok with your dad?" asked Lulabelle, now looking worried. "We don't want to make him angry."

"It's only dangerous in the Whispering Woods," replied Maeve. "That's why he was upset when we ran into you yesterday. There's all kinds of creatures that live there and some of them are quite nasty, I'm told. But it's the shortest way to the Central City so we'll take the wagon and stay on the main road when we have to." She hesitated, for the first time looking uncomfortable. "He doesn't *exactly* know I'm taking you to see the Cahir, but it doesn't happen that often. I'm sure he won't mind."

Lulabelle still looked uneasy as they reached the top of the hill and gazed down into a crater-shaped valley. Numerous black dots, which Kat assumed were people, flocked the hill across from them. In the center of the valley, forming three tight rings, stood a group of twenty or thirty horses and riders. In the middle of the rings, one lone figure on a white stallion appeared to be shouting directions. The horsemen were too far away for Kat to hear what was being said, but almost at once the riders scattered, half going to one side of the valley and half to the opposite.

The Harpers and Maeve found seats under an oak tree and watched the activities with fascination. As the two lines of horsemen galloped towards each other, Kat noticed that one group carried something that, from a distance, looked remarkably like spears. The two sides galloped past each other, and the horsemen hurled the spears through the air, where they were expertly caught by the other line of horsemen.

Kat felt a tap on her shoulder and Lulabelle passed her a pair of binoculars. "Here, you can have a turn. I used it for the last thing."

"Thanks, Lu."

Kat should've known Lulabelle wasn't joking about being prepared for all possibilities. She peered through the binoculars. The Cahir were taking turns racing toward two posts at the end of the valley closest to the Harpers. A small metallic ring hung from each post and as the first horseman drew near, he rose to his feet in the saddle and launched a spear through the ring. It struck the post with a dull thud. The horse cantered around the edge of the valley, the Cahir still standing upright. Kat's mouth fell open.

"That's unbelievable! How do they do that?"

Maeve grinned as she took a turn with the binoculars. "It's some kind of magic, sure enough. Da says it's a mix of learned skill and natural talent, and you either have it or you don't. I suppose that's why it's so hard to become one." She pointed at the man on the white stallion. "That's Cathmor. He's the leader of the Cahir and good friends with Da. Aren't the horses beautiful? They really are the best in the Hill province. Probably Ancora, too."

The horses were beautiful, no question; gray with black manes and tails, others chestnut or gold. Kat was about to ask Maeve which horse was her favorite when she felt a sharp rap on the top of her head. An acorn rolled into her lap, followed by another, and then another. Glancing at the trees, Kat spied a freckled face with a mop of unruly red hair gazing back at her.

"Aidan!" she cried, jumping to her feet. "What are you doing here?"

Aidan was stretched lazily out on a low branch, legs crossed, hands behind his head. His faded brown satchel, still shredded from the run in with the Bloody Bones, hung from the branch above him. He flicked another acorn at Kat, who caught it this time and threw it back at him, laughing.

"Aidan, we came back!" cried Rosie. "We came back, and we have new friends, and we drank Honeyfizz, and so many things have happened since we saw you!"

"It sounds like an adventure, sure enough." Aidan pretended to notice Maeve for the first time. "I told you the Hill folk would take care of you, didn't I? I suppose if you're the right sort you get the royal treatment, don't you now?" He laughed, but Kat detected a bite in his words that hadn't been there before. Maeve's eyes smoldered.

"It's you again!" She spat the words. "Tired of snatching chickens? Thinking of going for a Cahir horse? That sounds about right!"

"Have you two met?" Lulabelle asked hesitantly. She knew it was polite to introduce strangers but it didn't seem appropriate when one of the strangers appeared ready to clobber the other.

"Everyone in our village knows him!" scoffed Maeve. "He's the one I told you about—the no-good boy who's been stealing us blind! He pretends he's all about finding honest work, but we know better now, don't we?" She turned to the Harpers. "How do *you* know him, anyway?"

Lulabelle glanced at Kat and Rosie who were both wearing guilty expressions. "Well," she admitted, "we might've left out a few things about yesterday."

She tried to ignore Maeve's stormy face and launched into the story of getting trapped in Aidan's net. Kat jumped in to explain how Aidan had rescued Lulabelle and then proceeded to save them from the Bloody Bones, which she hoped made Aidan sound brave, but was afraid made him appear reckless. Maeve did not look impressed.

"You haven't lost another chicken, have you Maeve?" asked Kat, casting a worried look at Aidan, who smirked and tossed an acorn at the ground.

"No, but the Connallys lost one of their prize hens last night." Maeve's voice had sunk almost to a growl. "That's on top of everything else that's been stolen—jewelry, coins, all over the village. Everyone knows it's him, even if no one's caught him yet!"

"Now, Maeve," said Aidan, swinging down from his branch onto the grass, "it's not kind to accuse people of stealing things . . . although I'm sure whoever took that hen last night enjoyed it immensely. I bet they roasted it over an open fire until the skin was crisp and the meat was juicy and rich." Aidan licked his lips. "But that's all speculation, mind you, I wouldn't know anything about that."

"You think you're funny, don't you? You should stand in the village square and tell jokes, you should!" Maeve had turned bright red, which along with her hair, gave her the appearance of a very angry tomato. "But I suppose if I was worthless with no talents of my own, I might stoop to stealing chickens in the middle of the night, too!"

The Harpers stood awkwardly, watching the scene unfold. Kat wished she could jump in to defend Aidan, but she had a sinking suspicion that Maeve was right, at least about the chicken stealing. Aidan continued to smirk, but his eyes burned and Kat could tell Maeve's words had stung. A victorious cry sounded from the valley as one of the horsemen completed a difficult drill and Aidan glanced in the Cahir's direction. Maeve followed his gaze.

"Maybe the chicken thief has better plans for himself. Maybe you're thinking of joining the Cahir and becoming a great warrior. Is that why you're watching them? Hoping some of their talent and bravery will rub off on you?"

Aidan took a step towards her, fists clenched, but stopped himself. He gave a careless shrug. "I don't think it's all that hard, what they do," he said. "From where I sit, the horse does most of the work. All the rider has to do is not fall off."

Maeve crossed her arms and gave Aidan a nasty smile. "Then why don't you show us all how easy it is, Mr. Chicken Thief?" She pointed to their end of the valley, where a dozen Cahir horses grazed. "Those horses look awfully available. The Cahir can't see you, so you won't get in trouble—not like that's a big concern. And we can all watch in awe, amazed at how anyone can be a Cahir."

Aidan hesitated. He gazed down the valley at the riders, then back at the grazing horses. Kat thought he looked a little nervous.

Aidan took a deep breath. "Sure, why not. I could use some

excitement in my day, and I'm sure Lulabelle, Kat, and Rosie would like a bit of fun before you bore them to tears with walking tours of the Hill province." He stuck his hands in his pockets and set off down the hill toward the horses, whistling. Lulabelle turned to Maeve, her face worried.

"Is this really a good idea? Won't he get in trouble if they see him?"

"I'm not making him do it. It was a suggestion, that's all. Maybe this'll wipe that smug smile off his face!"

"But if they catch him, won't he mention it was your idea?" Lulabelle persisted. "Won't we all get in trouble?"

Kat had to admit she was with Lulabelle on this one. The thought of making a group of warriors mad, particularly ones with spears, didn't seem wise. She wondered whether Aidan had ever ridden a horse and if he would admit it if he hadn't. She watched as he reached the bottom of the hill and moved toward the horses.

"Do you think it's true?" Rosie said quietly. "Do you think Aidan really did steal the chickens and everything else?"

Kat and Lulabelle looked at each other. Kat knew they were both remembering Aidan's comments about finding a chicken for dinner.

Aidan was only a few feet from the horses now. Kat thought she heard him whistle, but the horses paid no attention.

"Ha!" Maeve plopped down on the grass triumphantly. The

horses had moved away from Aiden, their noses in the soft grass, their tails flicking back and forth. "They won't even let him come close. They must be excellent judges of character."

Aidan stood motionless, his hands clasped behind his back, his head bowed. Kat suspected he was praying for a giant meteor to strike the valley and distract everyone, but that was only a hunch. Minutes passed and nothing happened. Just as Kat was starting to think Aidan might have fallen asleep, one of the horses raised its head. Pricking its ears forward, it turned toward Aidan, as though noticing him for the first time. It was a beautiful horse, with a mahogany mane and tail, and a coat of white with red speckles. It studied Aidan for a long moment. Slowly, Aidan lifted one arm and the horse trotted over and put its nose in his hand.

The Harpers held their breaths as Aidan moved to the horse's side. Kat couldn't tell if he was speaking to it, but the horse's ears remained pricked. Grasping its mane with both hands, Aidan launched himself into the air and onto the horse's back. He gave it a pat and the horse trotted forward along the edge of the field.

"He's on the horse," said Maeve, and Kat could tell she was surprised. "I've never seen a regular person ride a Cahir horse. I didn't think it was possible."

They watched Aidan guide the horse in a slow circle. He grinned at them and gave a salute as he trotted by their hill. The Harpers waved back. Aidan made two laps around the small corner of field, then, picking up speed, guided the horse over to the wooden post where the Cahir's spears were still lodged. After several moments of wrestling, he successfully yanked out a spear, gave the horse another pat, and the two trotted off a little ways before turning back to face the post. Even from this distance, Kat could see the determination on Aidan's face.

Rosie gripped Kat's arm. "Do you think he can do it? What if he gets killed?" She covered her eyes with her hands. "I can't watch!"

Kat wasn't sure she wanted to watch either. Next to her, Lula-belle was exhaling deeply. "I read a story once, about a British nobleman who decided to take up spear-throwing as a hobby."

"What happened to him?" Kat couldn't take her eyes off of Aidan and the horse.

"Well, the story is called, '*The Bizarre Death of Sir Amos Gilly-wood*,' so there you go."

"Is he doing it?" squeaked Rosie from behind her fingers. "Did he fall off? He fell off, didn't he? No, don't tell me! I don't want to know. Just tell me he's not dead—he's not dead, is he?"

"He's fine, Rosie, he's not even going that fast," said Maeve pee-vishly, but even she looked anxious. The horse was galloping now, headed for the post, its mane flying. With quivering legs, Aidan rose to his feet in the saddle, grasping the spear, his face pale. Kat willed herself to keep her eyes on Aidan as he and the horse raced toward the post. When they were within striking distance of the metal ring, Aidan gave a tremendous heave and hurled the spear through the metal ring.

THWAP!

The spear soared cleanly through the middle and wedged itself into the post. Instantly, the horse slowed to a trot and Aidan dropped back into the saddle. Kat let out a cheer.

"He did it! He actually did it! Did you see that, Rosie?" She pulled Rosie's hands away from her eyes. "That was amazing! Lu, tell me you saw that!"

"Yes, I saw it," Lulabelle's voice was shaking. "I'm glad he's alive. He could've broken his neck."

"Don't think about that now," said Kat as they ran down the hill toward the field, Maeve trudging behind. Aidan brought the horse to a gentle stop in front of them, a smile threatening to take over his whole face. Rosie alternated between telling him how brave he was and how glad she was that he hadn't died, while Lulabelle sputtered something about the unfortunate Amos Gillywood and was quickly cut off by Kat. Aidan made a half-hearted attempt to shrug off the attention, but he couldn't stop beaming and petting the horse's soft mane.

"It wasn't that hard once I got the hang of it," he told them. "A little tricky at first, but Red Star and I managed fine." The horse gave an approving neigh.

"How do you know its name?" asked Lulabelle, holding out

her hand for the horse to sniff. The horse gazed at her with large brown eyes.

Aidan's smile flickered. "I guess I don't. It popped into my mind somehow, that she looks like a Red Star. And the funny thing is, I think she likes the name because she went a little faster when I said it."

"You can't name a horse that doesn't belong to you," retorted Maeve. "Only the Cahir name their horses—everyone knows that. And she no doubt went faster because she was trying to throw you off."

"Ah, Red, I didn't see you there," said Aidan, his smile even wider. "I'm sure you were hoping I'd get knocked off, weren't you? Break my neck? Maybe get dragged for a bit? Sorry to disappoint you, but it looks like I'm still standing." He gestured toward the horse. "Why don't you take a turn? After all, if a worthless, no-good, chicken thief can ride, surely an upstanding citizen like yourself can do it. What do you think, Red, are you up for it?"

Maeve looked like she was up for clubbing Aidan over the head with his own satchel, and for a second, Kat thought she and Lulabelle might have to keep their friend from throwing herself at Aidan and pummeling him with her fists. She glanced at Rosie, knowing how much her little sister hated fights. Rosie, however, didn't appear to be listening. Her breathing had slowed and her whole body had gone still. Her eyes were on the distant hills.

It was then that Kat saw it too. A shadowy mist moving towards them.

The shadow topped the farthest hill, disappearing into the valley. For the first time, Kat noticed that the sun, warm and bright only moments before, had been replaced by iron gray clouds. An icy breeze stung her cheeks as a trickle of dread slid down Kat's back. Everything was still, as though the entire Hill province was frozen. The dark shadow surfaced at the top of the next hill. It was moving towards them. Coming for them.

"What's that black mist?" she asked Maeve, but found to her shock that Maeve had gone completely white. For a long moment no one moved. Then, as another gust of cold air stung Kat's cheeks, Maeve turned to the Harpers with wild, scared eyes.

"It's the fog banshee," she whispered with barely concealed panic. "We have to get to the village. NOW!"

CHAPTER SEVEN

Attack on the Hill Province

W hy? What's going on? What is that thing?" Lulabelle
fought to keep the panic out of her own voice. Maeve
didn't answer, but grabbed Aidan's arm.

"You know what it is, don't you?" Aidan nodded, his eyes on
the mist.

"Then you know we have to get to the village and warn everyone!"

They all stared, mesmerized, as the black mist loomed closer.
Tendrils of fog curled in and out of the dark mass, like some kind
of smoky octopus. A low buzzing filled the air. With a start, Aidan
came out of his trance and bolted up the hill, snatched his satchel
in one swift motion, and sprinted down the other side, toward the

path that led to the village. Maeve and the Harpers did their best to keep up.

"I don't understand, what *is* that thing?" Lulabelle repeated, reaching for Rosie's hand and prodding Kat forward, although Kat needed no encouragement.

Maeve didn't look back. "It's a fog banshee—a demon monster from the North. If we can't get to the village, people won't have time to get ready, and if they can't get ready—" She shuddered.

"What happens if it catches us?" cried Kat, casting another glance behind her. She was fairly certain the answer wouldn't be a happy one.

"WE DIE!" Maeve had to shout to be heard. "It traps you in its fog and suffocates you! It nearly got someone last time and if we don't move faster, it'll get us!"

Over the relentless buzzing, Kat heard another sound—a steady thumping. The thumping grew louder and appeared to be coming from the same direction as the fog banshee. Aidan spun around.

"Stand back. Horses are coming."

The Harpers, Maeve, and Aidan scurried to the side of the path just as ten horses and riders thundered around the bend, the man on the white stallion leading the way.

"It's the Cahir!" cried Maeve, sounding relieved. The warriors skidded to a stop, dust and pebbles flying, and the man on the white stallion peered down at them. He was, without a doubt, the fiercest man Kat had ever seen. He had thick black dreadlocks that curled past his shoulders, a jagged scar over his right eye, and arms the size of boulders. In his belt was tucked a sinister looking knife. Kat knew at once she would never want to make him angry.

"There's not much time," growled the man. "The banshee will be here soon." He regarded the Harpers critically. "Have you ever been on a horse?"

Lulabelle, Kat, and Rosie nodded, although judging by the look on the man's face, Kat had a feeling their answers didn't matter.

"You'll want to hang on," he said. "We ride fast and we won't stop if you fall off. Not this time."

In the distance came the long blast of a horn. The man looked grim. "The village knows it's coming. Now pray we get there before it does." He made a clicking sound and the white stallion took off down the path.

Kat felt a strong hand encircling her waist as one of the warriors yanked her off the ground and onto the back of a grey speckled horse. She wrapped her arms around the man's middle, feeling a bit like she was hugging a brick wall. A black horse flew past and Kat caught a glimpse of Maeve, followed immediately by Lulabelle and her warrior. Rosie's warrior was so massive that Kat couldn't even see Rosie sitting in front of him. She looked for Aidan and spied a flash of red hair disappearing into the woods.

"Hold on!" barked her warrior and they were off, careening

toward the village before Kat had time to be annoyed with Aidan for deserting them.

The wind whipped her hair and stung her eyes. Kat's stomach felt like it was rocketing around somewhere in her throat. She buried her face in the warrior's back, clasping his middle as hard as she could. He barely moved, and Kat considered the possibility that he had glued himself into the saddle. She, on the other hand, felt like she was on a roller coaster with no seat belt, doors or brakes. The horse leaped over a tree branch and Kat gave a screech of protest as she bounced into the air. In front of them loomed the Hill village, the rainbow-colored buildings cheery and bright despite the approaching darkness. She peeked around the warrior's back, hoping for a glimpse of Lulabelle or Rosie, but their horses rounded another hill and disappeared from sight. She hoped Lulabelle had managed not to throw up.

A dull pounding filled her ears as the horses clattered across the bridge and up the deserted main street. The town was conspicuously absent of people, but Kat noticed something else in their place. Lots of somethings, to be exact. Piles of assorted odds and ends sat lumped together outside every doorway. Paintings, books, jewelry, furniture, even a child's bicycle, spilled onto the sidewalk like some bizarre garage sale. The horses came to a stop outside a shop with gleaming gold lanterns. Mrs. Stewart burst out of the door, followed by Mrs. MacDougal and Puddy, and Kat realized they were at the bakery.

Without warning, the warrior lifted Kat roughly off the horse, deposited her on the sidewalk, and galloped up the street before she could gasp out so much as a "thank you." She felt dizzy from all the bouncing and sank onto a nearby bench.

Mrs. Stewart hurried over. "Cathmor, did you see Liam? He went looking for Maeve when we spotted the banshee. I thought he might've run into you."

Cathmor shook his head. "I didn't see him, but it was chaos out there. It took all of my men to keep order and send everyone to the village. He might've gotten lost in the crowd."

"But you didn't see him on the path?" There was a tremor in Mrs. Stewart's voice. "What if something's happened? Shouldn't you go back to look for him?"

"You know I can't do that, Colleen," replied Cathmor in a gentle tone that seemed at odds with his wild appearance. "The rest of the province must be warned. Liam wouldn't want anyone risking their lives for him, and we both know he can take care of himself."

Cathmor leaned down to lock eyes with Mrs. Stewart.

"Whether or not Liam comes back, you know what to do. Get everyone inside, bar the door, and don't open it until that demon is gone!"

Mrs. Stewart bit her lip, nodding. Cathmor made a motion and the remaining group of Cahir disappeared up the street, the clattering of hooves echoing off the buildings. Surrounded by the Cahir, Kat had felt safe, in spite of the terrifying horse ride and the fog banshee bearing down. Now that they were gone, she felt more scared and confused than ever.

"Let's get inside, dearies." Mrs. MacDougal ushered them out of the street, glancing fearfully in the direction they'd come. "Don't you worry, everything will be all right." She tried to smile, but Kat thought she looked more afraid than any of them.

"Mam, where's Da? What do you mean he hasn't come back?" Maeve followed Mrs. Stewart into the shop as Puddy closed the heavy door and Mrs. MacDougal directed them to the far corner of the bakery.

"Your Da and I were getting ready to go into town when we saw it. I came on foot to warn the village, and your Da took Rumple and set off for the black rock. He knew you were meeting your friends." Mrs. Stewart gazed out the window anxiously, but the street remained cold and empty. Mrs. MacDougal began to stuff rags under the door, but Mrs. Stewart laid a hand on her shoulder. "Please, Ivy, let's give him one more minute." Mrs. MacDougal pursed her lips, but set the rags down.

"What happens if he doesn't come back?" Maeve's voice rose shrilly. "Da's too smart and too fast to get caught by the fog banshee, isn't he? And Rumple's the best horse in the valley. Of course, they can find somewhere to hide, somewhere safe—"

"Hush, child." Mrs. Stewart pulled Maeve close to her. "Don't worry about your Da. Cathmor is right."

At that moment, the lanterns lining the street shattered, glass shards exploding in all directions. Kat pressed her nose to the window pane, her heart pounding. The sky had turned black, as though an unseen hand had flipped a switch. The buzzing grew louder. From the window, Kat saw the eerie black mist approaching the village.

"It's here!" she croaked. "I see the fog banshee!"

But then, another figure caught her eye, cutting across the hill, directly in front of the monster. It was small and fast, coming from the west.

"It's Da!" screamed Maeve, clutching at the window. "Da's coming! He's right in front of it! He's trying to beat it, Mam!"

"Open the door, Puddy!" commanded Mrs. MacDougal. "Now!"

Mrs. Stewart rushed out the door, Maeve and the Harpers toppling after her. The frigid wind whipped Kat's hair, tearing up her eyes. The buzzing sound was at a piercing crescendo. Mr. Stewart hunched low in the saddle, urging Rumple on as the horse thundered over the bridge, moving so fast it seemed like it had eight legs instead of four. The fog banshee towered over them, tendrils of fog reaching out with grasping, claw-like fingers. If she stared hard, Kat thought she saw the outline of a face, mouth screaming, eyes red and burning. But then the fog rolled over itself and the face vanished in the blackness.

"Hurry, Da!" Maeve screamed above the buzzing as horse and rider hurtled toward the village. Mrs. MacDougal's eyes were closed, her lips moving in a silent prayer.

"He's not going to make it!" cried Puddy, "It's almost got him!"

The fog banshee was closing in on Mr. Stewart and Rumple, threatening to envelope them both. Lulabelle put her arms around her sisters, turning Rosie so she wouldn't see whatever horrible thing was about to happen. Kat felt as though time itself had ground to a crawl; everything was happening in slow motion. Above the relentless buzzing came a low, steady wail. It sounded so agonizing that it was all Kat could do not to scream. Mrs. Stewart stifled a sob and tears streamed down Maeve's cheeks.

"It's the death wail of the fog banshee!" screeched Puddy. "It's moving in for the kill, it is! Save us all!" Mrs. MacDougal stopped her praying long enough to slap him on the side of the head before he could say more.

All at once, the scene changed. To Kat, it felt like a movie that had been suddenly switched from slow motion to lightning speed. With a burst of desperation, Rumple charged up the street, his eyes white, his flank soaked with sweat. The fog banshee let out another piercing wail. It lunged once more but grasped only air. Rumple's last ditch effort to outrun the monster had been enough.

"Everyone inside!"

Mrs. Stewart shoved the children into the bakery, Mrs. Mac-Dougal and Puddy stumbling in behind them. Mr. Stewart leaped off the horse and hurled himself through the open door while Rumple took off in the direction of the hills. Mrs. MacDougal slammed the door.

"Quick, Puddy, stop up the cracks!" she directed, dropping a wooden bar across the doorway.

Mr. Stewart struggled to catch his breath, his chest heaving. Ignoring the protests of Mrs. Stewart and Mrs. MacDougal, he got to his feet and joined the Harpers at the window. One of his shirt sleeves was torn and a jagged red bruise was forming on his arm where the fog banshee had grazed him.

"Should only be a few seconds more," he panted, watching the street. "It moved faster this time."

"Will your horse be okay, Mr. Stewart?" asked Rosie, peering nervously after Rumple. Mr. Stewart nodded, his breath coming in short gasps. "Don't worry about Rumple, child. A fog banshee has little interest in a horse. Not when there's far more valuable things here." He tensed. "Here it comes. Everyone down."

The Harpers dropped to their knees obediently. Kat's heart was hammering in her ears but she couldn't look away. It was impossible to see the other side of the street through the thick darkness. The buzzing had faded into unnatural silence. The fog banshee drifted past the bakery and Kat watched the pile of goods outside the shop disappear one by one into the blackness. She raised her head to get a better look and saw that other piles lining their side of the street had also been swallowed up.

"Treasure for the fog banshee," Maeve explained in a low voice. "It's the only way to make one leave. You surrender your most valuable possessions. Once it has its treasure, it goes back to its home."

"But I thought you said it's been here before," Lulabelle whispered. "Why did it come back if it already has treasure?"

"We don't know—that's why everyone's so worried. It shouldn't have come back. This is the fourth time."

The Harpers watched a stained white apron float into the air and vanish in the fog. Behind them, Mrs. MacDougal choked back a cry.

"That was Mr. MacDougal's favorite apron, may he rest in peace. 'It's my magic apron, Ivy,' he used to tell me. 'It makes the pastries extra sweet.' He wouldn't let me throw it away, not for a minute, not even when it was more rag than apron. I should've put it out last time, I see that now, but I didn't think it was valuable to anyone else. Heaven knows it's dear to me, though." She sobbed quietly into her handkerchief while Puddy patted her shoulder.

"You did nothing wrong, Ivy," said Mr. Stewart as the fog

banshee scooped up a child's stuffed bear. "There's no telling what that demon wants. Money, jewels, an old apron . . . it takes them all and isn't satisfied with any of them." He stared out the window, his jaw clenched. "It's almost past now," he told them.

Just then, a thick strand of fog wafted past the window and fanned out along the glass, like a giant, spidery hand. Kat followed the fog hand up the window to the ceiling and saw with horror that darks wisps were pouring through a crack in the wall. She tried to scream but the fog was already pouring into the room. Within seconds, the fog was all around, blinding her. Instead of air, a burning, sour sensation filled her throat and Kat sank to the floor, choking. It felt as though someone was twisting her lungs into a knot. She couldn't breathe. She couldn't see. Everything was so white . . .

"Kat, are you hurt?"

She opened her eyes to see Mrs. Stewart bending over her. Maeve sat with her back against the window, her head between her knees. Lulabelle crouched on the ground, trembling. Kat blinked a few times and tried to clear her head. Had she fainted? Her lungs still ached, but the vise grip on them was gone.

"What happened?"

"There was a crack in the wall and a bit of fog got in." Mr. Stewart was sealing up the window with what looked like clay. "Maybe it thought there was treasure in here or maybe it couldn't resist an opening. It's gone now."

"Is that what it feels like to be caught by the fog banshee?" whispered Maeve.

Mr. Stewart shook his head. "That was only a taste, just an arm of the fog banshee, so to speak. If the whole monster had come in, none of us would be alive." He pounded hard at the clay.

"Rosie!"

Lulabelle's frantic cry cut through the noise and Kat turned to see her sister bent over Rosie's small frame. Rosie was lying on the floor, her eyes glassy. Her chest heaved as she struggled to draw a breath. Kat was instantly at her side, digging through her backpack for the inhaler.

"It's ok, Rosie, it's ok. Take a deep breath, everything's all right now."

Rosie's eyes fluttered. She had gone white as a sheet.

"Come on Rose, you can do it." Lulabelle lifted her off the ground and pulled Rosie onto her lap. "Can you feel how I'm breathing? That's what you need to do. Take long breaths." Lulabelle breathed in slowly, willing Rosie to do the same.

Kat threw all their snacks to the ground, searching for the familiar blue inhaler. Where was it? She turned the backpack upside down, her own panic rising.

"Hurry, Kat!" Rosie's lips were turning purple as she slumped in Lulabelle's lap. "You said you were packing her inhaler! Where is it?"

"I DON'T KNOW! I CAN'T FIND IT!"

Kat tried to remember what she had done in the kitchen that morning. It felt like a million years ago now. Lulabelle had shouted at her to bring the inhaler . . . it was on the kitchen table . . . she was deciding what snacks to bring . . . their mother had come in. Then she had run out to join her sisters. But surely she had put the inhaler in her backpack. There was no way it was still sitting on the table, useless and forgotten until now.

Kat stared at Lulabelle in dismay. "It's not here. I must've forgotten it!"

As the weight of her words hit them both, Kat felt like she had been punched hard in the stomach. Lulabelle tightened her grip on Rosie. "Come on, Rose, you can do it. You just have to take one breath, do you hear me? Just one good breath!" Rosie's whole body heaved with effort, but the breath wasn't there.

Kat knelt in front of her sister. Tears poured down her cheeks. How could she be so careless? It wasn't like forgetting a pencil or a toothbrush. Rosie *needed* her inhaler and Kat had been too busy with her stupid snacks that she hadn't given it a second thought. This was all her fault.

"I'm sorry, Rose, I'm so sorry!" she sobbed. "Please try to breathe. I know you can do it. Lu's here and I'm here and we really, really need you to breathe. Please!"

She was vaguely aware that the room had grown quiet. Mrs.

Stewart knelt down beside them. "What's wrong with the child? How can we help?"

"She has asthma," said Lulabelle, gripping Rosie protectively. "Her throat closes up and she can't breathe. It happens if she runs too hard for too long, but this time—"

"—The fog banshee did it," finished Mr. Stewart, kneeling down beside his wife. He put his hand on Rosie's forehead and felt her clammy skin. "And your medicine isn't here?"

Lulabelle shook her head. Mrs. Stewart stood up. "She needs a poultice to open up her chest. Liam, go to Flanagan's and see what they have. Ivy, we'll also need hot water. Do you have honey and ginger?"

Mrs. MacDougal sprang into action. "Of course we do! We're a bakery, not a blacksmith. Puddy, get the ginger out of the storeroom."

She put a clunky tea pot on the stove and set it to boiling. Lulabelle and Kat kept vigil over Rosie, who continued to gasp for air, her eyes closed. To Kat, it felt like the longest two minutes in the world until the tea kettle began to sing and Mrs. MacDougal mixed the honey and ginger into the hot water. She rushed a steaming mug over to Rosie.

"Sip a little at a time," instructed Mrs. Stewart, as Kat took the mug and held it up to Rosie's lips. "The honey and ginger will clear her throat and make it easier to breathe."

In between gasps, Rosie managed to get down the honey water, and soon her breathing grew steadier. By the time Mr. Stewart returned with a package tucked under his arm, the purple color was fading from Rosie's lips. Mrs. Stewart unwrapped the package and placed a warm, sweet-smelling cushion on her chest.

"Flanagan said this was the best treatment for breathing," Mr. Stewart assured Lulabelle and Kat. "It's medicinal oil from the Forest province. He says it works wonders."

Another few minutes and Rosie was able to sit up on her own. Her face was still pale, but she had found her voice and could tell Lulabelle and Kat that she felt better and to please stop looking at her like she was about to explode. While Mrs. MacDougal and Puddy ventured outside to survey any damage caused by the fog banshee, Maeve took advantage of their absence to explain (with a rather nervous eye on her father) that she and the Harpers had been watching the Cahir when the fog banshee attacked.

Mr. Stewart's eyebrows shot into his forehead. "Is that so? I seem to remember telling you—all of you—that if you returned to Ancora, you were to come to our house and nowhere else. So it's a bit of a puzzle to me how you ended up at a Cahir practice alone and—need I add—exposed to any number of dangers. Dangers like the one we just witnessed. The opposite, in fact, of what I told you to do. Am I missing something here? Would anyone care to enlighten me?"

Maeve glanced guiltily at Kat and Lulabelle, who likewise dropped their eyes. Only Rosie seemed peaceful, resting her head against Mrs. Stewart's shoulder and munching on cookies that Mrs. MacDougal insisted she needed.

At once, the whole story tumbled out: the Cahir practice ("It was a once-in-a-lifetime chance, I didn't think you'd mind!" pleaded Maeve), followed by Aidan's unexpected appearance ("That skinny red-headed boy who's been stealing from us, Da"), and finally, the attack of the fog banshee and the rescue by the Cahir.

"That's enough," Mr. Stewart said firmly, holding up his hands. "I understand. You children were excited and I can see how you might think it harmless to disregard my instructions, however briefly." He paused. "But you were careless and disobedient, and that disobedience might have had serious consequences—"

"We're so sorry, Da!" said Maeve. "We didn't know the fog banshee would come back and that you would come looking for us and almost get caught by it and we didn't—"

"She's right, Mr. Stewart," interrupted Kat. "Everything happened so fast. There wasn't anything we could do!"

"We're really very sorry," added Lulabelle. "We promise we'll do better from now on."

Mr. Stewart gave them all a hard look and everyone stopped talking. "Maeve Stewart, you will return home and muck out

Rumple's stall for the rest of the afternoon. Am I understood this time?"

Kat didn't know what mucking out a stall involved, but judging by the look of distaste that passed over Maeve's face, she imagined it was unpleasant. Maeve didn't protest. "Yes, Da."

"The three of you," continued Mr. Stewart, "will return home as well. I'll take you to the black rock myself. Rosie needs her medicine and for your own safety I think it best that you leave Ancora." Lulabelle and Kat nodded, although Kat couldn't mask her disappointment. She'd been sent to her room as punishment fairly often, but this was the first time she'd been sent back to her own world. It was very depressing.

Noticing her disappointed look, Mr. Stewart's stern expression softened. "I still mean what I said yesterday, child. You are welcome in Ancora and in our home. That will not change. But it's of the utmost importance that you do what I say from now on, am I clear?"

The Harpers nodded again. Mr. Stewart scratched his chin and sighed.

"The fact is, I'm partly to blame for all of this. I wasn't honest with you children yesterday. Had I been more truthful, none of this might've happened. I didn't want to frighten you and I thought I was protecting you in some way, but I see now that was a foolish decision." He glanced out the window before motioning for everyone to sit on the floor. Kat could still see Mrs. MacDougal outside the shop, surrounded by a group of village women, all talking and gesturing at the same time.

"I suppose," began Mr. Stewart as the Harpers waited expectantly, "that the best thing to do is to tell you the truth."

Chapter Eight
Mr. Stewart Explains

"I t began about three months ago," said Mr. Stewart, "around the beginning of spring. One of the Cahir spotted the banshee and made it back to the village to warn everyone. No doubt there would've been deaths if he hadn't acted as quickly as he did, for a fog banshee is one of the oldest and wickedest creatures in all of Ancora, not to mention one of the deadliest."

Kat gulped, wondering what the odds were that words like "death" and "wicked" meant different things in Ancora. Preferably cheerful things. She didn't think they were good.

"While there is much we don't know about fog banshees, we do know this—" Mr. Stewart paused to give his words greater effect. "— they're greedy and merciless and more than anything, they seek treasure from their victims. Once it has treasure, a fog banshee will leave, never to return. For reasons we don't understand, one came to our village. Then it came back again. Two weeks ago, it returned for a third time, and while no one was killed . . . we came close."

"Puddy MacDougal," whispered Maeve. "He tried to take back his treasure at the last minute and got caught in the fog, the idiot. He would've been a goner but for Da running into the street and pulling him out. Saved his life, he did!"

Mr. Stewart smiled thinly. "Thank you my girl, but it was a bit of luck we both didn't die. The fans at the shop next door came on at that moment and blew the banshee back long enough for us to escape. I'm afraid it had nothing to do with me."

"That's why Mrs. MacDougal gave you the cake?" Kat asked. "Because of what your dad did for Puddy?" Maeve nodded.

"Each time it returns, it's faster, stronger, more merciless than before," said Mr. Stewart gravely. "I fear it won't be long before someone dies or we become prisoners in our homes, which is nearly as bad. In short, the Hill province as we know it would cease to exist. I'm telling you all this because I see now that I should've warned you. I should've impressed upon you just how dangerous the situation is."

Lulabelle tentatively raised her hand, as though she was in school. "Sir, if a fog banshee never returns to a village more than once, why does this one keep coming back?"

"We don't know, Lulabelle." Mr. Stewart ran his hand over his eyes, looking tired and worn. "We're not a wealthy province and fog banshees are not known to value sentimentality over gold. This one is different. As you saw today, it's not picky about the treasures it takes. Mayor Digby and the village elders—of which I am one—feel that this can only mean one thing: the fog banshee is looking for a specific treasure and has not yet found it."

Mr. Stewart hesitated, as though trying to decide what to say next. He glanced at Mrs. Stewart, who gave him a slight nod. "There's something else I haven't told you and it is most important that you hear me."

The Harpers leaned towards him, eyes wide.

"A fog banshee never acts on its own. It must be summoned, a feat that is extraordinarily difficult. The conditions must be precise—two shadow moons in the last week of winter—and the spell requires a large number of ingredients that are difficult to come by, at least for most people. To further complicate matters, there must be an intense desire, an incredible focus of the mind that borders on obsession. And to top it all off, the summoner must be close to our village, since the demon cannot stray far from its master."

Lulabelle raised her hand again. "So you're saying that most people couldn't summon a fog banshee, even if they wanted to." Mr. Stewart indicated his agreement. "Well, sir, who *would* be able to do it?"

Mr. Stewart was quiet. When he spoke, it was in a voice that sounded very different and it took Kat a moment to figure out why. He was afraid and trying hard, in the way that grown-ups often did, to not sound afraid.

"We believe that only a dark sorcerer could summon such a demon. One with abilities the likes of which have not been seen in Ancora for ages."

"Do you have many dark sorcerers around here?" Kat couldn't help asking. Mr. Stewart chuckled for the first time.

"No, Kat, it may surprise you to learn that sorcerers aren't in the habit of jumping out from woodpiles or swinging down from trees. Nor do they walk around the village with helpful signs on their backs." He grew serious again. "But the fact remains that someone around here has summoned a fog banshee, and as hard as it is to believe, it could be a villager. As you might imagine, it has made people distrustful of their own neighbors and certainly any newcomers—*especially* newcomers. Rumors have already begun circulating that the fog banshee is the work of spies from another province, intent on destroying us. Therefore, anyone who's not from our province is considered suspicious."

"But we're just kids," said Kat. "How could anyone think we were spies or sorcerers? That's crazy!"

"Lies are often louder and brighter than the truth, child," replied Mr. Stewart sadly. "Truth can be quiet and dull. In this case, it's far easier to assume the worst of someone not our own than to accept the reality that we've been betrayed. Whether that someone is adult or child makes no difference."

Kat remembered the way some of the Hill people had glared at them the day before. She supposed if she had been attacked three times by a terrifying fog monster, she might be suspicious of everyone, too.

Maeve was sweeping the front steps when the Harpers arrived the next morning. With a shriek of delight, she dropped her broom and threw her arms around each of them as if they were long-lost friends.

"You can't think how relieved I am to see you!" Maeve cried. "I was afraid that you might not come back and I was trying so hard not to be disappointed, which was impossible, but now here you are!" Her words came out in a torrent, as though they had been pent up inside her brain for too long.

"I know Da did the right thing—telling you about the fog banshee—and I'm truly sorry we didn't tell you before because it's only fair that you know what's going on with dark magic and sorcerers, but I can't imagine how frightening it is to hear it said out loud and sudden like he did. It's true that this is rather a black time for us right now, but there's loads of wonderful things about our province, and it scraped on my brain to think that you might leave before I could show you how nice it can be—" She took another breath and looked like she wanted to hug everyone again.

"Maeve, it's ok," said Lulabelle quickly.

"There's Finian's Field, which has the most beautiful wildflowers, and Gulker's Itch, which sounds like a disease, I know, but is the loveliest spot for a picnic, and our Midsummer festival, which brings people from all over the province—" Maeve appeared to be picking up speed, as though she were an extremely talkative steam engine.

"Maeve, we're not going to leave!" It was Kat's turn. "We want to help you get rid of the fog banshee!"

"I have loads more to show you in town! We never got around to the toy shop and next to Piddlewick's, it's my absolute favorite. It's owned by Mr. Piddlewick's cousin, although they had a falling out, so if don't want to be cursed by a clurichaun, you can't mention anything about candy, chocolate, or any food at all—"

It took several more minutes of talking before Maeve calmed down. After that, it was another round of hugging and squeals of joy, which were so loud that they attracted the attention of Alberta inside the house. Kat waved in her direction; Alberta returned the favor by crossing her eyes and sticking out her tongue. It looked like the brownie still hadn't forgiven her.

The Harpers helped Maeve finish her chores, while Rumple, who had returned, peered benignly at them from his barn stall. Maeve explained that Mr. Stewart had left that morning for a meeting with Mayor Digby and the village elders.

"Da wouldn't tell us anything about the meeting," said Maeve in a hushed voice, "but he did tell Mam that Mayor Digby is beside himself. You met him, remember? He's such a jolly person, and he didn't count on demons and black magic when he was elected. More like cutting ribbons and chasing sheep out of the meeting hall. Da's worried he might lose control of the village."

Maeve put down the last load of firewood. "If you're sure you want to help with our troubles, I'm chalk-full of ideas for finding the sorcerer . . . or the treasure . . . or both, if we're lucky!"

Now that Maeve had enlisted allies, she was brimming with newfound enthusiasm. "The first thing we need to do is collect information. We should start with Eudora at our province library. She's a brownie and quite protective of her books so we'll have to compliment her something fierce if we want to do more than just peer at things, but I believe it's the best place to start. Thankfully, she's blind as a river troll and nearly deaf so it won't be any trouble to get you in."

Kat made a face, not sure which was worse: a building full of dusty books with crackling pages or another brownie she was likely to insult. Lu, on the other hand . . .

"A library?" Lulabelle's face was rapturous. "Where? How soon can we go? Do you have library cards? Could I get one?" Kat suspected that her sister was trying to figure out how many books she could fit in her backpack and whether they would make it through the black rock.

"But your dad—the fog banshee—" Rosie began but Maeve shook her head.

"I've already asked and they said it was fine as long as we took the path over the hills and stayed away from the village. It's a steep climb and it'll take us longer, but we'll be away from prying eyes. The fog banshee's never come back two days in a row."

Maeve ran into the cottage to tell her mother they were leaving, while Lulabelle and Kat stood off to the side, whispering together. Rosie, who was used to secretive conversations between her sisters, wandered over to the barn to see Rumple. With one final flurry of whispers, Lulabelle and Kat joined their younger sister in the barn.

"Rose," said Lulabelle quietly. Rosie stopped scratching Rumple's ears and looked up at them. "Kat and I don't think it's a good idea for you to come with us. We think it's better if you stay here and rest."

"It's not that we don't want you to come," broke in Kat, as Rosie, her eyes blazing, opened her mouth to argue, "but Maeve said the hill was steep, and we don't want to take the chance that you might have another attack."

"I have my inhaler this time!" protested Rosie. "Please let me go, I don't want to stay here by myself!"

"You wouldn't be by yourself," said Maeve, who was standing behind them, listening. "Mam's friend just arrived for tea and she brought her little girl along. Lil's a sweet thing and she's five, which is almost your age."

"I'm eight," said Rosie, looking wounded. She gave Kat a pleading look. "Please Kat, I want to go with you. It's not fair that I have to stay here!"

Kat shook her head. She felt bad about leaving Rosie, but an image of her little sister's pale face and shallow, gasping breaths filled her mind. They couldn't take the chance that anything like that could happen again.

"I'm sorry, Rose, but you have to stay here. I promise we'll make it up to you."

Kat tried not to think about Rosie's hurt face as she watched them leave. It wasn't as though they were trying to punish her, after all. Rosie had such a cheerful, happy nature that by the time they got back, she would've forgotten she was ever upset with them in the first place. Still, she and Lu would have to make it up to her. Maybe they could buy her a special treat from Piddlewick's. Yes, that would definitely help. There was no way Rosie would stay mad at them after that. Feeling better by the second, Kat hurried to catch up with the others.

CHAPTER NINE

Rosie Has Her Own Adventure

I'm not going to cry, Rosie told herself sternly. She stroked Rumple's soft nose, hoping to distract herself, but tears squeezed out the corners of her eyes and Rumple became a blur. Rosie wiped the tears away with the back of her hand, angry at her eyes for disobeying a direct order, but angrier with Lulabelle and Kat for leaving her behind. She wasn't a baby. She didn't need them deciding what she could and could not do.

"Rosie?"

Mrs. Stewart was standing in the doorway, smiling at her sympathetically. Rosie rubbed at her eyes again and tried to smile back, although she knew it must look a little crooked. Mrs. Stewart held out her hand and Rosie allowed herself to be led out of the barn and into the house. If Maeve's mother noticed Rosie's watery eyes and quivering chin, she didn't say anything.

Mrs. Stewart's friend, Mrs. Murphy, was a tall lady with serious eyes. Her daughter, Lil, hid her face in her mother's dress, too shy to speak. In her arms, she clutched a wooden toy that resembled some sort of horse. Rosie could tell from the look on Mrs. Murphy's face that she didn't quite believe the Harpers were new friends from outside the Central City and she was relieved when Mrs. Stewart sent her and Lil outside to eat cookies on the steps.

"How old are you?" asked Rosie, trying to be friendly.

Lil held up five fingers, lowered one, then held it up again.

"Wow, you're a big girl," said Rosie with an encouraging smile. After all, it wasn't Lil's fault that Rosie had been abandoned by her sisters.

Lil beamed. She inched her wooden toy in Rosie's direction, giving her a coy look.

Rosie took the hint. "I like your toy. What is it?"

Lil hid her face behind the wooden horse.

Rosie pretended to think. "Did someone make it for you?" Lil shook her head.

"Did someone buy it for you?"

A nod.

Rosie tapped her finger against her cheek. "Is it a bird?" Another head shake. "Hmm . . . I know! It's a chicken, isn't it?"

Lil dissolved into giggles. "No silly, it's a lumina!"

Close up, Rosie saw that it didn't look like a horse at all. Or rather, the body and legs were a horse, but the head was a dragon, with horns and jagged teeth.

"What's a lumina?" Rosie asked, handing it back to Lil. It seemed like an odd choice for a toy.

The little girl's eyes widened. "It's a big monster—scary and strong and fast as the wind. But it's a good monster," she added. "No one's seen them for years and years because they're a wee bit shy, but they're out there. Da says they're our special guardians and if ever we had to fight, the lumina would come out of hiding and help us."

She leaned closer to Rosie. "He bought this for me so I'd always feel safe. I named her Biddy 'cause she's a girl lumina. Mam and Da think she's only pretend, but she's not pretend. She's magic." Lil looked very pleased with herself. "And nobody knows except me—and now you."

Rosie decided to play along. "How do you know she's magic?"

"Oh, I know," said Lil wisely. "Tom—he's my brother—he tried to grab Biddy once, and as soon as he touched her, he tripped and fell in a puddle. When I was a wee thing, I lost her, but then I found her on my bed even though I had *already* looked there. And when I'm feeling scared of the dark, I sing and Biddy turns into my nightlight so I won't be scared anymore!"

"That's pretty amazing," agreed Rosie. They finished their cookies and lemonade and, searching for something to do, decided to follow a well-worn footpath that led into the hills behind the Stewart's house, pretending they were brave adventurers out to discover the secret hiding place of the luminas.

They climbed the hill, following the winding path through the trees until, with a start, Rosie realized they had lost sight of the Stewart's house. A wave of uneasiness set in.

"Come on, Lil," she said, taking the younger girl's hand. "Your mom may be looking for you and we don't want to get lost."

They were almost to the bottom when Lil stopped suddenly. She felt around in her pockets, searching for something.

"It's gone!" she cried, looking at Rosie in dismay. "My handkerchief—it must have fallen out when we were walking! Please, can we go back and look for it?"

Rosie hesitated. She wasn't used to being in charge like this. "Are you sure it was in your pocket? Maybe you left it in the house."

"I'm sure I had it! At least, I'm pretty sure." Lil's lip trembled. "Please, Rosie, can we go back and look for it? It's pink and my name is on it in fancy letters, like this." She made a swooshing motion with her hand.

"Ok, I'll go back and see if I can find it. You go straight home so your mom doesn't worry."

Rosie watched until Lil was almost to the Stewart's house, then turned and retraced her steps. The path was brown and dusty, but there was no sign of a pink handkerchief. Lil must have been wrong about dropping it.

Rosie started to head back down the hill, when all at once, a flash of color whizzed by and she jumped back in alarm. Another flash of color and she jumped back again. What was *that*? It had moved too fast for a butterfly. Was it a bird? No, wait—there it was! Flitting behind a tree was an unmistakable glimmer of gold. Rosie moved toward it, trying to be as quiet as possible. As she drew closer, she saw a pair of small, dark eyes watching her from behind the tree.

"You can come out," Rosie called softly. "I won't hurt you."

A furry golden animal about the size of a chipmunk crawled around the trunk, its wings fluttering. It shot into the air and took off through the trees, zig-zagging erratically from side to side, then up and down like a hummingbird. Without hesitating, Rosie plunged after it, swatting branches and brambles out of her way. All thoughts of finding Lil's handkerchief had disappeared. She kept her eyes fixed on the flash of golden fur, determined not to lose sight of it. Would it ever stop moving?

The creature and Rosie continued in this way for some time. Rosie was vaguely aware that she was climbing higher up the hill; she had long since left the main path. The creature disappeared suddenly through a narrow opening in a clump of bushes and Rosie ducked her head to avoid the thick foliage. She came out into a large, sun-lit clearing just in time to watch the creature shoot above the trees and out of sight. Almost at once, Rosie's disappointment at losing the golden creature gave way to another, more unpleasant feeling: she was completely, unmistakably lost. She bit her lip, determined not to cry. *You're not a baby*, she reminded herself, *you can find your way home.*

It was then that Rosie noticed the cottage in the middle of the clearing. The cottage was similar to the Stewart's, but without the window boxes filled with flowers. Sitting there by itself, it looked almost as alone as Rosie. She took a cautious step. Maybe whoever lived there could point her in the right direction. She hated the idea of bothering anyone, but every second she was gone was another second Mrs. Stewart would worry. She headed for the cottage, hoping that someone was at home. As she approached the front door, she noticed a pile of wood stacked against the side and next to it a basket that looked to be full of berries. Someone must definitely live here if—

Thwack! An axe sailed past Rosie's head and lodged in the woodpile. She screamed and whipped around in time to see a man—an angry man—striding toward her. He was younger than her dad but older than Aidan, with dark, curly hair that brushed against his chin, and dark eyes that glared at her under heavy black brows. His shirt was untucked with stains on it; he looked like he hadn't shaved in a long time. Rosie stood there shaking as he covered the distance between them in a matter of seconds.

"Care to explain why you're on my land without permission?" he barked, wrenching the axe out of the woodpile.

Rosie tried to locate her tongue but it appeared to be hiding inside her mouth.

"I said—" growled the man with even more annoyance, "—is there a reason you're trespassing on my land? Because I don't take kindly to strangers pushing their noses into my business. I have half a mind to make an example of you in case other Hill brats get the same idea." He gripped his axe and Rosie felt her chest tightening. "What do you think about that? Anything to say for yourself?"

"No sir," stammered Rosie, finding her voice at last. "I'm sorry, I didn't mean to trespass or—or bother you. I got lost and I don't know how to get back, so I thought maybe someone could help me, but—"

"So you thought you'd take a look around, is that it? Find a trinket and prove to your friends that you'd really been here? Or did you draw the short straw—send the little one to see what the hermit's up to?"

Rosie fought to keep the tightness in her chest from taking over her body. No one had ever talked to her like that. She wished with all her might that Kat and Lu were here so she didn't have to face this angry man by herself. She didn't understand what he was accusing her of, besides being on his property. She also wasn't sure what a hermit was, but it didn't seem like the right time to ask.

"No sir, no one dared me to come," she said through quivering lips. "I'm not from the Hill province so I don't know any other children, except for Maeve and Aidan, but I'm not sure if Aidan's from the Hill province or the woods—and I would never steal from anyone! When I was four, Carter Smith stole my favorite bear, Dr. Giggles, and he wouldn't give him back and I cried and cried until my teacher made Carter give Dr. Giggles back and then she made him sit in the corner—Carter, not Dr. Giggles." Rosie paused to take a breath. "So I know what it feels like and I would never do that to anyone—ever!" She wanted to say more, but the man held up his hand.

"Stop!" he commanded. "If you keep talking, I'll lose my mind."

He tossed the axe to the ground and crossed his arms. "Did it occur to you there's a reason I'm out here alone? That maybe I don't want to be bothered by children looking for directions?"

"Um, no sir," Rosie shook her head. "I got lost and I needed help finding my way back, that's all. I really didn't mean to make you mad and I wasn't going to steal anything. I would never, ever—"

"Yes, you've mentioned that." The man stood there silently, brooding at her with those dark eyes. When he next spoke, his voice was laced with a sliver of curiosity.

"Believe it or not, I think you're telling the truth. I accept that you're not here to spy on me and I'll even accept that you're not a thief. Not when you have a powerful story like 'Dr. Giggles' in your past. But if you're not from the Hill province, where *are* you from? How did you end up on my side of the hill?" He gazed at her with such intensity that Rosie momentarily lost her voice again.

"We're—we're from the Central City," she stammered, trying to remember what the Stewarts had instructed them to tell people. "I mean—not the Central City, but north—between here and there."

"There's more of you? Should I expect an endless number of children hammering on my door, demanding help?"

"No sir, there's only three of us—me—I'm Rosie, Lulabelle, and Kat. They're my sisters. We live between here and . . . there."

The man raised his eyebrows. Rosie had the distinct feeling that he didn't believe her but all he said was, "That's how it is, then. So you came to be lost how?"

More out of relief than a desire to explain, Rosie recounted the afternoon's events, beginning with her exclusion by Lulabelle and Kat, her adventure with Lil, and her encounter with the golden chipmunk creature.

"So, you see," she concluded, "I really didn't mean to make you mad. If you wouldn't mind pointing out the right way, I promise I'll never come back." She hoped she looked sincere.

The man sighed and glanced around the clearing.

"It's not much good to either of us if I point out the way only to have you lost again. With my luck, you'd end up back here and we would have this same delightful conversation." He turned and marched toward the tree line, waving his hand to indicate Rosie should follow.

"While I may be an ornery old gimp, even I don't relish the idea of a helpless lass like yourself wandering around alone. You could fall into a well, run into something dangerous—" The man held the brambles up and Rosie clambered through the narrow opening.

"I'm eight, so I'm not really little," she replied, careful to sound polite. "I know there are dangerous things around here. Me and my sisters were in town yesterday when the fog banshee attacked." The man didn't respond. Rosie couldn't tell if he was even listening.

"Have you seen the fog banshee?" she asked, trying to move as fast as he was.

"Yes, I've seen it."

"Aren't you scared to be out here by yourself? No one would be around to help you." Although the man had been so angry with her, Rosie hated the idea of anyone being left to the mercy of such a horrible monster.

"It hasn't attacked me yet so I haven't thought about it much. And no, I'm not scared to be alone, that's the point. I'm not a people person, as you may have guessed."

"But everyone was so scared yesterday!" Rosie shuddered, remembering. "The fog banshee took everyone's treasures and almost choked us to death!" She left out the part about her asthma attack. She didn't want to give this man another reason to think she was a baby.

"I would imagine I'm safe, then," said the man, turning left onto a narrow path. "I don't have any treasures to speak of, and I doubt the fog banshee's in desperate need of firewood."

Nothing else was said until they reached another footpath that sloped downwards, out of the woods and onto a large pasture. Across the pasture, Rosie could see the Stewart's cottage.

"Thank you for bringing me back," she said to the man, and she meant it. "I can go the rest of the way by myself. I won't ever get lost again. I'll wait for Lu and Kat to come back and we'll stay on this side of the hill. You don't have to worry about me ending up at your house because I couldn't remember where you live, anyway."

The man waved away her thanks. "It's over now. I expect I was rather harsh with you earlier. A downside to living alone, I'm afraid. I've become a bit of an ogre." He looked at Rosie intently. "Your sisters, they're older than you? And they went off and left you behind, is that it?"

"It's not that they're mean because they're really nice most of the time. They don't want me to get hurt, that's all. But I don't need them to keep me safe. I'm not a baby!" Rosie tried to keep the disappointment out of her voice, but found it was easier thought than done.

A curious expression flitted across the man's face. Without warning, he cupped his hands and made a whistling sound, followed by two short, low-pitched whistles, then another high-pitched one.

"What are you doing?" Rosie asked in surprise.

"Finding you some adventure." The man's eyes were on the sky. "I don't think it's fair that your sisters get to have all the fun, do you? Like you said, you're not a baby. You showed courage back at my place, standing your ground like a Cahir warrior. Ask any of the Hill brats—I'm a regular fog banshee myself so that's quite a feat."

The dark-haired man hesitated, then sighed and looked down at Rosie. "I also know a thing or two about being a younger brother."

"You had older brothers?" Rosie felt a sudden, unexplainable kinship with the dark-haired man, grumpy and strange though he was.

"Just one."

"Does he still treat you like you're a baby, even though you're grown up?"

The man's eyes grew shadowy. For a moment, he looked unbearably sad. "I'm afraid he died a long time ago."

Rosie tried to think of something to say, but at that moment she noticed a group of specks on the horizon, moving rapidly towards them. As the specks drew closer, Rosie had an odd feeling that she had seen them before.

"The flying horses!" she exclaimed. "Right? Me and my sisters saw them the first day we got into Ancora!" The thought of seeing the magnificent creatures again gave her a thrill of excitement. The man glanced briefly at her, then back at the sky.

"Kelpies, actually. Water spirits that take the forms of horses. They tend to stay around lakes or streams but if you know how to call them, they'll come from miles away." The man made another whistling sound and the kelpies separated into two lines. They were approaching very fast, with no signs of slowing down. The man took a few steps back and Rosie followed.

"Stand firm now. They won't hurt you, but they can be skittish. You don't want them to see you as a threat, that's the trick of it."

The kelpies landed around them with a thunderous clamor, their wings rustling loudly. Rosie squeezed her eyes shut and balled up her fists. "Be brave," she repeated to herself. "It's an adventure. They won't hurt you. It's an adventure."

She cracked her eyes open a tiny bit. The kelpies were grazing serenely in the field, oblivious to her presence. The dark-haired man smiled faintly.

"Magnificent, aren't they? You'd be hard-pressed to find their equal anywhere in Ancora." He made a purring sound and Rosie watched in amazement as a kelpie trotted over and let the man stroke its nose. He whispered to it in a language Rosie couldn't understand, while simultaneously beckoning to her. Hesitantly, she held out her hand and touched the glossy black side. The kelpie's wings flared and it stomped the ground.

"Not many in Ancora can say they've ridden on the back of a creature like this," said the man, still stroking the soft mane. "What do you think about that, lass?"

Before Rosie could muster an opinion on the subject of kelpie riding, the man had hoisted her onto the animal's velvety back. She sat there, blinking in shock, once again unable to form words. He gave her a challenging look.

"How's that for an adventure? Are you scared?"

Rosie gazed back at him as she gripped the sides of the kelpie with her knees. She couldn't tell if the feeling churning in her stomach was excitement or terror. Was he really suggesting that she ride this animal? The man's eyes bored into hers, as though he could read her thoughts.

"No shame in fear. It can be helpful—gives you the boost of adrenaline you need to do what you must. But you can't let it take over. You have to focus your mind and you have to make your decision. Do you want to ride it or not? If you don't, I'll lift you right off. But if you do . . . " The man leaned toward her. "Quite an adventure to tell your sisters."

Rosie took a deep breath and tried to keep her hands from shaking. What if she fell off? Would the kelpie catch her? What did she even hold onto? There was no saddle, no reins. If Lu were here, she would rattle off all the stories she knew about riding accidents and tell her to get off immediately. Kat, on the other hand, would ride the kelpie in a heartbeat. Rosie gritted her teeth. It wasn't fair that Lu and Kat had all the fun, while she had to wait at home. It wasn't fair at all. Heart pounding, Rosie looked at the dark-haired man with a determined expression.

"Yes, I want to ride!"

"Good for you," the man said. "Take care that you're sure. Once you've made your decision, there's no going back. Hold onto its mane with one hand, its neck with your other—that's right. Are you ready, now?"

Rosie had never felt less ready in her life, but she nodded before she lost her courage. The man made a clicking sound and the kelpie broke into a run. Rosie leaned forward, gripping the shiny mane with her left hand, while with her right, she grasped the massive neck. She felt the enormous wings behind her billow into the air and she braced for takeoff as the kelpie pushed off on its hind legs and soared into the sky. Rosie held on for dear life, her stomach flip-flopping in protest against this new, utterly strange sensation. On either side, the wings rose up and down, beating a steady rhythm. Below, the Stewart's cottage and barn resembled doll furniture, the dark-haired man a tiny plastic figure, waving up at her. In front stretched green hills as far as the eye could see and Rosie blinked against the glare of sunlight. With a jolt of surprise, she

realized that she wasn't scared at all. This was where she was supposed to be, gliding through the sky, the sun on her face and the
breeze in her hair. Rosie gave the kelpie a happy pat, and it tossed
its head, as though sensing her mood.

They looped around the top of a hill and Rosie saw even more
hills in the distance. Clustered here and there were miniature buildings that must be other villages in the Hill province and she marveled at how vast it all was. The kelpie neighed loudly and turned
back toward the field, its wings beating harder as it picked up speed;
Rosie buried her face in the animal's neck. The kelpie swooped
downward like a rocket and Rosie shrieked with exhilaration as the
ground came rushing at them. Her stomach was still doing flip-
flops and her heart was somewhere in her throat, but she didn't care.
She was flying!

"I can't believe you rode it!" cried Kat as she, Rosie and Lulabelle
walked back to the black rock. The Stewart house had been in a
state of panic when Rosie finally appeared, her cheeks flushed, her
soul victorious. Kat and Lulabelle had attacked her with hugs so
fierce that, for a few moments, Rosie thought her sisters' affection
might end up killing her.

She had been forced to repeat her story twice, once to her

sisters and the rest of the group, then later to Mr. Stewart, when he returned home. She had tried her best to be accurate, although it was possible she had exaggerated just how high and fast she had flown. Maeve had been incredulous, Kat had jealously asked for every detail, and Lulabelle—predictably—had sputtered something about safety regulations and parachutes that wouldn't open and then appeared to go into shock.

Rosie wasn't sure what Mr. and Mrs. Stewart thought of it all but they had both looked worried when the Harpers left. Rosie hoped the dark-haired man wouldn't get into trouble. He had refused to accompany her back to the Stewarts, but had turned on his heel and disappeared into the trees before she could even ask his name.

"I'm glad Rosie had fun but it was irresponsible of that man to let her do that. She could've been killed!" Lulabelle's voice was almost a squeak. "She barely knows how to ride a horse and he put her on a creature that flies hundreds of feet in the air? With nothing to keep her from falling off? What if she had fainted? What would've happened then?"

"I didn't faint!" Rosie huffed, but Lulabelle didn't seem to hear.

"Maeve said that the man is a hermit and won't have anything to do with anyone in the Hill province. When he does come into the village, he barely says a word. That does not sound normal."

Kat shrugged. "Who cares? Rosie said he was ok, just a little mean at first. Are you listening? Rosie got to ride a FLYING HORSE!"

Lulabelle and Kat continued to argue all the way to the black rock. Rosie trailed behind, her thoughts drifting back to her walk in the woods with the dark-haired man and the feel of the wind when she and the kelpie soared through the sky. She lowered her head and smiled into her chest. Lu and Kat could say whatever they wanted—it didn't matter. Today, she had gotten an adventure all her own.

CHAPTER TEN

The Realm

Over the next month, the Harpers devoted themselves to helping Maeve brainstorm ways of finding the sorcerer and ridding the Hill province of the fog banshee. This undertaking was greatly complicated by the fact that the Harpers knew very few people, had no idea what treasures the villagers owned, and had been forbidden to go anywhere without the express permission of Mr. or Mrs. Stewart. Lulabelle and Maeve spent hours poring over the books they had found in the province library. They hadn't uncovered much beyond what Mr. Stewart had already told them, although they had learned that fog banshees hated loud sounds and strong smells.

"Awesome!" said Kat as she waded in the stream that ran

alongside the Stewart's pasture, her jeans rolled up to her knees, trying to catch the sparkly crayfish-like creatures that nibbled at her toes. "So we find a bunch of smelly garbage cans, bang on the lids as loudly as we can, and then throw the garbage at the fog banshee. Easy enough!"

"It's just temporary, I'm afraid, and it only makes the fog banshee angrier." Lulabelle closed her book and reached for another one. She frowned. "*Get Saucy! Easy Sauces for All Occasions* . . . this can't be right."

Maeve looked up from the list she was making of possible treasures in the Hill province. "Eudora must have given me the wrong book. I said, 'sorcerers,' and she heard, 'sauces.' I told you she was nearly deaf. Save it, though. It's my night to fix dinner."

When they finally accepted that there was no more to be gained from books, the Harpers and Maeve turned their attention to the identity of the sorcerer. In this area, Maeve was much more helpful.

"There's Callum Donague from the next village over—he used to make faces at me in school . . . and Ronan O'Leary—I know he stole a slice of Mam's prize-winning cobbler at the Midsummer festival last year . . . and Lucinda Kelly—she sounds like a dying muskrat when she laughs . . . "

Lulabelle stopped writing. "Maeve," she said reproachfully, "do you really think one of these people is the sorcerer or do they just annoy you?"

"I don't see why that matters."

Lulabelle sighed and began to erase her list. She stared bleakly at the empty page. "If you can't tell who the sorcerer might be, you know we can't. We know almost no one!"

"What about the treasure?" Rosie was hanging upside-down from the tree branch over Lulabelle's head. "Maybe if we know what the fog banshee is looking for, we'll know who might want to find it."

"We tried that, remember?" Kat was also up in the tree, pretending she was riding a kelpie. "Every single thing Maeve could think of has already been taken by the fog banshee."

"I wouldn't put it past Olive McCutcher to keep something back," said Maeve, dropping down beside Lulabelle. "She's the richest woman in the province and mean as a snake. She pretends to be a grand heiress, descended from 'landowners,' but we all know her grandda made his money raising pigs."

"That's it!" cried Kat, leaping out of the tree. "We break into her house, look through—"

"No, Kat."

"Lu, you haven't heard my plan yet! Rosie doesn't mind being lowered down through the chimney, do you Rose?"

By the end of June, even Kat was feeling defeated. They were no closer to uncovering the identity of the sorcerer or the treasure; the only good thing was that Maeve had mastered several tasty sauces.

They watched Mr. Stewart's comings and goings, anxious to know what was being done by the village elders and whether they were having any success. Judging by the constant look of weariness on Mr. Stewart's face, the adults weren't faring any better.

Despite their frustrating search, the Harpers spent as much time as they could in Ancora. Every morning after breakfast, they filled their backpacks and set off for the black rock, waving goodbye to Mrs. Harper, who spent her days on the dock with her easel.

"I can't tell you how happy it makes your Dad and me to see you girls enjoying the outdoors," she told them. "You should keep a list of everything you find: rocks, insects, animals. You wouldn't believe how many interesting things are out there!"

There had been a moment of panic one Saturday when Mr. Harper insisted on accompanying them up the hill to make sure the cave was safe. Kat had a sudden burst of hope that he wouldn't be able to get in; the opening was too small for a grown-up, after all, but he found some footholds on the side of the rock and proceeded to astonish them with an impressive display of climbing ability. They waited in nervous anticipation as he came out of the tunnel, flicking off his flashlight. Their dad was humming, which seemed like an odd reaction upon finding another world inside an ordinary cave.

"Looks good, kiddos," he had smiled. "That's a pretty neat tunnel in there. I didn't see any spiders, but be careful. You don't want to run into something nasty."

"Maybe it's part of the magic," suggested Kat, when they were safely on their way to Maeve's house. "Maybe we're the only ones who can find Ancora. Maybe Dad can't see it because he's not supposed to get in . . . the way no one from Ancora can come into our world."

"Maybe so," replied Lulabelle pensively, "but I wish we knew more about the black rock. I have a feeling it might explain things."

Occasionally, Aidan joined them, strolling in from wherever he came from, an insolent grin on his face. Maeve scowled whenever she saw him, but had apparently decided not to risk her friendship with the Harpers. Although they were always happy to see Aidan, Kat couldn't help but feel a growing suspicion that something wasn't quite right. His hair was frequently messy, small tears appeared on his shirt and pants, and Kat spotted some painful looking bruises on his arms, which he shrugged off but didn't explain.

"What happened to you?" she gasped when Aidan appeared one afternoon looking particularly disheveled, a purplish bruise forming around his right eye, leaves sticking out of his hair, and a swollen lip.

"What, this?" Aidan appeared surprised. "It's nothing. I had a bit of a tumble with a tree, if you must know. I was setting a trap and I didn't tie it down tight enough. The branch sprang up before I was ready and BAM!" He touched his bruised eye and grimaced. "It was my first go at this trap, sure enough, and I've got a bit of a learning curve. No doubt the next try will be better."

"Are you sure you weren't in a fight?" Lulabelle couldn't help but wince at Aidan's maimed face.

"Now who would I be fighting with, little bird?" Aidan pretended to look offended. "I'm the very picture of peace and harmony." He saw Kat and Rosie staring at his bruised arms and hastily rolled down his sleeves.

"Peace and harmony, that's a laugh," scoffed Maeve. "I imagine there's a long list of Hill people who'd love to take a swing at you. I don't believe for a minute that a tree did that to your face. No doubt you got caught stealing eggs from a henhouse or boots from a back porch. I for one would like to know where you keep the things you nick from all of us because they haven't gone toward new clothes, that's the truth."

"Red, I'm crushed you would even think that," replied Aidan, clutching at his heart. "To suggest that I would take what doesn't belong to me . . . well, it's enough to kill the soul right out of a lad." He winked at her. "How are those hens of yours? Fattening up nicely, I imagine."

"Don't you even think of coming near my hens!"

"Where are you going Aidan?" said Rosie quickly, pointing at Aidan's satchel, which was bursting at the seams with hidden objects.

Aidan patted it. "Headed to the Realm for a sight of trading."

"What's the Realm?" Kat said, her curiosity aroused.

"A market of sorts, on the other side of the village just beyond those hills. It's a grand place for buying and selling. Money is welcome, but it's not necessary, not if you have anything valuable to trade." Aidan threw Maeve a sly look. "My guess is that any thief with half a brain would swap his goods there where it's more—shall we say, discreet? Theoretically speaking, that is."

"Don't let him fool you," Maeve told the Harpers. "The Realm is nothing more than a dirty, nasty bunch of falling down shacks filled with dirty, nasty people who will cheat you the first chance they get. A grand place, my eye! All of their wares are stolen, no doubt, and even if they're not, it's dangerous. No respectable Hill person would ever go down there."

Aidan's eyes narrowed. Two spots of color erupted on his cheeks.

"We can't all be respectable, can we Red? Some of us have to eat now and again. Not that your kind would know anything about that. I'd wager those 'dirty, nasty' folks you think so beneath you against a whole village of 'respectable Hill people' any day of the week. And I know for good and certain that your Mayor Digby himself has been spotted perusing the merchandise. So don't be fooling yourself—even a respectable Hill person will hold their nose for a good deal."

There was a tense silence that seemed to stretch on forever. At last, Rosie coughed quietly into her fist and Aidan came out of his angry haze.

"Right then, I'm off. Enjoy your afternoon of sunshine and rainbows."

He made as though to leave, then stopped. "Unless you'd like to come with me, that is. See a bit of the real Hill province. Not the kind that's all polished up."

Kat raised her eyebrows at Lulabelle. Lulabelle, frowning, shook her head. Kat knew she shouldn't want to go with Aidan, that Maeve could very well be right about the Realm and the people who traded there, but she couldn't swat away that feeling of intrigue that was flitting around her brain like a pesky gnat. What was the place like? Was it really dangerous or only slightly dangerous? It couldn't be that bad if Aidan wasn't afraid to go by himself. Could it?

Ignoring Lulabelle, Kat marched over to Aidan. "I'm going. We're out of ideas for finding the sorcerer and it could be fun. Don't look at me like that, Lu!"

Lulabelle sighed in frustration as Rosie joined Kat, but a second later she too was marching over. "Fine, count me in. I don't think it's a smart idea, but someone has to go and keep an eye on you two."

"Excellent! You're in for a grand treat," said Aidan, back to his cheerful self. "Last chance now, Red. I'll allow you to tag along, if you can muzzle that mouth of yours and keep from insulting folks. Otherwise, you'd best skip home and stick to safer things like cat's-cradle. Is that what you'd rather do?"

Maeve fumed but stood her ground. "You'd like to leave me behind, wouldn't you? You know I'm right about that wretched place, but you're too proud to admit it. There's a reason Da doesn't let me go with him down there, it's—" She clapped her hands over her mouth as she realized what she'd said.

"Oh ho!" Aidan crowed. "So even the upright Mr. Stewart isn't too good for the Realm! Enjoy your time alone, Red, we'll try not to miss your charming wit too much."

Throwing apologetic glances at Maeve, the Harpers turned to follow Aidan. They hadn't traveled far before Maeve caught up, red-faced and scowling.

"I still think it's a wretched place and we're foolish to follow that boy anywhere, but I'm not about to let you go alone. You're my guests as well as my friends, and it's not good hospitality to abandon either." She didn't say anything else, but kept shooting nasty looks at Aidan's back.

In her mind, Kat had pictured the Realm as a dark, grimy place filled with treacherous characters who could easily stab you in the heart if they were so inclined. The area where Aidan now led them presented a very different picture. Rows of tents formed three lines that wrapped around the foot of the hill, creating narrow pathways. Crowds of people milled around, inspecting the wares and making purchases. None of them seemed dangerous to Kat, although most looked like they hadn't taken a bath recently and several men carried menacing clubs. There was also a peculiar smell that Kat couldn't place—a flowery, sweet aroma that made her nose tingle.

Aidan moved through the crowd confidently, as though he had navigated this space many times before. The Harpers and Maeve hurried to stay close to him. He stopped in front of a dilapidated tent that appeared to be held together by rope and rapped on the counter. A stooped, ugly little man with a long nose and bald head emerged from somewhere within. The crabby look on his face changed into a smile, revealing yellowed, dirty teeth.

"Aidan me lad, always a pleasure to do business with ye!" he croaked in a voice that sounded like nails on a chalkboard. "What have ye got for me today, I wonder."

Aidan turned his back so the Harpers and Maeve couldn't see what he was removing from his satchel. He passed it to the man, who put on a pair of oversized glasses to examine it. Kat stood on her tiptoes, trying to get a better view and thought she could make out a thin, silvery object in the man's hand.

"Ha!" hissed Maeve's voice over her shoulder. "I bet you a week's worth of Honeyfizz he's got the Byrnes' candlesticks. They went missing two days ago and there's been no trace of them since.

It would be just like him!" Her lips narrowed in a thin line of disapproval.

The man seemed satisfied because he disappeared inside his tent and came out a moment later holding a drawstring bag, which Aidan slipped into his satchel. They whispered together in low voices before Aidan nodded and moved back into the crowd.

"That man back there," said Maeve glancing at the tent, "he—he wasn't a hobgoblin, was he?"

Aidan looked thoughtful. "You know, I think he might be on his father's side. I've met his mother and she's a nasty one, but she claims to be human. She makes old Grewter there seem positively radiant. And her face? Enough to scare the wool off a sheep. He's right lucky he got his father's looks."

"A hobgoblin?" repeated Maeve shrilly, forgetting to keep her voice down, although the size of the crowd made it unnecessary. "Don't hobgoblins eat human flesh?"

"I suppose so," said Aidan, shrugging. "But Grewter's only half hobgoblin, you see, and he's lived among humans ever since I've known him. I'm fairly certain he doesn't do that sort of thing anymore."

Aidan continued his trading with different sellers for the better part of an hour. He was obviously well known in the Realm as evidenced by the many cries of greeting that flew at him from both sides. The sellers were an odd assortment of characters. Some were human, others definitely not, and they regarded the children with guarded, skeptical eyes. But all of them, without exception, broke into genuine smiles when they saw Aidan and then they didn't seem nearly as scary, but rather like eccentric friends who happened to be missing most of their teeth.

"That's all for today," said Aidan at last, tucking what appeared to be a bridle into his satchel, which bulged even more than it had before. Maeve glared at him.

"Planning to do a bit of riding? Or do you imagine you can fit a horse into that bag of yours? They may be a sight harder to steal than you're used to."

Aidan managed to fasten the clasps on his satchel and smirked. "I suppose you'll have to wonder on that, won't you now?" He looked around, taking in the entirety of the tents and people with a satisfied air. "So, little sunshine club, what do you think of the Realm? A right cheery place to spend an afternoon, isn't it? Not as nasty as some people would have you believe?"

"It's interesting," said Lulabelle politely, her eyes on a creature covered in long hair. "Everyone seems . . . pleasant."

"I like it," Kat declared. It was an odd, unsettling sort of place in a lot of ways and she couldn't imagine many of the people here strolling down the main street of the Hill village. But at the same time, there was a scruffy charm to the Realm and the people in it that she found endearing.

Aidan looked proud. "What about you, little bird?" he asked Rosie, ignoring Maeve.

Rosie didn't answer; she was searching the crowd. "It's the dark-haired man! He's here!"

She pushed past them, elbowing her way through a throng of people. The dark-haired man was deep in conversation with a thin lady who was holding an object that emitted blue smoke, but he turned at the sound of Rosie's voice.

"It's you again," he said, his raised eyebrows the only indication he was surprised to see her. "You have a knack for finding your way into unlikely places, don't you?" He gave a curt nod to the lady, who placed a lid on top of the smoking object and handed it to him. He stowed it in a leather pouch as the Harpers watched curiously.

"I take it these are your sisters—the ones who left you to wander your way into my peace and solitude?"

"That's right, you haven't met them yet." Rosie introduced Kat and Lulabelle, as well as Maeve, who hovered behind the Harpers uncertainly. Kat noticed that, once again, Aidan had somehow disappeared. Where had he gone? She glanced around at the different booths.

"I don't know your name!" Rosie was telling the dark-haired man. "You never told me when we were back in the woods."

"No, I didn't." The man hesitated, as though trying to decide whether he wanted this conversation to continue.

"Donovan. My name is Donovan."

The words seemed uncomfortable for him and Kat remembered what Maeve had said about the man living as a hermit. Maybe he wasn't used to talking to people, especially children. Rosie didn't appear bothered by his discomfort; she smiled up at him.

"Nice to meet you, Donovan. Thank you again for everything. I'm glad I ran into you today so I could tell you."

"It was nothing," Donovan replied brusquely, looking even more uncomfortable. "But you should listen to your sisters and stay close to home from now on. You never know what may be out there." Without another word, he turned and disappeared into the crowd.

"He's . . . a little different," said Lulabelle as they watched him leave.

"I told you he's a wild man," whispered Maeve. "No one knows who he is or where he comes from. Two ladies went up to visit him last year with a basket of fruit and came running out of the woods an hour later, white as ghosts. They said he told them in no uncertain terms what they could do with their fruit and their busybody ways and then he yelled for a good long while. Now, no one goes near him."

"I don't think he's so bad," said Rosie defensively. "I think he can be nicer, when you get to know him."

Lulabelle looked worried. "I don't know, Rose. Until we know more about him, we should stay out of his way. He *is* a stranger."

"But Aidan was a stranger, too—" Rosie protested, but Kat cut her off.

"Where is Aidan, anyway?"

They scanned the market, but Aidan had vanished.

"Of course, he would leave us!" said Maeve, rolling her eyes. "He seems to have a talent for that sort of thing. Shall we head back home? Mam's making cookies and she promised to let us have some."

They were almost to the entrance of the Realm when Kat spotted a familiar figure standing off to the side, away from the busyness of the market. She started to yell to everyone that she had found Aidan, but something in his manner stopped her.

"Go on without me," she told them instead. "I'll catch up—I forgot something." She hustled in the opposite direction before Lulabelle or Maeve could say anything.

Kat retraced her steps to the back of the Realm, then looped around behind the tents to avoid being seen by the rest of the group. She approached Aidan quietly, not because she wanted to sneak up on him (not exactly), but because for some reason she felt like she should. As she drew closer, she heard a sniffling sound, followed by another sniffle, and then another, louder one. Kat stopped in her tracks. Were those sniffles coming from Aidan? Was he *crying*?

The realization froze her where she stood. What should she do?

She couldn't stand there and not say anything. Would it be better to turn around and leave him to his tears? Pretend she had never been here?

Sensing a presence behind him, Aidan whirled around and Kat was caught. For a brief, miserable second they stared at each other.

"Sorry!" Kat stammered while Aidan hurriedly wiped his eyes with the back of his hand. "We were leaving but we couldn't find you and I saw you over here, but I didn't know—I mean, it's ok if you want to stay here . . . we can find our own way back. I'm sure Maeve knows the way—and there's cookies at home, so . . . ." She broke off.

"No, no, that's fine, I won't be but a minute." Aidan's voice sounded like gravel. "My hay fever kicks up something fierce in the summer," he said half-heartedly, but Kat nodded like it made perfect sense. It was then that she noticed the wilted blue flowers that Aidan was clutching in his hand. In fact, there were flowers everywhere. They were stacked against each other in a tight circle like colorful dominoes, some fresh, others worn and faded. In the center of the circle burned three candles. It reminded Kat of a story she had watched on the news about the death of some famous person. People had come from all over to leave flowers and notes in memory of that person.

"Did someone die?" she blurted before she could stop herself. She expected Aidan to become angry, to tell her it was none of her business and to go away and leave him alone. Instead, he looked grateful, as though eager for the focus to be off himself.

"Her name was Birdie," he said, his eyes on the burning candles. "She sold things at the Realm. She was a bit like everyone's grandmother . . . always looking out for the other sellers, and the first to know if a chap needed food. She weren't much to look at— sort of a hunchback, Birdie was—with warts and only a few teeth left. She looked like she was about a thousand years old, but no one had a kinder, truer heart." Aidan sniffed again and wiped his eyes.

"You knew her well?" Kat ventured to ask.

"Birdie found me wandering in the Whispering Woods when I was a tyke. She took me back to her place and gave me food and somewhere to sleep. She saved my life, sure enough. I know those woods well enough to guess what would've happened if she hadn't found me when she did. But that was just like her, it was. She checked around to see who I belonged to, but when no one turned up, she let me stay with her and sell things at the Realm. We made quite a pair, Birdie and I did." Aidan's chin trembled and he kicked at the ground.

"What sorts of things did she sell?" said Kat quickly.

"Home remedies, mostly. Herbs, flowers, things like that. She was the one who taught me how to tell one from another and how to make them useful. She was a right good teacher but I don't know that I was the best student. Setting traps for critters is more my style."

"How did she die? Was she sick?"

As soon as the words left Kat's mouth she regretted them. An expression appeared on Aidan's face that she had never seen before on anyone. At first, she thought he was angry at her for bringing it up, but when he replied, it was like she wasn't even there.

"No, she wasn't sick. Birdie was strong as a kelpie, she was. She was murdered in her own stall. Some bloke bashed her head in, no doubt hoping for a spare gelding. She would've given them up, too, if she had any—which she didn't. She never set much store in those kinds of things. There was no need to hurt her. It was evil, nothing but pure evil!"

Kat realized that the expression on Aidan's face was rage, and for the first time since she'd met him, she felt afraid.

"He didn't even take anything! He ransacked her stall for spite and then he left her lying there." Aidan clenched and unclenched his fists. "If I had been there, I would've killed him with my bare hands before I let him walk away. He would've had to answer right then for how he'd hurt Birdie." He glowered at Kat and she knew he was serious. They stood there in silence for a moment, staring at the circle of flowers. Kat felt terrible. Terrible for what had happened to Birdie, terrible for Aidan's grief, and terrible that she had barged into his private moment.

"I should go and find the others," she offered, when she couldn't think of anything else to say. "I'm really, really sorry about Birdie. She sounds like a nice old lady. I hope whoever killed her is caught . . . and . . . punished very badly."

"They'll be wishing they were dead if I find them," said Aidan quietly. "I'll make sure of that." He fell silent and Kat took it as a sign that she should leave. She headed toward the entrance to the Realm, sneaking one quick glance behind her. Aidan was bending down to lay his flowers in the center of the circle.

"Where have you been?" demanded Lulabelle when Kat joined them minutes later. "We need to stay together, remember?" She looked down at Kat's empty hands. "Where is it?"

"Where's what?"

"You said you forgot something, where is it?"

"Oh, that." Kat shook her head. "No, I forgot to see something back inside, that's all. No big deal." She didn't feel like explaining her conversation with Aidan in front of the group. Lulabelle studied her suspiciously for a moment, but didn't press the issue. The two of them would talk about it later, when they were alone. Lu was good about keeping secrets.

They had just reached the familiar path that wound around

the Whispering Woods and into the Hill province when Maeve stopped short, her body rigid.

"What's wrong?" Lulabelle watched Maeve with concern. "Maeve, are you ok?"

Maeve's eyes darted from side to side. "Don't you feel it?" she said in a frightened voice. "It's close by, I can tell."

"What's close by?" Kat looked around them, but she could only see hills and woods. Nothing seemed out of the ordinary.

"Wait, not the—" Realization made Lulabelle's eyes as big as Maeve's.

Maeve nodded. "The fog banshee's here somewhere, it has to be."

"But . . . are you sure?" Kat blinked in confusion. "Everything seems normal to me. Look, the sky hasn't even changed color." There was no sign of the steely gray clouds or the cold wind that had seeped into her bones. Maeve shook her head, unconvinced.

"I know it's here."

They moved cautiously, pressed together, as though the fog banshee might materialize in front of them. Kat waited for the sound of a horn echoing around the hills that would indicate that this wasn't Maeve's overactive imagination, but there was only silence. If the fog banshee was here, no one else knew it.

They followed the path around a bend, still moving slowly. On their left, the Whispering Woods rose up, the trees still, as if they too were listening. On their right stretched the Hill province. For a moment, Kat wished she was standing in the middle of the village, safe and blissfully unaware of danger. The Whispering Woods, on the other hand—Wait! What was that? Kat could've sworn she saw movement out of the corner of her eye. She took a few steps toward the woods, trying to peer through the trees.

"Did you see something?" Maeve was right beside her.

"I thought I did, for a second."

"There it is!" Lulabelle pinched Kat's arm. "Behind that group of trees over there."

As they watched, black fog rolled out from between a cluster of trees about fifty feet away and Kat felt the hair on her arms stand on end. This time, she was positive she could see a face with red eyes in the middle of all the swirling black. A twig snapped and they watched, frozen, as a hooded figure approached the fog banshee from the other side of the woods. Kat wanted to cry out, to warn whoever it was that they were heading straight for the monster, but there was something about the way the figure moved that stopped her. It moved silently, almost stealthily, as though eager to avoid attention. The hooded figure stopped, and Kat, remembering how close the fog banshee had come to swallowing up Mr. Stewart and Rumple, braced herself for an attack. Instead of devouring the figure, though, the fog banshee hovered in front of it.

"I don't understand," whispered Maeve. "Why isn't it moving?"

"Who's that person with it?" said Rosie, squeezing her way between Lulabelle and Kat. "Why aren't they afraid?"

"Because—" said Lulabelle slowly, the way she always did when thoughts poured into her mind and she had to slosh through them, "he must be the one who summoned it. That's the sorcerer. He's disguised so no one can recognize him."

"Shouldn't we go tell someone?" breathed Rosie. "Someone like your dad, or . . . or a policeman."

Kat shook her head. "If we leave now, they might be gone before we get back. We should follow them so we can find out who the sorcerer is. Maybe we can make him send the fog banshee away."

"Kat, that's crazy!" Lulabelle gave her sister a disbelieving look. "We can't follow them! We could get killed! Rosie's right, we should find Maeve's dad. It's the safest thing to do."

Kat turned to Maeve. "What do you think?"

Maeve hesitated. "I don't rightly know. I'm not fond of going up against evil powers, but I don't want to see them get away, either. I agree with Kat, this may be our best chance to see who's behind all this darkness."

"It's too dangerous," protested Lulabelle, fighting to keep her voice down. "If it sees us, there's no way we could escape. You saw how fast it moves. There's nowhere to hide."

"Then we have to keep from being caught," said Kat. "C'mon

Lu, don't you want to find out who's behind this? If following it is our only choice, then that's what we have to do."

But before they could do anything, a pair of powerful hands grasped Kat's shoulders and shoved her to the ground. She put her arms out too late to break her fall and got a mouthful of grass. Rosie followed a second later. Looking up in bewilderment, Kat watched the same pair of hands force Lulabelle and Maeve to the ground as well.

"Are you really that stupid?" hissed a familiar voice, "or were you hoping to die today?"

CHAPTER ELEVEN

Secret Meetings

"G et down and stay quiet!" commanded the voice, which Kat found unnecessary since he had already knocked them to the ground and terrified everyone into silence. She raised her head and saw Donovan's dark eyes scowling back at her. He knelt behind them, finger to his lips, and Kat saw with alarm that the hooded figure had turned in their direction.

"Faces to the ground," murmured Donovan. "If we're lucky, they won't see us." Kat flattened herself against the grass and tried to ignore the soft blades tickling her face. After what felt like an eternity, Donovan straightened up.

"They've moved deeper into the woods. I don't think they've seen you."

The children scrambled to their knees and watched the hooded figure move silently through the trees, the fog banshee drifting behind like a pet following its master. Where were they going? Kat itched to follow, but was pretty certain Donovan would tackle her again if she tried anything.

"How did you know the fog banshee was here, Donovan?" said Rosie, trembling.

"I was behind you on the path. I wondered what you were up to—staring into the Whispering Woods like that—and then I felt it. That icy feeling that runs down your skin. So why didn't you run instead of standing here like idiots?"

"We were thinking of following it," said Kat, in what she hoped was a brave voice. "We thought we might catch whoever's been summoning it."

"That's a spectacularly stupid idea," replied Donovan flatly.

"Exactly what I said," muttered Lulabelle and Kat fought the urge to kick her in the shins.

"Do you have any idea what a fog banshee is capable of?" continued Donovan, glaring at everyone now. "Have you ever watched one drain a person of their last breath, slowly and painfully?" He didn't wait for a reply. "I have, and believe me when I tell you that, as unbearable as it is to watch, I can't imagine what it's like to experience. It's the stuff nightmares are made of."

"But we weren't going to catch the fog banshee!" Kat couldn't help arguing. "We wanted to catch the sorcerer that brought it here!"

Donovan let out a barking laugh. "If you can throw around the word 'sorcerer' like you're on your way to a picnic, then you have no idea what you're up against. Someone with that kind of power will know you're coming before you even get close to him. And what do you imagine he'll do when he sees you? Do you imagine you're fast enough to get back to the village and tell someone? Do you honestly think he would let you?"

Kat felt her face grow hot. When he put it like that, it did sound stupid. To her surprise, Maeve stepped forward. She looked like she might cry, but when she spoke, it was in a slow, deliberate tone very unlike her normal one.

"We know it's a bit risky," she said. "But you haven't been living in our village so you don't know how awful it's been for all of us. The fog banshee has taken our treasures, the things most dear to us, and it's made people mean and hard and distrustful. It's sucked the joy right out of our lives and it's only getting worse. Maybe we are stupid to think that we could stop it, but we can't always wait for someone bigger and stronger to step in and save the day later—not when we have a small chance to do it now."

Kat waited for Donovan to tell Maeve that it was pointless, that there was no way children could stop a fog banshee, but he was silent, considering her words. At last he sighed.

"You're naive is what you are, but I admire your courage, misguided though it may be. The fact is, I suspect you'll disregard whatever I say and go after the thing the moment I'm gone. Won't you now?"

Maeve and Kat looked at each other but didn't say anything. Lulabelle was practically turning her face into a pretzel attempting to get Kat's attention, but Kat ignored her.

"Fine."

Donovan got to his feet and everyone else followed. "We'll see if we can get a look at who's behind all this evil but we do it my way, is that understood?" Everyone nodded in unison. Donovan pointed at Rosie.

"Go straight to the village, find someone who looks trustworthy, and bring them back. If we happen to catch a sorcerer, I'd prefer to have an adult handy instead of a bunch of children."

"No, she should stay with us," protested Kat, forgetting her fear of Donovan for the moment. "She can't go by herself—"

"Her legs are too short," interrupted Donovan. "If we have to run, I don't fancy dying to save her. Now go!"

"But she doesn't know the way," added Lulabelle, grasping Rosie's hand. "She's too little and it's too dangerous."

"I'm not too little!" Rosie's face was pale, but resolute. "I know the way to the Stewart's house. I'm not afraid!" She wrenched her hand away from Lulabelle and set off toward the village before either Kat or Lulabelle could object. Donovan watched until she disappeared around the bend, then turned to Kat, Maeve and Lulabelle.

"Now then, you two stay behind me. Do as I say when I say it. You—tall one, what's your name?"

"L-Lulabelle."

"Lulabelle, you stay up front with me. Do you have a weapon?"

"A weapon?" Lulabelle looked petrified. "You mean, like the kind that hurts people?"

Donovan lifted up his trouser leg to reveal a dagger strapped to his ankle. He pulled it out and presented it to Lulabelle as casually as though he were offering her a stick of gum. "If you're attacked, you'll need to defend yourself." When Lulabelle continued to stare at the dagger, Donovan rolled his eyes. "It's the pointy end that's most effective," he added dryly.

"Can you kill a fog banshee by stabbing it?" asked Kat as Lulabelle took the dagger and held it like it was a bomb.

"Not at all," replied Donovan, motioning for them to follow him. "But even the most powerful sorcerer is human."

Everyone was silent as they crept through the Whispering Woods. Donovan moved like a cat stalking its prey, carefully, but with measured confidence. Behind him came Lulabelle, taking shaky breaths and exhaling as loudly as she dared. Kat wondered what sort of depressing stories she was telling herself to feel better.

Maeve, on the other hand, was bright-eyed and calm. Picking up a thick branch, she slung it over her shoulder.

"I'm not about to walk into this unprepared, am I?" she whispered to Kat. "I'm not sure Donovan won't abandon us to save his own skin. It may be up to you, me, and Lulabelle when it comes to it."

Kat wasn't sure she liked the sound of that very much. The hyperventilating sounds coming from Lulabelle weren't terribly reassuring, either. Kat scanned the ground before choosing a stick of her own, a skinny, smooth thing that didn't look like it would be much good against an irate squirrel, let alone an evil sorcerer and his trained monster. Still, it would have to do until she could find a better one. Kat was so busy searching for a more effective stabbing instrument that she didn't notice Donovan and Lulabelle had stopped. She collided with Lulabelle's back, causing her to whirl around.

"Sorry!" they cried at the same time, as Donovan raised his hand for silence. Ahead of them, nestled discreetly in the trees, stood a crumbling house. Moss covered the roof and vines snaked their way up and down the decrepit walls and into the cracks of the foundation. There was no door, only a gaping hole in the front where a door had once stood. Two gray knobs jutted out over the entrance, one on either side. Within there was only darkness.

"What is that?" Maeve whispered to Donovan.

"No idea. I've been through these woods once or twice, but I've never come across it before. It appears to be empty, but it's hard to tell." From his bag, he removed a silver object that looked to Kat like a small sword with a prickly ball on the end instead of a point.

"Wait here. I'll have a look—make sure they're not waiting for us inside. Don't move until you hear me tell you it's safe."

"What if they *are* in there?" said Lulabelle fearfully. "What should we do then?"

"I would advise running," replied Donovan, moving toward the house with slow, deliberate steps. "And do your best not to be killed."

"I don't think he likes us very much," remarked Kat, watching the back of Donovan's head.

They waited with breathless anticipation as he approached the house, his prickly weapon raised in front of him. Stopping to remove a small bottle from his bag, Donovan sprinkled whatever was in it over the prickly ball. The ball began to glow a pale blue color as he disappeared through the doorway. Kat wasn't sure if she liked Donovan, but she also didn't relish the idea of being left alone again. Lulabelle's hand slipped into her own and squeezed it. Kat knew there was nothing her sister could do if a fog banshee attacked them but she squeezed back anyway.

Donovan reappeared in the entrance and waved for them to join him. The house was made of stone and there were faded markings along the top and sides of the door frame. Looking up, Kat realized that the knobs jutting out above them were sculptures of two grim-looking creatures with curved horns and ferocious eyes. They had the heads of dragons, but with long horse-like bodies that didn't resemble any animal she had ever seen.

"Lucky for us, this place is abandoned," Donovan said. "But the fog banshee was here, no doubt about it. Come and take a look." He headed back inside and everyone followed close behind, relying on Donovan's glowing orb for light.

As Kat's eyes adjusted to the darkness, she saw the dragon creatures everywhere. Their faces were carved into the walls on either side of the room, mouths open as if they might lunge out of the stone at any moment. In between the faces were more markings that Kat couldn't read. The air felt heavy and a sour, musty smell permeated the room. Donovan lifted his light higher and Kat's attention was diverted to the center of the room where two piles—one large, one small—lay on the floor. The large pile was made up of books, dishes, clothes, even a wheelbarrow, and appeared to be thrown together without any apparent order. The smaller pile had similar objects, but the items were neatly stacked, as though someone had carefully handled each one.

"I'm not sure I understand," said Lulabelle, voicing Kat's thoughts out loud. "What is all this stuff? How do you know the fog banshee has been here?"

"Because these are our treasures!" gasped Maeve. "That wheelbarrow belongs to Mr. Murphy. He got it as a birthday present last year. That string of pearls is Olive McCutcher's. It came all the way from the Sea province and she's never let anyone forget it. That china vase with the crack in it belongs to Kieran O'Dell. It was his late grandmother's." Maeve walked around the large pile, pointing out objects and who in the village owned them while Donovan stood by, a somber expression on his face.

"I believe we've found the lair of the fog banshee," he told them. "It has to keep its treasures somewhere." He knelt down to inspect the smaller pile. "Very few people venture into this part of the Whispering Woods. This place is out of the way, and yet not so hidden as to attract suspicion. It's quite brilliant," he concluded grudgingly.

"Why do you think there are two piles?" said Lulabelle, crouching down beside Donovan and picking up an antique candle holder. He also reached for an object—a pewter cup—and studied it with an appraising eye.

"I don't pretend to know the thoughts of a fog banshee, but if whoever summoned it is searching for a particular treasure—and the fact that the fog banshee keeps returning suggests they are—then I would guess the summoner is going through these things and sorting valuable from rubbish." Donovan replaced the cup and got to his feet. "Interesting."

"What's interesting?" said Kat.

"It's interesting because it tells us that the sorcerer himself doesn't know what he's looking for."

A sudden noise outside made them jump. Donovan pointed to the back of the tomb, indicating that they should stay there, while he moved swiftly to the entrance and peered out into the woods.

"I don't see anything," he said at last, "but I'm going to check outside. It was careless of me to leave this place unguarded. Stay here until I get back." He was gone before anyone could think to ask him what they should do if he didn't come back.

"Well, I'm not about to leave empty-handed," declared Maeve after they had waited for a few minutes in silence. "These treasures belong to the Hill people and I mean to return as many as I can. It burns me up that the fog banshee sweeps in and steals them from us, then leaves them sitting here to rot!"

"No, Maeve, you can't do that!" said Lulabelle. "If the fog banshee comes back, it will notice that things are missing. It might attack the village again! You have to leave everything here so it won't know we've found its hiding place."

Maeve grew still. "I suppose you're right," she agreed with some reluctance. She stepped forward and whisked a tattered white apron from the larger pile. "At any rate, I can return Mrs. MacDougal's apron to her. It's only one thing and if the fog banshee's angry about that, it can attack me. I don't care!"

"Donovan's been gone a pretty long time," said Kat after a few more minutes had passed. "Should we go outside and look for him?"

"He told us to stay here," murmured Lulabelle. "I'm sure he'll come back soon. He's probably checking all around to make sure nothing's wrong."

"How do we know he's even here?" argued Kat. "He could've decided to take off and leave us in this weird tomb. We could be waiting for hours."

"I'm sure he wouldn't do that," said Lulabelle, although she didn't sound at all certain.

When Donovan still hadn't returned five minutes later, Maeve grew impatient. "I think we should see what he's about," she told them, grasping her stick. "He should've been back by now, and Kat's right, we can't stay here forever. What if he saw the fog banshee and decided to make a run for it? Leave us here like sitting ducks?" She crept over to the entrance and peeked around the side of the doorframe.

"I'm with Maeve," agreed Kat, holding up her own puny stick. "We have a better chance together. On the count of three, we all leave. Keep your eyes out for anything suspicious."

"But Donovan—" Lulabelle protested.

"Donovan may be gone, Lu, and if we stay here any longer the fog banshee might come back. You can try to have a friendly conversation with it, but Maeve and me are going."

"I don't even know how to use this!" cried Lulabelle, waving her dagger as the three of them hovered around the entrance. "What will I do if it's out there?"

"Stay behind one of us, obviously," replied Kat, searching for a glimpse of black fog behind a tree or bush. "Or tell it one of your miserable stories where everyone dies in the end. Maybe it will run sobbing away on its own."

"That's not funny. And they're not miserable stories, they're cautionary tales."

"Shh!" hissed Maeve. "Are we ready? Let's go!"

Huddled together for protection, they stepped out of the tomb, eyes alert for any signs of danger. There was no fog banshee or hooded figure in sight, but there was no sign of Donovan, either. It looked like he had indeed left them to fend for themselves.

"I see something!" squealed Maeve, gesturing at a cluster of trees. Kat spun around, her stick raised in what seemed like an appropriate battle position. Lulabelle hunched up next to her sister, eyes squeezed shut, and tried to remember some of the more aggressive moves from the karate class her parents had forced her to take the year before.

"I don't see anything, where is it?" cried Kat, trying to take in the entire woods at once.

"Right through those trees! I saw someone running," insisted Maeve. "I couldn't see their face but I'm positive they were wearing a brown hood."

Lulabelle's eyes flew open. "Did you hear that?"

"Hear what?" Kat strained to see the hooded figure.

"Just now. It sounded like groaning."

From somewhere close to them came a low moaning sound, like an animal in pain. It was coming from the back of the tomb, where a cluster of bushes and vines obscured the ground. The noise grew louder as they approached the biggest bush and they stopped and looked at each other. Whatever was making that noise was on the other side. With a sharp intake of breath, Kat grasped her stick and darted around the bush.

Donovan lay motionless on the ground.

"Donovan!" Kat dropped to her knees in front of the dark-haired man. His eyes were closed. Blood trickled from a nasty cut on his temple.

Maeve knelt down beside Kat and touched the back of Donovan's head. "He's got a whopper of a knot forming. I don't suppose anyone has a clean strip of cloth so I can wrap it for him?"

"Yes, we do!" Lulabelle unzipped her backpack and pulled out a roll of gauze, along with a tube of antiseptic. "Can you use this?"

It was at times like this, reflected Kat, that Lulabelle's obsessive need to prepare for every emergency was a good thing. Maeve applied the ointment to Donovan's bleeding cut and expertly wrapped the gauze around his head. He uttered a low moan from time to time, but otherwise didn't stir. Kat felt bad that she had suspected him of leaving them to the fog banshee. As Maeve finished wrapping the gauze, securing it with tape from Lulabelle's backpack, Donovan's eyes fluttered open. Blinking in confusion, he struggled to sit up.

"How long was I out?"

"We found you like this," said Kat. "We waited for you inside the tomb, but you never came back so we decided to look for you. We thought you might have left us."

"You have a nasty gash on your head," added Maeve. "I've done the best I can, but you should have it treated properly." Donovan gingerly touched his bandaged forehead, then reached around to feel the knot forming in back.

"I remember now. I heard a noise from over this way. I was standing here, listening, when there was another noise behind me and someone got me from the back. I went down, but not before they landed another blow to my temple." Donovan winced, rubbing the bandage. "Everything went dark after that." He shook his head and tried to stand up.

"Do you think it's a good idea for you to move around?" said Lulabelle, grabbing for Donovan's arm as his legs buckled. Maeve caught his other arm and he leaned against a tree to steady himself. "You might have a concussion—or maybe internal bleeding."

"No, I'm right enough." Donovan smiled weakly. "Believe it or not, this isn't the worst bump I've had and I'm sure it won't be the last. It seems my head's too thick for any lasting damage. I only wish I could've gotten a few blows in myself. I don't fancy being taken by surprise like that."

"Look at this!"

Kat had spotted a heavy rock lying a few feet away. A dark liquid was splattered on it. She picked it up, dabbing at the liquid with her finger. "Donovan, I found the weapon. Do you want to see it?"

"No, thanks," replied Donovan, his eyes closed. "We've met."

"We need to get you to the village," declared Maeve, tearing her eyes away from the bloody rock. "It's not safe to stay out in the open like this."

"I couldn't agree more." Donovan pushed himself away from the tree with some effort while Lulabelle and Maeve lurked on either side of him like nervous bodyguards.

"Shall we help you?" asked Maeve uncertainly. "It's a fair walk back."

"No need, I'll be myself in a minute. I just need to clear the cobwebs from my brain."

"Are you sure?" Kat was doubtful. "You look like you might throw up." Lulabelle gave her an annoyed look.

"Perfectly sure." Donovan took a few sluggish steps. "Do me a favor, though, and don't include me in your next plan to track down sorcerers. I prefer to keep my skull in one piece."

They made their way slowly out of the Whispering Woods and

down the path that led into the village. They had almost reached the bridge when Maeve gave a cry.

"There's Rosie! She found Da and some others, thank goodness!"

Mr. Stewart was marching towards them, Rosie at his side. Behind them came a group of ten or twelve men. Kat recognized Aifric Digby, the Hill province mayor, and Cathmor, the leader of the Cahir, among the group. Maeve ran to her father and flung her arms around him.

"We're safe, Da! We're safe but we found it! We found the lair of the fog banshee! It has all our treasures in the Whispering Woods!"

"Maeve, what do you mean by this? What's going on?" Mr. Stewart pulled Maeve away from him and frowned into her eyes. "Rosie tells me that you saw the fog banshee and meant to follow it into the woods. Surely you wouldn't be so foolhardy as to go after a demon like that on your own. Not when you know what it's capable of."

"We weren't on our own, Da," explained Maeve. "Donovan came with us. He's the reason we found the lair and all of our treasures. If you go right now, you'll see what I mean."

"Am I to understand, sir, that you took these children into the woods after a fog banshee?" Mr. Stewart was staring at Donovan now, his voice dangerously calm. "You took them all the way into its lair with no protection but yourself? Are you mad?"

"It's more like they took me into the woods after the fog

banshee," Donovan replied in an even tone. "As you can see, it did not end particularly well. If anyone was in need of protection, it was me."

"Please don't be mad at Donovan," cried Lulabelle as several Hill men cast furious looks in his direction. "He tried to stop us but we wanted to find out who's been summoning the fog banshee and this seemed like our best chance. The truth is that we would've gone with or without him. He went along to keep us safe . . . and he did, too, even though he got hurt instead of us."

Kat thought it was nice of Lulabelle to make it sound like they were all to blame for what had happened instead of pointing fingers at Kat and Maeve. Maeve must have thought the same thing because she made a face that was more than a little guilty.

"I see," said Mr. Stewart, giving Maeve an exasperated look. "I suppose that shouldn't surprise me. You have shown yourselves to be a determined bunch." He turned to Donovan. "I apologize to you, sir. I judged too hastily just now. It seems I should be thanking you for keeping my daughter and her friends safe on this foolish escapade of theirs. I am most grateful."

Donovan shrugged away Mr. Stewart's thanks. "It's nothing. My day had been a bit too quiet anyway."

"Please, Mr. Stewart," Kat urged, "you have to go right now. The sorcerer may still be there. You might be able to catch him. We can go with you if you like—to show you where the lair is."

Mr. Stewart's expression was similar to one her own father had given her when Kat had volunteered to drive him to work one day. "That is not an option, child," he said simply. "You have put yourselves in enough danger. You're to go back to our home and wait for me there." No one attempted to argue. "Now tell me about this place you found."

As quickly as they could, Kat, Lulabelle and Maeve described the house with the strange creatures. When Maeve got to the part where the hooded figure had fled into the woods and they had discovered Donovan bleeding and unconscious, Mayor Digby let out a bleating yelp.

"Good gracious!"

His face was red and he was breathing heavily, as though hearing about danger was more than enough to frighten him. Kat couldn't imagine he would be much help if confronted by a sorcerer.

"Right then, we'll go there now." Mr. Stewart's face was grim. "If there's anything to be found in those woods, we'll find it."

"But Liam, it may not be safe," whined the mayor, clutching his red hat. "We're no match for a fog banshee, after all. If there's a sorcerer, who knows what sorts of black magic he might send our way!"

"I understand, Aifric," replied Mr. Stewart, "but as foolish as these children were, they were right about one thing. This may be our best chance to discover who's behind this evil. More than likely, whoever summoned the monster and ambushed this man is long gone, but there's no harm in trying to find out all we can."

Aifric Digby looked like he thought there was a good deal of harm, but he nodded and murmured, "You're right, of course, Liam." Kat felt a twinge of pride that Mr. Stewart agreed with them, although she wished he would stop using the word "foolish."

Mr. Stewart turned to Cathmor, who had removed his dagger from its sheath and was cleaning it with the hem of his shirt. "Cathmor, are your men ready if we need them?"

"They're standing by as we speak. The horses, too—say the word and I'll call them."

Kat wondered how he planned to do that when there were no horses or Cahir warriors anywhere to be seen, but Cathmor didn't offer an explanation.

"Let's not waste any more time," Mr. Stewart said to the men gathered around him. "I suspect we have a small window to find anything. You, sir," he added, addressing Donovan, "please allow my wife to dress your wound. It's the least we can do to thank you. I suspect she'll also gift you one of her famous fruit pies in additional thanks. I would advise you to accept as they're quite famous in this part of Ancora."

For a brief moment, Donovan's dark eyes flickered and Kat detected a softening of his sharp features. But almost at once, it was replaced by the familiar guarded look. "That's unnecessary. I must be getting back, I have a great deal of work to do."

He started to push past the group of men but stopped. "Please accept my thanks for your kindness." He said the words haltingly, as if he had not practiced those sorts of pleasantries in a long time, before trudging away in the direction of his hill.

The next hour dragged on. Lulabelle paced back and forth in front of the Stewart's cottage, while Maeve talked incessantly, although it was unclear who she was talking to, if anyone. Just when Kat had convinced herself that time must actually be moving backward, Rosie sat up from her position in the Stewart's hayloft and pointed at a figure in the distance.

"Your dad's back, Maeve!"

As Mr. Stewart grew closer, Kat saw that Mayor Digby and Cathmor were with him, but there was no sign of a hooded figure or anyone who looked remotely like a sorcerer. Mr. Stewart wore the same grave expression as before, while Mayor Digby—to Kat's surprise—seemed relieved. Cathmor, on the other hand, looked irritated. Kat had a sinking feeling that something was wrong.

"Da, did you find the lair?" Maeve called as the three men strode across the yard, gravel crunching under their boots. "What about the treasures? Was there any sign of the person who hurt Donovan?"

"Yes and no," replied Mr. Stewart heavily. "We found the house. Cathmor tells me it's a lumina shrine . . . but it was empty. There was no sign of the fog banshee or its summoner."

"How is that possible?" said Lulabelle. "What about all the treasures we found?"

"There were no treasures, Lulabelle. We looked in every corner, I assure you." Mr. Stewart's eyes were troubled.

"That's impossible," said Kat. "We saw it for ourselves! There were two piles of treasures from the village. Donovan says the person who called the fog banshee doesn't know what he's looking for and he's trying to figure out what's valuable and what's not."

"Does he?" growled Cathmor, staring hard at Kat. "What do you know of this Donovan? What do we know of you for that matter?"

"Cathmor," said Mr. Stewart sharply. Kat's mouth dropped open in shock. Her eyes flashed.

"You think he's lying? That he made all that up and hit himself in the head? You think we had something to do with this? THAT'S CRAZY!" Kat knew she was shouting—and at a grown-up, no less—but she didn't care. "HOW COULD WE CALL A FOG BANSHEE?" She felt Lulabelle's hand squeeze her shoulder and she shook it off. "Did you even look for the sorcerer? He might have still been there, you know! There's probably clues everywhere and YOU'RE NOT EVEN LOOKING!"

Mr. Stewart held up his hands for calm. "No one thinks you called a fog banshee, child. Such an idea is ludicrous and we all know it. No one is saying Donovan is lying, either." He shot a glance at Cathmor, who scowled. "He was obviously attacked in the woods by some unknown person. What I believe Cathmor means is that until we have more facts to guide us, we must be careful not to assume anything. I have no reason to think Donovan is anything other than honest, but I also can't vouch for someone I don't know."

"And I'm not about to accept the words of outsiders without more evidence than what we have," growled Cathmor.

The mayor gave an embarrassed laugh. "Now, now, there's no need to argue, is there? The fact is the whole village has fog banshee on the brain, don't you know? It's understandable that a group of children, out for a nice walk, might let their imaginations get the better of them and think they see something in the woods . . . a trick of the light, perhaps . . . or a very large rabbit . . . "

"We know what we saw—" Kat began but Maeve interrupted excitedly.

"I almost forgot! I took this from the pile of treasures. It's Mrs. MacDougal's apron from the last time the fog banshee came. This proves we're telling the truth!" She thrust the piece of white cloth at Mr. Stewart, who examined it carefully before passing it to

Cathmor. Mayor Digby rocked back and forth on the balls of his feet, looking distressed.

"Oh dear, this is most upsetting! If people find out the fog banshee's lair is nearby and the demon is still here . . . we'll have riots in the streets! There's only one thing to be done. We must tell everyone to gather up whatever treasures they have left and take them to this lumina shrine. A final offer of appeasement, you see. Whatever it takes to send it away!"

"I don't think that's the answer just yet, Aifric," replied Mr. Stewart, handing the apron back to Maeve. "The only way to stop the fog banshee is to find out who summoned it and what they're looking for. Until we know that, no one is safe and this nightmare will never end."

"Then you believe us?" said Lulabelle. "You don't think we're imagining the treasures or the hooded figure?"

"I have always believed you, that was never a question," Mr. Stewart assured her. "But from now on, I want all of you to stay out of the woods. Whoever was there saw you leave. How else to explain the empty shrine? We may not be any closer to finding this dark person, but they don't know that. If they feel cornered, they may become desperate."

"I think we need a meeting!" squawked Mayor Digby. "We must call a council of the Hill province elders . . . with her, naturally. She said to inform her of any new developments. If today's events aren't new developments, I don't know what is!"

"I agree. Cathmor, how soon can one of your men find her and bring her back?"

"Within the day. I believe she's in the Lake province now."

"Fine. Once she's here, we'll convene a meeting of the elders." The three men moved away, talking quietly between themselves. Kat strained to hear what they were saying, but it was obvious the conversation was meant to be private. She leaned over to Maeve.

"Who are they talking about?"

"I think it must be the Enchantress," Maeve replied. "She was here after the fog banshee attacked the first time and then after the third time, but I haven't seen her since. She left in a hurry to gather information. I don't know where she went or what she's been doing."

Kat knew the proper emotion at the moment was pure terror. Not only was the sorcerer still out there, but he had probably seen them—all of them. What would he try to do? Would he send the fog banshee after them? Kat knew these questions should frighten her and that a more reasonable, normal person like Lulabelle would obey Mr. Stewart's instruction to stay close to the Stewart's cottage. But those were not Kat Harper's thoughts. All she could think about was this mysterious Enchantress. What had she discovered? When and where would the secret meeting be? Most importantly, how could she, Lulabelle, and the others find a way to sneak inside?

CHAPTER TWELVE

Legends, Tokens and General Sneaking Around

T he next day was Saturday. The Harpers sat at their kitchen table, eating breakfast and trying hard not to feel disappointed. Mrs. Harper had announced they were to spend the day as a family "soaking up the beauty of nature." She seemed puzzled that this idea wasn't met with the enthusiasm she had expected. When even the mention of ice cream aroused half-hearted interest, she felt Kat's head to make sure there wasn't a fever going around.

"It's not like we're missing anything," said Lulabelle glumly when they were alone. "We wouldn't have been able to go to the meeting anyway."

Kat pushed her plate away, her appetite gone. It was driving her crazy to think that something was happening in Ancora without them. The Enchantress might have important information and they would never know. The grown-ups certainly wouldn't tell them.

Lulabelle looked at her watch. "Maeve will be waiting. One of us should go and explain."

"I'll go." Kat stomped out of her chair, fighting the urge to kick something (or someone) as hard as she could. "We should be trying to save the Hill province from the fog banshee, but we've decided to 'soak up nature' instead. I hope Maeve understands!" The back door slammed behind her.

Kat returned home in remarkably better spirits, although she said nothing to Lulabelle or Rosie. Her meeting with Maeve had given Kat the tiny kernel of a plan, but it required some thought. Plus, telling Lulabelle now would only give her sister time to come up with a laundry list of objections. No, she needed to think. There had to be a way.

"Sneak out? Are you insane?"

The Harpers sat next to each other on the boat their parents had rented for the evening, eating fried chicken and baked beans on paper plates. Kat had tried to bring up her plan casually, as though it was the most reasonable idea in the world. Lulabelle, however, was staring at her sister as though she'd suggested they light each other on fire for fun.

"It's the only way, Lu. Maeve told me that the meeting is tonight at eleven. The Enchantress was late so it couldn't be earlier. This is our chance, we have to be there!"

"It won't work, Mom and Dad will hear us. You know what a light sleeper Dad is. And Kat, the quieter you try to be, the more you knock into things . . . you know it's true. There's no way we can make it out of the house without being caught."

"Why do we have to be in the house at all?" said Rosie. "Why don't we ask Mom and Dad if we can camp in the back yard? That way, we don't have to sneak out of the house and we don't have to worry about getting caught."

Kat and Lulabelle stared at Rosie. She gazed back at them innocently.

"But where would we get a tent?" Lulabelle sputtered.

"There's one in the hall closet. I found it when I was looking for supplies."

Kat and Lulabelle looked at each other. Lulabelle furrowed her brow and pursed her lips, trying to come up with a reason why Rosie's plan was unacceptable. At last, she sighed and gave Kat a look that Kat recognized all too well. Lulabelle, against her better judgment, would go along with the plan. Kat leaned over and pulled Rosie's brown ponytail affectionately.

"Rosie," she said, "you are absolutely brilliant." Rosie smiled and took another bite of fried chicken.

"Kat, wake up. It's time." Kat opened her eyes and tried to rub the bleariness away, her brain foggy and uncomprehending. It took her a moment to remember where she was and why Lulabelle was bending over her, her face contorted by the flashlight's glow. It all came back to Kat with a rush—the fog banshee, Maeve, the secret meeting with the Enchantress—and she sat up, her mind focused. Next to her, Rosie yawned and blinked her eyes.

"We have to move now. Mom and Dad's light has been out for half an hour and they checked on us right before that. I pretended to be asleep and you were snoring, so we should be safe."

"You didn't sleep at all?" Kat had intended to stay awake the whole time and she felt irritated with herself for dozing. She put her sneakers on and reached for her backpack.

"One of us had to stay up. We're on a schedule and we can't be late." Lulabelle tapped her watch for emphasis. Kat had to hand it to her sister—on the rare occasions that Lu agreed to break the rules, she did it with a strong sense of punctuality. They unzipped the tent flap and climbed out, careful not to make a sound. Through the tops of the trees, Kat could see thousands of tiny stars twinkling down on them and she took a deep breath to calm her nerves. This was really happening. Lulabelle hesitated, her eyes scanning the forest. Kat suspected she was having second thoughts.

"Come on Lu, no turning back now." Kat grabbed her sister's arm and tugged her up the hill.

"It's just—" Lulabelle looked pained. "I once read that half of all murders committed by psychopaths happen in densely wooded areas."

"Then we'll just have to hope we're the other half!" replied Kat, impatient to be on their way. "Let's go!"

Ancora was cloaked in stillness when they came out of the black rock and onto the grassy hill overlooking the meadow. Rosie gasped in delight.

"I've never seen so many stars! They're all different colors!"

Millions of lights covered the inky blackness, some so tiny you could barely see them, others so big they looked like planets. Blue, green, white, gold, red. Every color of the rainbow was there above their heads, shining for all of Ancora. It made the stars in their own world seem dull by comparison.

"There you are!"

Maeve appeared from behind the black rock. She had pulled her curly red hair into a cap and in the glare of the flashlight, her freckles stood out against her pale skin. She motioned for them to follow her down to the path, where Rumple waited patiently with

Mr. Stewart's wagon. Maeve lowered the back of the wagon and Lulabelle and Rosie climbed in while Kat opted to sit up on the driver's bench with Maeve where she wouldn't miss anything. They rode in silence until they came around a bend and Kat saw a few tiny lights in the distance. Almost there.

All of a sudden, Maeve drew in a sharp breath. She tugged on the reins and Rumple came to a stop. "Someone's coming," she told them.

"How can you tell?" Kat couldn't see anything in the darkness. Behind her, Lulabelle shifted in her seat.

"What's wrong?"

"I think it's a horse," said Maeve. "I can make out the sound of hooves." From up the path came a faint clicking noise. Kat marveled at the fact that Maeve had detected it at all. She supposed that living in a place where the nights were deathly quiet must sharpen your hearing. Another few seconds and Kat could see the dim outline of an approaching rider. Whoever was coming toward them was moving at a steady, but not urgent pace.

"Who do you think it is?"

"I have no idea. Not many people have purpose to go out at night . . . well, unless they're us."

"What if it's the sorcerer?" Rosie whispered. The thought had crossed Kat's mind as well. What would they do this far from the village? There was no way a wagon could go faster than one rider on a horse.

"I have an idea."

Lulabelle was on her knees behind the bench, hoisting the flashlight between Maeve and Kat like she was pointing a gun. "When whoever it is gets close to the wagon, I'll shine the light in their eyes. Maeve, you drive as fast as you can to the village. Maybe it will give us a few extra seconds to get away. At any rate, it's all we have."

"What kind of magic is that?" said Maeve in an awed voice, her eyes on the flashlight. "How does the fire stay inside? Won't it burn your hand?"

"It's a flashlight," Kat whispered hastily. "It's like a lantern, but brighter. Anyway, we don't have time to get into that now."

The clicking noise was louder. Any second would bring the mystery rider into view. Kat held her breath, Maeve clutched the reins, and even Rumple pawed the ground. The rider's outline loomed large in front of them and Lulabelle yelled, "Now!"

The flashlight beamed on, catching the horse and rider full in the face.

The horse reared up with a sharp neigh as the rider grabbed for the reins with one hand, shielding his eyes with the other.

"Blast it all! Blind a lad, why don't you? For the love of a river troll, put that lantern out!"

"Aidan?"

Lulabelle lowered the flashlight as Aidan put his arm down and gave them a look that was half annoyed, half amused. He had another purplish bruise, this time around his left eye, but that seemed like the least of their problems at the moment.

"Were you expecting another visitor out for a moonlit ride? Or did you think you'd plant yourselves here and blind anyone who comes along?"

"What are you doing?" Kat stammered, her heart not yet back to normal speed.

Aidan grinned. "Word around the village is there's to be a meeting tonight. Very hush hush. Lots of talk about the fog banshee, sure enough. I had a hunch that you lot would try to worm your way in somehow, and since you're about as sneaky as a herd of stampeding kelpies, I thought I should come along for the occasion. Lend you my expertise and all that. Then it was a matter of watching Red here to see when she left—nice work with your Da's wagon, by the way—and finding my own means of transportation so I could join you."

"We don't need your help!" retorted Maeve, looking like she would happily run over Aidan with the wagon. "We're doing fine, thank you, and you'll no doubt get in the way." Her jaw dropped as she noticed the horse for the first time.

"Is that one of the *Cahir* horses?"

Aidan lifted his chin in defiance. "What if it is?"

"That's the one you rode, isn't it?" said Rosie. "The pretty one with the red mane." The horse gave a soft neigh, as though appreciative of the compliment, and trotted over to the wagon so Rosie could rub her nose.

"Are you thick in the head? Do you know how serious that is? It's bad enough to ride their horses without permission, but to steal one? You'll get us all in a heap of trouble!"

"That's a bit rich coming from you, Red. Where'd that wagon come from again?" Aidan leaned down and stroked the horse's mane. "I'm borrowing her for an hour or two, that's all. Red Star was happy for some exercise."

"I suppose you consulted with her before you hopped on?"

"Maybe I did."

"We should be going," Lulabelle reminded them. "The meeting will start any minute."

When they crossed the bridge into town, Maeve guided the wagon off the path into a cluster of trees. Jumping down, she looped the reins around a low branch and fed Rumple an apple from her pocket. The village was still, the shop windows black with sleep. A few lanterns flickered along the main street but there was no sign that anyone was awake.

"Aren't you going to tie your horse?" Maeve demanded as Aidan touched his forehead to Red Star's nose and gave her a carrot.

"Don't need to," he replied, patting her side. "She knows what we're about. She'll wait for me." Maeve rolled her eyes and led the way into town, heading for a part of the village the Harpers had never seen. At last, she stopped and pointed at an imposing stone building on the end of the street. Unlike the other buildings, it had no window boxes filled with flowers or colorful awnings, although it did have an imposing wooden door .

"That's our village hall. That's where the meeting will be. We'll go the back way, there's less chance of us getting caught."

She ducked into a narrow alley that ran between two shops and everyone hurried after her. There was no lantern burning at the end of the street and the area surrounding the village hall was blanketed in shadows. Maeve darted across the cobblestones and disappeared around the side of the building, the Harpers and Aidan behind her. There was another door, smaller than the front door, but Maeve didn't bother trying the knob.

"They always keep it locked, even in the daytime," she explained, sinking to her knees and jiggling a row of metal bars that covered a large square hole. With one tug, the bars came loose, and Maeve lifted the cover and set it on the ground.

"This used to be an old wash chute," she said, wiping her hands on her dress. "Whenever they had parties or fancy dinners, they would load up all the dirty dishes in a tub and send them down this chute to be washed outside. Of course, now they have a kitchen in the hall so no one uses the wash chute anymore. But it's a right useful thing to have."

"Have you used it before?" asked Lulabelle, regarding the hole with distrust.

Maeve's eyes twinkled. "Once or twice, but only for the most important things. Don't worry, it's roomier than it looks. . .ok, after me, and try not to bang too much."

Maeve climbed into the hole and disappeared up the chute. The others climbed in after her, the metal cool against their palms. Kat hoped the hollow echo of her knees against the chute wasn't as loud as it sounded. Another few seconds and Maeve stopped crawling, pivoted onto her bottom, and slid out of sight. Kat did the same and found herself standing in a darkened room lined with boxes. The door was cracked open and a sliver of light was coming from somewhere close by, along with the murmur of voices.

"Beyond there is the meeting hall," Maeve whispered, as the others slid out of the chute. "We'll be able to see and hear everything if we sit on the landing. It's a bit rickety but I imagine it's safe."

"What do you mean, you *imagine* it's safe?" Lulabelle said, but Maeve had already slipped into the hall.

Once out of the kitchen, Kat saw that a massive partition separated them from the rest of the meeting room, forming a hallway filled with more boxes and a few pieces of furniture. While the partition prevented Kat and the others from seeing into the meeting hall, it also had the lucky effect of keeping those in the meeting from seeing them, making it easy to get to the stairs undiscovered. The landing was really an elevated stage, about ten feet high, surrounded on all sides by a railing, and covered by a blanket. The thick layer of dust on the blanket implied the landing was not used very often and Kat had a fleeting suspicion that might have something to do with its safety, regardless of what Maeve said, but it was too late to worry about that now.

Maeve lifted the blanket and everyone wiggled underneath, pulling themselves forward on their elbows so they could crawl to the edge and peer over the side. A circle of chairs was set up in the center of the meeting hall, and in each chair sat a person who Kat assumed was one of the Hill province elders. As she watched, Mayor Digby got to his feet and clapped his hands to get everyone's attention.

"Thank you ladies and gentlemen for coming on such short notice and at such a late hour," he began. "As many of you know, there have been new developments in the last two days of a most disagreeable nature . . . terrible, just terrible. It's imperative that we discuss these new developments and what action should be taken. Our very survival is at stake!" The mayor stopped, clearly overcome, but recovered quickly. "First, we shall hear a report from the Enchantress, who will hopefully shed light on this grave situation. Enchantress, if you please."

All eyes turned towards someone sitting out of Kat's line of sight. She craned her neck as far as she could but was unable to see the Enchantress over the edge of the railing.

"My dear friends," the Enchantress began in a voice so rich and smooth it reminded Kat of melted chocolate. "I apologize for my late arrival but I'm afraid it was unavoidable. Aifric has informed me of the disturbing events that occurred yesterday, and while it is worrisome to know that the fog banshee is still here, it does confirm suspicions that many of us have had for some time. Namely, that this particular demon is searching for something not valuable to the naked eye, but rather unique and specific. This means that whoever summoned it is not interested in gold or riches. After consulting with the circle of Enchanters and studying the old legends with new eyes, I believe I now know what the fog banshee and its summoner seek."

The room was so quiet that Kat felt afraid to breathe.

"They are seeking ultimate power," the Enchantress said quietly, "and with that power, the ability to rule, not only the Hill province, but all of Ancora."

The meeting hall hummed with worried, confused voices. "But Enchantress, how is that possible?" said a man with straw-colored hair. "There's nothing in the Hill province with that kind of power. Surely we would know if we had it?"

"What sort of object?" asked another man. "Can you give us some idea?"

"I'm afraid I don't have the answer to that question yet. But there is no doubt in my mind that it is an object of extreme power."

"Perhaps there's been a bit of a mix-up," volunteered Mayor Digby. "If any province has a magical object, it's the Forest province. Isn't there a way we could tactfully point the fog banshee in that direction? Suggest it look there?"

"And have Achak and his people at war with us? I would rather face the fog banshee again," muttered a grumpy looking man. There was a chorus of agreement.

"What do you know of the one who summoned it?" said an older lady with glasses. "Are we any closer to discovering their identity? Surely that's as important as finding this object."

"Yes, it is."

Kat thought she heard hesitation in the Enchantress's voice. "While I'm afraid I don't know who is responsible for summoning the fog banshee, I believe—and my fellow Enchanters agree—that it could only have been the work of a Spellbinder."

A collective gasp filled the room. The gray-haired lady shuddered and put a handkerchief to her face. Mayor Digby's mouth dropped open and Mr. Stewart lowered his head gravely. The Harpers exchanged glances. Hadn't Aidan said something about Spellbinders the first time they had met him? Something about them dying out long ago? Or not existing at all? Kat turned to Aidan, but his eyes were on the Enchantress, his face stone. The landing gave a sudden creak and Kat felt it sag. This wasn't good. The talking stopped as heads turned in their direction and everyone ducked under the blanket. After a moment, the talking began again and Kat sneaked a peek. It appeared they were still hidden.

The Enchantress held up her hands for quiet. "I realize this comes as a dreadful shock but I'm afraid it's the only possible explanation; the level of magical skill involved, the intensity of the darkness, the obscurity of the potion which was thought lost to the ages. No one but a Spellbinder would be capable of that type of power . . . and I believe no one but a Spellbinder would have that desire."

"But I thought those sorts of people were the stuff of legends!" cried Mayor Digby, his mouth still open. "Are you saying they actually exist? That one of us—" he swung his arms around the room, presumably to include everyone present, "—one of us is a Spellbinder? That's impossible!"

"We knew it had to be a sorcerer, Aifric," Mr. Stewart reminded him. "No one else could pull off that kind of magic."

"Yes, but I assumed it was just your garden-variety sorcerer. Spellbinders are an entirely different situation!" Mayor Digby looked like he was on the verge of a nervous breakdown. "And let's not forget, no one believed they were real!"

The Enchantress was silent until the voices grew quiet. "In order for you to understand, I must tell you a legend. It's a legend that I suspect most of you heard as children. I have come to believe over the past few weeks, though, that it's more than a simple story. It is absolutely true." Every eye in the room, including the ones on the landing, were glued to her.

The Enchantress moved into the center of the room. Her hair was the color of wheat, mixed with tendrils of red, and flowed nearly to her waist. She wore a simple white gown that sparkled as she walked and when she turned to face the other side of the room, Kat saw her face for the first time. It was a beautiful face, with porcelain skin, and a mouth that looked like it could smile warmly. Now her mouth was serious, her eyes steady but worried.

"The legend I'm referring to is that of the Two Princes and the Lost Tokens of Ancora."

She paused again while more shock and confusion settled over the room. Kat didn't notice any of their expressions, for at that moment, the landing gave another creak and dropped several inches. Someone screamed as a cloud of dust rose into the air. Another creak and part of the railing gave way and toppled to the floor.

"It's going to collapse!" cried Aidan, squirming out from under the blanket. "Everyone get back!"

With a flash of panic, Kat realized that it was too late. The heavy blanket, which had been so effective at hiding everyone, had now turned against them, making it impossible to escape. The landing gave one final groan, then buckling under the weight of too many people, came crashing to the floor of the meeting hall, directly at the feet of the Enchantress.

CHAPTER THIRTEEN

A Tale of Two Princes

Through a haze of dust, Kat peered at the roomful of people with shocked expressions on their faces. She wished she could pull the blanket over her head and pretend to be invisible.

"Maeve?" said Mr. Stewart. "Kat? What on earth . . . " He appeared at a loss for words and Kat couldn't really blame him.

"Yes, Da, it's me—us I mean," replied Maeve in a small voice, climbing out from the wreckage of the landing with difficulty. Mr. Stewart and another man rushed over to help.

"Us, too, Rosie and me," said Lulabelle as she took Mr. Stewart's outstretched hand and stood up, shaking dust and wood fragments from her jeans.

One voice was conspicuously absent amidst the chaos. A quick glance was enough to tell Kat that Aidan alone had escaped. Stealing a look at the landing, she thought she detected a shadow hovering around the darkened stairs. Kat didn't know whether to feel glad that he hadn't been caught or anger that, once again, he had left them to fend for themselves.

"Are these your children, Liam?" The Enchantress was looking at the Harpers and Maeve with her serious eyes.

"This one here, Enchantress—that's my Maeve," said Mr. Stewart in a tone that sounded like he was debating whether to claim her. The shock appeared to be wearing off and his eyes were daggers.

"And these other children? Do they belong to anyone here?"

"No, Enchantress, these are the children I told you about."

"The ones from outside Ancora!" added Mayor Digby in an excited voice and immediately looked sorry he had spoken. Mr. Stewart grimaced as the murmur of voices rose and Kat knew that the secret was out. Mayor Digby rose to his feet, trying to recover from his slip of the tongue. "This is most unusual," he said, wringing his hands. "I didn't expect . . . that is . . . "

"They should be sent home at once," said a voice from behind Kat. A thin woman in a purple dress was giving them a disdainful look. She had elaborate curls styled on top of her head and her mouth was pinched, like she had eaten a lemon. "This is a private meeting. I don't know what you're teaching your daughter, Liam, but if I had a child I would expect better behavior than this. It's disgraceful! How did they even know to be here? I was under the impression this meeting was confidential." She turned her withering glare toward Mayor Digby, who popped out of his chair like a jack-in-the-box.

"Yes, no doubt about it!" he agreed hastily. "That is, I may have mentioned it to Ivy MacDougal when I stopped in for some mutton pastries this morning, but aside from that . . . "

"That explains it then. Honestly, Aifric, you might as well hand out leaflets in the center of town than tell Ivy anything in confidence. That woman couldn't keep a secret if her life depended on it, although apparently she's not the only one."

"You've made your point, Olive." Mr. Stewart held up his hands for peace. "And you're correct, the children had no business sneaking in as they did. Maeve—" he began, but Maeve cut him off with a pleading look.

"Please don't make us go, Da! We're sorry for barging in and I'll muck out Rumple's stall for a month as punishment, but please let us stay. We won't make a sound. You won't even know we're here." Rosie sneezed just as Kat stepped on a piece of railing, breaking it with a sharp crack.

"This doesn't concern you," snapped the woman named Olive. "This is secret Hill province business and it's no place for a child. Particularly children from outside the Hill province." She gave the Harpers another nasty look.

"But it does concern us!" Kat heard her own voice cry out. She was tired of all the secrets and the unjustness of the situation was more than she could stand. "We want to stop the fog banshee as much as you do! And we almost did yesterday! What have you done besides hide?" She stopped before she could get them into even more trouble. Why had she said that? Why couldn't she be quiet for once?

"The child is right, they should stay."

The Enchantress spoke quietly but it was clear her words ended the matter. Olive made another lemon face, while a few others grumbled under their breath, but the older lady with glasses smiled at Kat. Some of the men brought chairs and Kat found herself seated on one side of the circle, between Maeve and Rosie. Aifric Digby, more flustered than ever, made hasty introductions.

"This is most irregular—you know Liam, obviously—" Mayor Digby went around the circle, introducing a dozen people to the Harpers, until he ended with the nasty lady in the purple dress. "—and last but not least, Olive McCutcher—" The woman drummed her fingernails on her lap impatiently, looking annoyed.

"I believe that's everyone!" finished Mayor Digby with forced cheerfulness. He plopped onto his seat, wiping his forehead.

"I apologize again for the intrusion, Enchantress," said Mr. Stewart, taking his seat as well. The look he gave them from across the room told Kat they were definitely in a heap of trouble. She decided to focus on the Enchantress, standing in the center of the circle.

"According to the legend," she began in her chocolate-like voice, as though there had been no interruption, "there was a time, long ago, when Ancora was led by a royal family. This royal family presided over a council from all the different provinces—Hill, Lake, Mountain, Sea, Caves, Forest, Southern, and the Central City. It was not a perfect system, but for the most part it worked well and was a time of great peace and prosperity.

"But then a king rose to power, and this king had two sons. The older prince, as was the custom, would ascend the throne after his father's death, while the younger prince assumed the role of liaison between the provinces and the royal family. He was beloved by many in Ancora, who saw in him a genuine love for his people and his country. The older prince was different. He cared not what the rest of Ancora did, as long as they left him alone. Battles might be fought, but he preferred others to fight them. Arguments might need settling, but he wished others to settle them."

Kat thought this older prince sounded like a first-class wimp, but she kept that thought to herself.

"When the king died and the older prince assumed the throne, troubles quickly multiplied. The older prince was incapable of leading the council and had little interest in anything but his own pursuits. Provinces began to quarrel and quarrels led to serious disagreements. The younger prince found that his attempts to bring peace fell on deaf ears. At last, one province, angry at its neighbor for a perceived wrong, attacked the other province and several on both sides were killed. The younger prince could take it no more. His beloved Ancora was tearing herself apart and if his brother would not intervene, then his brother must go."

The Enchantress paused and her eyes flicked past Kat to something behind her head. Had she seen Aidan? Kat turned to follow her gaze and thought she detected the same shadow in the doorway.

"The younger prince knew his brother would never give up the throne, for he enjoyed the power that came with his office, even if he cared nothing for its responsibilities. The older prince also had allies on the council— those who took advantage of his disinterest to further their own ambitions—and overthrowing the king could lead to civil war. No, if the king were to be removed, it must be permanently and it must look like an accident."

"You mean kill him?" interrupted Kat.

The Enchantress inclined her head to indicate that was exactly what she meant. Kat felt a timid pinch on her arm and Maeve leaned over to whisper, "Sorry, that's from Lulabelle. She says to be quiet."

"Before long, a rare poison from the Forest province found its way into the older prince's goblet. The poison was odorless, tasteless, and therefore, impossible to detect. As the older prince had always been in poor health, no one questioned his death. The younger prince assumed the throne, and hope was restored to Ancora. The provinces believed they were entering a second golden age, a return to the prosperity of former days.

"As a testament of good faith, each province created and presented a token, an object unique to that province that reflected its desire for unity. The objects were filled with powerful magic—magic that would remain strong so long as the tokens were joined together. Should the tokens be separated, however, the power bestowed on them would be broken, although each token would retain a glimmer of its former glory. No one gave much thought to that at the time, for the people knew their beloved prince would always use their tokens for good. He would never betray them . . . or so they thought.

"But power has a way of bringing out the darkness that lurks at the bottom of our souls. The younger prince had sacrificed so much for Ancora; now he would do whatever it took to preserve her. He grew anxious, even more so than when his brother ruled the provinces, and decisions once left to the council became his alone; who else could he trust with his precious Ancora? Friends became enemies and every word, no matter how innocent, grew suspicious in his mind. By the time sixteen years had passed, the younger prince's heart was so filled with poison that he was much worse than his older brother had ever been.

"There was still hope, though. The infant son of the older prince had reached the age when he would assume the throne. The boy, although only sixteen, was nothing like his father and everything like his uncle had once been: humble, kind, with an eager spirit and a gentle heart. With great joy and much relief, the provinces made preparations for his coronation.

"But the younger prince was no longer prepared to relinquish the throne. Ancora was his obsession and he trusted no one else to lead it. He was not alone in these thoughts. Over the years, he had acquired followers from all eight provinces who loved Ancora the way he did. They called themselves Spellbinders, for they had found ways to uncover ancient, dark magic that allowed them to control Ancora. They schemed to murder the young heir on the night of the coronation and reclaim the throne, once and for all. They believed their dark magic, coupled with the power of the tokens, would make them unstoppable."

Kat shifted in her seat. This legend was sounding less promising by the minute.

"All was not lost, though, for the heir had his own support-ers, men and women sworn to protect the royal line. They were known as Light Seekers. When the Spellbinders laid siege to the Central City on the night of the coronation, they found the heir to the throne had vanished. The prince was furious. He ordered his Spellbinders to locate the heir and destroy him. Ancora descended into chaos, for the Spellbinders were powerful and their magic was black. So the people of the provinces did the only thing they could, what they should have done years before . . . They fought back.

"They came together and defeated the prince and his Spellbinders through sheer courage and determination. They removed the tokens from the Central City, breaking their power, and each token went back to its own province, never to be seen again. The prince died on the battlefield and the few remaining Spellbinders were scattered. The eight provinces became what they are today—lands that keep to themselves, with little thought for the others. Never again has there been a leader to unite Ancora."

Lulabelle, sensing the Enchantress had come to the end of her story, gingerly raised her hand. "Excuse me, but what about the heir? What happened to him?"

The Enchantress nodded, as though expecting the question. "No one knows. Some believe he died before he could assume the throne, but I believe he chose to stay hidden. Perhaps he was afraid of what power might do to his own soul, or perhaps he wished to lead a quiet life and now had the chance. Whatever the reasons, he never came forward and not one of the Light Seekers ever revealed his location."

"There've been rumors over the years, haven't there?" said the man with straw-colored hair, Mr. Quigley. "Rumors that the royal line is alive. That somewhere out there is the rightful heir to the throne of Ancora, whether they know it or not."

"That is correct, but I'm afraid that's all they are—rumors.

Some also believe that a group of Light Seekers still exists, that through these many years there has remained a secret group dedicated to protecting the royal line. But those remain rumors as well."

"What of the tokens, Enchantress?" Mayor Digby was on the edge of his seat, like a toddler eyeing a bowl of ice cream. "What do they have to do with the fog banshee?"

"Thank you, Aifric, I was coming to that. Although the tokens, like the heir himself, were never seen again, the legend claims they are still hidden in their respective provinces. Should they be found and reunited, whoever possessed them would have the power to control Ancora."

"This is ridiculous!" scoffed Olive McCutcher. "We all know that legend is a child's fairy tale. Princes, tokens, Spellbinders! It's too farfetched for words!"

"I agree," said the old man sitting next to her. "I remember my mam threatening to send a Spellbinder after me if I was a naughty lad. They're bogeymen, nothing more."

There were grumbles of assent from around the room. The Enchantress waited patiently for everyone to grow quiet. Mr. Stewart cleared his throat and the grumbling ceased.

"I understand the disbelief," he said. "I too have always thought this legend to be simply that—a legend. Any basis in fact had long since been cluttered by exaggeration . . . too many late-night tellings around a campfire with a jug of ale." A few of the men smiled in understanding. "To entertain the notion that it's true requires a good deal of faith. It's no easy matter when a fairy tale becomes real because that means it's no longer safe. Unlike a story, we can't control what happens next. I confess that I don't understand everything, but I trust the Enchantress. If she believes the tokens are real, then I am inclined to believe as well, even if my understanding is incomplete."

"But Liam, surely you don't believe this nonsense about Spellbinders?" Olive McCutcher scoffed. "You honestly think dark sorcerers are plotting to take over Ancora as we speak? Even if there were Spellbinders once, they would've all died out long ago. Are you really implying that some deranged individual is calling himself a Spellbinder and learning black magic?"

"Someone knew enough to summon a fog banshee, didn't they?" growled the grumpy man, who had been introduced as Mr. Corley. "You think anyone could do that? Gaffney Culkin? Puddy MacDougal?"

Olive sniffed disdainfully.

"I don't know if there's a ring of new Spellbinders out there or not," Mr. Stewart conceded, "but it's safe to say there's at least one and he's powerful enough to summon a fog banshee."

"Quite right, Liam, you make a good point," agreed Mayor Digby. "If we only knew what the token looked like it might save everyone a great deal of trouble." He looked at the Enchantress hopefully. "I don't suppose you've discovered some sort of list in your research, have you? Perhaps one of the scribes kept a detailed record of notes?"

"I'm afraid not, Aifric, more's the pity," said the Enchantress, trying not to smile.

"If the legend is true, and I'm inclined to agree with Liam that it could be," said a man named Mr. Gaffney, "that means the Hill token is hundreds of years old, doesn't it? Shouldn't we be searching for something ancient? Made of stone, perhaps?"

The Enchantress frowned. "That's a logical thought but you must remember that the tokens still contain traces of magic and this magic might transform an ordinary object. I consulted with the other Enchanters and we could not agree what the token might look like now, or if it would even be altered. I'm sorry to say that, until we learn more, we must assume the token is anything that can be held in your hand."

"That's rather vague," muttered Olive McCutcher.

"For once, Olive and I agree," said the lady with glasses, Mrs. Tully, in a mild voice. "It seems unlikely that we can find this token with the little information we have and time is of the essence. That brings me back to my original question: what of the person who summoned it? If he's indeed a Spellbinder, can he be that hard to identify? Indeed, that may be far easier than searching for this token."

Mr. Stewart looked troubled. "I think we should be careful, Aileen, lest it turns into a witch hunt where good reputations are ruined."

"I understand Liam, but I'm afraid that's what we have now." The brisk, no-nonsense way Mrs. Tully spoke made Kat think she must have been a school teacher in her younger days. "People are turning on each other and it's only getting worse."

"A Spellbinder here?" whined Mayor Digby. "I can't imagine that any of us would be part of such wickedness. I vouch for all of my neighbors in the Hill province any day of the week!"

"Then maybe we should start looking outside the Hill province," said Mr. Corley, his dark eyes fixing the Harpers in a cold stare.

"We've been over this before," replied Mr. Stewart with a touch of irritation. "These children are not responsible for what's happened. To even suggest that they're capable of dark magic is ludicrous."

"Maybe not these children, but there are others, aren't there?" Olive McCutcher dismissed the Harpers with a wave of her hand. "What about that wild man who lives in the hills? And the Realm? There's all sorts of undesirable people there. Has anyone thought to investigate them?"

She snapped her fingers. "What about that red-headed boy who slinks around town? I have it on good authority that he's no more than a dirty thief, yet he's out roaming the countryside. If he has parents—which I doubt—they don't seem at all interested in raising him. It's anyone's guess as to what sorts of dark things he's involved in."

At the mention of Aidan, Kat felt hot anger bubbling inside her. She balled up her fists and wrapped her ankles around her chair to keep from jumping up and yelling at Olive McCutcher. Even worse, more than a few people were nodding in agreement. She wondered how many of them had lost things to the mysterious Hill province burglar. Her question was answered by a chorus of voices.

"That's a fact, sure enough. My best fishing pole was snatched right off my porch and I saw him hanging about only moments before."

"Two raspberry pies in my back window! I could've sworn the thief had red hair."

"I felt sorry for the lad and gave him a bit to do around my barn. How did he repay me? Made off with my favorite harness, he did!"

The grumbling grew louder. Kat fought the urge to turn around and see if Aidan was still hiding in the shadows. She didn't want him to hear what people were saying.

"Ladies and gentlemen, if you would please quiet down!" Mayor Digby was on his feet again, attempting to restore order. "I agree with Liam that we shouldn't rush to judgment when it comes to Spellbinders. It would be most unfortunate to accuse someone wrongly." Mayor Digby shot a sideways glance at Mr. Stewart. "However, I do think it prudent to keep an eye on, shall we say, certain ne'er-do-wells who may or may not be involved somehow . . . "

"He's a boy, Aifric," said Mr. Stewart firmly, "not much older than my Maeve. Is he a thief? Perhaps, although no one's caught him stealing. But a Spellbinder? It's as ridiculous as accusing these children. He's no more involved in dark magic than I am." He gave Olive McCutcher an exasperated look. "And he can't help where he comes from or who his family is."

Olive McCutcher was unmoved. "But that's the point, we don't—"

The Enchantress held up her hand and Olive fell silent, although she gave the Harpers another nasty look and resumed drumming her fingernails on her dress. One of her elaborate curls had come loose and bobbed up and down against her cheek. Kat wished she could lean over and yank it good and hard.

"I have told you everything I know so far," the Enchantress said. "I wish that it was more helpful, but at least we know whom we are facing and what they seek and that knowledge may help us in ways we don't yet realize. For my part, I will do what I can to learn more of the Hill token. As to how you proceed in finding the Spellbinder, I leave that to your discretion. But remember this: the legend tells us that Spellbinders are adept at hiding, often in plain sight. They may not appear as you imagine a sorcerer should for they are masters at deception and can look and act as anyone else. The original Spellbinders were able to move freely for so long because no one thought to suspect them of dark magic. We must not make that mistake again."

Mayor Digby rose to his feet as the Enchantress returned to her chair. "I suppose now we enter into the brainstorming phase of our meeting, so to speak. I'm quite open to any suggestions. Shall we alert our neighbors to the east and west, do you think? Surely the Mountain province would be helpful."

"Ragnar would want to know," agreed Mr. Stewart, "although I doubt his men would fare better against a fog banshee than the Cahir."

"Quite right. What of the Lake province? Shall we send word to Rumpkin? Seek his counsel?"

There was a pause and then the entire room erupted into laughter. Kat had no idea what was so funny, but apparently it involved someone named Rumpkin. Mayor Digby, realizing his words had prompted the amusement, chortled louder than anyone.

"Good gracious, what am I saying? Seek his counsel, indeed. Yes, by all means, let's see what wise words the honorable lord protector Rumpkin has to offer!" There was a wave of fresh laughter. When the laughter died down, Mr. Stewart stood up, indicating that Maeve and the Harpers should stand as well.

"Thank you, Aifric, it's nice to know we can still find humor in times such as these," he said, smiling. "I will leave the meeting in your capable hands. These children must be returned to their home."

Kat wanted to plead with Mr. Stewart to let them stay, but it was clear he was in no mood to argue. They followed him out the heavy front door, a collection of whispers trailing after them. Kat cast one more glance in Aidan's direction, but the shadow hovering around the stairwell was gone.

CHAPTER FOURTEEN

The Midsummer Festival

T his has got to be the most disgusting job ever," declared Kat
as she and Lulabelle helped Maeve shovel horse manure out
of Rumple's stall and into a large bucket. "How much poop does
one horse make?"

"Da says he eats enough for ten horses, sure enough," replied
Maeve, wiping the sweat from her forehead and leaving a dark mark
that Kat hoped was dirt. For someone on poop duty for the second
time that summer, Maeve was surprisingly upbeat. The walk back
to the wagon had been a painful one. No one had uttered a word.
Maeve had refused to look at anyone, choosing to stare straight
ahead like a prisoner being led to her death. Kat expected Mr. Stewart to yell, lecture, or at least wave his hands around, but he hadn't

spoken, not even when he discovered the wagon and Rumple still tied to the tree. Red Star and Aidan were nowhere to be found. It was only when they reached the black rock that Mr. Stewart turned to speak to them, huddled together, miserably awaiting their fate.

"To say I am disappointed in you would be an understatement," he said. In one hand he held a lantern, and the quivering flame made him seem even more terrifying. "While I don't suspect the elders of dark magic, secrets have a way of getting out, which means if the Spellbinder wasn't already aware of your presence, he will be." Mr. Stewart sighed. "I'm afraid I can't help that now, but what I can do is try yet again to impress upon you how serious this situation is. You are not my children but while you're in Ancora you are my responsibility, and therefore I'm going to treat you like my own. You haven't listened to talking so we shall try another tactic."

He put the lantern down. "Report to our house tomorrow morning at nine o'clock sharp. Wear old clothes."

"At least there's three of us, so it'll go faster," said Lulabelle, heaving another shovelful into the bucket. She was wearing her rain boots and an orange poncho that made a crinkling sound every time she moved. She was also wearing her goggles from a science lab the year before that, for reasons Kat couldn't begin to imagine, Lulabelle had felt compelled to pack in her suitcase. Rubber gloves from under the kitchen sink completed her outfit. Lulabelle had offered to find a poncho and goggles for Kat as well, but Kat had dismissed her with, "No thanks, I don't want to look like an idiot."

Maeve had politely declined Lulabelle's offer of goggles and gloves, but had chosen instead to attach a clothespin to her nose, which Kat was quick to inform her, looked even weirder than Lulabelle and a lot more uncomfortable. Now as Kat rubbed the sweat out of her eyes and examined the dirt (please let it be dirt) under her fingernails, she was forced to admit that they were both on to something.

"I still think it's unfair that Rosie gets off scot-free," she complained. "She was at the meeting too. How come she doesn't have to shovel poop?"

"You know the barn makes her allergies worse," said Lulabelle, adjusting her goggles. "It's not like she's getting out of it. Mr. Stewart is still making her do work."

Kat glanced out the barn door where Rosie was pulling weeds in Mrs. Stewart's garden. To her eyes, it looked more like Rosie was creating necklaces out of the weeds than anything else. Not fair! If they were all going to be punished, it was only right they be equally miserable.

"Water break in five minutes," said Mr. Stewart from the doorway. They all breathed sighs of relief. "When you've finished here, I promised Mrs. Tully you would muck out her barn. Mr. Tully's laid up with a bad back and they could use the help."

A collective groan followed. Kat was positive Mr. Stewart

smiled as he turned away. She attacked her pile of manure angrily. "Maeve, how many horses do the Tullys have?"

Maeve shot her a despairing look as she dumped another shovelful into the bucket. "Mr. Tully trains horses for a living. They have at least five." More groans.

When they weren't mucking out stables or weeding flower beds, Kat, Lulabelle, and Rosie spent the rest of their time with Maeve, watching the preparations for the Midsummer festival from a distance (but a distance greatly helped by Lulabelle's trusty binoculars) and listening to Maeve describe past festivals as if they were Christmas, Halloween and summer vacation all rolled into one. When the day of the festival arrived, Kat couldn't contain her excitement.

"What should we eat first?" she asked as they turned onto the dirt road that led to the Stewart's house. "Maeve says Mr. Piddlewick always makes a special batch of Honeyfizz so we have to remember to try some. Oh, and don't forget the giant peppermint snaps that are shaped like real peppers and try to bite you. I think I want one of the flaming lamb kebabs so we can pretend they're torches—"

"It's not only about food," Lulabelle reminded her. "There's going to be all kinds of dancing and acrobatics. Maeve said the brownies put on an amazing show and I don't want to miss it because we're trying to find you a flaming lamb kebab."

"Please can we try the games?" begged Rosie. "I want to win a stuffed troll!"

The Hill province was awash in sunlight as the Stewart's wagon bumped along the road toward the festival. Decorations hung from every cottage, the doors and windows strewn with purple and gold. People walking along the side of the road called out greetings to each other, but Kat couldn't help but notice their smiles looked forced, their eyes nervous. A cloud of anxiety hung in the air. The wagon crossed the red bridge, but instead of turning towards the village, Mr. Stewart left the main road and climbed a much smaller hill, where he came to a stop under a tree. Below them, Kat saw an enormous field teeming with hundreds of people. Tents of all sizes dotted the field and the faint strains of music floated upward, as well as the salty, smoky aroma of meat.

The entrance to the Midsummer festival was a flowery archway with two full-size statues of horses on either side. At least, Kat thought they were statues, but when she leaned in for a closer look, she realized the statues were made of chocolate. Mayor Digby stood in the center of the archway, wearing a plum-colored hat with a gold feather. His eyes lit up at the sight of the Harpers.

"Welcome, welcome!" he cried heartily. "This promises to be

quite a show, no doubt about it! Not even a fog banshee can keep us down for long!" He gazed out at the festival, his smile dimming. "I'm afraid it's much smaller than last year's, don't you think, Liam? Not as many vendors. Or people, for that matter. Do you know, I had to beg the brownies to open the festival this time around, and it was all I could do to come up with enough compliments to please every one of them. Extremely taxing!"

"People are still scared, Aifric," Mrs. Stewart reminded him. "You must give them time. You've done a wonderful job. We need to get out in the sunshine and have a bit of a normal life. We can't hide forever."

"Until we can be sure the fog banshee's gone, it will be difficult for anyone to relax," added Mr. Stewart.

"I suppose so, but it's been over a month since it came. Surely that's a good sign . . . maybe it's finally gone." Mayor Digby sighed. "But there's still the matter of the Spellbinder running loose and that's what's doing it. If we could only capture *him*, then people would feel safer . . . ." He trailed off, lost in thought.

As though realizing where he was, he shook his head and smiled broadly. "But what am I doing? These children are here for fun, aren't you? And fun you shall have!" His eyes widened. "Dear me, I must go find Mr. Piddlewick! The horses are starting to melt and I'm sure I told him to use an anti-warming enchantment. It's only a matter of time before they look like they've met a gruesome death. Not at all a pleasant way to welcome people!" He disappeared into the crowd.

"Right then, shall we see what there is to see?" Mr. Stewart smiled at the Harpers. They nodded, speechless with eagerness. As they followed Maeve into the center of the festival, the tents rising up around them, the aromas of buttery popcorn and toffee mixing with a symphony of voices and other sounds, Kat had to pinch herself to believe it was real.

She stopped in front of an oversized tent covered in gold fabric, where a tiny man who resembled Mr. Piddlewick perched on the counter, juggling balls that changed color every time they touched his hands. Behind him were stacks of toys that reached to the top of the tent. A variety of wooden animals sat on the counter and Kat reached out to touch one of them. The animal didn't look like any creature Kat had ever seen, but it was also strangely familiar. It came to her at once—the animal was the same one from the tomb they had discovered with Donovan, although then it was carved into stone rather than wood. Kat examined the toy, which was painted red and green. What an odd creature.

"It's another lumina," said Rosie, picking up a rainbow-colored one from the counter. "It's just like the one Lil has. This one's a little prettier but I would never tell her that."

"What are they?" asked Lulabelle, reaching for a purple and gold lumina with a bow around its neck. "They were all over that shrine we found."

Rosie explained what Lil had told her about the luminas acting as protectors of the Hill province, waiting to defend its people from danger. Maeve nodded her agreement.

"When I was little, I would imagine I saw luminas hiding behind trees, watching me play. It's another one of our legends, but I can't remember all the details. It did make me feel safer, thinking there might be good monsters ready to protect us." Maeve studied Lulabelle's lumina critically. "Rather on the ugly side, though, aren't they?"

"It's too bad they're not here now," said Kat, replacing the wooden toy on the counter. "We could use their help getting rid of the fog banshee."

They made their way through the rest of the tents, stopping at several of the most interesting ones. At last, they came out onto the open field where most of the festival goers were gathered. Another row of tents stood off to the side and the tantalizing smells drifting from that direction made everyone's mouths water. In front of the tents sat a group of tiny men dressed in green, blowing on horns that were twice their size. There was a bang and a shower of gold coins erupted from the horns and landed on the ground.

"We're rich!" cried Kat as the watching crowd clapped

appreciatively and the tiny men took turns bowing. She dropped to her knees, trying to collect as many coins as she could. "They must be leprechauns!"

"Not rich, I'm afraid," said Lulabelle, taking a bite of her coin. "They're toffee, I think."

Kat took a bite and shrugged happily. "Close enough."

For the rest of the morning, Kat felt like she was floating in some kind of wonderful dream. The brownies put on an entertaining show that involved various complex flying formations, disappearing and reappearing spontaneously, and for a grand finale, fireworks that formed pictures in the sky. When they finished, Kat, Lulabelle, and Rosie clapped until they thought their hands would fall off, while the brownies fluttered around collecting items given to them by people in the crowd, their little faces bright with pleasure.

Maeve opened a pouch hanging from her dress and removed a ball of rubber bands, which she presented to a skinny brownie in a purple robe. The brownie bowed before moving on to the next object, a rusty spoon. Noticing the Harpers' questioning looks, Maeve laughed.

"It's a bit odd, sure enough. Most people want flowers, but then brownies aren't people, and I suppose their idea of treasure is different from everyone else's. When Alberta first came to live with us, Mam made the mistake of giving her a new dress for her birthday—you've never seen such disappointment! I thought Alberta might really turn us out of our own house. But then she saw the needle and bit of thread Mam used to make the dress and that became her present instead. Who knows? Maybe they see something the rest of us can't. As for me, if people ever toss things at my head, I hope they're diamonds."

They had just gotten their food—four flaming lamb kabobs— and were looking for a place to sit when Rosie nudged Kat and pointed in the direction of one of the food tents. A figure slouched against a tree, taking in the festival from the safety of the shadows. His hat was pulled down over his eyes but Kat recognized the brown satchel with the claw marks. Signaling to Lulabelle, the three of them headed in the direction of the figure, Maeve trailing behind. Kat reached him first, careful to hold her flaming lamb kabob at a distance to avoid setting her hair on fire, although she wasn't worried about burns. Maeve had shown them that it was just an enchantment and not really hot, a fact she demonstrated persuasively by running her hand back and forth through the flames.

"Aidan, is that you?"

They hadn't seen him since the night of the meeting. Kat wondered whether he was avoiding them on purpose. She hoped he hadn't heard the angry words directed at him.

"You don't miss a thing, do you little bird? I should take you hunting with me next time. You're better than a bloodhound."

He pushed his hat up on his head to see them better and the Harpers gasped at a red, jagged cut on his temple. Aidan touched it tenderly, sensing their shock.

"Not to worry, it looks a sight worse than it feels. Anyway, I stitched myself right up and it's healing rather nicely."

"You gave yourself stitches?" Lulabelle looked horrified. "Did you use a sterile needle? Did you clean it with alcohol? What about—"

Rosie threw her arms around Aidan's waist. "Where have you been? We missed you!"

Aidan sucked in his breath, a pained expression on his face. He patted Rosie's back, then gently removed her arms, exhaling as he did. "Careful there, little bird, my ribs are a touch sore at the moment. Either that, or you're too fierce for me." He tried to smile but it was obvious he was in pain.

"Aidan, what's going on?" Kat demanded. "Every time we see you, you have bumps and bruises and cuts. What are you doing? Is someone hurting you?"

"No one's hurting me." Aidan leaned against the tree, his eyes closed.

"If you're not going to tell us, at least have lunch with us," said Kat in a grumpy voice. She took out her anger on her lamb kabob, blowing on it until the flames dwindled into tiny sparks. Aidan watched the crowd of Hill people milling around before pulling his hat over his eyes again.

"I'm not sure I'm the most welcome lad right now. Everyone seems to think I'm a Spellbinder, out to destroy the Hill province. Isn't that right, Red?" He laughed, but it sounded unnatural and Kat's heart sank. He *had* heard everything.

Maeve glared at him. "I wouldn't put it past you. Although, truth be told, you seem like the type who would steal things yourself, rather than send a monster to do it for you."

"We don't think you're a Spellbinder!" Lulabelle said quickly, before Aidan could reply to Maeve's insult. "No one's paying attention, anyway. Just keep your hat on and stay close to us."

Reluctantly, Aidan followed the Harpers and Maeve to a bench, where they sat down to watch the next performance. Everyone divided up their food to share with Aidan, although Maeve chose the very smallest chunk of lamb and passed it to him grudgingly. Aidan insisted he wasn't hungry, then proceeded to devour the lamb in a way that made Kat question when he'd last eaten. A few benches away, Mr. and Mrs. Stewart sat chatting with friends. From time to time, Mr. Stewart glanced in their direction, but if he recognized Aidan he chose not to say anything.

The performance ended and the dancers—a troupe of Hill province women in fancy dresses—curtsied to enthusiastic applause.

Mayor Digby, clutching a gigantic bullhorn, announced that it was now time for the Midsummer games. There was a ripple of delight and within minutes, the crowd had tripled in size. Kat caught a glimpse of Cathmor, along with two burly men who looked like they must be part of the Cahir. All three wore somber expressions and were scanning the crowd. Kat remembered what Mayor Digby had said at the meeting—that he couldn't believe anyone in the Hill province was a Spellbinder. She thought he had a point. It was hard to imagine that one of these happy, laughing people could have summoned something so evil.

Olive McCutcher, the nasty, lemon-faced lady, was impossible to miss. She wore a poofy gold dress that made her look like a candle on a birthday cake, and a hat with feathers all over it. As she moved through the crowd, people stepped back to give her a wide berth. At first Kat thought it was because Olive's dress was so massive, but when she settled herself daintily on a bench, Kat saw that she was leading two peacocks on a leash, their plumes brushing against people's legs. One of the peacocks chose that moment to unfurl its feathers, whipping a cloud of dust right into Olive's face. She erupted in loud, ragged sneezes that caused her hat to fall off, where it was promptly stepped on by the other peacock. On the other side of Lulabelle, Rosie stood up to wave to Lil, the little girl she had befriended at the Stewart's cottage.

"Look, Mam, it's Rosie. Hi Rosie!" Lil ran over, dragging her toy lumina behind her on a purple ribbon, and hugged Rosie's neck. "Isn't this grand? It's my first festival and I'm going to stuff myself with candy and stay up past my bedtime every night!" She settled herself on the ground in front of them as a horn sounded, the contestants entered the clearing, and the crowd burst into applause.

The games went on for the better part of the morning. There were all sorts of contests: barrel rolling, in which men pushed heavy barrels up and down the field; rope climbing, in which contestants shimmied up ropes held in the air by brownies and rang a bell at the top; and a throwing contest, where contestants hurled objects at a moving target. Kat wasn't sure whether this tested strength or accuracy, or simply gave people an excuse to throw rocks at things, but she found herself clapping and cheering along with everyone else. Maeve appeared to be having the time of her life, yelling out encouragement to her favorites and screaming like a maniac when one of them did well. Aidan was strangely quiet, never once taking his attention off the games or the contestants. From time to time, he would make a sudden movement, as though imagining himself in the middle of it all, competing with the others.

At last, Mayor Digby announced the final event of the games and a new set of contestants took the field. Maeve leaned over to explain that this contest was the most difficult, as it required contestants to balance atop barrels and roll around the field until they either got tired or fell off. Fifteen contestants each claimed their barrel and the whistle blew to start the event.

Within seconds it became clear that the contest was meant to entertain the crowd as much as show off the contestants' skill. Three people immediately fell off their barrels and rose to their feet, laughing at their clumsiness. Two contestants ran headlong into each other and flew backward, the barrels spinning off in opposite directions and knocking two other contestants off their own barrels. Rosie pointed out Puddy MacDougal in the middle of the field, swinging his arms crazily, as though fending off a swarm of psychotic bees. Mrs. MacDougal's piercing voice could be heard over the laughter of the crowd, yelling instructions at Puddy (which only seemed to make things worse). His barrel lurched forward suddenly, plowing through five more contestants and sending them flying. Puddy let out a high-pitched shriek as he and his barrel hurtled off the field, narrowly missing Mayor Digby, who leaped out of the way just in time. Picking up her skirts, Mrs. MacDougal ran after Puddy, still yelling instructions as the crowd howled.

The two remaining contestants, an older man and a brownie, continued to roll their barrels around the edge of the field for the next five minutes, careful to stay out of each other's way. Finally the older man, breathing hard, hopped off his barrel and bowed to the crowd, pointing at the brownie to acknowledge him as the winner. People stomped their feet, cheering and whistling their approval; the brownie fluttered to the ground, smiling a wrinkly smile.

The contest winners filed onto the field as Mayor Digby presented each with a garland of flowers and a small certificate. When he reached the brownie, he paused, unsure what to do.

"This is surprising indeed! I don't believe a brownie has ever won the barrel roll before. What is your name, little fellow?"

The brownie tinkled an answer.

"Barnaby! Well done, Barnaby! I think a special victory deserves a special prize. What do you say, ladies and gentlemen?"

There was a great deal of applause and Barnaby's smile deepened as Mayor Digby cast around for something to present to him. A few people held up random objects: coins, a bottle cap, an empty paper bag. Barnaby frowned, studying each one. All of a sudden, his gaze fell on the Harpers and his eyes lit up. To Kat's alarm, the little brownie rose into the air and flew as fast as he could toward their bench, arms outstretched, eyes bulging gleefully. What was happening? What was he doing? Was it the Harpers? Did he want to claim one of the Harpers as his prize? Barnaby reached their bench and, with a triumphant squeak, he snatched at the wooden lumina in Lil's arms. She screamed in terror, grasping at the string as Barnaby tugged the toy away from her.

"You can't have that! It's mine!"

The brownie snarled and pulled harder. The Harpers and Maeve sat there, stunned. In fact, the entire crowd appeared to be frozen, too shocked to move. Aidan was the first to recover; leaping off the bench, he shoved Maeve to the side and wrenched the lumina out of Barnaby's hands. Lil burst into tears and ran to her father, who had come out of his shock and was racing towards them. Barnaby tried to pull the lumina back, but Aidan held on tightly. The brownie exploded into furious tinkling as Mayor Digby came puffing over and everyone began talking at once.

"Dear me, I was not expecting this! Now little sir, there's no cause to be upset. There are plenty of other prizes to choose from . . . equally wonderful." Barnaby squeezed his eyes shut, his small fists pounding the air.

Mayor Digby looked around desperately. "I'm sure you can find another prize, my dear fellow. You must understand that we can't allow our contest winners to violently grab things from small children!"

Barnaby lunged toward Aidan once more, but it was obvious he was no match. Just then, a squeaky voice rang out from somewhere in the crowd and people drew aside to let someone pass.

"Have no fear! I have what you need—pardon me, madam . . . sir, please excuse me, coming through! Coming through, I say!"

A little man with a fat face appeared out of the crowd. Kat recognized him as the juggling leprechaun (or was it clurichaun?) from the toy tent they had passed earlier. He was holding another toy lumina in his arms, a silver one with red and blue flowers all over it. He held it out to Barnaby, bowing.

"If it's a toy you seek, allow me the honor of presenting you with the best that Snugglewump's Superior Toys has to offer!" The little man held the lumina up for the crowd to see. "At Snugglewump's, every toy is hand carved and made to order—truly excellent crafts-manship, as you can see for yourselves. No more of this bickering, everyone wins at Snugglewump's!"

Barnaby made a pouty face. He glanced once more at the lumina in Aidan's arms, but seemed to realize he was not going to get it. Glumly, he took the toy offered by Mr. Snugglewump. The spectacle over, the crowd dispersed as music played from somewhere close by. Aidan returned the lumina to a tearful Lil, who hugged it more tightly than ever. Mayor Digby clapped him on the shoulder.

"Nicely done, lad! Very quick reflexes, I must say. Perhaps I misjudged you before, you're a useful fellow to have around." He waved goodbye as they moved away from the field and back into the throngs of festival goers. "Enjoy today while you can!" he called after them. "Chance of rain tomorrow, you know!"

"This was one of the absolute best days in the whole world!" Kat declared that afternoon, as she, Lulabelle, and Rosie climbed out of the black rock. They were tired and sweaty and everyone's stomachs hurt from all the sweets they had eaten, but they couldn't help grinning at each other.

"I hope Lil's okay," said Rosie, her expression clouding. "She was so upset when that brownie tried to take her toy. I wonder what got into him."

Kat shrugged. "Who knows? Maeve says that brownies get excited about weird things."

Lulabelle's expression was thoughtful.

"What is it, Lu?"

"I was wondering about that brownie, Barnaby, trying to take Lil's toy. I'm sure Maeve's right. It's just odd, that's all."

"It's over now," said Kat, ready to be done with the topic. "He got another toy, which is what he wanted, and Lil got her lumina back, so there's no harm done. Hey, did anyone else see the tent with the DANGER signs all over it? I think it had a skull and crossbones. We should go there first tomorrow!"

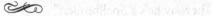

The sky was gray and overcast when they arrived in Ancora the next day, the air filled with a spitting rain that dampened their hair and faces. The grass felt soggy under their feet; Mayor Digby's warning about possible rain had come true. Maeve paced in front of the cave, her shoes making a squishy sound every time she whirled around. Her eyebrows were furrowed in deep concentration, her lips pursed so tightly they appeared invisible. She jumped when she saw them, startled out of whatever thoughts had consumed her.

"There you are, I've been waiting here forever! I thought you'd never come. I even tried knocking on the rock . . . I don't know what I was expecting, maybe for a door to open. Oh, I'm so glad to see you!"

"Were we supposed to meet you here?" asked Lulabelle, looking confused. "I thought we had agreed to come to your house after lunch—"

"Yes, but none of it matters right now," Maeve said hurriedly. "The festival's been rained out for the afternoon. No, we have to get to the town hall before it begins—there's no time to spare!"

"Before what begins? Maeve, what are you talking about?" A vague sense of dread gripped Kat. "Is something wrong?"

"You could put it that way!" Maeve took a deep breath, forcing her voice to slow down. "It's Aidan. He's been arrested for murder. They say he's a Spellbinder!"

CHAPTER FIFTEEN

Things Take a Bad Turn

"I t happened this morning," Maeve said, hurrying along the path. The rain was coming down harder, as though determined to soak them thoroughly before they reached the village. The umbrellas packed by Lulabelle were only mildly helpful. "Someone—I don't know who—left a note on Cathmor's doorstep. The note said that the sorcerer could be found in O'bannon's shack, along with evidence of their crimes."

Seeing their blank expressions, Maeve explained. "O'bannon's shack is an abandoned horse stable at the edge of town. I think someone owned it years ago, but now it's no good for much of anything. I don't know why they don't tear it down. Anyway . . . Cathmor and some of his men came looking for Da—that's how I heard about it—and when they got to the shack, they found Aidan. Da wouldn't say what evidence they found, but it must have been terrible because Cathmor arrested him on the spot, and Da came home all worried and then he and Mam went into their room and shut the door. I tried to hear what they were saying," continued Maeve, without the slightest bit of guilt, "but they kept their voices low. Then Da left to see Mayor Digby, but he told me there's a hearing this afternoon to decide whether Aidan should stay in jail. He said if we wanted to come, he wouldn't send us away. He knows that *you* all like him."

"That's stupid!" said Kat, blinking the rain out of her eyes. "How could anyone think Aidan's a Spellbinder? He's just a kid, like us. The Enchantress said that Spellbinders know more dark magic than anyone, didn't she? Aidan doesn't know dark magic. They're making a huge mistake!"

"It doesn't make any sense," agreed Lulabelle. "Whoever this Spellbinder is, they've been very careful up until now. No one knows who they are because no one's seen them. We saw a person in a cloak and a hood that day with Donovan, but we never saw their face. In a province like this one, where everyone seems to know everyone else, it would be hard to stay hidden like that for so long . . . and they've summoned the fog banshee four times without anyone figuring out who they are. So if Aidan is the Spellbinder—"

"Lu, are you kidding? There's no way—"

"I know he's not the Spellbinder, but listen for a minute. Why would he mess up now? Why would he take all this evidence—whatever it is—to some old shack that everyone knows about? Why keep any evidence around at all? It's careless. It doesn't add up." Lulabelle bit her lip. "If Aidan really was the Spellbinder, there's no way he would have let himself get caught like this. Maeve, you have no idea what they found in the shack? Who do they say he murdered?"

"We'll find out at the hearing. Why can't the walls in our house be thinner!" Maeve yelled into the rain.

"Why are you so interested anyway?" said Kat sharply. "I didn't think you liked Aidan."

"I can't stand him. I think he's a smug, arrogant, no-good thief who owes me three chickens. But something big is going on and I hate not knowing what it is."

"But they have to let Aidan go, don't they?" Rosie's lip was quivering, her eyes threatening to overflow. "We know he didn't do any of those things. They can't keep him in jail forever."

"Don't worry, Rose, I'm sure it will all be sorted out," said Lulabelle reassuringly. "We'll have to make them see he's innocent, that's all." Kat hurried on, oblivious to the fact that her body now felt like a wet sponge. Aidan was innocent, without a doubt, but how on earth were they going to prove that?

By the time they reached the meeting hall, the Harpers and Maeve looked as though they had walked through a medium-sized hurricane. Rain dripped from the ends of Kat's hair and the tips of her fingers, forming a puddle on the wood slats of the floor. They stood for a moment in the dark entranceway, listening to a clock ticking from somewhere close by.

"This way then," urged Maeve. She led them down a narrow hall which appeared to be deserted except for one door at the end, under which a thin ribbon of light was visible. The Harpers followed, trying to be as quiet as possible, although the squishing sound of their waterlogged shoes made it difficult. They reached the end of the hallway and Maeve knocked softly on the door. When no one answered, she pushed it open.

The hearing room was lit with two immense iron chandeliers, each one holding at least forty glowing candles. In the back of the room were three rows of chairs that sloped upward onto a platform; only the first row of chairs was occupied, and Kat recognized some of the faces from the meeting with the Enchantress. A few uncomfortable looking benches sat on either side of the room. As the Harpers and Maeve stood dripping in the doorway, Mr. Stewart rose from where he sat with Mayor Digby and hurried over to them.

"I thought you might come," was all he said, leading them to a bench in the front row. Someone else found blankets and Kat wrapped herself in a musty smelling gray one that was surprisingly warm. Mr. Stewart knelt on the floor, his face worried.

"I don't know if I'm doing the right thing by letting you stay. The hearing will start shortly, and I have to warn you . . . there's a bit of evidence against the boy. Serious charges, I'm afraid. Not what I'd prefer for you to hear. But the lad could use a friend or two so I'm inclined to let you stay for his sake."

"He's not a Spellbinder, Mr. Stewart, we know he's not!" Kat's voice was louder than she intended and a few people turned to stare. "They're making a huge mistake," she added even more loudly, scowling at them.

"It doesn't make sense, sir," repeated Lulabelle. "Aidan's not a sorcerer. If there's evidence against him, there has to be an explanation. Or someone wants us to think he's guilty."

"I tend to agree with you, Lulabelle, but I'm only one person. The truth is, Aidan does not have many friends in this province right now. People are suspicious of him for other things." Mr. Stewart did not elaborate, but there was no need. They were all thinking about the thefts in the village. "Keep in mind, this is an informal hearing, not a trial. The elders will decide whether there's enough evidence against the lad to keep him in jail for now. It's not the final word, no matter what you might hear. The best thing you can do is support your friend . . . and please try to refrain from yelling at the council." He directed these last words in Kat's direction, a trace of a smile on his lips.

Mr. Stewart returned to his seat on the platform as the room quieted; there was an air of tense expectation. Mayor Digby sat in the center chair, shuffling papers nervously. On one side of him were Mr. Stewart; the grumpy man, Mr. Corley; the older lady with glasses, Mrs. Tully; and another man Kat didn't know. On the mayor's other side was the man with straw-colored hair, Mr. Quigley; two ladies Kat recognized from the previous meeting, and to her disgust, Olive McCutcher, looking as sour as ever.

Although their side of the hearing room remained empty, Kat noticed that a number of people had shuffled in and were sitting on the benches across the way, waiting for the hearing to start. She supposed they were there out of curiosity . . . or did Aidan have more friends than he let on? As she studied the people on the other side of the room, she realized they all looked extremely angry. Her heart dropped.

There was a sharp knock as Mayor Digby pounded his desk with a gavel and shuffled his papers once more. "I believe we're ready to get started. Are the hearing members all present? Shall I take a roll call?"

"Just look around you, Digby," barked Mr. Corley. "There's only nine of us. You know we're all here."

"Yes, of course." Mayor Digby colored. "Let me remind you

that the purpose of this hearing is to determine whether there's sufficient evidence to keep the lad in jail. We will not be conducting a full trial, that will come later—may come later, that is—" he corrected himself. "Certainly we all want this matter dealt with as soon as possible. People need to know that our province is safe, that the Spellbinder is behind bars and the fog banshee is gone for good. They must know that they can count on us to keep them safe. This hearing is our opportunity to do that."

Mr. Stewart frowned and shifted in his chair while Kat crossed her arms in annoyance. That sounded suspiciously like Mayor Digby wanted to keep Aidan in jail. Even worse, most of the council appeared to be in agreement, if their nods were any indication; only Mrs. Tully and Mr. Quigly looked uncomfortable at his speech. The hearing hadn't even begun, Aidan hadn't even had a chance to defend himself, and most of the council were against him. Kat could feel heat welling up inside her. *I will not yell*, she reminded herself. *I will not lose my temper.*

"If no one else has anything to add, I believe we're ready to begin," Mayor Digby said. "Please tell Cathmor to bring in the prisoner—lad, I mean."

The door opened and closed again with a resounding thud that filled all the quiet spaces in the room. Kat caught Lulabelle's eye and Lulabelle gave her a tight smile. Her hands were gripping the bench so tightly that her knuckles had turned white. There was a loud creak as the door swung open and Cathmor strode down the aisle, followed by two beefy men. They stopped at the front of the room, their hands clutching their daggers. Two other Cahir marched down the aisle; between them, his face pale, looking skinnier than he ever had, was Aidan. The warriors led him to a little box surrounded by a railing and he sat down hard on a bench. Kat could see that his wrists were bound together. The Cahir seated themselves behind Aidan, at the end of the bench from Kat and the others. Cathmor and the two men with him sat down across from Aidan, their eyes never leaving him for a second.

"Why are there so many guards?" Kat whispered to Lulabelle. "Do they really think he's going to escape?"

"They think he's a Spellbinder," Lulabelle whispered back. "They probably expect him to use dark magic. The evidence must be really bad."

Mayor Digby pounded his gavel on the desk again, even though it was unnecessary. Aidan turned in his seat and glanced back at the Harpers. He had dark circles under his eyes and his hair was matted, bits of straw clinging to the ends. Kat tried to smile, to make him see that they were his friends, but her face wasn't cooperating and she could only stare helplessly back at him.

"Now then," Mayor Digby was saying, "before we consider the evidence, let's get some preliminary information out of the way." He peered over his desk at Aidan. "Young man, would you please state your name and age for the hearing?"

"Aidan, sir." Aidan's voice didn't sound at all like it normally did. It was softer, scratchier. "I'm thirteen, but I . . . I'm not sure of my birthday."

Mayor Digby scribbled on a paper. "And your surname, if you please."

"Um . . . my what, sir?"

"Your last name, son," said Mr. Stewart in a kind voice.

Aidan lowered his head and scuffed his feet against the floor. "I don't have one—that is, I don't know my last name, sir. My parents died before . . . before they could tell me."

"So they *are* dead? You're an orphan. No one has raised you properly." Olive McCutcher sat back in her seat, triumph written on her face. She gave Mr. Stewart a look that plainly said, 'I told you so,' and Kat wished with all her might that she could punch Olive in her nasty, good-for-nothing nose.

"It's no matter," said Mayor Digby as he continued writing. "It's not a crime to lack a surname, after all. It's the least of the problems facing us today. We'll stick with your first name, shall we?" He smiled weakly. "As far as your address, I don't suppose . . ."

"I'm a bit all over, sir . . . mostly in the woods, unless it's raining or cold."

"Where do you live then?"

"Wherever I can find—someone's barn or an old shed. As long as it's dry and keeps the wind out. I've stayed at that shack for weeks at a time."

"O'bannon's shack? Where they found you this morning?" Mrs. Tully adjusted her glasses, distress in her eyes. "That's not even habitable. Loose nails, rat droppings, broken bottles . . . and it must be covered in grime. Do you mean to say that you live there, young man?"

"It's not so bad as you might think, ma'am. When that cold north wind comes over the hills in the winter, I'm glad for a bit of shelter. I'm not one to be picky, sure enough. Where else would I go? Who would have me?"

A silence filled the room. The council members exchanged embarrassed glances. Mr. Stewart sat back in his seat, looking sad. Mayor Digby, who seemed more flustered by the minute, picked up his gavel and moved it to the other side of his desk, as though desperate to do something with his hands. A funny, lumpy sort of feeling settled in Kat's throat. She had imagined Aidan's life as one of excitement, full of adventure, with no one to tell him what to do or where to go. A dirty old shack with rats and broken bottles? Was that really where he lived?

Mayor Digby coughed. "I shall make a note that you have no fixed address and we'll leave it at that, how does that sound?" He didn't wait for a reply. "Now that we have the preliminaries out of the way, why don't we get to the business at hand. Cathmor, if you would please take us through the events in question?"

"This morning, as I was leaving for dawn patrol, I discovered this note—" Cathmor took a crumpled paper out of his pocket and held it up "—under a rock outside my door. The note provided information on the sorcerer and where we might find him. It also indicated we would find evidence tying this person to additional crimes."

Cathmor opened the railing gate and delivered the letter to Mayor Digby, who examined it carefully before passing it to the other council members. Kat caught a glimpse of messy, slanted writing that took up the entire page.

"Did you recognize the writing?" asked Mrs. Tully. Cathmor shook his head.

"I assume it was meant to be disguised."

"Did that not strike you as odd?" said Mr. Stewart. "If I'm not mistaken, the reward for information regarding the sorcerer is up to one thousand geldings. Why would a person with such valuable information choose to be anonymous? Why not contact you directly, as so many have done?"

"I can't answer that, Liam. But I agree, it is odd."

"I don't see anything odd about it," sniffed Olive McCutcher. "It's quite obvious that whoever left this letter was afraid the boy would find out and send the fog banshee after them. I don't blame them a bit for wanting to stay hidden, no matter what the reward. After all, money isn't everything."

At the end of the bench, Maeve snorted, then tried to disguise it as a cough. There were a few titters from the other side of the hearing room as well. Olive McCutcher, it seemed, was universally unpopular.

"Now Olive, let's remember this is merely a hearing. The question of ultimate guilt is for another day," Mayor Digby reminded her. He frowned at Cathmor. "Nevertheless, I must agree with Olive's first point. Why does it matter who the letter writer was? The fact is, he led us to the boy, which is most important. Cathmor, if you'll continue . . . "

"After I read the note, I rounded up a few of my men, and we went to fetch Liam. I wanted to have a council member as a witness. When we—"

"Why Liam?" Olive McCutcher interrupted, looking offended.

"Because I trust him. And I like him the best."

In spite of the seriousness of the moment, Kat stifled a giggle. Olive McCutcher glared frostily at Cathmor, who didn't appear at all bothered by her hostility. Mayor Digby motioned for him to go on with his story.

"The note said the sorcerer would be found in O'Bannon's

shack, along with evidence of his treachery. When we arrived, we found the lad asleep."

Cathmor pulled a piece of rope out of his pocket and set it on the table. "When the boy emptied his pockets, we found this. It's a tether for leading horses. It's one of ours, I know the markings." He addressed Aidan for the first time. "Where did you get this, lad?"

Aidan stared at his hands. "I don't know, sir. It was there when I woke up."

Perhaps it was the altered tone of his voice, or the way he refused to meet Cathmor's eyes, but Kat had the sinking feeling that Aidan was lying. Cathmor studied Aidan for a long moment, before placing the tether in his own pocket.

"I must say, this does not look good for you, my boy, not good at all," murmured Mayor Digby, shaking his head.

"Let's not forget the other things that have been stolen," added Olive McCutcher. "If I'm not mistaken, this boy is the prime suspect in a string of thefts around our village. I see plenty of people in this room who have lost something of value—" She gestured to the onlookers sitting on the benches across the aisle, most of whom were shooting hostile glances at Aidan. "Are we really going to waste our time wondering whether someone else is to blame?"

"It's a fair stretch to go from thief to sorcerer," said Mr. Stewart shortly. "I would hope that we can examine the evidence on its own merits and not be swayed by what the lad may or may not be guilty of in other matters. I remain skeptical that anyone his age is capable of black magic."

"Very well, Liam, your opinion is always valued," replied Mayor Digby. Kat had the distinct impression the mayor was eager to end the hearing. He made a motion to Cathmor, who picked up a small bag and withdrew a glass bottle filled with purple sand. Reaching into the bag for a second time, Cathmor brought out a thin leather bracelet with a gold stone in the center. He held both objects up for the council members to see before handing them to Mayor Digby. Cathmor reached into the bag for a third and final time, removing a torn scrap of paper.

"When we found the lad, these items were also on him. This paper was stuffed in his pocket and the bracelet and bottle were in his satchel."

Mayor Digby took the scrap of paper and squinted at it quizzically. "I don't understand. *A tablespoon of ground snakeroot, two drops of devil's helmet, three pinches of bogbean pollen, one crushed wolfsbane root*— what on earth is this?"

Cathmor clasped his hands behind his back and bowed his head. Kat had a horrible feeling that whatever he was about to say would not help Aidan. "I'm afraid what you have is a partial list of ingredients for a particularly evil spell, a spell that very few in our province had ever heard of until four months ago."

The mayor's eyes widened in horror. "You don't mean?"

"I'm afraid I do. It's known as the Daemonium Nebula. The Demon Fog. It's the spell for summoning a fog banshee."

Chapter Sixteen

The Evidence Mounts

For a second, Kat thought she might tumble off the bench. In front of her, Aidan dropped his head into his hands. Mayor Digby stared at the piece of paper as though it might transform into a fog banshee on the spot. The rest of the council sat stunned, with the exception of Mr. Stewart, who leaned back in his chair, his eyes fixed on a point at the back of the room.

"How can you be sure?" Mrs. Tully said when she had regained her voice. "It's only a scrap of paper and most of it's missing. Surely there are other spells with those same ingredients?"

"With the same ingredients? It's possible, but unlikely. Every plant listed on that paper is highly lethal. Many medicinal potions may call for one in a trivial amount, but I'm not aware of any other potion that would use so many. After the fog banshee came the first time, I did some research in my private library; as you know, I have quite a collection of old books and texts concerning Hill province lore."

Cathmor paused as every eye in the hearing room remained riveted on him. Kat wasn't sure what was more shocking—the fact that such an evil spell had been found on Aidan, or that this rough, scary warrior was also a bookworm.

"I could find little on the history of the fog banshee and less on the spell to summon it," said Cathmor. "What I found I've already shared with this council. However, when I looked again, I found a reference at the bottom of one text that I had missed. The reference sent me to another, more obscure book. In that book were listed the ingredients to bring forth a fog banshee, although not the quantities. When I saw the paper in the lad's pocket, I recognized the ingredients at once. There is no doubt in my mind that it's the Daemonium Nebula."

"And this?" One of the council members held up the bottle of purple sand.

"According to the texts I found, the finished potion must be combined with an extraordinary level of heat, most likely a fire. Only then can the summoner bring forth the fog banshee. The heat crystallizes the liquid in the potion, leaving behind the purple sand. I've examined the sand as closely as I dare, and I can say with a great deal of certainty that it points to the darkest of magic."

"How can you be sure?" Mr. Quigley examined the glass bottle with horrified fascination. "Is it still harmful?"

In reply, Cathmor rolled up his shirt sleeve and raised his arm for the council to see. There was a sharp intake of breath as they gaped at a cluster of red, raw blisters on the inside of his wrist. Mr. Quigley quickly put the bottle down and pushed it away.

"That's only a few grains," said Cathmor, rolling his sleeve down again. "Any more and the results would be far worse."

"Why would the sorcerer keep the sand? To use as a weapon?"

"Perhaps. Like I said, the ingredients are dangerous by themselves. However, I don't think that's why the sorcerer held onto this bottle."

"Why then?" Mayor Digby couldn't seem to take his gaze off the innocent looking jar of sand.

"Because, from what I've learned, this sand can be used to summon a second fog banshee."

"What?" Mayor Digby lost his balance and nearly fell out of his chair. "Do you mean to tell me the bottle you found in this boy's possession can—can bring another one?"

"That's what I just said. Once a fog banshee is summoned, it will not leave until it has treasure or its summoner releases it. But the sand retains all the ingredients of the original potion. You only need a fire . . . and the right intentions."

"And you found this vile thing in the boy's satchel." Olive McCutcher gave Aidan a look of utter loathing. Most council members seemed more frightened than angry; one lady shrank away from him, murmuring what sounded like a prayer. On the other side of the room, a rumble of angry voices grew louder. Mayor Digby banged his gavel on the desk.

"This is disturbing, without a doubt." He held up the leather bracelet with the gold stone in the center and the room grew silent. "I'm almost afraid to ask what this is, but I know I must. Is it also part of the spell?"

"No, it's not part of the spell and it doesn't belong to the sorcerer."

Cathmor's voice had changed. An undercurrent of rage sliced through each word. Aidan went rigid, his eyes on the bracelet.

"I have reason to believe this bracelet belonged to a peddler by the name of Birdie O'Malley. She had a booth at the trading post east of town, commonly known as 'the Realm.' She was murdered back in March and we never found her killer. She sold various herbs and plants for medicinal uses and according to her friends, often stayed in her booth late into the night. It was thought that the killer was hoping for geldings and surprised Birdie—Ms. O'Malley, I mean. When she wasn't willing or able to hand over her money, he murdered her, then ransacked her booth . . . at least, that's what we thought at the time."

Cathmor paused, either to take a breath or to control his anger. The entire hearing room waited breathlessly.

"After I discovered the ingredients to the Daemonium Nebula, I went back and looked at the inventory from Birdie's booth. Without exception, every single one of the ingredients could be found in her supply of herbs. This leads me to a new theory."

"Yes?" Mayor Digby's voice had sunk to a frightened whisper.

"The one who murdered Ms. O'Malley was not looking for geldings. He was looking for ingredients to summon a fog banshee. Ms. O'Malley was considered an expert in finding and harvesting numerous plants and if anyone had the right ingredients, she would. I think the sorcerer killed her, took what he needed, then ransacked her booth to disguise his theft."

"Where does the bracelet come in?" Mrs. Tully was wiping her eyes with a handkerchief.

"I told you that nothing else was taken from Birdie's booth, but that's not entirely true. When we interviewed the other vendors, they mentioned that she always wore a leather bracelet with a gold stone in the middle. She claimed it belonged to someone else and she was keeping it safe until that person returned. There was no trace of the bracelet in the booth or in her house—until this morning, when we searched the lad's satchel."

There was a sudden scraping sound as Aidan shoved back his

bench and leaped to his feet. The paleness in his face had been replaced by a deepening red.

"IT'S A LIE!" he yelled. "I would never hurt Birdie, she was like a mam to me! She gave me food and shelter and took care of me—I owe her my life, sure enough! Anyone who thinks I would hurt her is a bleedin' fool, I WOULD DIE FIRST!" He pointed at Cathmor, who surprisingly, made no move to stop him. "What do you care about Birdie, anyway? She was just some poor old lady to you, not good enough for your fancy lot! I'm surprised you bothered to investigate at all, seeing as how she wasn't your type! How much time did you put into finding her killer—an hour, maybe two? It wasn't until the fog banshee threatened all your precious treasures that she became a bit more important, didn't she?"

Cathmor's jaw tightened but he remained silent. Mayor Digby fumbled around for his gavel while the grumbling in the room grew louder. Aidan paid no attention but kept going, his words ragged and wild.

"I don't know how that bracelet got into my satchel! It's hers, sure enough, but she would've given it to me if I asked for it. She would've given anyone anything if they were in need. That's how good she was!" Tears streamed down Aidan's face, but he made no attempt to brush them away. "Someone put that bracelet in my satchel, just like they put those other things. That's who you should be looking for! Lock me up for being a thief or a sorcerer if it makes you feel better, I don't care, but don't think for a second that I killed Birdie! DON'T THINK FOR A SECOND THAT I HURT THE ONLY PERSON WHO'S EVER BEEN TRULY KIND TO ME!" He took great gasping breaths, wiping his eyes with the hem of his shirt.

"Order! Order, I say!"

Mayor Digby pounded the gavel on his desk, struggling to be heard over the commotion; the whole room chattered excitedly, and as far as Kat could tell, seemed divided over Aidan's guilt or innocence. More than one onlooker had tears in their eyes.

"Kat!" Maeve took advantage of the chaos to lean across the bench. "Did you know about Birdie?"

Kat shot Lulabelle a quick glance. She had told her sister about the conversation with Aidan at the Realm, but they had agreed not to mention it to anyone else. Aidan was their friend, and as Lulabelle had pointed out, if he really wanted them to know about Birdie, he would've told them himself instead of waiting until Kat snooped around and all but forced it out of him (Kat strongly disagreed with this last part but she did admit that Lu had a point about everything else). Now, she didn't think it mattered. She hurriedly told Maeve and Rosie about finding Aidan at the Realm, the circle of flowers for Birdie, and what Aidan had told her.

"I know he's innocent!" Kat told them as the room quieted and

Mayor Digby's gavel broke apart from his incessant pounding. "You didn't see him at the Realm. There's no way he could've done what they say he did. He cared about Birdie too much."

Rosie's eyes widened. "Donovan's here!"

In spite of all the people crowded into the hearing room, Kat recognized Donovan's lanky frame and curly black hair. He stood off to the side, away from everyone else, leaning against the wall and watching the proceedings with the same unreadable expression on his face.

"Why do you think he's here?" said Lulabelle. "I thought he didn't want anything to do with the village."

"He doesn't," replied Maeve. "I've never seen him at any gathering before. I wonder what made him come today."

"Maybe he's here to support Aidan," said Rosie hopefully, giving Donovan a small wave that he seemed not to notice.

Their discussion was cut short by Mayor Digby, who had at last regained control of the hearing room and was speaking to Aidan.

"There now, lad, there's no cause to get carried away. You're understandably upset, but we are nothing if not fair, and we must look at the evidence in front of us. It's a matter of public safety— yours and the village—and we must take it seriously. Whatever the outcome of the vote, you will have a chance to defend yourself properly later on, if it comes to that." He glanced around at the rest of the council for affirmation. "If that's all the evidence, why don't we go ahead and take a vote. A 'yes' vote if you think the evidence is enough to . . . er . . . detain the lad for the time being, and a 'no' vote if you think he should be released. Olive, why don't we start with you."

Olive McCutcher wrinkled her nose. "Absolutely, without question, yes."

"There's a big surprise," Kat muttered to Lulabelle.

Mr. Quigley was next. The sympathy on his face gave Kat a flash of hope, but then he said, "While I have my concerns, I'm afraid I must vote yes, at least today."

The two ladies next to him voted yes as well and Kat wanted to shake them. Aidan remained standing, his chin raised, as though determined not to show fear. The man to the left of Mayor Digby was practically hyperventilating and squeaked out a 'yes' before the mayor could even call his name. Mrs. Tully, on the other hand, cast her 'yes' vote with an air of regret; apparently, Aidan's impassioned words about Birdie had touched her.

"Liam?"

Mr. Stewart sighed. "I agree that the evidence against the lad is serious. I don't fault my fellow council members for voting the way they did. But the evidence, while incriminating, is a good deal too convenient. It flies in the face of all we know about the sorcerer and his secrecy so far and it raises the question of how a thirteen-year-old lad could master such dark magic. I'm also bothered by the anonymous note left on Cathmor's doorstep and why the one who wrote it refused to come forward. In our haste to find the culprit, let's not be so quick to pin the blame on a boy . . . particularly a boy who has no one to defend him. I vote no."

"I vote no as well," grunted Mr. Corley. Kat suspected his vote was more out of a desire to be disagreeable, but she felt a rush of gratitude, nonetheless, especially when she saw the look of irritation on Olive McCutcher's face.

"I suppose that leaves me, then." Mayor Digby pressed the tips of his fingers together thoughtfully, although Kat was pretty sure he had made up his mind long ago.

"While I too don't wish to blame the boy unfairly, the evidence is much too serious for me to ignore. What if we let him go and then something else happens? No, I think it's better to be safe than sorry. My vote is yes. If no one has anything to add, the hearing is adjourned. Cathmor, please take the lad into custody and . . . er . . . see that he's comfortable."

So that was it. The hearing was over and Aidan would stay in jail. Anger flooded through Kat's brain like a tidal wave. She wanted to yell at the council that they were being stupid, that Aidan couldn't be a Spellbinder and certainly not a murderer, but even she knew it was pointless.

They watched Cathmor place a hand on Aidan's shoulder and whisper in his ear. He and Aidan marched back down the center of the room, the rest of the Cahir falling into step behind them. Aidan didn't look at the Harpers as he passed by, but he cast a glance over his shoulder before he reached the door and gave them a wan smile and a wink. Kat thought she might cry. Next to her, Rosie sniffed hard and rubbed her eyes. Now that the excitement was over, people milled around, discussing the evidence and adding their own opinions as to how they would have voted. Lulabelle jumped to her feet, her eyes on the door.

"Quick, we need to catch him before he leaves."

"Before who leaves?" Kat and Rosie rushed to keep up with Lulabelle as she pushed her way through the crowd of people.

"Donovan. He might be able to help us—and Aidan."

"How?" said Kat, but Lulabelle was moving too fast to reply. They squeezed out the door and zig-zagged their way down the long hall, trying to avoid the villagers clustered together. Kat was relieved to see that the rain had stopped. Half a block away, a lone figure was striding down the street.

"Donovan!" called Rosie.

Donovan turned to wait for them to catch up. Everyone looked at Lulabelle expectantly.

"Mr . . . um . . . Donovan, we—I wanted to ask you about the fog banshee. You told us that day in the woods you had seen one before. I wondered if you could tell us anything that might help Aidan."

Donovan cocked his head as he considered the request. "Such as?"

Lulabelle hesitated, trying to decide how to ask her next question. "Maybe you could tell us what you know about sorcerers. In the woods, you made it sound like you knew more about them than—than most people might. We know Aidan's not a Spellbinder or a murderer, so that means the real Spellbinder is trying to make it look—"

Donovan cut her off. "How do you know your friend's not a Spellbinder? What makes you so sure?"

"Because it's stupid, that's why!" Kat retorted. "Aidan would never do anything that evil. He's not like that. And even if he was, he doesn't know enough to call a fog banshee. Plus, the real Spellbinder killed Birdie and she took care of Aidan for years. She was like his mother—or grandmother. He would never hurt her for a minute!" She glanced at Lulabelle who nodded emphatically.

"You have a lot to learn about Spellbinders," Donovan told them. "They never look or act the way you'd expect. They don't lurk in dark alleyways, waiting to curse you as you pass by. Don't be naive enough to think a Spellbinder is a shriveled old man hiding behind a cauldron. It's more likely to be the nice lady selling pies in the bakery. Or a teenage boy, for that matter. The sooner you learn that, the better."

He eyed them appraisingly. "But, for what it's worth, I don't think your friend is a Spellbinder. Not because he's incapable, but because a true Spellbinder doesn't reveal himself until he's ready. All that business with the potion list and the sand and the old woman's bracelet? Foolishness. Distractions. But it keeps everyone good and busy and I imagine that's the point."

"So how can we find the real Spellbinder?" persisted Lulabelle. "As long as they think Aidan's guilty, they won't bother looking for anyone else. We're the only ones who believe him, so it's up to us to find out who the dark sorcerer is and prove Aidan is innocent. We need you to help us."

Donovan regarded Lulabelle with an expression that almost resembled respect. They all waited hopefully, on the off chance that he might give them a name, or at least some practical tips, but his next words deflated them like tears in a balloon.

"That's a question I can't answer. Like I said, you're not going to find the Spellbinder, not if he doesn't want to be found. A Spellbinder could be right under your noses and you wouldn't know it. But I will tell you this—if everyone is looking in one direction, and you know that it's the wrong one, then I would suggest going in the opposite direction." He turned away from then, heading across the cobblestone street and toward the hills.

"What does that mean?" Kat called after him, annoyed. She wasn't a fan of riddles and certainly not a fan of people who talked in them. "What direction should we be going in?"

"Stop thinking about the Spellbinder and start thinking about what he's after," replied Donovan without breaking his stride. "A fog banshee won't leave until it has its treasure or the summoner releases it. If you assume the treasure is still out there, you can assume the Spellbinder hasn't released the banshee. Find the treasure and you'll find the Spellbinder. Or better yet—he'll find you. And when he does, for the love of a clurichaun, don't come knocking on my door!"

CHAPTER SEVENTEEN

The Dueling Clurichauns

S o how are we going to break him out?" Kat said as the Harpers made their way along the path and into the Hill province the next morning. The sun had chased away the wet dreariness of the day before and the sky was back to its normal shade of vibrant blue.

"What are you talking about?" replied Lulabelle, catching herself before she stepped into a soupy mud patch.

"Aidan! We can't leave him in jail, he's innocent!"

Lulabelle gave her a shocked look. "Are you serious, Kat? You want to break Aidan out of jail? That's insane."

"Why? They do it all the time on detective shows. I bet it's not even that hard."

"This is real life, not a detective show, and it would never work. The entire Cahir is probably guarding him."

"That's true, we need a distraction. Maybe Rosie could do her tap dance routine in front of the jail while the two of us sneak in. You remember your routine, don't you Rose?"

"I think so. Would I have to wear my costume?"

"No, just the routine is good. Lu, we'll also need your smoke bombs. You know, the ones you saved from that fireworks show last year."

"Why would I have smoke bombs?"

"How should I know? Why do you have science goggles, a giant box of glitter, and a book on medieval sword fighting? You bring all kinds of weird stuff wherever we go."

"And you think I happened to pack smoke bombs in my suitcase? Just to have for a rainy day?"

"Did you?"

Silence. "Yes."

Lulabelle sighed, ignoring Kat's satisfied look. "So you're planning to terrify the Cahir, take over the jail, and free Aidan with some smoke bombs and tap dancing? That sounds like a fantastic plan. I'm sure Aidan will thank us when we all end up in the cell next to him." Rosie started to laugh, but at Kat's scowl, changed course and pretended to choke on her apple.

"Ok, what's your idea to break him out?"

"I don't have an idea because it's ridiculous. There's no way we're going to break him out, not when the whole Hill province thinks he's the Spellbinder. And if we did manage to get him out, it would only make him seem guiltier. I don't like that he's in jail either, but at least he's safe for now."

Kat stomped her foot in frustration and drops of mud spattered onto her legs. She hated it when Lulabelle was right, which was most of the time. "What should we do? We have to do something!"

"I know. I've been thinking about what Donovan told us yesterday and it makes the most sense. We have to find the Hill token before the fog banshee does. If we find it, the Spellbinder will show himself and then everyone will realize Aidan's innocent."

Kat groaned. "And you think my plan is crazy? How are we going to find this token? You heard the Enchantress, it could be anything. Anything! And if we find it, how do we keep it safe from the Spellbinder? He knows a ton of magic, plus he has a fog banshee. All we have are smoke bombs . . . and Rosie's tap dancing."

"I have to think about it some more," said Lulabelle firmly. "The token can't be anything. It has to be unique to the Hill province. Something you hold in your hand. There's got to be a way to narrow it down . . . " Her voice trailed off as her eyes took on a faraway glaze.

"We need to narrow it down fast," said Kat, dodging another

puddle. "Aidan doesn't seem like the type of person who enjoys cages."

The ride into town for the Midsummer festival felt very different than it had that first day. Gone was the excited laughter; the Harpers and Maeve sat clustered together, whispering furiously about the identity of the Spellbinder, the evidence against Aidan, and what might happen to him. Not surprisingly, Maeve was less than sympathetic.

"Of course, I don't think he's a Spellbinder or a murderer or anything like that, but it won't hurt him to spend time thinking on his actual crimes! The jail's not so bad, either. It's clean, warm, and they give him three square meals a day, which is more than he usually gets."

When no one appeared convinced, Maeve tried again. "Da says Cathmor agreed to let him stay in the yard today because the weather's so nice. It's fenced in, obviously, but he has plenty of room to stretch his legs and get fresh air. He'll no doubt decide he likes it more than slogging around the woods and then he'll never want to leave."

Since there was nothing more to be said about Aidan, the talk turned to finding the Hill token. Maeve suggested knocking on doors and compiling a list of the most valuable treasures that the fog banshee hadn't claimed yet, but Lulabelle objected on the grounds that it looked suspicious and might alert the Spellbinder to what they were doing. Kat wondered if they could get the same information by sneaking into people's homes while they were at the festival and taking a peek into their closets, but one look from Lulabelle made it plain that idea was off the table.

"How do we know the token is still out there?" asked Rosie. "We haven't seen the fog banshee in over a month. Maybe it's not coming back because it already has the token. Or maybe the token was destroyed a long time ago. What if we're too late?"

As if by silent agreement, they all turned to Lulabelle.

"I've thought about that," Lulabelle said carefully, "but I don't think it has. When we found the fog banshee's lair, there were two piles of treasures, like someone was sorting through them to find the token. Then, when Mr. Stewart and the others went back to look for clues, everything was gone. I think the Spellbinder moved the treasures because he didn't want them found before he had a chance to examine them. Why would he go to all that trouble if he already had the token?"

"Maybe he found it after that," said Kat, not wanting to think about the possibility that Aidan might stay in jail forever, with no way to prove his innocence.

"Then why bother framing Aidan? No, I think Donovan's right.

The Spellbinder put that evidence in Aidan's bag so everyone would think he was responsible—and it worked. Now the real Spellbinder can focus on finding the token without anyone suspecting. It's still out there, I know it is. We just have to put our heads together and find it before the Spellbinder does."

Lulabelle gazed at them with such determination that Kat, Maeve, and Rosie couldn't help but look equally determined. The token *was* out there and they would find it if they had to dig up every inch of the Hill province. Aidan's fate depended on it. The fate of everyone depended on it.

Mayor Digby was standing at the entrance to the festival again, greeting people with even more enthusiasm than before. "Welcome back, welcome back!" he called, shaking everyone's hands and beaming. "Couldn't ask for better weather, especially after that dreadful rain yesterday! Watch where you step, though. It's still a mite wet in places."

He waved at a family passing through the entrance. "Not even noon and already we have twice as many as the first day!" he declared. "I do believe the boy's arrest was a turning point—people are coming out of their houses again. Oh, I know you have your doubts, Liam," he said before Mr. Stewart could speak, "but it's hard to argue with the evidence when it's staring us in the face. I only wish it didn't have to be the lad. He seemed like a good sort, but I guess you never can tell."

"Digby!" Two men approached the mayor wearing identical frowns. Mud covered their boots and the bottoms of their pants. Mayor Digby's smile faded at the sight of their appearance.

"Gentlemen, how is the set-up for the firefly picnic coming?"

One of the men shook his head. "That part of the field's a bleedin' mess. Mud everywhere . . . and it's not likely to dry out before the evening. We need to move it somewhere drier."

"Oh dear, a back up location—I never thought . . . well, if you think it best." Mayor Digby turned away to confer with the men and Mr. Stewart motioned to the Harpers and Maeve to follow him into the festival.

More tents had sprung up along the field and Maeve led them toward a massive gold tent with fireworks erupting from all sides. A sign spelled out "Piddlewick's Gourmet Sweets" in blinking purple letters. Mr. Piddlewick himself stood on the counter, dancing a jig as he poured Honeyfizz into glasses for a crowd of eager customers.

From somewhere close by came a loud pop and Maeve clapped her hands. "He's arrived! It's about to get good, it is!"

Another tent had appeared directly across the way. This tent was an even brighter gold and instead of fireworks, confetti and flowers shot out of the top. A short, fat man who resembled Mr.

Piddlewick danced his own jig on the counter, blowing a loud horn, while above him a blue sign with fancy white letters announced "Snugglewump's Superior Toys." Kat recognized him as the one who had given Barnaby a lumina. Balloons floated out of the horn and into the air and Rosie gave a squeal of delight as toys rained down in front of the tent.

"I don't think Mr. Piddlewick is very happy about that," remarked Lulabelle as the candy maker scowled at Mr. Snugglewump. Several bottles of Honeyfizz dangled precariously above his head.

Maeve grinned. "It drives him batty. You should never make a clurichaun jealous and that's the truth. They do this every year, though, so I imagine they're both used to it by now. It's grand entertainment for the rest of us!"

Mr. Snugglewump blew more balloons out of his horn and the crowd cheered. Mr. Piddlewick stamped his foot on the counter, lifted his arms, and white clouds materialized in the air between the two tents. There was a clap of thunder and snowflakes trickled toward the ground as children came running.

"This one tastes like raspberry!" a boy yelled, catching a snowflake on his tongue.

"This one's caramel!" cried a small girl.

The people gathered in front of Mr. Snugglewump's tent hurried back toward Mr. Piddlewick. The portly candy maker bowed and shot his own devious smile at Mr. Snugglewump, who shook his fist. Turning to the wooden toys stacked on shelves behind him, he pointed at each one. With a puff of pink smoke, soldiers, luminas, bears, goblins, and other creatures climbed onto the counter and leaped down to the grass, where they proceeded to form a parade around the festival goers.

Mr. Piddlewick snapped his fingers and a shower of gold coins exploded out of his tent. Most of the gold coins landed on the field where they were picked up by the laughing crowd, but some inexplicably veered off course, knocking down several of the wooden toys. Mr. Snugglewump bared his teeth and pointed a silver tipped cane at Mr. Piddlewick threateningly. Mr. Piddlewick stuck out his tongue and made a rude gesture.

Pointing his own cane at a massive teddy bear slouched against the side of his tent, Mr. Snugglewump directed the bear onto the grass, where it did cartwheels to the delight of the crowd.

In reply, Mr. Piddlewick enchanted his chocolate butterflies, which fluttered around the field in formation before dive bombing the bear in his furry backside.

The toy maker twirled his cane and an army of miniature toy soldiers marched onto the counter, dropped to one knee, and took aim at the butterflies. There was a series of tiny pops and the butterflies fell to the ground.

"Maeve, children, over here!" Mrs. Stewart beckoned to them.

Maeve let out a groan and swallowed the last of her Honeyfizz.

"Right when it was about to get good! Pretty soon, they'll stop enchanting the candy and toys and just start throwing curses at each other."

"Isn't that dangerous?" said Lulabelle, as they followed Maeve away from the tents where the two clurichauns continued to battle. One of Mr. Piddlewick's candy dragons had set fire to Mr. Snugglewump's hat and the toy maker was furiously stamping it out. "Someone might get hurt."

"I suppose so," said Maeve. "They have lost quite a few toys and sweets over the years. But they would be heartbroken if anyone made them stop—they spend months preparing. I do believe Mr. Piddlewick used the fire dragons last year, though. I'll have to tell him he needs new material."

The Stewarts had arranged a picnic in a sunny spot on the field, where they were joined by numerous friends, all cheerful, laughing, and ready to gossip about the arrest of "that red-headed boy."

Lil and her parents were some of the first to gather, and Mayor Digby joined them halfway though, red-faced and flustered. From the little she heard, it sounded to Kat as though the search for a back-up location for the evening picnic had not gone well. In the end, the picnic had been moved to Mayor Digby's own yard, a decision which did not appear to please the mayor. Lunch had just ended when the music from the festival struck up again and they leaped to their feet.

"Not so fast, little lady," said Mr. Murphy, swinging Lil up into his arms as she made to follow the Harpers and Maeve toward the sound of the music. "A big morning for a wee bird like you means an even bigger nap. Especially with the firefly picnic tonight."

"But I'm not tired!" protested Lil, stifling a yawn.

"We'll look for you this afternoon," Rosie promised her. "You can walk around with us then."

Lil smiled sleepily and tucked her head into Mr. Murphy's shoulder, her toy lumina nestled in her arms.

"Ever since that brownie tried to take it, she's been scared to death of losing it, poor dear," murmured Mrs. Murphy to Mrs. Stewart. "I've tried to tell her that we could get another one, but she won't have any of it. It's her own special treasure, though I don't see the attraction myself. I was hoping she'd take to a bear or a bunny rabbit."

Out of the corner of her eye, Kat noticed a rustle in the trees. She whirled around in time to see a brownie's wrinkly face peering down from one of the branches. It locked eyes with Kat for a split second before flitting speedily away. She watched it go, unable to shake the feeling that she had seen the brownie before.

"Maeve," she cried, pulling on Maeve's elbow to show her the back of the fleeing figure. "Isn't that the brownie from the barrel contest? The one that tried to steal Lil's toy?"

Maeve squinted after it. "I can't really tell . . . maybe."

"They said his name's Barnaby," added Lulabelle.

"I think he was spying on us—or maybe on Lil. Do you think he still wants her lumina?"

"Brownies are odd, no doubt about it," shrugged Maeve. "He must really think it's treasure. But I wouldn't worry. He's not foolish enough to take it from her twice—"

There was a crash behind them. Mayor Digby had dropped a plate onto the picnic bench. He stood for a moment, startled, before hastily picking up the pieces.

"So sorry, Colleen! Clumsy of me, I'm sure. Don't know what I was thinking!"

"Don't trouble yourself, Aifric," said Mrs. Stewart soothingly. "It's no great loss."

"Very gracious of you." Mayor Digby picked up the remaining glass shards, his face pink. "Well, I must be off . . . have to prepare for the picnic, you know. My yard is in a shocking state—it'll take all afternoon to get it ready."

"Let us help you, Aifric," said Mr. Stewart. "We can do it in no time, if there's enough of us."

"No, no, that's quite unnecessary." Mayor Digby seemed eager to be gone and away from the embarrassment of the plate. With a quick goodbye, he hurried away, losing his hat only once.

For the rest of the afternoon, the Harpers and Maeve roamed the festival. The duel between the clurichauns had ended and both Mr. Piddlewick and Mr. Snugglewump lay sprawled across their respective counters, snoring loudly.

Maeve stopped in front of a booth that promised hideous stuffed hobgoblins to anyone who could hit a moving target with a slingshot, and yanking Lulabelle to her side, they took turns aiming pebbles at the target while Rosie cheered them on. Kat tried to join in, but her mind kept wandering to Aidan. What would happen if they couldn't find the token? What if Aidan was found guilty? Would they keep him in jail forever or (Kat gulped) did they chop off people's heads, the way they used to in France? What if the Spellbinder discovered the Hill token before they did? From what the Enchantress had told them, the tokens weren't as powerful by themselves. But together, they could make whoever had them supremely powerful . . . and if that person happened to be a Spellbinder . . .

Kat was so lost in her thoughts that at first she didn't hear the excited commotion coming from the festival entrance. People were running and the music had stopped playing. The noise grew louder.

"What do you think's going on?" said Lulabelle, puzzled.

Then a woman screamed.

The Harpers and Maeve exchanged startled looks and sprinted in the direction of the screaming.

As they drew closer, they saw that everyone was gathered around the screaming woman, who was now weeping softly while other women knelt by her side, patting her shoulders.

"I can't see—what are they saying?"

"Come on, this way."

Kat, Lulabelle, and Rosie followed Maeve in and out of the crowd until they reached the front of the circle. Cathmor was kneeling in the center, talking to the weeping woman. And the woman he was talking to . . . Kat was shocked to see that it was Mrs. Murphy, Lil's mother.

"I know you're upset, Eily, but I need to understand what happened," Cathmor was saying in quiet, even tones. "You put Lil down for her nap at what time?"

"A bit after lunch," said Mrs. Murphy in a tremulous voice. "She was so tired from all the excitement. We set her down and left Minnie to keep an eye on her. She's so reliable, Minnie is, such a dear little thing . . . " She broke off as her eyes filled with tears again.

"Who's Minnie?" Kat whispered to Maeve.

"Lil's nanny. She's been with them for ages."

"We came down to enjoy the festival, Quinn and I did. When we returned home the door was open. There had been a fight—broken glass everywhere, pillows shredded, books thrown out of the shelves! And blood—" Mrs. Murphy stifled a sob, "—blood all over the floor. Our poor Minnie was lying outside Lil's room. She must've tried to protect her, poor thing, but she's—she's dead!"

A gasp rose from the crowd of people. Mrs. Stewart and another lady put their arms around Mrs. Murphy, comforting her.

"And Lil was gone?"

"Yes, we've looked everywhere—called her name, checked her favorite hiding spots—she's nowhere to be found. Quinn's searching for her down by the brook." Mrs. Murphy cast pleading eyes on Cathmor. "Why would someone take my Lil? She's only a child. She must be so frightened!" She burst into tears again as Cathmor stood up and began to issue directions.

"You men there—" he ordered in a voice that presumed obedience, "—head down to the brook and help Quinn. You men over there, check the far pasture. Whoever took her might've gone that way instead. The rest of you spread out across the village and keep your eyes open. Hopefully, they won't have gotten far, but there's no time to waste."

Cathmor pointed at two rugged looking Cahir. "We'll go to the Murphy's house and see what we can find. There may be something there that will help us locate the child. We'll find her Eily, I promise you."

Mrs. Murphy nodded, her face tear-streaked. "I'll come with you. I want to take care of Minnie." Her eyes flared as Cathmor started to protest. "Don't even think of telling me no, Cathmor O'Connell! Someone murdered Minnie and took my child, I'm not about to sit on my hands!"

Cathmor smiled faintly. "Alright then, Eily, let's go." He helped her to her feet as the crowd began to disperse, everyone hurrying to carry out Cathmor's directions. Kat could see Mr. Stewart leading a group of men in the direction of the brook.

"I can't believe it," Maeve was saying over and over again, a shocked expression on her face. "I just can't believe it. First a fog banshee, then black magic, and Spellbinders . . . and now this! It's like the whole province is falling to pieces. How anyone could hurt Minnie . . . and Lil—if they've hurt Lil . . . ."

"I wish we could help," cried Rosie, wiping away her own tears. "There's got to be something we can do."

"Maybe there is." Lulabelle's eyes were bright. "Maeve, do you think we can take a look at Lil's house? Get inside it, I mean?"

Maeve looked doubtful. "I don't know, I don't see Cathmor letting a bunch of kids poke their noses anywhere they please."

"Why do we need to go to Lil's house, Lu? What are you thinking?" interrupted Kat.

"I'm not sure yet. I need to check first."

"Right, let's go." Maeve seemed as mystified as Kat, but the intensity of Lulabelle's desire was contagious. "There's nothing for us to do here, anyway."

The Murphy's house was a neat stone cottage on a narrow lane outside of town. The front yard was empty, but the door was open and Kat could hear men's voices coming from inside. They crept around to the side of the house and peered through an open window.

Mrs. Murphy and Cathmor were kneeling over a brownie that lay motionless on the floor. Mrs. Murphy stroked the figure's head and smoothed her little dress. Kat felt an unexpected lump in her throat. That must be Minnie. She had never seen a dead body before, human, animal, or . . . well, otherwise. Minnie was so small and helpless. She couldn't have put up much of a fight. Brown stains covered her dress and there was a pool of the same brownish-red color around her head, like some kind of gruesome halo. Cathmor gently prodded Minnie, examining the blood stains on her dress. He frowned as he lifted her lifeless head.

"It looks like whoever did this struck her from behind. There's no other wound that I can find. Wherever this blood came from, it's not hers."

He bent over Minnie again, his fingers on the brownie's neck. He tilted his head close to hers, listening, then sat up, relief flooding his face.

"Eily, she's not dead! I can feel a pulse — it's barely there, but it'll do. Kallen, take her to the doctor right away. Right now, she's our only witness. Call Thunder and go as fast as you can, man!"

A burly, fair-haired warrior hurried over and scooped Minnie up in his arms. As he stepped through the open front door, the children dropped to the ground behind a pair of rose bushes. The warrior named Kallen planted himself in the middle of the lane, his eyes on some point far in the distance. From time to time, he glanced down at the still form of Minnie; Kat could see snow white hair tied in a neat bun, and a small wrinkly face. Minnie must be a very old brownie. What kind of person would attack such an old, helpless thing?

Her attention returned to Kallen. What was he waiting for? Why didn't he go to the doctor like Cathmor had ordered? Just then, a sound ruptured the stillness—a rhythmic clicking that moved steadily closer. Kat peered around the corner of the bush in time to see a beautiful chestnut brown horse thundering down the lane toward Kallen. Pebbles exploded as the horse came to a stop in front of him. Kallen climbed onto its back in one quick motion, still cradling Minnie in his arms, and galloped back down the lane in the direction of town. There was no time to process this strange scene; voices were coming from inside the Murphy's house again.

"Why would someone want to make it look like Minnie had been stabbed?" Mrs. Murphy was saying. "If it's not her blood, then whose . . . ?" She broke off, her eyes frantic.

"Don't go there, Eily," said Cathmor before she could finish. "Right now, we're trying to make sense of it all. There's no blood anywhere in Lil's room, which is a good sign. It's all here and by the door. It's curious—" He stopped talking, his eyes on the blood-stained floor. Motioning to the other warrior, they hurried out the front door and into the yard.

"This way," Maeve made a motion with her shoulders. "They went around to the other side—come on."

Sneaking single file around the back of the Murphy's house, they had nearly reached the side when a sharp cry rang out.

"It's another one! Quick, before he bleeds to death!"

Maeve fell to her knees and crawled the rest of the way, followed by the others. Kat breathed a silent prayer of thanks that the Murphys were so fond of rose bushes.

Cathmor was reaching into a small bin that appeared to hold firewood. Kat could see more blood on the ground in front of the bin. When he straightened up, he was holding something in his arms.

"It's the brownie from the contest!" hissed Lulabelle in disbelief. "The one that wanted Lil's toy—Barnaby!"

Carefully laying Barnaby on the ground, Cathmor stripped off his vest and wrapped it around the little body. "He's bleeding here, from his side. I don't think it nicked anything important, but that doesn't matter if he keeps losing blood. You take him, and I'll stay here—see what else I can find. Make Eily go with you, I want her there if one of them wakes up."

The other Cahir picked up Barnaby and disappeared around the house. Cathmor remained on the ground, examining the blood stains. The faint sound of a horse's hooves grew louder, and then, after a few seconds, faded away and Kat knew that yet another Cahir horse had come for the warrior, Barnaby, and Mrs. Murphy. All of a sudden, Cathmor looked up.

"You might as well come out. I know you're there."

Nervously, they stepped out from behind the rose bush. Cathmor sighed impatiently. "What do you want? This is a serious matter, not a child's game. You shouldn't be here."

"Please, Cathmor, we didn't mean to spy on you," begged Maeve. "We were worried about Lil, that's all. She's our friend. We thought we might be able to help."

"Were you here when she was taken?"

"Er . . . No."

"Then I don't see how you can help," retorted Cathmor. "If you want to be useful, go into town and look for her there. I'm busy."

"Are those brownies going to die?" said Rosie. Her lip quivered and she bit it to make it stop.

Cathmor got to his feet. "I don't know, little one. But Maeve will tell you that our doctor is the best. If anyone can save them, she can."

"Did Barnaby attack Minnie?" Kat preferred not to irritate Cathmor further, but she couldn't stop herself from blurting it out. The whole situation was so bizarre. If Barnaby *had* attacked Minnie, then who had taken Lil? And who had stabbed Barnaby?

"I don't know yet. I'm trying to piece it together."

"Barnaby was really upset when he couldn't have Lil's toy," said Lulabelle. "Do you think maybe he came here to try and take it again?"

"Or maybe he tried to steal the lumina," added Maeve, "and Minnie wouldn't let him so they fought and she stabbed him with a kitchen knife, but then he hit her on the head and . . . "

"—And decided to hop into the wood keep and bleed to death?" Cathmor scowled at them. "Does anyone else have a theory they'd like to share or may I get back to work?" He wheeled around to go back in the house but the faraway sound of a horn blast stopped him in his tracks. The sound was long and mellow and seemed to last forever.

"Kat, look at the sky!" Lulabelle pointed to a line of steel gray clouds rapidly moving across the horizon in their direction. The words had just left her mouth, when Kat felt an icy wind whip across her face, stinging her eyes. The coldness seeped into every part of her body, as though she had been plunged into a bucket of ice. She had experienced that feeling once before, earlier in the summer.

"There it is!"

Cathmor's voice lacked either panic or fear, but was filled with an urgency that Kat remembered all too well. Rolling down the crest of a faraway hill, making straight for the village, was a blanket of seething, moving blackness.

"It's the fog banshee," cried Cathmor, pushing them roughly toward the house. "Everyone inside!"

CHAPTER EIGHTEEN

The Return of the Fog Banshee

"Close the windows!" ordered Cathmor, slamming the front door. "Make sure nothing's open, not even a crack. Don't give that demon any means to claw its way in here."

While Kat, Lulabelle, and Rosie ran around the house, pulling the windows shut, Cathmor yanked the curtains off one of the windows, tore them in half, and began rolling them into a long strip. Maeve remained frozen.

"Cathmor," she gasped, "Mam, Da—they're down at the field. What if they don't hear the horn? What if they can't get away in time?"

"They heard it, sure enough. The rest of the Cahir will sound the alarm for anyone who didn't." He opened the front door and squinted at the sky. The icy wind was starting to blow more force-fully.

"Aren't you staying with us?" However intimidating Cathmor could be, the thought of him leaving filled Kat with panic.

"I must ride to the field and get people to safety. The fog ban-shee's deadly enough when we're in our homes. An open field full of people with nowhere to go? Someone will die. As long as you stay here and stay down, you're safer than most. Plug the door with this when I leave."

Cathmor held up the strip of torn curtain.

"With any luck, it won't come this way." He removed a necklace with a crystal stone from around his neck. "In case it does come, I'll set this out . . . . A few pieces of china as well, I'm sure Eily won't object." He grabbed two bowls and tucked them under his arm.

"Remember, you're to stay here. Under no circumstances should you leave this house. I'll come back for you when it's gone." He slammed the door behind him and they immediately pushed the torn pieces of curtain into the cracks on the top and bottom of the door. Peeking through the window, Kat wasn't even surprised when, seconds later, a snow white stallion came hurtling towards the house, its mane flying. The horse raced past, yet somehow Cath-mor pulled himself onto its bare back and he and the horse vanished from sight.

Kat planted herself by the window, praying that the fog banshee would stay away, but also hoping that everyone at the festival was safe and the Cahir would reach them in time. Rosie joined her and together they stared out at the narrow lane, neither of them speaking. Rosie's left hand clutched at her pocket; Kat knew she was feeling for her inhaler, just in case.

"As long as we're here, do you think Cathmor would be angry if I took a quick peak in Lil's room?" The way Lulabelle said it indicated she was pretty sure of the answer.

Maeve was folding and refolding Mrs. Murphy's blankets, piled in a basket against the sofa. "I suppose you might as well. Cathmor can't accuse us of messing with things when he's shut us in the house and told us not to leave."

"What are you trying to find?" said Kat, following Lulabelle into Lil's small bedroom. Lil's bed was pink with fluffy pillows, and filled with an assortment of stuffed toys. Lulabelle gave them a brisk glance before crouching down to look under the bed. She got back up, frowning, and went over to Lil's dresser, hesitating only a second before opening the drawers and lifting the clothes packed inside.

Lulabelle closed the last drawer. "I don't know," she replied, "it's an idea I had. But I have to think about it some more before I can be sure."

"At least tell us what you're looking for!" Kat was becoming more impatient by the minute. "Maybe we can help."

"No, I could be wrong."

"You're never wrong—" Kat started to say, but the sound of breaking glass cut her off. They rushed back into the living room to see Maeve staring at them in horror; pieces of shattered china lay at her feet.

"I just remembered," Maeve said faintly. "Cathmor put Aidan in the outside yard . . . because it was so nice. But he didn't know, he couldn't have known—the fog banshee—we thought it might be gone . . . we hoped it was . . . ."

"Where's the outside yard?" demanded Kat, hoping beyond hope that it was anywhere but actually outside.

"In the middle of the village, right off the main road! If the fog banshee comes through again—"

"It'll run into Aidan," finished Lulabelle breathlessly. "And if the Cahir have left for the fairgrounds, he'll be trapped. He won't be able to escape."

It was truly a sign of how much they liked Aidan that not one of them (even Maeve) thought twice about disregarding Cathmor's warning and yanking open the front door. Steel gray clouds still covered the sky and the wind was bitterly unforgiving. In the distance were faraway noises that sounded to Kat like people screaming. She closed her eyes. Surely Cathmor and the Cahir would get to the festival in time. The Stewarts, Mr. Piddlewick, Mayor Digby, Mrs. MacDougal and Puddy . . . . Their faces flashed before her and she tried not to think about them, or what might be happening at that moment.

No one said anything until they reached the village. The main street was deserted except for a few scattered piles of treasure. Maeve pointed in the direction of a brown stone building a block away.

"That's the jail. The outside yard's behind it."

She led them through an alley and into a courtyard, in the middle of which was a fenced-in area about the size of the Harper's garage. Sitting on the ground with his back against the fence was . . .

"Aidan!" Kat cried, relieved beyond words.

Aidan jumped to his feet at the sight of them. He still had straw in his hair and dark circles under his eyes.

"Well, little birds, it appears the tables are turned, sure enough. Now I'm the one in the trap, aren't I Lulabelle? It'll be a mite harder to cut me out of this one, I'm afraid. I'm awfully glad to see you lot, even you, Red, especially with all this going on." He nodded his head upwards where the clouds swirled unnaturally. "It's back I take it, the fog banshee?"

"Yes," replied Lulabelle, examining the steel lock and chain wound tightly around the fence. "We don't know where it is, but we have to get you out of here in case it comes back."

"I couldn't agree more," agreed Aidan cheerfully. "I suppose I'll have to cancel my afternoon tea with the Cahir, but I'm sure they'll understand, seeing as how it's a matter of life and death." He whistled a tune under his breath.

Maeve gave Aidan a dirty look. "I'm glad all the trouble you're in hasn't dulled your ability to make jokes. We came as fast as we could to rescue you. We even risked our own lives, I'll have you know, as well as Cathmor's wrath, which is about the same thing. And now we're going to break you out, which will land us in a heap of trouble, although you don't deserve it!"

"Ah, Red, and I'm glad to see danger hasn't dulled your sweet spirit."

"Where are the Cahir, anyway?" said Kat. "I thought they were guarding you."

"They were indeed, but when the horn sounded, they took off for the festival. One of them promised to come back, but as you can see, I'm quite alone in my castle." A sudden gust of wind made the grin slide off his face. "Did you feel that?"

Kat shivered. An icy chill was seeping into her skin and a low buzz had filled the air. Above them, the clouds churned in a frenzied mass of gray and white, as though ready to burst. Lulabelle didn't look up but continued to examine the lock with increasing frustration.

"I can't budge it at all. We need the key. Do you think it's inside?"

"Probably, but the Cahir keep the door locked at all times."

Aidan pressed his face against the bars of the jail, trying to see the lock for himself.

"Then we have to open the lock without the key." Lulabelle felt around in her pockets before unzipping her backpack. "We need a hairpin or a safety pin or something."

"If you find one, I can pick the lock," said Aidan as another gust of wind broke over them. For the first time, Kat detected a flicker of fear in his eyes. The buzzing sound grew louder, the clouds more chaotic.

"There's the fog banshee! Down by the river!"

As though caught in slow motion, they all turned to follow Rosie's outstretched arm. A strange feeling swept over Kat. It felt as though her whole body was suddenly stuck in molasses and try as she might, she couldn't make herself move. The mass of black fog was rolling toward them as the buzzing increased to a fever pitch, yet for some unexplainable reason, she could only stand there and watch.

"I can't find anything!" cried Lulabelle above the buzzing. "There's nothing here! I can't believe I didn't bring any safety pins!" She picked up her backpack and shook all the contents out, sifting through them desperately; Maeve bent down to help her.

"You have to get away, it'll be here in a minute." The color had drained from Aidan's face but his voice was calm.

"We're not going to leave you!" Kat yelled. Her head was

throbbing from the relentless buzzing. "You'll die!"

"Don't be crazy!" Aidan shot back. "I'm not worth you lot dying, too. You have to go now!"

"We can't!" Rosie was crying. "We can't leave you, Aidan!" Her breath came in sharp gasps and she fumbled in her pocket for her inhaler.

Kat's mind swirled. What could she do? Leaving Aidan was not an option. The keys—they had to have the keys. Without stopping to think, Kat raced back up the alley, only faintly aware of voices calling after her. She charged up the steps of the jail and rattled the doorknob. Locked. Pressing her nose against the window pane, Kat caught sight of something that made her heart soar. In the center of a large desk was a silver ring with several keys. One of them had to be the right one. Kat stepped out of her shoe, yanked off her sock, and slid the sock over her hand. There was no time to think about how furious the Cahir would be or what laws she was breaking. They had to save Aidan. She balled up her fist and punched the glass as hard as she could.

"Here it is!"

Kat came running, waving the ring of keys in one hand. Lulabelle was pounding away at the lock with a pair of sewing scissors. Kat skidded to a stop in front of the fence and Aidan pointed at a large gold key in the center of the ring. "That's the one, I watched them lock me in."

Kat's body was rigid, her eyebrows knit in concentration. The wailing had reached a crescendo. Was it only her imagination or was the air in her lungs being twisted out of her body? Rosie puffed on her inhaler, her eyes fearful. The dark mass whirled closer. Already, black tendrils of fog were curling into claws, reaching for them while a low wail sounded from somewhere in its depths.

"Go!" Aidan yelled again. "You can't do it, it's too late!"

"SHUT UP YOU STUPID BOY!" screamed Kat, struggling to fit the key in the lock. "WE'RE TRYING TO SAVE YOUR LIFE!" She pulled the lock as hard as she could. It fell away with a snap. The door swung open and Aidan leaped out, not a second too soon.

"This way! Run!"

Aidan pulled Rosie onto his back and with a speed that would have rivaled the Cahir horses, he sprinted up the alley, the others close on his heels. Behind them came a piercing shriek. Kat glanced back to see the mass of fog flood the courtyard, encircling the fence and crushing it into a splintered mess. They came out onto the main street, their hearts thrashing inside their chests; Aidan leaped up the steps of the jail two at a time and they darted through the open door, slamming it behind them. Maeve and Lulabelle hastily covered the shattered windowpane with papers from the Cahir's desk, while Aidan stood guard at the window and Kat marched Rosie to the back of the room, as far away from the fog banshee as possible.

When several minutes had passed with no sounds of wailing and no glimpses of black fog, Aidan joined Kat, Lulabelle, Maeve, and Rosie in a circle on the floor. "No sign of it now," he said, leaning against a chair and closing his eyes. "Everything's quiet as a tomb. Wherever it is, it's not here."

"It's weird, isn't it," said Lulabelle pensively, "the way the fog banshee disappeared like that. It didn't even bother to take the treasures outside. If it's searching for the token, why leave them? And what happened at Lil's house? Did Minnie stab Barnaby before he hit her? But then where's the knife? And who took Lil? None of it makes sense . . . " She lapsed into thought.

Rosie got to her feet and went to stand by the window. "I'm worried about Lil," she said. "Whoever kidnapped her might not know about the fog banshee. They could be heading straight for it."

"The Cahir are out there," said Lulabelle. "I'm sure they'll find her before long. The kidnapper won't get far, not with the whole Hill province looking for them."

"But the Hill province isn't looking for them! The Cahir's not, either. They're too busy making sure everyone's safe from the fog banshee. By the time they start looking, it may be too late." Rosie crossed her arms and jutted out her chin. "We should look for her ourselves."

"What?" cried Kat and Lulabelle together.

"It's way too dangerous," protested Lulabelle. "If the fog banshee finds us, we could be trapped—"

"We don't even know which way they went," added Maeve, giving Rosie a sympathetic look. "These hills spread out for miles. I'm all for finding Lil but it would be like a needle in a haystack, I'm afraid."

"No, it wouldn't," Rosie insisted. "You could track her, Aidan!"

"Me?" Aidan's eyes shot open and he glanced around the room, as if expecting to see someone else with his name sitting in a corner. "You want me to track the little bird?"

"Why not? You track animals, don't you? Why can't you track a person?"

"I suppose, but . . . "

"Footprints are footprints," declared Rosie with authority. "If you don't want to help, I'll go by myself. But I can't wait here and do nothing when Lil's out there. We rescued Aidan, didn't we? Because he's our friend. Well, Lil's my friend and she's in trouble. She needs help so I'm going to help her!"

Rosie marched towards the door, Lulabelle and Kat hurrying after her. Lulabelle lunged in front of Rosie, trying to block her path.

"Rosie, I'm not letting you go. I'm responsible for you. I'm the oldest and—-what are you doing?" Her gaze shifted to Kat, who was leaning around her to open the door.

"I'm going with her," Kat said simply. "Rose is right, we can't stay here while Lil is out there. We have to try and find her."

"I'm not about to stay here with a chicken thief while you have all the fun!" Maeve jumped to her feet. Aidan grinned at her, then shook his head.

"I'd like to see the lot of you track a little bird without a tracker. You'd end up going in a bleedin' circle. Poor little bird wouldn't ever be found. But I suppose it's the least I can do, seeing as how you saved me from an agonizing death."

Lulabelle looked from Rosie to Kat and then back again. She sighed and made a face that she only made when accepting defeat; Kat recognized it because it almost always had something to do with her.

"Fine, I'll go too. I want to find Lil as much as you do, Rose, but we have to be careful. The fog banshee's still out there and next time we might not be as lucky."

Rosie smiled happily. "We'll be careful, Lu, I promise."

The wood keep where Cathmor had found Barnaby was still open and the drops of blood had dried into dull brown. The Harpers and Maeve stood back while Aidan inspected the grass. He squatted down, touching the wilted blades lightly, running his hands across the patches of dirt in front of the wood keep, then retraced his steps around the house to the front door, his eyes on the ground. He repeated this process two more times, while Kat shifted from one foot to the other and tried not to think about how long he was taking. When he retraced his steps for a third time, she couldn't handle the suspense any longer.

"Are you done yet? Can you tell which way they went?"

Aidan straightened up and stuck his hands in his pockets.

"It's odd, no doubt about it. There was a struggle, sure enough, although from the look of things, just one person was doing the struggling. There's only one set of shoe prints from what I can tell, and they're all in a mess . . . like whoever was here was turning around over and over again—"

Lulabelle's face brightened. "Because one of the people could fly," she said, hurrying to the wood keep and sticking her head in before popping back out again. "What if whoever took Lil was fighting with Barnaby? That would explain why there's only one set of prints, wouldn't it? Barnaby was flying around the whole time."

Aidan nodded. "That makes sense. If the brownie was fighting from the air, then whoever he was fighting would have to defend himself from all sides. That's why the prints are such a mess—he had to turn around like this—" Aidan pivoted from side to side, his arms in the air, fighting off an imaginary attacker.

"I guess that's how he ended up in the wood keep, poor fellow," said Maeve sadly. "He tried to fight off Lil's kidnapper and got stabbed for it. Barnaby's a strange one, but at least he tried to help her."

There was a moment of silence while they reflected on the very weird, yet now endearing brownie.

"I wouldn't be too sure of that, Red," said Aidan, who had moved a few feet away to inspect another patch of dirt. "He might have helped more than we think."

"What do you mean?" They crowded around Aidan to stare at the dirt patch, although no one had the slightest idea what they were looking at. A small shoe print lay outlined in the middle of the dirt.

"Is that Lil's print?" asked Rosie hopefully. Aidan nodded.

"They start at the front steps and come out this way. I didn't see them at first. Since they're small, they're covered by the other, bigger ones. Near as I can tell, she ran out of the house and someone ran after her . . . or maybe they took her out and made her march in front of them . . . it's a bit tricky. But then whoever took her stopped—because of the brownie most likely—and Lil kept going alone. No other prints lead down the hill in that direction."

Aidan indicated the valley stretched out in front of them, beyond which lay the Whispering Woods.

"Then she got away?" Kat wasn't sure whether to be glad or worried. It was a relief to know that Lil might have escaped from her kidnapper, but that meant she was alone and defenseless, with a fog banshee on the loose.

"Seems that way. I don't see the bigger prints anywhere, but he might've cut her off later. Only one way to find out. Are you sure you want to do this?"

Everyone nodded.

"Fair enough," said Aidan, his eyes on the small prints disappearing down the hill. "Let's track this little bird."

It was rather, thought Kat, like playing a very strange game of follow-the-leader, only the leader was an invisible five-year-old, they had no idea where she was taking them, and a monster might attack at any moment. Aidan appeared to have gone into a trance, so focused was he on following Lil's prints, and the Harpers and Maeve hung back, not wanting to distract him. Instead, they kept a lookout for any traces of black fog lurking in the trees or over the next hill.

Occasionally, Aidan stopped, his brows furrowed in a clear sign of confusion. When that happened, the others exchanged worried glances, holding their breaths until Aidan let out a satisfied whistle and the search resumed; only Rosie seemed content to let him work, the trust never wavering in her brown eyes.

"He's going to find her, I know he will," she confided to Kat during an especially long waiting period in which Aidan walked around in a circle, cursing under his breath. Kat didn't say anything but hoped with all her heart that Rosie was right.

When they came at last to the edge of the Whispering Woods, Aidan stopped.

"It's clear the little bird went this way. See where the grass is smashed? She dug her heel into the blades—turning 'round to see if she was being chased, I bet—then she kept going. I wonder why . . ."

"Isn't it obvious?" said Maeve in surprise. "To get away from her kidnapper."

"Then why not run that way, to the village?" Aidan motioned toward the long stretch of valley behind them. "Or what about the festival? The field is right over that hill. It makes more sense than coming here, where there's no one to help her."

"She's only five," said Lulabelle. "She was scared. She wanted to run away and there's lots of places to hide in the woods. Maybe she thought she could find somewhere safe until help came."

Aidan didn't look convinced.

"At any rate, she'll be easier to track," was all he said.

The minutes ticked on as they continued their careful, painstaking chase deeper into the woods and a feeling of uneasiness sprouted in Kat's chest. Where was Lil? What had happened to her? Had the fog banshee . . . ? No, the fact that the footprints continued was a good sign. They were getting closer. They had to be getting closer.

Up ahead, Aidan stopped. A few yards away stood an old, crumbling building. On either side of the doorway perched two fierce looking stone creatures with the heads of dragons.

"It's the lumina shrine!" exclaimed Lulabelle. "How did we end up back here?"

"I knew we walked a fair piece, but I didn't realize it was that far," agreed Maeve. "We must be miles from the village by now."

Aidan whistled again. "You mean to tell me you know about this? I found it a few years back, but never had much use for it myself. A bit on the creepy side for my taste. Too many holes in the roof to keep the rain out, and frigid in the winter to boot."

As quietly as she could, Lulabelle told Aidan about their adventure in the woods with Donovan, their discovery of the shrine, and the figure in the cloak. When they reached the doorway, Aidan gave them a significant look.

"From what I can see, the little bird's prints lead here. I can't find any bigger prints, but that doesn't mean someone's not in there with her." He grimaced. "My knife would be handy right now, but unfortunately the Cahir don't allow prisoners to keep weapons, so there you have it. Look sharp and watch yourselves, all right?"

The smell of mildew greeted them as they entered the shrine. It wasn't as dark as the last time; slivers of sunlight pierced the cracks in the walls and ceiling. The grotesque faces of the stone luminas gaped at them from all sides and Kat did her best to avoid looking at them. She understood why Aidan might've preferred O'Bannon's filthy shack to this ghoulish place, no matter the number of rats. As far as Kat could tell, the room was empty. There was nothing here but a bunch of scary, stone luminas . . .

. . . And a dark lump huddled against the wall in the farthest corner.

The lump suddenly moved and they all screamed (even Aidan, Kat noted, although he later denied it).

"Lil," said Rosie, her voice shaking with the sudden scare. "Lil, it's me—Rosie. We came to find you and take you home."

"Rosie?" The lump lifted its head, revealing Lil's tear-streaked face. She rose unsteadily to her feet.

"I was so scared," she whimpered as Maeve hurried over and wrapped her arms around the little girl. "When the man tried to grab me, I was so scared . . . I ran as fast as I could . . . I didn't want him to catch me."

"I know, little one, but you're with us now," crooned Maeve. "We won't let him hurt you."

"He hurt Minnie, too!" Lil continued tearfully. "He hit her on the head and she fell down and didn't wake up! Then he tried to grab me, but the other brownie hit him and I ran outside." She gulped, stifling a sob. "The man ran after me and he grabbed my arm and he tore my dress." She showed them a patch of torn fabric. "But the other brownie hit him again and then he hit him back . . . and then they were fighting . . . and I kept running. I think the bad man hurt the brownie because he was bleeding . . . he's very, very bad!" Lil dissolved into frightened tears and Maeve hugged her tightly.

Lulabelle knelt down beside Maeve. "Lil, you've been really brave but I need to ask you an important question. Ok?"

Lil lifted her head from Maeve's shoulder. She sniffed her assent.

"When the bad man came into your room, are you sure that he tried to grab *you*? Or was he trying to grab your lumina? Can you remember?"

Lil scrunched up her eyes. "I—I don't know. I was lying in bed and he put out his arm, and he tried to grab me . . . he was very, very bad," she reminded them solemnly.

"But were you all by yourself or were you holding your lumina?"

For the first time, Kat noticed the wooden toy clutched in Lil's arms.

"I was holding my lumina," said Lil, pressing it against her chest. "I always sleep with it, always. It's magic."

Lulabelle sat back on her knees. Even in the dim light, Kat could tell that her sister's face was pale.

"I know it's magic," she said in a shaky voice, "and I think the Spellbinder knows it too."

"What are you talking about?" Maeve looked from Lulabelle

to Lil. "How can a wooden lumina be magic? Mr. Snugglewump doesn't enchant the toys he sells, I would know if he did."

"Because it's not one of Mr. Snugglewump's luminas," Lulabelle replied, "and it's not a wooden toy. Unless I'm very wrong, we've found the lost token of the Hill province."

"WHAT?"

The echo of their voices bounced off the high stone ceiling as everyone crowded around Maeve and Lulabelle, hoping to get a better look at the toy in Lil's arms. Lil shrank back against the wall and stared at them like they had all gone crazy.

"That's impossible," stammered Maeve. "Lil's had that toy since she was a baby. It's nothing special. How could it be the token? It would be hundreds of years old!"

"I don't know," replied Lulabelle. "But remember what the Enchantress said? Each token still has magic in it. No one knows what the magic might do—it might preserve the token somehow. She also said that each token was unique to the province it came from, and in the legends, luminas were the protectors of the Hill province, weren't they?"

Maeve nodded, speechless.

"So that's what the Spellbinder's been trying to find this whole time?" repeated Aidan incredulously. "All this mess with the fog banshee, all those treasures it took . . . was to find that?" He looked skeptical. "It doesn't seem to have a lick of magic about it."

"But it does!" Lil cried, finally grasping the meaning of their conversation. "It's got loads of magic! It told me to come here, that I would be safe."

Now it was Kat's turn to be incredulous. "Does it talk?"

Lil giggled. "No, silly, it can't talk! But when I was running away from the bad man, I could feel it. It kept pulling me this way and when I saw this house, I knew it wanted me to come inside."

"That's why you came here instead of the village," said Rosie.

"I think we have a bit of a problem," said Aidan, frowning at the lumina. "How exactly do you plan to prove it's the Hill token? It doesn't look at all magical."

There was a silence as they all thought hard.

"Wait a minute," Rosie said suddenly. "Lil, didn't you tell me your lumina was a night light? That when you're scared of the dark, you sing to it and it glows? Can you sing to it now?"

Lil sat the lumina on the stone floor. She began to sing in a soft, sweet voice and Maeve smiled.

"I know that song. It's an old Hill province lullaby. I haven't heard it in ages." She sang along with Lil, the slow, haunting melody reaching to the ceiling.

"It does sound familiar somehow," said Aidan. "I think I may have heard it when I was a lad, but it's fuzzy . . . "

Lulabelle gasped. From the center of the wooden lumina, in the place where its heart would've been, a faint blueish light glowed.

The light grew brighter and bigger, spreading through each of the lumina's four legs and into its snarling head. It was unlike anything Kat had ever seen, and as Maeve and Lil finished the lullaby, the room grew quiet again. The lumina continued to glow for another minute, before the light gently faded and was gone. Lil picked up the lumina and returned it to the safety of her lap.

"I told you it was magic!" she said triumphantly.

"We have to get this to the village," Lulabelle told them. "The Enchantress has to know."

"Oh, now, I don't think that's necessary, not at all," came a cold voice from behind them. "Not when I've worked so hard to find it."

They whirled around, stunned. Standing in the doorway of the shrine, his face hidden in shadows, was the hooded figure.

CHAPTER NINETEEN

The Man in the Cloak

M-Mayor Digby?" said Maeve as the hooded figure stepped into the light. "You're—you're the Spellbinder?"

Mayor Digby sighed, regret flitting across his face. "I'm afraid so, Maevie my girl, although I must say, I didn't intend for you to find out this way. But you forced my hand, you see, and here we are."

He swung his arms back and forth, surveying the lumina shrine with interest. "Do you know, I had my doubts that this would be a good hiding spot—a tad too musty in my opinion—but the fog banshee took to it and who was I to argue?" He laughed a short, bleating laugh. "And it did work, for awhile at least, although you know how that story ended . . . such a shame, I was growing rather fond of these hideous luminas."

"Then it was you that day in the woods," said Lulabelle in a raspy voice. "You were the one we saw with the fog banshee."

"You hit Donovan with the rock!" exclaimed Kat accusingly. "You framed Aidan, too! I bet you were the one who left that note at Cathmor's doorstep. You wanted everyone to think he was the Spellbinder!" Mayor Digby held up his hands, looking guilty.

"Now, now, I didn't want to hurt your friend. I'm not a violent man. But he was sniffing around outside and it was only a matter of time before he discovered our hiding spot. There was a third pile of treasures, and we thought . . . I thought . . . they had real possibilities . . . that one might be the token." Mayor Digby shrugged. "I was wrong, of course. The token was right under our noses the whole time, but you see the difficult position I was in. As for Aidan, I'm afraid that was necessary as well, but I had no doubt he would ultimately be cleared—the council is quite reasonable. I really am sorry, though," he added.

"We thought you were Da's friend!" spat Maeve. "You betrayed all of us!"

"No, no, no, I haven't betrayed anyone, don't you see?" Mayor Digby looked hurt. "I'm setting our beloved province on a far better path. When this is all said and done, you'll be thanking the Spellbinders, mark my words."

"Thank an evil, nasty sorcerer who sends monsters after innocent people? Never!" yelled Kat. Her fear had given way to a dark, explosive anger; Lulabelle reached out and grabbed the back of her shirt before she could run at Mayor Digby and pound him with her fists.

Mayor Digby shook his head. "You see, that's what I'm talking about. We've been led to believe that Spellbinders were wicked, intent on taking over Ancora and ruling through terror and violence. Or we dismiss them as villains in ancient legends who never existed at all. But the legends are lies, nothing but lies! Spellbinders don't want to terrorize Ancora, they want to bring it together. They want to unite the provinces, just like in the old days. How could anyone object to that?"

"Yep, peace, sure enough," muttered Aidan. "Except you left out the part where they'll be running the show, telling the rest of us what to do."

"Someone will have to be in charge, that's true, but I assure you it will be strictly benevolent . . . more of an advisory council, no different from what we have now."

Mayor Digby smiled broadly, clasping his hands behind his back as though about to deliver a lecture. "It all started last year when I . . . er . . . borrowed a book from Cathmor. As I was taking it off the shelf, I noticed a smaller one wedged between the shelf and the bookcase. I daresay Cathmor never knew it was there; he inherited quite a few books from his father. I don't know what possessed me to take it, but it was most fortunate that I did, because it contained ancient writings—true writings—about the Spellbinders. They didn't bring fear and oppression, but peace and stability. It was only when a misguided rebellion separated the tokens and murdered the Spellbinders that things became worse. And look at us now! What do we have? A good deal of hills and grass and sheep, that's what. We have no protection, no wealth, nothing of any value."

"That's not true!" Maeve's eyes sparked with rage. "We have lots of good people who love our province and love Ancora! We have kindness and generosity and courage."

"You don't understand, none of that will go away. The Spellbinders love Ancora even more than you do. That's the only reason they wish to be in charge—to see it prosper!"

"It's hard to prosper when you're busy hiding from a fog banshee!" retorted Kat. Mayor Digby bowed his head.

"I *am* sorry about that, but it was the only way to find what I was looking for. After I finished the book, I realized how important it was to recover the Hill token. For the Spellbinders to unite Ancora, it was vital that we recover all the tokens, of course, but we . . . I . . . had to start somewhere. But how to find it?

"I'm afraid the book was rather vague on the token's identity, and completely silent as to its whereabouts. I searched as best I could, but had no success. It wasn't a total waste, however; I used the time to learn the old spells and other . . . er . . . useful magic that would allow me to become a Spellbinder. And in the end, it was that magic that let me summon the fog banshee, which is no simple task, if you don't mind my saying so."

"That doesn't make sense," said Lulabelle slowly. "The Enchantress told us that sort of magic is complicated. And Mr. Stewart said it was extremely hard to summon a fog banshee, even for a Spellbinder. How did you teach yourself all that in only a few months?"

For the first time, Mayor Digby seemed uncomfortable. "Naturally, I'm a very quick learner," he bleated, dropping his gaze to the floor. "I have an excellent memory and the book itself was quite useful — more of a step-by-step guide, if you will."

"I never would've thought you were a Spellbinder," Maeve snarled. "I can't believe it of you!"

"Why, because I'm not clever enough?" Mayor Digby's round face twisted into a pout. Without his usual big smile, he looked petty and disagreeable. "That's what everyone thinks, isn't it? Jolly old Aifric, only good for cutting ribbons and kissing wee babies! Don't allow him to make hard decisions, no, that's what more intelligent people are for. People like your da and Cathmor and Angus Corley. Even Olive McCutcher commands more respect! As for me? I'm left to twirl my hat and make speeches for people who think me no more than a fool!" Mayor Digby was working himself into a tizzy.

"But none of them found the token, did they? None of them were clever enough to summon a fog banshee. They won't be laughing when I'm exalted far above them! They won't be sniggering over my intellect then."

"Except that you weren't the first one to discover the token," said Kat evenly. "That brownie, Barnaby, did. He knew right away it was special. That's why he tried to take it from Lil that day he won the contest. Maeve told us that brownies see value in things that we don't. Barnaby knew a treasure when he saw it."

"I will grant you that," admitted Mayor Digby, his temper returning to normal. "Brownies are clever creatures. It was Barnaby that made me realize the lumina was the token, in fact. The little fellow was so upset when he couldn't have it the first time. When I saw him in the tree . . . well, I should have realized it long before, but better late than never. I thought I could take it while the child was sleeping, but I'm afraid I underestimated Barnaby yet again. He's really a persistent fellow."

"You're a bad, bad man," declared Lil, peeping out from around Rosie. "You hurt Minnie and that other brownie!"

"Now, now, child, I didn't want to," Mayor Digby protested. "I'm not a violent man."

"That's a lie," said Aidan in a tight voice. "You killed Birdie, the kindest, most generous person in the world because she got in your way. Don't kid yourself that you're all about peace and harmony and whatever bunk you tell yourself to feel righteous. In the end, you're a coward and a murderer, nothing more."

Mayor Digby blanched. He appeared to be at a loss for words.

"Did you even talk to her before you murdered her?" Aidan went on, his voice rising. "Did you shove a lot of pretty words at her about Spellbinders and unity and everyone in Ancora holding hands? She would've seen through you in a second. But she wouldn't have laughed at you, not Birdie, she was too kind. She would've sat you down, made you a cup of tea, and tried to convince you all that mess about Spellbinders saving Ancora is rot. But I doubt you even had the courage to look in her eyes. I bet you knew what she would say and you killed her rather than have your fine ideas come crashing down on your head. Just like you skulked around in the shadows, waiting for us to find the token for you."

"That's ridiculous!" Mayor Digby refused to meet Aidan's eyes. "I would never intentionally kill an old woman! I meant to knock her unconscious—to tie her up so I could take what I needed. But she turned at the last minute and I must have brought the rock down harder than I thought . . . " He struggled to regain control of his voice. "It was a tragic accident, but it was not murder, my lad."

Aidan made a move as though to attack but Mayor Digby held up a hand. "I wouldn't advise that. I'm not a violent man, but I will resort to violence if you do anything rash."

"Maybe I don't care about myself," growled Aidan, his fists clenched.

"I wouldn't harm you," corrected the mayor, "but I might have to harm Lil here, or the little one with the ponytail, I forget her name." He nodded in Rosie's direction as Lulabelle and Kat moved protectively in front of their sister. Aidan gritted his teeth, not willing to test Mayor Digby's words. He closed his eyes and bowed his head, as though praying or, more than likely, thought Kat, trying to keep himself from clawing Mayor Digby's eyes out.

"What about the heir?" squeaked Rosie from behind Kat and Lulabelle. "Doesn't the legend say there's a royal family out there? That's the one who should unite Ancora, not the Spellbinders!"

Mayor Digby shook his head. "Everyone knows the royal line died out years ago. There's no long lost heir . . . not all legends are true, I'm afraid."

"Just the ones that benefit you!" Maeve shot back.

"Enough!" Mayor Digby had finally snapped. "I'm not going to defend myself to a bunch of children. The token, if you please."

Lulabelle, Kat and Maeve exchanged worried glances. Aidan's head remained bowed, his eyes closed; he didn't seem to be aware of anything going on in the shrine. Maeve pulled Lil gently toward her.

"Little one, we're going to have to do as he says." Lil stifled a sob and hugged her lumina. "I know it's hard, but you must be extra brave. It's the only way the bad man will let us take you back to your mam. We won't let the mayor get away with this, but we have to pretend for a little while."

Lil sniffed. "I'm a good pretender."

"Then let me have your lumina, little one."

Reluctantly, Lil offered the toy to Maeve, who presented it to Mayor Digby with a glare so intense that Kat thought he might melt on the spot. He accepted the lumina reverently, his face glowing with greedy excitement. He held it up to the light, turning it around in wonder.

"Marvelous," he murmured, "so simple, yet so elegant. I can't think how it never occurred to me until today. The luminas of the Hill province—our great protectors. To think, I once believed the token was one of Olive McCutcher's old hair pins!"

"We gave you what you want," said Kat crossly. "Can we go now?"

With a great deal of effort, Mayor Digby pulled his gaze away from the lumina. He stared at her for a moment with a blank look then let out a hollow laugh, as if Kat had told a mildly funny joke and he was trying to be polite.

"Let you go? Oh dear, I'm afraid I can't let you go. You see, I didn't intend to reveal myself until much later, when I had recovered the rest of the tokens. It wouldn't matter what anyone else tried to do then, don't you see? But now . . . " Mayor Digby clicked his tongue. "Now, if I let you go, you'll sound the alarm, and Cathmor will toss me into that hole of a jail and leave me to rot. No, that doesn't sound agreeable at all."

"So what are you saying?" said Maeve angrily. "You're going to lock us in here while you make your grand escape to wherever it is worms like you go?"

"No, I can't do that, either." Mayor Digby shook his head. "Too many things could go wrong and I simply can't take any chances. No, I'm afraid the solution must be a bit more permanent."

As the meaning of his words sank in, an ominous chill crept down Kat's spine. At first she thought it was only in her mind, but when Rosie shivered and Lulabelle rubbed her hands up and down her arms, she knew it wasn't just her. The temperature in the room had dropped. That could only mean one thing.

"You're going to kill us?" said Lulabelle in a shaky voice, putting her arms around Rosie.

"Of course not, child! I told you, I'm not a violent man." The sorrowful look on Mayor Digby's face deepened. "You must understand that I don't have a choice in the matter—you forced my hand. No, I won't kill you . . . .But I'm afraid it will."

A gust of frigid air hit them with the force of a brick wall. Behind Mayor Digby, the entrance to the lumina shrine went dark. As they watched in horror, a black arm of fog twisted and curled toward them, reaching through the doorway. A face with burning red eyes loomed out of the fog, its mouth stretching open as it emitted a piercing wail that shook the stone walls.

"You won't get away with this!" screamed Kat, her ears ringing from the wailing right outside the doorway. "They'll catch you! Mr.

Stewart and Cathmor and the Enchantress—they'll figure out that it was you and then you'll be sorry! You're a terrible, awful man and the Spellbinders will never win no matter how much you want them to—not when there's good people who'll stop them!" There was far more that Kat wanted to scream at the mayor but the wailing had grown so loud she could hardly hear herself. Mayor Digby adjusted his cloak and replaced his hood, a sinister sign that the conversation was over.

"I truly am sorry about this," he repeated. "For your sake, I'll ask the fog banshee to be quick so you don't suffer. As mayor, I'll have a plaque made in your honor, detailing your heroic sacrifice in trying to save Lil. I promise it will be lovely!" He hurried out of the shrine.

"What now?" Kat yelled as they moved closer together, forming a tight huddle.

"We have to run for it!" Aidan had come out of his trance and was staring past them at the doorway where Mayor Digby was speaking to the fog banshee.

"How?" Maeve clenched Lil's hand in her own. "We're trapped! If we try to leave, the fog banshee will kill us and if we stay here, it'll come in after us and smoke us out—"

"We don't have a choice," argued Aidan. "If we stay together and hold our breaths, we might have a chance!"

"What is it, Lu?" Kat shouted at her sister, who had gone very still, her eyes wide, her hands stuffed inside the pockets of her jeans. There was a movement from the doorway. The fog banshee rolled toward them, its fog arms outstretched, screaming that unearthly wailing sound. Kat could feel the oxygen draining from her lungs. Instinctively, she reached for Rosie's arm.

"It's ok," Rosie gasped, as though reading Kat's mind. "I can hold my breath, I know I can."

"Everyone behind me!" ordered Aidan. "Grab hands and stay close to the wall. When I say go, we run for the door!"

"Wait, I have an idea!" cried Lulabelle. Reaching into her pocket, she brought out a handful of little white tadpole-shaped balls. Picking up two of the balls, she hurled them at the ground. There was a sharp crackle as smoke filled the air and a charred, burned smell hit Kat's nostrils. The fog banshee reared back in surprise, its claw arms tearing madly at the air. Lulabelle threw three more balls at the ground and there was another crackling sound as the smoke intensified, making Kat's eyes water.

"The smoke bombs!" she yelled in surprise. "I forgot you had them!"

"They're working! I don't believe it!" Maeve gaped as the fog banshee retreated into a corner, an ear splitting wail still pouring from its wide open mouth.

"Now's our chance, go!"

Aidan bolted for the doorway, one arm outstretched to ward off an attack, the other grabbing onto Lil. Maeve took the little girl's other hand, at the same time reaching for Rosie, followed by Kat and Lulabelle. The combination of the acrid smoke and the suffocating fog made Kat's stomach churn and she hoped very much that she wouldn't throw up all over the floor before they made it out. With a screech of anger, the fog banshee lunged at them and Lulabelle hurled the rest of the smoke bombs with all her might. As she and Kat barreled through the doorway, they could hear half a dozen pops and crackles followed by more wailing.

Aidan tore through the woods, the others at his heels. They ran until the lumina shrine was out of sight and the trees hid them from view. Glancing around, he pointed at a hill some distance away.

"We've only got a bit of time before it comes after us. Get to that hill over there and I'll meet you as soon as I can."

"Where are you going?" said Kat, struggling to catch her breath.

"To get that token back, sure enough. The mayor was heading the other way through the woods. If I go fast, I can cut him off. You worry about getting to that hill."

"Why, what's on the hill?"

"Help," said Aidan shortly. "Now go!"

"But how will you get the token back?" Kat called after him. Aidan turned and grinned at her.

"Shouldn't be all that hard— Mayor Digby was heading straight for one of my traps. Maud won't let us down!"

The Harpers and Maeve hurried through the Whispering Woods until they reached the edge of the tree line and came out onto a flat stretch of grass. In front of them loomed the hill where Aidan had promised to meet them. In the distance the village beckoned and Kat felt a flicker of hope. Maybe they could reach it safely before the fog banshee overtook them. But the vast expanse of field and stream separating them made her realize such an attempt would be futile. No, they would have to make it to the meeting spot and trust that Aidan's help would be there, whatever that meant.

They had nearly reached the top when an unexpected sound stopped them in their tracks. It was coming from the other side of the hill: a soft snorting noise, followed by muffled stomping. Puzzled, they tiptoed the rest of the way, unsure what was waiting for them at the top. Could anything be worse than the fog banshee?

"Thank goodness," said Lulabelle with relief as they reached the meeting spot and gazed down at the other side. "They're horses."

"Not any horses," said Maeve in surprise, "those are Cahir horses. I recognize their markings."

A white horse with red specks and a mahogany mane and tail trotted over, tossing its head. It gazed at them with its soft brown eyes, then stomped the ground. Kat had the strangest feeling that it was trying to tell them something.

"It's Aidan's horse," said Rosie delightedly, stepping forward to let the animal nuzzle her hand. "I think he calls it Red Star." The horse lowered its head so Rosie could stroke its nose.

"What are they doing here?" said Kat, patting the horse's side. It seemed like too much of a coincidence that Red Star and the other horses happened to be grazing in the same spot where Aidan had told them to meet.

"That's easy enough," said a voice behind them. Aidan was holding the wooden lumina and smiling through gasps of air. "They're here because I called them."

"You what?" cried Kat, Lulabelle, and Maeve at the same time. With a whinny of recognition, Red Star ambled forward and rubbed its nose against Aidan's shoulder.

"That's impossible!" said Kat. "You've been with us the whole time. There's no way you could have left to get horses!"

"Look, it's a bit of a long story and I don't fancy going into it here," replied Aidan, oblivious to the fact that everyone was gaping at him. "If we make it to the village, we'll sit around a cheery fire and I'll tell you everything. But there's no time now and you have to trust me on that!"

"At least tell us how you got the token back from the mayor," said Kat as two other horses trotted over and Aidan hurriedly checked each one, tightening saddles and reins.

"He pulled a bit of a Lulabelle," Aidan told them with a wink.

"I was right about old Maud. I put her down last week hoping for a deer and Digby stepped right into it. He dropped the token and happily, I was there to pick it up. I left him cursing my name, but at least we know where to tell Cathmor to find him."

"Then you didn't—" Lulabelle hesitated but everyone knew what she wanted to say.

"I wanted to," Aidan said, his eyes sad but clear. "He deserved it, for what he did to Birdie, what he tried to do to us, but I couldn't. I guess I knew what Birdie would say and she wouldn't want me to. I wasn't there to help her when she needed me, but maybe I can make her proud another way, by doing what she would've done." Aidan leaned down on the pretense of checking Red Star's stirrups and they heard a sniffle.

"Look!" cried Lil, pointing towards the Whispering Woods. A man had burst from the trees and was racing towards them, while from the woods came another long wail, louder this time.

"It's Donovan!" exclaimed Rosie as he bolted up the hill and came to a stop next to them, his chest heaving. No one spoke, too shocked to say anything.

"Oh good, you're alive," was all he said.

"How did you know we were here?" said Kat. This day was getting more surreal by the second.

"On the other side of the hill . . . heard the horn sound . . . saw the fog banshee and the man in the cloak . . . decided to follow them—" Donovan sucked in air and wiped his forehead. "I got as far as the tomb when I saw all of you come tearing out." He did a double take as he noticed the lumina in Aidan's hands for the first time. "Don't tell me that you actually found . . . "

"It's the token, Donovan!" cried Rosie. "We found it! The fog banshee was after it, too, just like you said!"

Another blast of cold wind blew over the hill, followed by a faint buzzing. Donovan shook himself out of his trance.

"It's still after it, by the sound of things." A curious expression passed over him. To Kat, it appeared as though Donovan was weighing a decision he didn't particularly want to make. When he spoke, it was with a great deal of reluctance.

"If you trust me, I can take the token instead . . . cut across from the other side. You ride as fast as you can to the village. If we're lucky, the fog banshee will come after me. It's risky, but it might give you more time."

Aidan tightened his grip on the lumina, a wary look in his eyes. "Sorry, chap, but I don't trust you. I don't know you and we've already lost the bleedin' thing once. I don't fancy losing it again."

Donovan smiled briefly. "Fair enough, I would do the same. Trust is a dangerous weapon if you don't use it wisely." His gaze fell on Lil. "Then let me take the little one. If I carry her, you'll have a better chance." A biting gust of wind slapped against them; the buzzing had reached a feverish peak.

"Come on now!" barked Donovan. "We're out of time! Ride as fast as you can!"

Without waiting for anyone to agree or object, he swung Lil over his shoulder and disappeared down the other side of the hill, running almost as fast as he had by himself. There was no time to wonder if they had made the right choice—Donovan had made the choice for them. Aidan swung into action; in one swift motion, he lifted Rosie onto Red Star's back.

"He's right!" he yelled over the buzzing. "We have to get to the village!" He helped Kat onto the second horse, then Lulabelle. Kat grasped the reins so tightly that her knuckles turned white; behind her, she could feel Lulabelle's heart thudding against her back. Maeve swung herself onto the third horse and took the reins, her face resolute.

"Now then," said Aidan, pulling himself up behind Rosie and taking Red Star's reins, the lumina sandwiched somewhere between them. "Follow me!"

He dug his heels into Red Star's side and the horse took off down the hill, Maeve's horse behind it. Kat gave hers a tentative kick, but found it was unnecessary. The horse, sensing urgency, broke into a run. She and Lulabelle bent down and did their best to hold on.

From behind them came a chilling shriek. Kat glanced back in time to see the fog banshee stream out of the Whispering Woods.

She caught a glimpse of its face hovering in the blackness and she prayed that it wouldn't see them, that somehow they could avoid its piercing gaze. But even as Kat thought this, the fog banshee turned its red eyes in their direction, let out a scream that made her ears ring, and swept toward them just as the horses reached the bottom of the hill.

With Red Star in the lead, they streaked across the field, the horses' legs a blur against the green grass. The air was so cold that Kat could no longer feel her face. On the other side of the field lay the village. It was there, waiting to protect them, if they could only make it in time. The grassy plain separating them appeared to grow wider by the second.

"It's getting closer!" Lulabelle screamed into Kat's ear. "We have to go faster!"

As though it understood Lulabelle's words, their horse surged forward and they grabbed at whatever they could find to keep from falling off. Out of the corner of her eye, Kat could see the black mass covering the distance between them with lightning speed. The village was so far away; there was too much field between them.

They would never make it.

"Kat, help!"

At the sound of Lulabelle's terrified cry, Kat whirled around. A black claw of fog was snaking itself around Lulabelle's neck, choking her. An identical shout rose up nearby where another fog arm had encircled Maeve and was trying to pull her off the horse.

"No!"

Kat kicked her horse as hard as she could and the horse darted sideways, almost throwing Kat and Lulabelle off its back, but releasing the fog banshee's grip on Lulabelle, who dissolved into a fit of coughing. Maeve's horse darted the opposite way, and the fog banshee fell back with a shriek of rage.

"Just a little farther!" yelled Aidan from up ahead—or at least, that's what Kat thought he was saying; his words were lost in the cacophony of hoofbeats and shrieking. On the other side of the field, a row of dark specks hurtled toward them with the same pounding rhythm of the horses—wait a minute, could it be? Kat's heart surged with hope. Those *were* horses, big horses, and in the front was a snow white stallion, racing across the field with ferocious energy. The horses drew closer and Kat saw that each one was carrying a large, stone-faced warrior, and in each warrior's hand was gripped a spear.

"It's Cathmor!" Kat yelled over her shoulder to Lulabelle. "It's Cathmor and the rest of the Cahir! They're coming to help us!"

"Kat!"

Lulabelle's cry was strangled and Kat turned to see the snake-like arms of the fog banshee wrapping around Lulabelle once again. The arms were pulling Lulabelle off the saddle and into the writhing mass of black fog that was on top of them. The fog banshee's face loomed overhead, and as Lulabelle fought to free herself, a high-pitched wail poured out of its ghostly mouth.

"No!" Kat screamed hysterically. "Leave her alone!" But even as the words left her, she could feel air being squeezed from her lungs. The black fog swarmed over them so that she could no longer see the Cahir rushing to their rescue, and the buzzing sound filled her head so intensely that it was all she could do to form coherent thoughts. The fog was pouring into her eyes. Lulabelle's arms around her waist were slipping away. White dots mixed with the fog. Aidan and Rosie were mere shadows through the haze and Kat had a fleeting thought that maybe, just maybe, they would get away . . . they would escape. Maybe Rosie would make it back through the cave, back to their parents. But it was too late for her and Lu . . . they had tried . . . they had done their best . . . but the fog banshee was too strong . . . their horse was brave, but not fast enough . . . it wasn't fast enough . . . poor horse . . .

Their horse. What was happening to their horse? From the swirling void of pain and unconsciousness, Kat felt a sudden jolt. Her eyes shot open and she sat up in her seat as though struck by lightning. Something was happening to their horse, she could feel it. A pulsing energy coursed through them, starting with the horse's legs, running up to its head, into its haunches and through its tail. A faint blue light was coming from somewhere around them and it took Kat a moment to realize that it was coming from inside the horse. What was happening? Was this some sadistic trick of the fog banshee? Some last torture before it finally killed them?

But no, it couldn't be, for even as the thought occurred, the horse leaped away from the fog banshee and the icy grip on Kat's chest lessened. She heard Lulabelle's ragged breathing, and her sister's arms tightened around her waist once more.

Kat clutched at the horse's bridle as it shot across the field with the force of a bullet. Reaching down for a better grip, she saw that the black mane and coat of the horse had disappeared. In their place was a covering of smooth, greenish-yellow scales, and instead of hooves, there were now enormous claws. The horse (but could it really be a horse anymore?) gave an earth-shaking roar and Kat's eyes widened at the sight of a head that no longer resembled anything like a horse, but was compact and muscular, with green eyes and powerful jaws. Where the horse's ears had been, two horns now curved upward.

"What's happening?" she yelled to Lulabelle.

"It's happening to Maeve's horse, too!" Lulabelle yelled back.

Kat twisted her head around to see the same greenish-yellow skin, powerful claws, and dragon-like head in the place where a dappled gray horse had been only moments before. Up ahead, Kat could tell that Red Star had undergone the same shocking transformation. Almost instantly, another realization hit her—she had seen these creatures before in the lumina shrine. But they had only been stone, snarling at her with gray, sightless eyes.

"They're luminas!" she cried, not sure whether to be ecstatic or terrified. "The Cahir horses are turning into luminas!"

A chorus of loud roars filled the air. The line of horses racing at them from the other side of the field had also transformed, their claws tearing up the earth, their green, dragon eyes narrowed. They were now close enough for Kat to see Cathmor and the other warriors clearly; as she watched, each warrior raised his spear over his shoulder and dropped lower into the saddle. Only Cathmor remained upright. With one hand, he beckoned to them, urging them forward.

The row of luminas let out another roar and tongues of fire shot into the air. Kat and Lulabelle screamed, even though the fire was clearly aimed at the fog banshee, which shrieked in fury. There was a hot brush of air as the row of Cahir swept past them and straight at the monster, then more roaring, followed by a shriek so chilling that Kat counted to ten before daring to peek over her shoulder. The luminas had reached the fog banshee, which had risen high into the air. For a split second, the spectral face loomed out of the blackness. Then, with one last heart-stopping wail, it swirled upward and disappeared in an explosion of blue and purple sparks.

Chapter Twenty
Answers and Questions

I can't believe I didn't see it before yesterday," remarked Lulabelle. They were sprawled on the grass in front of the Stewart's cottage, munching blueberry tarts from Mrs. MacDougal's bakery. Word of the fog banshee's defeat and the recovery of the Hill token had spread like wildfire through the village (due in large part to Mrs. MacDougal herself), and the Harpers had arrived that morning to discover so many cakes and pies had been left for them by grateful villagers, that the Stewart's cottage now resembled the bakery more than a house.

"What didn't you see before yesterday?" Kat turned over on her stomach, wincing slightly. Her ribs were still sore from where the fog banshee had squeezed her.

"I can't believe I didn't realize the Cahir horses were the luminas from the legends. It's obvious now that I think about it. The luminas were supposed to be the protectors of the Hill province, just like the Cahir watch over it now. The Cahir horses are known to be special, and there was definitely something horse-like about the stone luminas in the shrine. What are they exactly, half horse, half dragon?"

Maeve nodded as she swallowed the last of her blueberry tart.

"Plus, the fact that the lumina shrine even existed in the first place should have been a clue that there was more to them than an old legend. I can't believe I didn't put the pieces together sooner."

"But you put everything else together," said Rosie admiringly. "You figured out that Lil's lumina was really the token. I never guessed that at all."

"Yeah, Lu, how *did* you know?" When they had returned to the black rock the previous evening, escorted by the entire band of Cahir warriors, they had been too exhausted to talk much. It had taken every ounce of energy they possessed to get through dinner without making Mr. and Mrs. Harper suspicious, so that by the time Lulabelle and Kat collapsed into bed, comparing notes about their eventful day was the last thing on their minds. But now it was different and Kat found herself bursting with unanswered questions.

"I think it must have come to me at the same time it came to

Mayor Digby," answered Lulabelle, staring across the open field at the distant hills. "When you caught Barnaby spying on us, it got me to thinking about Lil's lumina and how he wanted it so badly. But why? It was a toy, after all, and as Rosie pointed out, it wasn't even that pretty."

"But brownies like weird things," said Kat. "They get excited about stuff no one cares about—and Barnaby was happy to take the other lumina that Mr. Snugglewump offered him. So how did you know Lil's lumina was the token?"

"That's the thing, Barnaby wasn't happy to take the other toy. He did it because he had no choice, but it was Lil's that he wanted. So when you saw him spying, I remembered what Maeve had said about brownies seeing value in things that we can't, and it made me wonder what was so special about Lil's lumina. That made me think about luminas themselves — how they were part of the old legends, which meant they might have been around when the tokens were created. If the tokens were unique to their province, then why not create a token in the form of a creature that protected the Hill province?"

"That's brilliant!" declared Maeve. Lulabelle blushed.

"I might have been right about the lumina, but I never once suspected Mayor Digby was the Spellbinder. I wish I could've seen that coming."

"None of us did, I'm afraid. When I think of all the times he's been in our home, I still have trouble believing it of him." Maeve's eyes darkened. "We've been afraid for so long, and all because of what he did. I do believe if he were standing in front of me, I would strangle him myself, without the help of any fog banshee!"

"It came so close to killing us," whispered Rosie, "and it would've done it too, if you hadn't thought to throw those smoke bombs, Lu. You saved our lives!"

"How did you know the smoke would scare the fog banshee?" asked Kat, remembering the way the monster had shrunk away from the crackling noise and the acrid smell.

"I didn't, not really. I was so scared when Mayor Digby said he was going to let the fog banshee kill us that I couldn't move. But then I heard Maeve say something about how it was going to smoke us out and I . . . well, I sort of . . . " Lulabelle stared at her knees, embarrassed.

"What?" Kat prodded.

"Well . . . " Lulabelle reddened even more. "You know how weird my mind can be. I always remember horrible stories whenever I'm scared and this time was no different. I remembered something I'd read about a lady circus performer whose act involved juggling firecrackers that she kept hidden in pockets all over her costume, but it all went south when she accidentally got shot from a cannon—"

"How did she accidentally—"

"It's a long story but she ended up with the nickname, 'Smokin' Sally,' and I couldn't help but wonder what sort of nickname I'd have after all this and then I remembered what I'd read in the book from the library about fog banshees not liking loud sounds and smells, and then I remembered the smoke bombs. They were in my pocket—"

"Ha!" Kat felt suddenly vindicated. "You did have them! You didn't think my plan to free Aidan was so bad after all!"

"No, your plan was awful and would've failed miserably. But I thought the smoke bombs might come in handy somehow . . . and, I don't know . . . I like to be prepared . . ." Lulabelle ducked her head. "Stupid, I know."

"It's genius!" Kat declared. "I wish I had thought of it."

Lulabelle grinned bashfully.

"Someone's coming," said Rosie and they jumped to their feet. Three figures were moving in the direction of the cottage.

"It's Da and Cathmor, I think," said Maeve, squinting into the bright sunlight. "And someone else, but I can't tell who."

Kat caught a glimpse of long golden hair and at once knew the identity of the third figure. "It's the Enchantress!"

Maeve's mouth dropped open.

"The Enchantress? Coming here? To our cottage?" She glanced around the small yard nervously. "Does it look all right, I wonder? Shall I sweep up a bit? Maybe plant a few flowers? I wonder if she expects tea." She lunged in the direction of the nearest broom, but Kat pulled her back.

"Don't be silly, your house looks fine. There's no time for tea or gardening, anyway, they're almost here."

Maeve still looked apprehensive. Rosie, who had been watching the approaching figures with interest, gave an excited yell. "Aidan's with them, too!"

A shorter figure with red hair and a familiar sauntering gait marched behind Cathmor. Kat saw with relief that he didn't appear to be handcuffed. After the disappearance of the fog banshee, Cathmor had insisted on returning Aidan to jail until he had sorted out the jumble of facts surrounding the day's events, despite Kat's loud protestations and repeated foot stomping.

"How's Lil?" said Rosie anxiously when the group reached the Stewart's house. An hour after they had returned to the village, Donovan had come staggering down the main street, covered in sweat, a sleeping Lil in his arms. From where they sat, covered in warm blankets and sipping steaming cups of tea, the Harpers watched Lil's parents rush over to Donovan, both weeping with happiness. Donovan, after a few short words with Mr. Stewart, had vanished into the hills.

"Lil's fine," Mr. Stewart reassured them. "Her da tells me she doesn't remember much of yesterday, which is for the best. She's at home resting now, but seems to be unharmed. Mr. and Mrs.

Murphy would be most grateful to have a word with you later. I imagine they want to thank you in person for saving their daughter's life."

The Harpers and Maeve smiled at each other. It hadn't occurred to any of them until that moment that they had saved Lil's life. It was a nice feeling, to be a life saver.

"What about the brownies, sir?" said Lulabelle. "Are they . . . ?"

"Barnaby and Minnie are going to be fine as well," said Mr. Stewart. "Thanks to the Cahir's fast riding, our doctor was able to save them. Mrs. Murphy has insisted they be moved to the Murphy's house where she can tend to them herself, so they're in excellent hands."

"Did they tell you anything?" blurted Kat, unable to stay quiet any longer.

"They did," replied Cathmor. "Minnie was hit from behind and never saw her attacker. Barnaby admits that he followed the Murphys back to their home, hoping for a look at the toy. He found the door open and Minnie lying on the floor. He saw Digby bending over Lil's bed and tried to defend the child, getting himself stabbed in the process. Lil ran out of the house and Digby broke away from Barnaby long enough to go after her. Barnaby tried to revive Minnie, but when he couldn't, he chased after Digby and they fought again in the yard. The last thing Barnaby remembers is Digby throwing him into the wood keep."

"Poor thing!" cried Rosie in dismay and Kat felt renewed sympathy for Barnaby, in spite of his tendency toward creepiness. Lulabelle cleared her throat.

"Did Barnaby tell you why he wanted Lil's lumina so badly?"

"You mean, did he know it was the lost token?" Mr. Stewart shook his head. "He says not and I'm inclined to believe him. He seemed genuinely surprised to learn of its importance, as did the Murphys. Mr. Murphy bought it from a traveling vendor years ago but never believed for a second it was anything other than a child's toy. In the end, I think we shall have to accept that Barnaby saw its value, even if he didn't recognize what it was."

"So it really is the token then, Da?" said Maeve in a hushed voice. "The legend is true?"

Mr. Stewart and Cathmor both turned to the Enchantress. In the daylight, Kat thought she looked even more beautiful and regal than she had the night of the meeting.

"Yes, child, it is all true. The legends and the stories are real. The tokens are out there and whoever finds and unites them will possess tremendous power."

"That's what Mayor Digby told us yesterday," said Lulabelle quietly. "The Spellbinders want to take over Ancora and make it better for everyone. He said they're not bad, not the way people think."

"Aye, and a snake doesn't always look dangerous, but it can

poison you just the same if you're not careful," scoffed Cathmor. "Digby is a traitor and a coward, nothing more."

"He told us that he found a book—a book about Spellbinders—in your library . . ." Lulabelle said tentatively, with a nervous glance at Cathmor. Kat could hardly believe her sister's nerve, especially given the size of the Cahir's knife. For a moment, Cathmor looked angry, but almost at once, his expression changed to one of sadness.

"My father was many things, but he was no Spellbinder. I don't know where Digby got hold of such an evil book, but it was not from my library. One more of his many lies, I'm afraid."

Mr. Stewart's eyes were sad. "I was a fool not to have seen him for what he was. Aifric was always drawn to power, to those he regarded as important. In the last few months, he had become quite interested in the old legends—research he called it—to fight the fog banshee . . . and I didn't question him . . . ."

"Because he always seemed a bit of an idiot, that's why!" growled Cathmor. "No one thought Digby had the brains to find his way home, let alone become a Spellbinder. He fooled everyone."

"It's not your fault, Da," insisted Maeve. "You were friends your whole life—of course you didn't suspect him. I think it's noble, not foolish."

"Thank you, Maevie, but it's because we were friends for so long that I more than anyone should've seen his flaws. If I had, perhaps things would have turned out differently."

"Did you find Mayor Digby?" asked Lulabelle anxiously. Cathmor scowled.

"Not a trace of him and my men have scoured the Whispering Woods. I don't see how he did it—the lad's trap was quite good, but somehow he managed to free himself. I wouldn't worry too much, though," he added, noticing Lulabelle's worried face. "He won't dare to show his face around the Hill province, or anywhere else for that matter. Not if the Cahir have our way."

"Does that mean you're letting Aidan go?" said Kat, in what she hoped was a calm voice. Cathmor raised his eyebrows, although Kat was positive she saw a twinkle in his fierce eyes.

"If I say no, are you planning to yell some more?" Without waiting for a response, he motioned Aidan forward. "Yes, the lad has been cleared of all charges. No jury would convict him, not after what Digby confessed in the shrine. He was set up from the start, plain and simple."

"We went to Aifric's house last night," added Mr. Stewart. "We found traces of the purple powder that he used to summon the fog banshee, as well as some items that have gone missing from people's houses . . . a last attempt to find the Hill token, no doubt, at least until he came upon Lil's lumina. We believe Aifric must have followed Aidan back to O'bannon's, waiting until he fell asleep before putting the incriminating items where he knew they would be found."

"Then there's the small matter of the treasures buried in Digby's back yard," added Cathmor, stroking the ominous knife at his side, as though longing to use it on the mayor. "Everything taken by the fog banshee was buried under Digby's root cellar like a bleedin' dog bone."

"I understand why Aifric was hesitant to move the firefly picnic to his backyard," said Mr. Stewart. "Once you discovered the treasures inside the lumina shrine, he knew they had to be moved. I imagine he thought the bottom of his root cellar was as good a place as any, and he was right. No one would ever have dreamed of looking there for the fog banshee's lair. But the firefly picnic, the entire village feet away from the treasures? It had to have worried him to no end."

"May I ask another question?" said Lulabelle. "When Mayor Digby was telling us about the Spellbinders, he made it sound like there were more of them—like they're out there, plotting to take over Ancora. Aren't you worried they'll try and get the token back?"

Cathmor and Mr. Stewart exchanged swift glances but remained silent. The Enchantress bowed her head, pondering Lulabelle's question.

"The circle of Enchanters has considered that possibility," she said at last. "But the majority feels that Mayor Digby was acting on his own in a misguided attempt to return Ancora to its former glory. The circle does not believe that other Spellbinders exist, at least not outside of the mayor's mind. To be sure, there have been no rumblings of dark magic in any of the other provinces. I'm afraid Cathmor is right—Aifric fooled all of us."

Sensing their unease, the Enchantress smiled again. "As for the token, it is safe and will remain within the circle for the foreseeable future. Wherever Mayor Digby is, he will not be able to get to it again, nor do we believe the fog banshee will return. It is finally over."

"The luminas must have scared it off," said Kat but Cathmor shook his head.

"Nothing can defeat a fog banshee. We only meant to distract it long enough for you to escape. We intended to buy you time, that was all. If the fog banshee left, it was because Digby knew it was over and released it."

It took a moment for Kat to fully digest what Cathmor was saying. The Cahir hadn't ridden across the field because they thought they could fight the fog banshee, but in order to protect them. They had been prepared to sacrifice themselves if it meant the Harpers, Maeve, and Aidan would be safe. She swallowed hard.

"Did you know, Cathmor?" said Maeve at last. "Did you know that the horses were really luminas?"

"We've always suspected there was more to them, but we didn't know for sure. In legends, the luminas rose up in times of great peril for the Hill province in order to protect its people. I imagine the recovery of the token hastened their transformation. They have returned to their horse form now." He rubbed a burn on his wrist. "It's just as well, the fire-breathing would've put a damper on our practices."

All the talk of luminas reminded Kat of something that had been lurking on the edges of her mind since their dramatic escape.

"Are you finally going to tell us how you called those horses?" she demanded of Aidan. "Does it have anything to do with your bruises? You've been acting sneaky about them all summer."

For the first time, all eyes fixed on Aidan. He hung back, his own eyes on the ground. At first, Kat thought he was trying to avoid looking at her, but when he stole a furtive glance at Cathmor, she realized it was the Cahir leader that was causing him to hesitate.

"Go on, lad," Mr. Stewart encouraged him. "We would all like to know your secret."

Aidan dug the toe of his boot into the ground. "I don't know that I can explain it, sir. It happened that day we saw the Cahir practice, when I rode one of the horses. I wasn't sure if I could . . . I know it's near impossible, but I heard a voice in my head, telling me I could do it, that I was meant to do it."

"You hear voices in your head?" interrupted Kat and then immediately clutched her side where Lulabelle had elbowed her. Aidan flushed.

"Just one voice. I thought I was going a bit soft, but the voice kept on at me and then I realized the voice was coming from the horse—from Red Star." Aidan tensed, as though waiting for them to laugh. When they didn't, he relaxed.

"If I concentrated quite hard, I could make her understand what I was saying without speaking a word. She told me . . . she told me . . ."Aidan lowered his voice. "She told me I could be a Cahir warrior—that it was in my blood, if I would only practice and stop showing off for . . . people."

"That's how you got the bruises?" said Maeve, looking impressed in spite of herself.

"I thought after my first ride, when I put the pole through the ring, that everything else would be easy, but it was a sight harder than I expected. Red Star's the best horse there is and I might have given up, if she hadn't made me keep practicing." Aidan sneaked another glance at Cathmor. "And I had to be a bit secretive about . . . borrowing Red Star."

Cathmor gave Aidan a searching look. "If what you say is true, lad, then you indeed have a rare gift. It's a gift I haven't seen in ten years, and never in one so young. Each Cahir has a unique bond with his horse, and the bond is so strong that words become unnecessary—or distance, for that matter." Cathmor studied Aidan. "You have no idea who your parents were? Where they came from?" When Aidan shook his head, Cathmor frowned. "The gift of the Cahir tends to run in families. Whoever your da or mam was, they might very well have had the same gift." Aidan said nothing, but Kat thought she detected pride in his eyes.

"Does this mean you're not going to throw him in jail for taking Red Star?" she said quickly, crossing her fingers behind her back.

"Stealing a Cahir horse is serious and not something we take lightly. The last lad who tried as much spent five nights in the stocks to help him remember. But if you do indeed possess the gift of the Cahir, it would be a crime in itself to waste such talent. Meet us at the training field tomorrow morning and we'll see whether you deserve the stocks or a horse."

Kat thought that sounded more than a little ominous, but to her surprise, Aidan appeared excited rather than nervous. He grinned and stood up straighter.

"Aidan, you're going to be a Cahir," Rosie informed him, beaming. "I know it! Just like we knew you weren't a Spellbinder, and you didn't do any of those things they said you did."

Mr. Stewart put a hand on Aidan's shoulder and Aidan's grin vanished as he took in the somber expression on the older man's face.

"It's true lad, that you were framed for the more grievous crimes by Mayor Digby. Not one of us doubts that. But there have been other thefts around our village—other things stolen. If you desire to be a trustworthy lad, deserving of a place in the Cahir, you must be truthful with us now. Were you the one who stole them?"

Aidan stared down at his feet.

"You must look me in the eye, lad." Mr. Stewart's voice was kind but firm. "No matter what may happen in your life, you must always look a man in the eyes, for your own dignity as well as his."

Aidan didn't say anything. For a long moment, Kat thought he was going to stand there silently forever. But at last, he raised his head and locked eyes with Mr. Stewart.

"Yes, sir, it was me—I took them."

"My chickens, too?" said Maeve hastily, as though wanting to be sure the dignity of her chickens was not forgotten.

"Those too."

"What did you do with all those things, lad?"

"I . . . I sold them down at the Realm . . . for food, mostly, but other things I needed, too."

Mr. Stewart nodded. "Then it would seem the only way to make things right is to repay those from whom you stole. You cannot give them money perhaps, but you can work it off until your debt is paid."

Relief flashed across Aidan's face. "Yes, sir, I can do that, sure enough. I'm not afraid of hard work."

"And where will you live, Aidan, while you're working off your debt?" The Harpers jumped at the sound of Mrs. Stewart's quiet voice behind them. She must have joined the group at some point in the conversation, but Kat had been so engrossed she hadn't heard her.

"I'll find someplace, ma'am, no worries about me," replied Aidan heartily. "There's plenty of shelter in the Whispering Woods, and O'bannon's shack, if I'm in a pickle. In the summer, there's nothing like nesting in one of those great oaks, even if they are on the scratchy side."

"But how can we be sure you won't tire of working and run away when it suits you? You're asking us to trust you with no guarantee you will keep your word." Mrs. Stewart's voice had a hint of sharpness to it and Kat stared at her, surprised.

"I won't run away, ma'am, I swear to you I won't," Aidan began but Mrs. Stewart stopped him.

"I think to prove yourself trustworthy, you must stay where we may keep an eye on you. Our barn is simple, but it's clean and warm. We can put down blankets and pillows to make it more comfortable. You may earn your meals by helping Maeve with the gardening and Mr. Stewart with the farming, in addition to your other work. Does that sound agreeable?"

Aidan nodded eagerly, leading Kat to suspect that he wasn't as ambivalent about returning to the woods as he had led them to believe a moment ago.

"That's settled then." Mrs. Stewart smiled at Aidan, then at her husband, who smiled conspiratorially back. It occurred to Kat that perhaps the Stewarts had planned this conversation earlier, but she had no time to think any more about it because her attention was suddenly drawn to Maeve, who was making painful gasping sounds.

"You mean he's going to live here with us?" she croaked, her face contorted into an expression of horror. "But that's—he can't—what about . . . " She floundered, unable to find words sufficient to convey her disgust. "We don't know how much he'll eat—and Alberta should be consulted—and . . . "

"Maeve, that will be enough," said Mr. Stewart in a voice that brimmed with finality. Maeve looked as if she wanted to argue further, but settled on giving Aidan a mutinous glare and mumbling something about people who didn't respect chickens.

"If we've settled everything here, I'll be getting on," said Cathmor. "The Cahir are closing down the festival tomorrow and we have a bit of practicing to do. Enchantress, allow me to escort you back to the village?" He offered his arm to the Enchantress, who smilingly accepted. They had only gone a few steps when Cathmor stopped and, fishing around in his pocket, withdrew a dark pouch. He tossed it to Aidan.

"I've been holding onto this since the hearing, but now that you're in—shall we say—a better spot, I believe it's time to return it."

Aidan opened the pouch and took out a leather bracelet with a gold stone in the center. Kat recognized it as the same bracelet that Cathmor had shown the council at Aidan's hearing—the one that had belonged to Birdie. Aidan gazed at it for a long moment.

"Am I right, lad? Birdie's friends tell me she was holding onto it for someone. It was you, was it not?"

"Yes," whispered Aidan. "I was wearing it the day Birdie found me in the woods—when I was just a tyke. When I left her, that last time, I told her . . . I told her I didn't care to have it, that it was nothing to me, but she said—" Aidan's voice cracked with emotion. "—She said that it was part of my past and that I should have it to remember. She said that memories were one of the most sacred things we could ever have. Then she said she would keep it safe for me until I came back." His eyes sparkled, as though something was in them, and he wiped whatever it was quickly away.

"That sounds like Birdie," said Cathmor. His jaw twitched and Kat noticed that his own eyes sparkled too.

"You knew her?" said Aidan with surprise. Cathmor smiled sadly.

"You're not the only one she was kind to, lad," was all he said.

CHAPTER TWENTY-ONE
The End of the Beginning

It was amazing, thought Kat, how much friendlier people were when they didn't suspect you of black magic. She, Lulabelle, and Rosie sat with Maeve on one of the many benches along the perimeter of the field, watching the last performances of the Midsummer festival and sharing a basket of muffins that Puddy MacDougal had sheepishly presented. Mr. and Mrs. Murphy had stopped by earlier with Lil, their arms full of apples from their small orchard. Mrs. Murphy had cried and hugged them all, and Mr. Murphy, his voice cracking, had thanked them repeatedly for saving Lil, which brought tears to Lulabelle and Rosie's eyes and made Mrs. Murphy hug them all over again.

"Here's the new lumina Mr. Snugglewump gave me!" beamed

Lil, holding up a pink toy covered in silver sparkles. "It's almost as good as my old one, but the Enchantress is keeping that one safe now. She said it's the most important lumina in Ancora and she's proud of me for taking care of it. It has to be in a special place now where Mayor Digby can't ever find it."

The last group of performers, a raucous band of acrobatic leprechauns who had obviously stopped by the Gilded Thistle beforehand, bounded off the field. An excited murmur rose up from the spectators.

"It's the final performance of the festival," Maeve explained to them. "It's always the Cahir and it's always the best."

A sound like approaching thunder rumbled through the crowd as the Cahir horses came galloping from all sides, leaping over benches, tables, and anything else that happened to be in the way. They trotted around the field while the warriors, dressed in black with silver sashes, rose to their feet in the saddles, each twirling his spear as if it was a mere baton. The crowd responded with whoops and whistles and the Cahir acknowledged the applause by hurling their spears into the center of the field where they lodged in the ground. Steering their horses into two lines, each warrior proceeded to do a back flip while the crowd yelled its approval.

"There's Aidan!" cried Rosie over the noise. "He's there with the rest of the horses!"

Kat caught a glimpse of Aidan on the side of the field, watching the Cahir. As several riders trotted off the field, he hurried over with water, his face eager. With smooth, practiced hands, he helped remove the saddles and pat dry the sweating horses.

"Only an errand boy, I see," scoffed Maeve, as they watched Aidan dash off for another bucket of water. "Not quite the grand warrior. He'll be lucky if Cathmor lets him anywhere near Red Star after all the sneaking around he's done."

"Oh, hush up," said Kat spiritedly. "You're just mad that he's going to live with you."

"I'll thank you to stop reminding me. I feel a bit ill in my stomach when I think of it."

"Cathmor must've liked what he saw at practice," murmured Lulabelle. "I can't imagine the Cahir would let him stay if he hadn't shown some talent."

A large hoop, the size of a grown man, was carried onto the field and the Harpers watched with interest as the Cahir took turns leaping through it and landing on their horses. Mr. and Mrs. Stewart joined the group while the warriors completed one daring stunt after another to wild cheers and enthusiastic foot stomping. Kat's attention was suddenly caught by a lone figure leaning against a tree some yards away. Donovan looked remarkably different from the last time she had seen him. His shirt was clean and tucked in, his boots shiny, as though recently polished, and he had tied his messy black hair into a ponytail. Catching sight of them, he made his way over to Mr. Stewart, who reached out to shake his hand.

"I confess I'm surprised to see you, sir," said Mr. Stewart pleasantly. "You're welcome, of course, but I didn't think you cared much for village life."

"Solitude has its limitations," replied Donovan, his eyes on the Cahir. "There is much to be said for community—the right kind of community. I've been alone for so long that I'd almost forgotten."

"I hope your solitude isn't due to any trouble," said Mrs. Stewart with concern. "You shall find there are plenty here who would extend a hand, if needed."

"You're kind, but any troubles of mine are entirely self-inflicted." Donovan was quiet and Mr. and Mrs. Stewart said no more. Kat knew she shouldn't listen, but it was hard to will her mind elsewhere.

"Do you think it's gone for good?" said Donovan. He didn't specify what the "it" was, but there was no need.

"The Enchantress is hopeful," replied Mr. Stewart quietly. "The fog banshee must stay close to its summoner and there's no sign of Digby anywhere. Cathmor and his men have searched extensively and are satisfied he's left the Hill province. The token itself is in a safe location outside the province, so it's unlikely the monster would return and even unlikelier that Digby would show his face again. It appears that we are safe, thank goodness."

Donovan gave Mr. Stewart a searching look. "I admire your hope," he told him. "It's a rare gift in this world." He nodded at Mrs. Stewart and disappeared into the throng of spectators.

The Cahir's performance came to an end and the Harpers pushed their way to the field, where Aidan was removing saddles and bridles from the panting horses. He waved when he saw them, then turned to speak to Cathmor, who patted his back. Aidan gazed up at him in admiration.

"A grand show, sure enough!" he cried, wiping his forehead. His face was flushed and sweaty but Kat had never seen him look so happy. "Did you ever see anything like it in all your days? Cathmor said I could stay with them . . . keep the horses cool and dry . . . fetch what was needed. Important business like that!" He puffed out his chest proudly.

Maeve bit her lip. Kat knew it took every ounce of her self-control not to spit out a sharp retort.

"How was the practice yesterday?" asked Lulabelle. "Are they going to let you join them?"

"Easy as rolling off a log," said Aidan breezily, then stopped himself. "Maybe a bit harder than that," he admitted and grinned. The Harpers grinned back. "Cathmor brought Red Star out and I had to give her commands—all in my mind, you know. It took every drip of concentration I had, but Red Star was magnificent. Cathmor said he'd never seen a lad my age with the gift."

"So you're going to be a Cahir?" asked Rosie.

"Not officially. Cathmor won't let me start training 'till I'm sixteen, but he said I'm to take care of the horses and learn some of the simpler tasks—sort of a junior Cahir."

"It seems as though you've turned over a new leaf, haven't you?" Maeve smiled at Aidan, although her voice was a little too sweet to sound genuine. "I expect you'll be running for mayor soon. I hear the elders are looking for someone."

"Ah, Red, I was wondering when you would overcome that timid spirit of yours and chip in," said Aidan, winking at her. "Now if you'll excuse me, I have a bit of Cahir business to tend to. They're counting on me, you know." He sauntered off in the direction of the field, whistling nonchalantly.

The end of summer came much too quickly. Why was it that time streaked by in a blur when life was the most fun, yet plodded on relentlessly when it was most unpleasant? Kat considered the question as she, Lulabelle and Rosie made their way up the hill and into the black rock one final time. The Harper's car was packed, the cabin empty and lonely looking. They had said their goodbyes to Mr. and Mrs. Stewart, Mrs. MacDougal, Lil, and what felt like the entire village the day before, and Kat felt a teary sadness even now as she thought about their smiling faces. *We will see them again*, she assured herself, *we will come back*. Maeve had refused to say good-bye, insisting they meet her at the black rock before they left. With a good deal of huffing, she had mentioned that Aidan might show up as well, if it wouldn't annoy anyone too much.

Sure enough, Aidan's red hair and gray eyes were the first thing the Harpers saw as they stepped out of the rock. Maeve stood nearby, wearing a look of both nervousness and pleasure. As Kat's eyes adjusted from the darkness of the cave, she realized why. Standing between Maeve and Aidan, as beautiful and ethereal as ever, was the Enchantress herself. She smiled at the Harpers, her eyes crinkling at the surprised looks on their faces.

"I'm glad to see you again, children," she said in her warm, chocolatey voice. "I was hoping to see you once more before you left and Maeve and Aidan were kind enough to allow me to join them."

Maeve shot a jealous glance at Aidan, less than pleased to share recognition. Aidan pretended not to notice.

"The entire Hill province is in your debt," continued the Enchantress. "Because of your bravery, loyalty, and quick thinking, you not only saved the people of this province and their dearest treasures, but you stopped a grave miscarriage of justice."

Aidan's face clouded. Kat wondered if he was remembering the hearing. He had never mentioned that day and no one would ever bring it up. He also hadn't talked about Birdie. Kat suspected those memories were either too sad or too happy to share. Maybe both.

"We were glad we could help," said Lulabelle shyly, "but it wasn't just us. Maeve and Aidan saved everyone, too, and Cathmor, and Donovan . . . it's not like we were extra special or anything."

"Your humility is a credit to you, child," smiled the Enchantress, "but I'm afraid I must disagree. You are quite special, perhaps more than you know." She hesitated and Kat had the strangest feeling that she wanted to say something else. The moment quickly passed and the Enchantress remained quiet.

Maeve stepped forward, her eyes watering.

"I'm going to miss you so much," she sniffed, putting her arms around the Harpers. "You have to find a way to come back—do you hear me? I won't let you forget about us!"

"Not like they could if they wanted to," drawled Aidan. "Just say the word, little birds, and I'll make a special trap for Red—keep her up in the trees where she can chatter with the squirrels instead of driving the rest of us out of our minds."

He held out his hand, but Rosie ignored it and threw her arms around him, followed by Kat, and then Lulabelle. When they broke apart, Aidan looked both embarrassed and pleased.

"Go on, keep this up and you'll have me blubberin' like Red here," was all he said.

"This can't be the end," declared Kat as the Harpers came out of the cave and onto the hill overlooking the cabin. "We have to convince Mom and Dad to come back next summer. This can't be goodbye forever."

"I agree," replied Lulabelle. "I'm sure if we put our heads together, we'll come up with something. We have all year to brainstorm."

"No need, I already have a plan. But we'll need fifty bags of sand, a unicycle, and a small llama."

"Tell me you're joking."

Seriously, Lu, do you think you can ride the unicycle? Because that may affect the plan."

"Do I really have to answer that?"

"It's either that or ride the llama. Rose, what do you think?"

"I'll ride the llama if Lu won't."

"Have you two lost your minds?"

Still arguing, they made their way down the hill to the car.

EPILOGUE

H e had lit a fire, again. Although it was September and the first frost was a month away, the Spellbinder couldn't help himself. There was something intoxicating about the flames—the combination of delicate beauty with infinite danger, the potential for warmth and safety, fused with pain and destruction. Within the confines of his campsite, the flames gave him the illusion of control, but one gust of wind into the nearest tree and the fire's true power would be unleashed. The Spellbinder sat back on the hard ground. It had taken time to sort through the tangle of the last few months, to know whether to congratulate himself on his triumph or curse his foolishness. Maybe both were in order.

He had made a mistake with Digby, that much was clear. Digby with his pathetic lust for importance. He had seemed a convenient ally at first: someone who knew the Hill province, who might find the token more easily, who had a modicum of intelligence (a generous assumption), but could also shield the Spellbinder from the rest of the province, although he hadn't bothered to mention this to Digby.

It had also been a mistake to frame the boy, though at the time it seemed a clever distraction. Digby had suggested it and the Spellbinder agreed, primarily because he was curious what the other children would do to save their friend. They had not disappointed him. And the bracelet—what of the boy's bracelet? It was a cheap bauble, and yet something (a memory?) had stirred in him when he saw it on the dead woman's wrist. Was that why he had taken it? He would have to think some more.

Then Digby had discovered the token's identity and panicked. Instead of waiting for the Spellbinder's orders, he had tried to take it from the little girl and had made one stupid decision after another. Never trust a man who panics under pressure. That was the point at which the Spellbinder cursed his own failure. He wouldn't make the same mistake again. Digby had come simpering back to the Spellbinder that night, sputtering excuses and begging for one more chance, but it was too late. The Spellbinder didn't give second chances. And unlike the old peddler's death, he didn't feel regret in the slightest.

But the children, now that's where things turned interesting. The children had managed to find the token where he could not— find and return it at great risk to themselves. Other men might feel embarrassment, but he was not like other men. He had underestimated the children and that was another shortcoming. He would not make that mistake again, either.

All things considered, the Spellbinder was content. True, he would've preferred to have the token, but when the moment was right, he would reclaim it. Not for the first time, he pondered the prophecy, the one he was quite sure no one had mentioned to the Harpers. And why would they? If the children knew they might never return. But if the prophecy was true, if the Harper sisters were indeed part of Ancora's destiny, they would most certainly be back. The rest of the tokens were out there, and they would be the ones to find them. It was for that reason alone the Spellbinder had released the fog banshee, had realized, watching from a distance, how useful the children would be and decided to spare them.

For now, he would simply wait.

THE HARPER SISTERS RETURN
FOR A NEW ADVENTURE IN

Ancora

The Frozen Flame
of Vallengard

COMING SPRING 2021

Acknowledgments

(in which I thank all the people who helped me not quit writing)

SHARON NEHLS - for agreeing to read my original, 195,000 word first draft and doing it with kindness, enthusiasm, and lots of helpful suggestions (a good editor being one of the first).

JENNY BOWMAN & JESSICA MACLEISH - editors with yoda-like skills who patiently helped me polish and refine this manuscript. If it shines even a little bit, it's because of you.

SEUNGWAN HAN, KATIE JIMENEZ, KATHY MARCH, ELLIOTT MILLER AND ANNE PURDY - my incredible beta readers who faithfully went on this adventure with Kat, Lulabelle, and Rosie and then answered all my questions about it. I would give you a million Honeyfizzes if I could!

KELLEY MCMORRIS - an absurdly talented illustrator who created the most amazing book cover I could ever have hoped for. I don't think it's exaggeration to say that this is absolutely, without a doubt, the best cover art in the history of the world. Ever.

LISA VEGA - for taking things like, "font preference," "line spacing," and "first-letter drop cap," and turning them into works of art. I will never look at book design the same way again!

MICHELLE RAPPAPORT & BETSY EKLE - ladies who offered wisdom and encouragement at exactly the right time. Thank you for helping me take a flying leap off the cliff (note: if you're still reading, please know that this is a metaphor—I don't actually jump off cliffs and I really don't recommend it. I'm with Lulabelle on this one).

MOM AND DAD - for helping to make this dream a reality in every single way and reading, then re-reading . . . and then reading some more. You're the best of the best and I love you more than you know. Also, I owe you a trip to Switzerland.

CHASE, MARY CHASE, KATHRYN, AND JANE - my heart and soul. You make me thankful every single day that I get to live in the same house with you and share life together. You've made this whole crazy experience worth doing a thousand times over and I love you all to the moon and back.

ABOUT THE AUTHOR

Miriam Pittman has always loved escaping into a good book, ever since she stepped through the wardrobe with Lucy as a child. Her writing career began at the age of eight when she wrote a story about a girl who eats too many gumdrops. Her mom loved it. This was followed by stories about pioneers, kidnapped grandmothers, and aliens. Her mom loved those, too. She now lives in Tennessee with her husband, three daughters and two stray cats that refuse to leave. She enjoys chocolate, hot tea, bonfires, and any excuse to avoid laundry. Ancora: The Fog Banshee's Curse is her first novel (and her mom still loves it). You can follow her at miriampittman.com.

CPSIA information can be obtained
at www.ICGtesting.com
Printed in the USA
BVHW080710130121
597521BV00006B/82